1 986949 21

LAST
PROPHECY

BI

Renfrewshire
Council

The library is always open at
renfrewshirelibraries.co.uk

Visit now for library news and
information,
to **renew** and
reserve online, and
to download
free eBooks.

Phone: 0300 300 1188
Email: libraries@renfrew

D1369158

Also by Iain King:

Fiction
Secrets of the Last Nazi

Non-Fiction
How to Make Good Decisions and Be Right All The Time
Peace at Any Price

LAST PROPHECY OF ROME

IAIN KING

bookouture

Published by Bookouture

An imprint of StoryFire Ltd.
23 Sussex Road, Ickenham, UB10 8PN
United Kingdom

www.bookouture.com

ISBN: 978-1-910751-75-6
eBook ISBN: 978-1-910751-74-9

To the 5,230 refugees who died during 2015,
trying to reach a better life in the West.

'If all the barbarian conquerors had been annihilated in the same hour, their total destruction would not have restored the empire of the West...The story of its ruin is simple and obvious; and instead of inquiring *why* the Roman Empire was destroyed, we should rather be surprised that it had subsisted for so long.'

Edward Gibbon, *The History of the Decline and Fall of the Roman Empire*, 1776-88

'...in the course of human events it becomes necessary for... people to dissolve the political bands which have connected them...'

From the first sentence of the US Declaration of Independence, 1776

DAY I

CHAPTER ONE
Rome, Italy

It was the wrong place for a holiday.

The crowds, the hassle, the noise...

Myles looked around and tried to be impressed: so this was Rome.

He gazed at the magnificent statues: gods, emperors and senators. He saw the Colosseum, where gladiators brawled and died. He studied the city walls, which tried but ultimately failed to keep out the enemy. He even visited the old grain stores, Rome's strategic stockpile of food, which kept its citizens plump. Stores once filled by harvests from across the sea, until barbarians overran the land now known as Libya...

Helen grabbed his arm. 'Shall we see the Pantheon?' she suggested. She was still trying to lift his mood, and he could tell. 'You ought to teach this stuff to your students, Myles...'

Myles shrugged. She was right: Rome was an empire built on war and conquest. Perfect material for a military historian. He should teach it.

But he knew he couldn't. And the reason why was something he could never explain to her.

They passed a fast-food outlet, an ice-cream seller and a man hawking plastic sunglasses for five euros a pair. School groups trampled over the ancient squares. Great artefacts were being smothered by chewing gum.

As they crossed a piazza towards the Pantheon, Myles looked up at the sandstone columns guarding the entrance, then hauled open the oversized wooden doors to go inside. Helen followed close behind.

Their eyes adjusted to the gloom. The only illumination came from the single window in the centre of the ceiling. They moved towards the middle of the patterned marble floor, directly below the light. Then their gaze slowly fell down to the alcoves and statues around the side of the circular building. Constructed in 126AD, Rome's heyday, this was a church built for worship of all the gods – long before Emperor Constantine converted to Christianity and ordered the whole Roman Empire to come with him.

Bang.

Myles flinched, hunching his head into his shoulders. He crouched down and scanned around.

No one else had reacted. A few people even looked at him as if he was odd – which he knew he was.

Helen saw it first. She motioned with her eyes: the huge doors to the Pantheon had been slammed shut, and the domed ceiling amplified the sound.

Myles calmed himself.

Helen put her hand on his face, and asked if he was OK.

He was. It was just instinctive. His body had adapted to behave that way in Helmand. It would take time to unlearn.

The army thought it had cracked Post-Traumatic Stress Disorder. In a change since Vietnam and the Second World War, troops were now flown from the frontline in groups. They were given time in an isolated place where they could drink away their memories – together, with people who had experienced similar things. By the time they returned home they had already half-forgotten their wars.

Not Myles. His experiences had been unique, and nobody but Helen had any idea what he had been through. When he saw a street, his first thought was to wonder where someone would place a machine gun to control movement. When he saw a patch of grass, he feared an improvised explosive device – a deadly IED – could be buried underneath. When he heard a bang, he flinched.

The symptoms would be obvious in anybody else, and therefore treatable. But for Myles, an unorthodox specialist in war and a misfit by any standard, it was hard to say what behaviour was normal.

Afghanistan hadn't made him violent. Myles would never be that. Nor had his experiences made him hateful, which was a common expression of combat trauma. But Afghanistan had turned his imagination against him. He used to dream up solutions. Now he dreamed up enemies.

'Myles, you need to get back to the hotel,' said Helen.

They turned around. Away from the spectacles of the long-gone empire into the commercialised narrow streets and the crowds.

They passed a homeless man in one of the alleyways. He looked tired and hungry. Myles could tell the young man didn't have much – unshaven and with ruffled hair, he'd probably been sleeping rough for weeks. So Myles found some change and threw it towards him. The man thanked him with a nod.

Outside a Hard Rock Cafe they saw men and women in business suits. They were standing about and chatting nervously, like they didn't belong there. Obviously foreign. Myles picked up their accents: American.

Some of them recognised Helen, but none of them reacted. Myles guessed they were used to dealing with famous people.

Then he realised: these people worked in the American Embassy, which was opposite. He could faintly hear a fire alarm, which explained why they were all outside.

Myles smiled at them. Some of them smiled back, others just ignored him. None of them were worried.

Then he looked up to see a very large cardboard box suspended from a rope. A man in dark glasses was manoeuvring it from a second-floor window of a nearby apartment block.

The man lifted his glasses.

Myles caught a sinister look in his eye. He grabbed Helen's arm and pointed. 'A bomb,' he whispered. 'It's got to be a bomb…'

Helen tried to work out how Myles could know the dangling box contained explosives. But Myles was already amongst the crowd. 'Move away – quickly,' he warned. 'It's a bomb.'

The Embassy workers took time to react.

He was flapping them away with his long arms. A few started to move slowly, until two or three started to run. Then everybody began to run with them.

'Helen – RUN!' Myles could see this was the perfect terrorist trap: set off the Embassy fire alarm then blow up all the staff as they muster outside.

'But Myles…' queried Helen.

'Quick!'

Senior executives, mid-level diplomats and all their support staff: they all began to flee. Helen reluctantly moved back with them.

They started to gather at the far end of the street. From there they could see what would happen – but not at a safe distance if the Englishman's warning was right. They all watched: half-curious, half-alarmed.

Myles found himself alone in the street. He looked up at the window.

The man hauling the cardboard box was sweating nervously now. Suddenly he left the box to swing on the rope and darted into the building.

Myles rushed over to where the box was hanging. *Damn the consequences.*

This was one terrorist he was determined to catch…

CHAPTER TWO
New York, USA

Salah had told his wife nothing about what he was planning to do.

She had been suspicious – she had quizzed him about one of the books he had been reading. But he'd managed to conceal most of the material under his baby daughter's bed. It was the only place to hide things in their tiny New Jersey apartment.

His best information had come from the internet. He had discovered why so many terrorists had achieved so little. Now he understood how to do so much more, since his contact in Libya had explained to him the secret of 'smart terrorism'.

Small terrorist attacks were doomed to fail. Blowing up a few people or a single building could be explained away as the work of a lone psychopath or a disgruntled former employee. They might dominate the news for twenty-four hours, but not much longer. A celebrity romance or a scandal on Capitol Hill would soon squeeze them off the television.

Larger terrorist attacks also failed. For an Oklahoma bombing, a Mumbai massacre or even a 9/11 to succeed, it could only ever be known about after the event. That meant only survivors would hear about it – the very people whom it had failed to break. It just made them ever-more defiant and patriotic.

American patriotism – the thought of it made Salah retch. *They won't be singing 'America the Beautiful' after this one…*

Salah had studied previous attacks against New York: the attempt to destroy the World Trade Centre with an underground car bomb in 1993; the feeble bomb attempt in Times Square of May 2010. Even planes flying into the twin towers had done less damage to America's financial system than a few greedy traders playing with hedge funds and derivatives…

As his contact had explained, the secret to successful terrorist attacks lay not in the devastation they caused, but in the future they forced people to imagine. Smart terrorism meant convincing the public that much worse was to come.

Salah looked across at his wife. She was sleeping soundly. Quietly he slipped out of bed and moved to dress in the very ordinary clothes he had picked out several days before: jeans, a white shirt and a workman's fluorescent vest.

Careful not to wake his seven-month-old daughter, he pulled his newly acquired American passport and flight ticket from under her cot. He placed them in his daysack, along with a spare set of clothes, a toothbrush, toothpaste, shaving foam and a disposable razor.

He'd thought hard about whether to leave a note, but eventually decided against it. She would never understand what he was trying to do. Even if she did, she would never forgive him.

And there was a greater danger – any note might be discovered before he had done his work. Salah's wife had been an American twice as long as him. Unlike him, she had taken seriously the mantras they were taught in citizenship classes. Unlike him, she had disowned her roots in Africa.

Salah knew, if she discovered what he was going to do, she would report him.

Instead of a note, he left behind his keys. He wouldn't need them again.

Taking a last look at his baby daughter, still snoozing serenely, he walked backwards out of the apartment. Silently he closed the door behind him, pulling it into place with a click.

He walked down the stairs and out to his delivery van. Alone in the first light of the morning, he surveyed the vehicle, walking round all four sides to check nobody could have interfered with it. He examined the tires and looked under the hood to see the engine. Everything was still dirty, which was good: it meant the FBI weren't on to him.

Finally, he climbed into the driver's seat and, taking another look in the street to confirm he was still alone, he bent down to check the device. Still strapped in place above the foot pedals: the bomb remained untouched.

With a last glance at his family home, he turned the ignition key, let the engine settle for a few seconds, then drove off towards the centre of New York's financial district. To Wall Street.

On test runs over the previous weeks, Salah had noticed the scars that still marked the walls on 23 Wall Street, the former offices of JP Morgan. In 1920, it had been the site of a bomb concealed in an old cart, led by a tired horse. The carriage had been parked by a man who stepped down and left quickly – some witnesses said he looked Italian. His hundred-pound dynamite bomb had killed thirty-one people instantly, with two more dying from their wounds.

Like the Italian Wall Street bomber of 1920, Salah would never be caught. But his bomb was different. It would not leave scars on walls, but in people's minds.

He crossed the bridge into New York State, along famous roads clogging up with the morning traffic. He drove into Manhattan with the sun behind him.

As planned, the journey was taking him ninety minutes. Perfect. He spent the time focussed – concentrating on his driving, and being grateful for the money and advice he had received from his contact back in Libya.

Finally, he turned into Wall Street, trying to stay calm as his vehicle slowed to a crawl. He heard the horns blare and watched the taxi-drivers gesticulate against the traffic jams.

Then he smirked. The jam meant he had arrived at exactly the right time: in the middle of the rush hour, when the impact would be greatest.

Soon he was opposite number 23, the site of the bomb blast from almost a century earlier. Here he manoeuvred his van onto the sidewalk, turned off the ignition, and put his daysack on his shoulder. Deliberately, he didn't look again at the bomb under the dashboard. He just stepped down, onto the tarmac.

He closed the door behind him, locked it, and pulled on the handle to check it was locked.

Then he began walking away into the morning rush of suited bankers, city traders, treasury officials – and all the cleaners, baristas and shop assistants who worked to support them in their jobs but whom Salah knew were paid much, much less.

He was a full two hundred yards away when he first turned around to check his vehicle again. Over the heads of the walking crowds, he could see it remained in place, and was not yet causing any alarm.

No one was on to him. His contact in Libya had been loyal: the secret of the bomb had been kept.

So Salah pulled out his mobile phone, turned it on and waited for it to register a signal.

Then he dialled the number he had memorised. The number which would set off the most powerful bomb Wall Street had ever seen.

CHAPTER THREE
Via Veneto, Rome

The bomb dangled outside the second-floor window, which was now empty. Myles had to reach it.

He ran to the door underneath and grabbed the handle. It was locked. He tried ramming it with his shoulder – twice – but it stayed firm.

He looked up. The explosives were still spinning on the rope above him, out of reach. He wondered whether the terrorist could escape through the back.

Then Myles saw someone emerging from the house next door – an old woman. He rushed over. 'Move away – there's a bomb,' he warned. The neighbour looked confused. Myles tried to remember his Italian. 'Una Bomba!' He gestured 'an explosion'.

The woman put her hands to her mouth in shock. Myles grabbed her and pointed her towards the crowd of Embassy staff, huddled at the end of the road. Helen came over to guide the confused woman away.

The house next door gave Myles an opportunity – could he run through the old woman's house to chase the terrorist?

Myles was about to try when the door beneath the bomb opened. He looked over – the terrorist was about to run out. Sweat covered the man's forehead. Myles caught his eye again: this time he looked scared.

The man sprinted down the road, towards the American Embassy staff. He overtook his elderly neighbour, almost knocking her over.

Myles did the same, but turned to check the woman was OK as he rushed past.

American Embassy staff were blocking the road in front of the terrorist. Myles called out to them as he ran. 'Stop him…'

Some of the younger office workers came forward. Having watched the whole chase, they wanted to help.

But then the terrorist slowed down and allowed himself to be caught.

One of the Americans grabbed the man's arm while two more patted him down for explosives. Others gathered round, cutting off any chance of escape.

The terrorist just looked confused. He tried to talk back to the Americans in Italian, panicking but polite. 'Dove si trova la bomba?' he asked.

Once Myles caught up with them he was desperate to make sure the man couldn't use any electronic devices to set off the bomb.

One of the Embassy men retrieved some keys attached to a small remote control transmitter from the Italian's pocket. 'What's this?'

The Italian gesticulated in an attempt to explain, but was gabbling too fast for anyone to understand. The man reached for the transmitter in desperation.

Myles tried to grab it first. 'Don't let him press it!'

But it was too late. The terrorist put his thumb to the red button and pushed.

There was no explosion. Instead, the lights on an Alfa Romeo parked not far away blinked, matched by a faint sound from the horn.

One of the Americans asked him about the hanging box.

'Si tratta di una lavatrice,' answered the man.

It was a washing machine. The man had been dangling it into the building by rope because it was too big to be carried up the small Italian staircase.

CHAPTER FOUR
Via Veneto, Rome

Myles lowered his head, paused, then simply sat down in the street. He tried to apologise to the man, but the blare of approaching police sirens meant nobody heard what he said.

The Embassy staff began drifting back to their offices, and within minutes police were swarming everywhere. They checked and confirmed that the hanging box was indeed a washing machine. It was soon swung inside the house. One of the police even helped fit it into place.

Helen put an arm on Myles' back. Myles just sat there, thinking through what had happened. 'I really thought it was a bomb…'

Helen knew it was best not to answer. She just nuzzled her head onto his shoulder in consolation.

A policeman approached and began speaking English with only a mild accent. 'Are you the one who caused the disturbance?'

'Sorry. I thought it was a bomb,' replied Myles.

'You understand you caused a serious panic. The old lady is being taken to hospital with chest pains – she could have died from a heart attack.'

Helen and Myles could both tell the Italian policeman was playing it up, but Myles answered calmly. 'Sorry officer. I just tried to do the right thing.'

'There are professionals to deal with bombs.'

Myles was about to answer back but Helen stopped him. This was a time for discretion. She put her hand on his arm and spoke for him. 'Thank you officer. We're sorry. We won't cause another alarm,' she promised.

Myles wasn't sure she was right. If he came across another 'bomb' he would try to tackle it again. Maybe the same way. Alone, if he had to. He still distrusted the authorities – all authorities.

He had never trusted them, at least not since his mother had been diagnosed with bowel cancer. Myles had seen medical bureaucracy deny her the early surgical treatment she really needed. He saw her battle against authorities, both public and private, who cared only for their reputations. And he saw her fight the withering poisons of the chemotherapy they gave her. By the time she eventually died, in the week of his fourteenth birthday, Myles had no faith left in 'the authorities' at all. Everything since had just confirmed his view.

Even before his mother's death, Myles had been different. As a child, he was uniquely brilliant at most academic subjects, but unable to read aloud or distinguish his left from his right. He hadn't been able to tie his shoelaces until he was twelve, and he had no natural ability to empathise. His condition might have been labelled as dyslexia or even Asperger's syndrome. But there was never a need for diagnosis – Myles was nice to everyone, just a little other-worldly. He had found juvenile pleasure in performing magic tricks for people and helping them solve puzzles. At school he would happily share his always perfect answers with his many friends, none of whom were close. He learned to empathise as an acquired skill and he was soon empathising more naturally than almost everybody else.

But he knew he would never fit in. He'd gone on to study history at Oxford – a university full of oddballs, but even there he felt like an outsider.

In the military they'd put him in intelligence. With his overpowered brain and lack of physical skills it should have been the perfect fit. But Captain Munro could never settle into being a normal officer. Some seniors said he had no discipline. Others said he had too much sense. In the doomed war of Iraq, his military career had ended in disgrace.

Myles had retreated into academia – where else could he go? – accepting a junior lectureship on military history back at Oxford University. There, the students loved him – partly because of his attitude, but mostly because his views were unorthodox. In his ever-popular lectures he would explain why most military historians were wrong. It annoyed the other military historians, and it gave Myles a certain reputation.

A reputation which meant nothing to him at all.

CHAPTER FIVE
Wall Street, New York

Reputation mattered to Richard Roosevelt because he knew his reputation could never be truly earned. People thought they already knew about him, just from his name.

It wasn't the two presidents which framed people's impressions. Dick Roosevelt didn't remind people of Theodore or Franklin Delano, the boldest Commanders-in-Chief of their generations. Richard Roosevelt had been eclipsed by a far more historic personality, and one who was still alive: his father, Sam.

Even though Senator Sam Roosevelt would probably never run for the White House again – twice was enough – everybody knew of his heroism in the Vietnam War. He had been even more courageous on the floor of the Senate, where he had driven the Roosevelt-Wilson Act into law. It meant US citizens could be tried for crimes committed abroad, 'Because the laws of the land must reach beyond the sea,' he famously explained. The senior Senator frequently appeared on early evening news shows, talking to the 'common American' in straight language – often very straight language, which left interviewers shocked. Sam Roosevelt was loved by the American people. And some of that affection tumbled down onto his only son, Richard. Now aged thirty-one, Dick tried his best to deserve what people thought of him.

'This way, Mr Roosevelt, sir,' ushered a staffer.

'Call me "Dick",' he replied.

As Richard was led into the Treasury building opposite number 23 Wall Street, he leant over to his executive assistant. 'Remind me of the brief. How many people do we have working here, again?'

'Seventy-eight on duty at the moment, a total assignment just under two hundred, sir.'

Dick nodded, then straightened his back. He readied himself to meet more of the men and women employed by Roosevelt Guardians, the private security company established by his father, of which he was now the Chief Executive.

It was as he was entering the lobby that he first noticed someone in a Roosevelt Guardian uniform looking concerned. One of his security guards – alarmed?

Dick remembered words from his speech:

'Your job is to allay fear, so Roosevelt Guardians, you should appear calm and assured at all times...'

Dick stopped to watch. His small entourage stopped with him, knowing great men often noticed important things others missed.

The security guard had gone outside. He began pulling hard on the locked door of a delivery van. The door wouldn't open.

One of the men beside Dick nervously tried to explain it away. 'Er, routine procedure, sir, er, Dick, sir...'

But Richard Roosevelt kept watching. The delivery van was certainly parked in an odd place.

Then, just as the guard was about to give up in bemusement, the spectators saw another man approach. The man was foreign-looking, perhaps North African. He said something apologetic to the security guard as he took a set of keys from his pocket and went to unlock the vehicle.

The Roosevelt Guardian stepped back as the North African man climbed into the van. 'Thank you for moving along, Sir.'

The North African man nodded as he closed the door, then contorted his body to reach something beneath the dashboard.

Sweat reflected from the man's forehead. Both Dick and the guard could see the driver was agitated.

The security guard opened the door to speak to him. 'There's parking further down and to the left, sir,' he volunteered. But as he said the words, the guard spotted something and began to react.

Suddenly the driver turned and kicked the security guard in the face. As the guard recoiled, the man in the vehicle slammed the door shut and locked it.

The sight of one of his staff being assaulted shocked Richard Roosevelt. He marched out of the lobby, and broke into a run. Roosevelt rushed up to his employee, who was reeling on the pavement with a bloody nose. 'What did you say to him?' he asked.

'There was a bomb, sir,' came the reply.

Barely believing, Roosevelt looked through the van's window at the driver. The man's face confirmed the worst.

Roosevelt tried the door on the vehicle, but it was locked.

Quickly he grabbed a briefcase from someone passing by and swung it into the glass. The window shattered. Roosevelt flung the case to the floor, pulled up the lock and yanked open the door, catching the driver by surprise.

Roosevelt climbed into the vehicle beside the man, then dragged him from the bomb, and pressed him hard against the seat. The driver tried to unpick Roosevelt's fingers, which were grabbing his shirt. But it was no good. Within moments the man found himself flung out of the door and crashing down onto the street. He collapsed into a gathering crowd of uniformed Roosevelt Guardians.

'There's a bomb in here,' called Roosevelt through the broken window. 'I'm going to have to drive this someplace safe.'

'But sir…' The Guardians watched as their Chief Executive clunked the vehicle into gear and moved off into the traffic. He was soon driving down Wall Street.

Roosevelt's men called the police immediately. Within a minute Roosevelt was being led by a police car. Within two minutes an impressive escort had formed around the van. Loud sirens and flashing lights started clearing the traffic away, allowing the bomb-laden delivery truck to move ever faster.

Overhead a helicopter, more used to reporting on traffic jams for the New York breakfast TV shows, started to broadcast the events. 'This must surely be the fastest anybody's ever driven during Manhattan's morning rush hour…'

As news leaked that the van was being driven by none other than the son of Senator Sam Roosevelt, the feed was piped live onto national TV.

The first confused reports said that Richard 'Dick' Roosevelt was driving a bomb around Manhattan. But the rolling news ticker soon provided the clarification: he was actually driving the bomb *away*. Dick Roosevelt was single-handedly saving New York.

The police escort knew where to guide him and Roosevelt followed: off Wall Street, down a side road, along another road, into an open area. About as open as it gets in Manhattan.

As he turned onto the broken ground, Roosevelt saw a young bomb disposal expert already starting to put on his protective clothing. Over the noise of police sirens and helicopters, he heard instructions from a loudhailer. 'It's safe here, sir – you should leave the vehicle and run away.'

Roosevelt saw the policemen flee their cars, not even bothering to shut their doors as they ran. So undignified. And on live television, too…

Instead, Dick Roosevelt calmly parked the van, turned off the ignition, opened the door, and magnanimously stepped down onto the ground.

He dusted off his hands and turned back to look at the vehicle one last time, before walking on towards the hastily assembled control area. No point running – this was his moment of majesty.

The bomb disposal expert rushed passed him – going towards the van as Roosevelt walked away from it. 'Can I help some more?' queried Dick.

'No thank you, Mr Roosevelt, sir – just professionals from here on.'

It was a snub Roosevelt accepted. He had done enough already. He looked across at the crowd of policemen and agents gathering a safe distance from the van, being joined by the first news crew on the scene. They beckoned and Richard Roosevelt came. As he reached them he was mobbed by pats on the backs, applause and other praise.

But the congratulations were soon cut short. A deep boom and a sudden rush of air knocked them all to the ground.

The delivery van had been obliterated and the bomb disposal expert blown completely away.

It took several seconds for the crowd to recover themselves, and realise the sky around them was full of confetti.

Richard Roosevelt grabbed at the air and caught one of the fluttering bits of paper. He read it.

And, like the police and the assembling news crew around him, he wondered whether the message it contained could possibly be true…

CHAPTER SIX
Rome

Helen stayed with Myles, both sitting on the concrete as the crowds drifted away.

She had known him for less than three months – first meeting him on a training course, where he had been able to solve difficult problems but not tie his shoelaces properly.

Straight away she'd known he was different. But it was a good sort of different: even his clumsiness had a charm to it. He had a uniqueness which she found far more attractive than his height, his looks or his peculiar intelligence. To an American working in the media, where the men wore make-up and false smiles, Myles was abnormally genuine. In all her time reporting for CNN, in many places and many tough situations, Helen Bridle had never met anyone quite so special.

'Next time a terrorist hides a bomb in a washing machine, you're the man!' she said with a smile, trying to console him. She was disturbed by the Embassy staff reaching for their pagers. Their mobile phones all started ringing at the same time. Something was happening.

Myles was alert again. 'What is it?' he asked.

Then Helen's phone rang. She raised her eyebrows to Myles, as if to say 'you're about to find out'. She pressed the green 'accept' button to answer. 'Helen Bridle here.'

It was one of her producers. There had been a bomb in New York. One dead, but it could have been much worse – they'd tried to blow up Wall Street.

Helen registered the information. Was this news? One dead in a terrorist bomb was a tragedy, and a bomb in New York was certainly a headline.

Her producer's voice was animated. 'And get this, Helen. There was a sort of confetti in the bomb. And it said, "America is about to be brought down like the Roman Empire"!'

The producer was eager to give Helen more details: about Senator Sam Roosevelt's son Richard driving the bomb away, escorted by police live on TV. But Helen was more sombre. 'Do people think the warning is true?'

'Nobody knows, Helen, but it's a great news story…'

She winced to hear one dead and a threat to civilisation described in that way, putting the mobile on speakerphone. She let the producer continue talking while she summarised what had happened for Myles. 'So, you were right about a man with a bomb. You just got the wrong city.'

Myles was absorbing the report as the TV producer cut to the chase. 'Helen, you're in Rome, right? With that historian boyfriend of yours? The Brit, right?'

Both Helen and Myles smiled at the notion of Myles being a 'boyfriend'.

'I am, yes.'

'Well, we need to interview him now – on air, to talk about the Roman Empire and the USA.'

Helen was about to say no, to shield her partner. But Myles refused the protection. He nodded.

'OK, he's here with me now. Shall I put him on?

'Yes, thanks Helen.'

Helen passed the phone to Myles.

Myles tried to stand straight, immediately made nervous by the prospect of a live television interview. He tried to listen down the phone, but it was silent. 'Er, hello. Myles Munro here,' he offered. More silence. He was beginning to think they'd changed their minds – no interview after all.

Finally the machine clicked back to life again. Then a very professional-sounding voice spoke from the other end. 'Myles Munro, thank you for talking live on CNN.'

'Er, thank you.' Myles could tell his voice sounded amateurish. He was no natural TV pundit.

'Mr Munro, you're a historian from Oxford University, currently in Rome, Italy. Tell me, could the USA *really* be brought down like the Roman Empire?'

Myles tried to do the question justice, which meant there was no simple answer. 'Well, yes, I suppose it could, if we actually knew how the Roman Empire was brought down.'

Silence, while the anonymous interviewer in a faraway studio tried to come up with the next question. 'And what do *you* think brought down the Roman Empire? What should people prepare for?'

'I'm afraid there are over two hundred theories on why Rome fell. Some historians reckon it was lead poisoning.'

'Lead poisoning?'

'Yeah, the Romans used lead in a sauce for their food. Other people reckon it was the plague. Several epidemics struck the empire, including things like smallpox. But bubonic plague was the most deadly.'

'And what's your favourite theory, Mr Munro?'

Favourite? A favourite reason for the collapse of a whole civilisation? Myles tried to remain polite. 'Well, there are three *leading* theories,' he explained. 'First, Rome suffered a series of attacks – from Persia and from lots of tribes in the East.'

'Persia – that's modern Iran, right?'

'Yes, and they fought over where Syria and Iraq are today. The theory goes that there were simply too many attacks for the Roman army to cope with. The Empire was overwhelmed.'

'So, multiple attacks from the Middle East, huh? What's the second theory, Mr Munro?'

'Well that has to do with migration. For centuries, when it was on the rise, Rome welcomed new tribes into the Empire – including people they'd conquered. But when thousands of refugees, who'd been forced from their lands by war in the East, tried to settle in Europe, Rome treated them very differently. It was cruel to them. The refugees became enemies, and it was a migrant tribe, the Vandals, who eventually broke into Rome and destroyed the city.'

'And that's where we get the word "vandalise" from?'

'That's right. Rome's last big military operation was against the Vandals, and their new base in Libya. It was a disaster, and it left the Empire bankrupt.'

'A refugee crisis. Very interesting. OK, so the third theory…' There was a pause on the other end of the line. Then, 'Sorry, Mr Munro, we're going to have to wait on that third theory on why the Roman Empire fell. We're about to go live to a press conference with Dick Roosevelt, son of Senator Sam Roosevelt, who drove the bomb away in those live television pictures we saw earlier and thwarted a major terrorist attack that would have ripped through the heart of New York and claimed thousands of lives…'

CHAPTER SEVEN
Via Veneto, Rome

The phone line went dead. Myles gave the handset back to Helen.

Helen was still curious. 'Why do you think a bomber in New York cited the Roman Empire?'

Myles turned his head to one side – he was trying to make an educated guess. 'Could be because the US was founded with the Roman Empire in mind. Your Senate, Capitol Hill, the eagle as a national symbol, even the rule of law – they all came from ancient Rome.'

'But America doesn't have an empire?'

'Not a normal empire, no. But, like Rome, you dominate the known world. Some people resent you for it.'

Helen nodded, accepting Myles had a point.

The phone rang again. Helen looked at the screen and frowned: an unknown number from Washington DC. 'Hello, Helen Bridle speaking.'

'Sam Roosevelt, Senator. I understand you're with that British historian, Myles something.'

Helen was shocked. As a television journalist she often met powerful people. But a call from Senator Sam Roosevelt was quite a surprise, even to her. 'Er, yes, Senator.'

'Well, I want to speak to him,' growled the voice. 'Put him on.'

The Senator's voice gave commands naturally. Something about his tone made them hard to disobey. Helen handed the phone over to Myles again, who raised his eyebrows in surprise.

'Myles Munro speaking.'

'Mr Munro, its Senator Sam Roosevelt here. You may have heard of me.'

'Yes, I've heard of you. I think most people have heard of you, Senator.'

'You know about this "Roman Empire" thing?'

Myles paused, and scratched his head. 'The threat, Senator?'

'Yes, and it is a threat. It's a threat to the whole United States…'

The Senator raised his voice to emphasise points and spat out the important words. Myles could tell he wouldn't like to spend much time with the man.

'Mr Munro, we've got intelligence which says this threat is blackmail.'

'Blackmail, Senator?'

'Yes. Someone is trying to hold the whole USA to ransom.'

Myles paused before he asked the obvious question. 'Do you know who it is?'

'Yes we do,' came the reply, confident and instant.

'Well, can you tell me?'

'No I can't, Munro.'

Myles was more bemused than angry. 'So, how do you want me to help you?'

'Mr Munro, I need you to come with me to sort this out.'

To Myles, the request seemed absurd. He thought, then answered carefully. 'Why me, Senator?'

'Because I've just heard you on TV, Myles, and you know the Roman Empire.'

Myles let out a frustrated wheeze of breath. Whatever the Senator was planning, it had the makings of a fiasco. 'Senator, I don't know the Roman Empire. I don't know who's blackmailing you, and I'm not American. You'll be able to find someone much better.'

There was the sound of shock at the other end of the line: the Senator was not used to people saying 'no' to him. Myles could hear the Senator exhaling very deliberately. 'Munro, there is also another reason.'

'Well, what is it?'

'It's a reason I can't explain over an open phone line. Few people get a chance to serve their country like this.'

Myles refused the bait. 'Senator, I've just served my country, in Afghanistan. I've got nothing against Americans – I'm even dating one…' He saw Helen smile. 'And there will be lots of Americans far better than me for what you have in mind.'

Myles was about to offer help finding someone else. But the Senator had already ended the phone call.

CHAPTER EIGHT
Washington DC, USA

The Senator was furious. He pushed the phone across his desk, away from him. 'You said this guy understood the military,' he boomed. 'He should know why some things can't be said over the phone.'

Susan hadn't yet learned that the Senator was not to be corrected. 'I said he gave lectures about the military, Senator.'

'I read the brief. It said he'd worked closely with Military Intelligence,' huffed the Senator. 'Is this what the British call "intelligence"?' Senator Roosevelt tossed the thin briefing folder in the air.

Papers fluttered down all over the office. Susan tried to read them as she gathered them up. She soon realised the Senator was right and she was wrong.

The Senator put his head in his hands, scratching his scalp through his white hair. 'Don't we have any Americans with a long-lost connection to this Juma guy or his Ivy-League wife?'

The words 'Ivy-League' were said with a sneer. Susan, a Harvard-alum herself, tried not to take the bait. 'No, Senator,' she answered, squarely.

The Senator picked up a photo which had fallen onto the floor. He held it close to his face as he studied it, looking at the man eye-to-eye. 'So this is Juma,' he mused. Roosevelt had seen many photos like this when he was chair of the Senate Foreign Affairs Committee. It had obviously been taken with a long-distance lens, which meant either spooks or Special Forces. Juma was someone they couldn't get close to. Sam Roosevelt ignored the man's muscular physique. He registered the way Juma held his gun, but it was the expression on his face which struck him most: Juma had a recklessness about him, as though he didn't care about anything. 'This is the pirate who thinks he can send a bomber to the Big Apple…'

'Through his wife, Senator – Homeland said the messages sent to the bomber were all from Juma's wife, not Juma himself.'

'OK. So Juma – or his wife – sends a bomber to New York. They write ransom demands on little bits of paper and think people will listen because they put the confetti in a bomb. Then the bomb goes off in a different place to where it's supposed to and the bomber gets caught.'

'Yes, Senator.'

'And they still send a text message to his phone? *After* he's been caught?'

'That's right. Even though their bomb was foiled, they still made the demand.'

The Senator paused and thought. Text messages and a bomb plot which went wrong. It seemed very amateurish. 'Read me out the text message again.'

Susan checked her paper and read from it. 'It said: "If you don't want America to suffer the same fate as Rome, then send a delegation to meet me, and I will set out my terms. I will only talk with Senator Roosevelt. He should bring a representative from his old firm, the Roosevelt Guardians, and the Oxford University historian, Myles Munro. No one else."'

The Senator absorbed the information again. 'Who does this pot-chewing pirate from Libya think he is?'

'Er, it's called "Qat", Senator. And he is from Somalia. He's only been in Libya for a few years.'

The Senator looked confused, a facial expression that demanded an explanation from Susan.

'Qat, Sir. It's the drug they chew. Not pot, Senator, Qat.' Susan smiled quietly to herself.

The Senator let her small victory pass. 'OK. But why did Juma move from Somalia to Libya?'

Susan had read up on this. 'In 2009, the Libyan dictator Colonel Gaddafi tried to develop a navy, so he invited in a whole bunch of Somali pirates,' she explained. 'Juma was one of them. Later, Gaddafi paid them to fight for him as mercenaries. But when Gaddafi was killed in 2011, the mercenaries were abandoned. Some left Libya, but many stayed and turned to crime.'

'Was this guy Juma involved in murdering our Ambassador Stevens and his staff in the Benghazi consulate attack on September 11th, 2012?'

'I don't know, sir,' Susan replied. 'He may have been complicit.'

Senator Roosevelt frowned at her – not knowing was bad, and speculating was worse. 'Just stick with the facts, missy. Do we know whether Juma still leads a bunch of Somali pirates?'

'More than that, Senator. Juma leads one of the militias which rival the defence forces in the New Libya,' she explained. 'Juma's got many of the Africans who came to Libya to work for the oil firms.'

'Migrant workers, you mean?'

'If they can find work. Many try to escape to Europe – every few days a boatload of them sinks in the Mediterranean. And if they make it to Italy they just get sent back. Juma doesn't need to offer them much to bring them into his gang.'

'So Juma's leading a band of slaves, huh?' Senator Roosevelt nodded to himself. 'A real modern-day Spartacus...'

'He'd like to think so, sir. The new authorities in Libya – the guys elected after Gaddafi – have tried to round them up but failed. And no one knows where Juma lives.'

Senator Roosevelt didn't notice Susan agreeing with his assessment. He began thinking aloud. Susan took it as a good sign – it meant he trusted her. 'OK, so our first choice is: do we let Juma dictate who's on our team?'

'Sir, if we do, we need to handle the media on it,' insisted Susan. 'It would mean both negotiating with terrorists and giving in to their first demand before we'd even started.'

'Agreed.' Then the Senator waved his hand. 'But I've talked with all sorts of crazies over the years. If we try to send a different team, then he'll refuse to meet us and do something stupid. For the media, just say it was an old man doing peace talks. Something like that.'

'OK, Senator.'

'Next, Juma's gonna let us bring a Roosevelt Guardian along. But which one should I take?'

Susan nodded. Her expressions made clear that she was very keen to accompany him.

'I suppose you want to come along.'

'Yes, Senator. Although I'm from Homeland, I'm on your staff. I could count as a Roosevelt Guardian.'

The Senator pulled a thinking face. Then he smiled like a father about to disappoint. 'No. I'm sorry. Two reasons. You're too official – if this goes wrong, it's got to look like the independent peace mission of a has-been hero.'

'I could resign from Homeland Security, and just work for you, sir.'

'If you resign from Homeland then you're no good to me.'

Susan pretended to ignore the insult. 'And the second reason, Senator?'

'You're a woman.'

Susan tried to hide her astonishment. Could anybody really be that sexist anymore? Then she remembered who she was talking to. Sam Roosevelt had no trouble at all being sexist.

The Senator tried to console her. 'It's not me. I know you could do it,' he said, eyebrows raised. 'It's them. The terrorists. They won't take you seriously.'

Susan didn't look convinced. The Senator rammed the point home. 'We've got to remember our mission: we're not going to enlighten them about gender equality. We're going to stop them killing Americans.'

Susan had to accept the logic. 'So who will you take?'

The Senator looked at the photographs on his wall: faded pictures of himself as a young football star, a Marine, a Junior Senator in Iowa where he came close to winning his party's presidential nomination… Then he settled on a family picture. 'Dick. I'll take Dick. He's become a five-minute hero in New York. If he's going to inherit my Senate seat he needs foreign affairs experience.'

Then the Senator smiled like a gambler about to play the same bet twice. 'And don't think I've given up on this British guy…'

CHAPTER NINE
JFK Airport, New York

Together, Myles and Helen collected their bags and walked off the plane. Through the arrivals corridor of Terminal One, they followed the other passengers until they reached passport control. There the corridor split: one way for US citizens, another for aliens. Myles waved off Helen as they joined different queues.

'Meet you at the other side,' she called, blowing him a kiss as she left.

He smiled back to her, then approached his own line. Soon he was giving his landing card to the female immigration official and allowing his iris to be scanned.

'Do you intend to stay long in the United States, Mr Munro?' asked the American official.

'Er, no, not really.'

The border officer smiled at his English accent while she swiped his passport. 'You travelled to Afghanistan recently?'

Myles nodded.

'Military?'

'No, but with the military. I study war.'

The official accepted his answer, then waited for her computer to give the all-clear. But something flagged up. She frowned. 'Mr Munro – there's a special message for you. You need to report to that room over there.' She pointed to one of the interview rooms at the back.

'That one?'

'Yeah.'

Myles thought of asking what it was, but realised he might as well find out for himself.

An American woman with an ID badge around her neck introduced herself with a handshake. 'Susan from Homeland Security,' she said, welcoming him into the room. 'Good to meet you, Mr Munro.'

Myles took in the room around him: no windows, just white walls.

Susan invited him to take a seat. 'Would you like a drink?' She was wrestling a plastic cup from a dispenser, which she filled from a water cooler in the corner of the room, then brought it to him.

'Thank you. Will I be here long?'

Susan didn't answer. Instead she reacted as if to say 'you'll find out soon enough'.

Then the door opened again.

In walked an ageing but very fit-looking man. Smaller than Myles had expected, but with a face he recognised immediately. Sam Roosevelt.

Myles remembered Sam Roosevelt's bids to be President – and his famous campaign slogan: 'We're all going bust if we ain't got trust.'

Roosevelt had stood out in the crowd of political wannabes. In one of the Presidential TV debates, he'd famously distinguished himself by daring to agree with Bill Clinton's line on Bosnia. Other candidates had tried to call him a coward for it, but the charge could never stick: Senator Roosevelt's personal story was far too glorious for that. As a marine, he'd won the Congressional Medal of Honor in Vietnam for rescuing a small army of American POWs from the Vietcong. He had led a team of only five men to take on more than twenty. Roosevelt, then only a junior officer, had planned the audacious assault on the position himself. His actions that day in 1971 were still studied at West Point as an example of tactical brilliance. Myles had even referred to them in his Oxford University lectures.

Myles stood up to offer a handshake. The Senator motioned to a chair, directing Myles to sit back down again. Myles obeyed.

As he sat down, a younger man entered the room behind the Senator. The two men plus Susan were squaring up to him like an interview panel. Sam Roosevelt waited until everyone was seated before he started at Myles. 'So you're the guy who said "no" to me on the phone, huh?' he said.

Myles refused to be intimidated. 'Correct, Senator. But I can help you find…'

'No.' The Senator had cut him off, then paused, sizing Myles up before he offered more. 'Mr Munro, America needs you.'

Sam Roosevelt explained what he couldn't say over the phone: the threat that 'America will be brought down like the Roman Empire' had come from Libya. From a Somali pirate based there called 'Juma'. And Myles knew his wife. 'You studied history with her – when you were an undergraduate at Oxford University.'

'So you want me to help because I once knew his wife – when I was a student?'

The Senator shook his head. Myles wasn't getting it. 'No, Munro. The pirate sent a bomber to New York. The bomber was caught, and my son, here, drove the bomb away from Wall Street.'

Roosevelt waved his hand in the direction of the young man sitting beside him. Dick Roosevelt was about to introduce himself formally but his father ignored him and continued. 'Then they sent their demands,' said Sam. '*After* their bomber had been caught. And they demanded that the negotiation team include…' The Senator poked Myles with his finger as he completed his sentence '…you'.

Myles looked to Dick and Susan for a reaction. There was none. They were watching for his.

Myles offered a response. 'So you're going to talk with this man?'

'Yes, absolutely.' The Senator answered without hesitation. He had no doubts at all. Myles could tell Dick Roosevelt was less sure: negotiating with terrorists made the young man uneasy.

The Senator continued. 'We've already got a plan for this...' The Senator outlined his ideas and Myles listened. The plan seemed simple: fly to Cairo in neighbouring Egypt, drive in US Embassy vehicles up to the Libyan border, then cross into Libya under the protection of his own Roosevelt Guardians. They would come out the way they went in. There were even back-up options, in case something went wrong.

Sam Roosevelt clearly missed the front line. Trips with the Armed Services Committee and campaign season might come close. But it was nothing like tactical planning for real. Like all politicians who had made their reputations in the military, Senator Sam Roosevelt relished the details of war-fighting. Neither Myles nor the Senator's son were surprised as Sam went through the specifics.

Myles allowed the Senator to finish, then cocked his head to one side. 'OK, but what if this "Juma" guy...' Myles made eye contact with Susan and Dick to check he had Juma's name right. 'What if "Juma" doesn't want to talk?'

Sam Roosevelt became enthusiastic at the question. 'We know he wants to meet a delegation because he's asked for one. But we don't want namby-pamby diplomats putting this in wordy speak. So the answer will come from me.'

The Senator put out a hand as a surgeon might ask for a scalpel. Susan placed a fountain pen on his palm. Maintaining eye contact with Myles, the Senator grabbed a sheet of clear white paper from his assistant and began to scrawl.

Juma.

You have threatened the most powerful nation on earth.
One of your men has exploded a bomb here.
We will meet you to talk. We may also blast you to hell.

Sam Roosevelt

The Senator screwed the lid back on his pen and passed the paper back to Susan. 'Make sure he gets that.'

'Yes, Senator.'

Sam Roosevelt concentrated back on Myles. 'Good thought, Mr Munro. We'll work well together. So you're in, then?'

The Senator was in full persuasion mode. His charisma was compelling. Myles could see how donors, voters and just about everyone this man met said 'yes'. How could Myles say 'no'? He looked at Dick and Susan – they were fully behind the Senator, encouraging Myles to come into line too. Everybody was just waiting for him to agree…

Myles faced Sam Roosevelt squarely as he answered.

'No, Senator.'

CHAPTER TEN
JFK Airport, New York

Sam Roosevelt frowned, staring at Myles, but still hoping to persuade the Englishman. 'Why won't you come with me?' The Senator paused, trying to size him up. 'Money? How much do you want?'

Myles shook his head. He didn't care about money.

'You're scared?'

Again, Myles shook his head.

The Senator's frown deepened. 'Then please explain.'

'Well, Senator – you've told me how you're going to get there and get out again, but nothing about the crucial part: the talks themselves.'

The Senator nodded respectfully. 'OK. First, we find out whether this guy's serious. If he is, we stop him doing whatever he has in mind.'

Myles thought before coming back. 'And how could we stop him, Senator?'

'Not by trying to invade Libya,' assured the Senator. Everybody knew the Senator had been a sole voice on the Senate floor warning against America's doomed intervention in Somalia in the early 1990s. Sending US troops into Libya, now supposedly 'free' after the Arab Spring, threatened to repeat the humiliation of Black Hawk Down.

The Senator indicated to Susan, who pulled some files out from under the table which were marked 'confidential'. The

Senator offered them to Myles. 'If you want to read more, we've got plenty of material for you.'

Intrigued, Myles glanced at a CIA briefing on Juma. Myles picked it up and began to read:

```
Juma is the leader of a group of Somali pirates,
now based in Libya. From his headquarters in
Sirte, on the coast – a lawless city which refuses
to accept Libya's new government – he has rapidly
come to dominate Libya's underworld...
```

The brief explained how Juma had first caught the attention of the CIA. As an impoverished teenager in Somalia, he'd been lured to Istanbul by a criminal gang who promised to buy one of his kidneys. After the surgery, Juma had been flown back to Mogadishu with the promise there'd be someone waiting there to pay him. There wasn't. One kidney down, and no money to show for it, the young Juma refused to be taken for a fool. He had smuggled himself on a cargo vessel back to Turkey without a visa. There, he'd tracked down the gang, killed a few of the middlemen, then threatened the gang leader. The gang leader – frightened for his own life – agreed to go back to Somalia with him, where all his money was signed over to Juma. The gang leader then disappeared, presumed dead. The cash enabled Juma to hire some local muscle in Somalia and establish a gang of his own. In 2009, Colonel Gaddafi invited Juma and his pirates to Libya. When Gaddafi's regime began to crumble in February 2011, Juma's men became mercenaries for the dictator. Several died fighting for him, and some were arrested when the dictator was killed in October of that year. But most escaped. They revelled in the lawlessness of 'Free Libya' – the Arab Spring meant they didn't need to take orders anymore. Untouched by the new rulers of the country, Juma had become the brutal leader of a large criminal network…

The CIA's psychological assessment was blunt: 'Presumed Psychopathic'.

The Senator, Dick and Susan had waited silently while Myles read the paper. Dick Roosevelt broke first. 'So you know this guy's wife from school?'

'I don't know,' shrugged Myles. 'Who's his wife?'

Without words, Richard Roosevelt passed another piece of paper towards Myles, then watched the Englishman's face.

Myles tried not to react, although when he re-read the name he found himself swallowing in shock. He hesitated before answering. 'You're telling me this "Juma" guy is married to Placidia?'

Dick nodded.

'Then yes,' Myles admitted. 'I do know her.'

Dick leant forward. 'How well did you know her, exactly?' The question was snide – half accusing Myles of something, half voyeurism.

Myles ignored it. 'She was a Rhodes scholar. We studied the history of the Roman Empire together – Placidia was my tutorial partner for a term. She was much cleverer than me.'

Dick Roosevelt had heard of the Oxford university tutorial system, where just one or two students were taught in person by a world expert in a subject. 'And you became friends?'

'Yes, we did. We were very good friends.'

'Just friends. Really?' Dick Roosevelt was trying to probe.

'Yes. But after her year in Oxford she went back to Harvard, and I lost contact with her. I've not heard from her for a long time now.'

Dick checked with his father that he still had permission to ask questions. He did. 'So, Myles, why do you think a highly educated half-American woman has hitched up with a psychopathic pirate in the third world?'

Myles raised his eyebrows. 'I don't know. Only explanation I can think of is...' He hesitated.

Dick urged him on. 'Is...?'

'Well, love.'

Myles' answer disarmed Dick, who began looking through the CIA briefing pack to see if there was a sheet on the woman. He double-checked the whole file: there was nothing. As Dick leafed through his sheets, Myles glimpsed the top of a page the younger Roosevelt was trying to keep covered.

```
Myles Munro: Oxford University Lecturer of
Military History
Exceptionally Intelligent (top 0.1%) but problems
with some basic tasks...
Distrustful of bureaucrats...
```

Myles was curious. He pointed the sheet out to Dick. 'Mind if I read that?'

Dick looked to his father for advice.

Sam Roosevelt shook his head, taking charge. 'Myles, look,' he levelled. 'Your name was in a text message sent to the mobile of someone who planted a bomb in the middle of Manhattan. Don't be surprised there's a confidential CIA briefing on you.'

'Well, can I read it?'

'I'm afraid you don't have the security clearance.'

'And yet you still want me to go with you, to meet this madman in Libya?' Myles was moving his body to indicate he was about to leave the room.

The Senator put his hand on his shoulder. 'Mr Munro. America needs your help, and – hell – I need your help. Come on. Please.'

Myles didn't respond.

The Senator knew he still hadn't Myles won over. He paused, then hunched his shoulders a little, ready to change tack. 'You know, Myles, your ex-girlfriend has got herself mixed up with a terrorist. I can only imagine she asked for you because she needed your help.' He stared into Myles' eyes. 'Placidia needs your help, Myles.'

Myles absorbed Sam Roosevelt's plea. He looked at Susan and Dick, whose expressions were underwriting Sam's words – that Placidia really *did* need him.

He turned back to the Senator. 'OK,' he said. 'I'll help.'

The door burst open. It was Helen, with an apologetic immigration official trailing behind her. The four people in the room were as surprised to see her as she was to see them. 'Myles, so this is where they took you…'

She acknowledged the Senator, who responded on Myles' behalf. 'Ma'am, your boyfriend is about to become a hero,' said Roosevelt senior.

Helen wasn't buying it. 'Senator, my "boyfriend" needs a rest.'

The Senator was about to get angry, but Myles intervened. 'I'm still young enough to be a "boy"-friend?' Everybody relaxed. Myles put his hands on Helen's elbows and spoke slowly. 'I've got to do this. I'll be back soon.'

'You've got to?'

'Helen… I must.'

'Must?' She winced as she said the word. It was probably the most meaningless explanation Myles had ever given her.

'Yes, Helen, I must.'

Helen surveyed the room. She wanted to fight it, but she could tell she was outnumbered and that the decision had already been made.

She turned to the Senator. 'Senator, keep him safe. Please.'

Sam Roosevelt nodded but said nothing.

The Senator made no promise to keep Myles safe at all.

DAY II

CHAPTER ELEVEN
Cairo International Airport, Egypt

Myles was woken by the noise of the wheels folding out from under the commercial airliner. A stewardess was standing over him: he needed to put on his seatbelt. The aircraft was about to land.

A wave of applause swept through the plane as it touched town with only a few bumps. The passengers – half of whom were Egyptians returning home – were glad to have landed safely.

As the plane taxied over the smooth tarmac, Myles saw the terminal buildings of Cairo's main airport through the windows. White paint was peeling from sun-soaked walls. He saw some scaffolding not far from the runway, and an old bus probably used to transport people into passport control. Four airport workers were standing around a fuel tanker – they seemed to be lighting cigarettes.

Dick Roosevelt saw the men and winced. 'How dangerous is *that*?'

Myles just smiled. Different places, different people.

A team of airport workers rolled a set of aircraft steps up to United Airlines flight 9856. The door was soon open, while the captain announced a standard greeting over the intercom. 'Welcome to Cairo, capital of Egypt, where the temperature today will reach 105 degrees Fahrenheit...'

Myles kept looking outside: two well-built white men in suit jackets, chinos, neat blue shirts and sunglasses appeared at the bottom of the steps. With a sense of authority, they breezed up to the plane's door as it swung open and invited themselves onto the passenger jet. Barely acknowledging the cabin staff, they were soon standing in front of Myles – and the Senator. 'Senator, we're from the Embassy, sir.'

Sam Roosevelt ignored the IDs offered by the two men. His body language responded as if the men's arrival was completely normal. 'OK, thanks guys.' He had already taken his bag from the overhead locker and moved out to join the men.

'Anything in baggage, sir?'

'No. We won't be staying here long.'

The two security men took the Senator's jacket and bag, and guided him to the steps. With Myles and Dick behind, the five men were first to leave the plane.

Myles was struck by the air outside: colder than he had expected. But it was dawn in Cairo – the same latitude as Houston, Texas. Within an hour the sun would have risen. Everything would heat up soon.

Myles saw Dick reach for his passport, but one of the two security men gestured with his hand: he could put it away.

'We've arranged a diplomatic passage for you, sir.'

Dick raised his eyebrows, acknowledging the pleasant surprise. His father didn't react at all.

Three white SUVs drove over the runway to meet the five men at the bottom of the aircraft steps. Diplomatic plates, special antennae on the roofs, heavily tinted bulletproof-glass windows: US Embassy vehicles.

One of the security men opened the door to the middle vehicle. Sam Roosevelt climbed inside, leaving Myles and Dick to enter the same vehicle through other doors. As soon as the last security man was in the rear car, the convoy was off, soon picking up speed and driving straight out of the airport. Uniformed Egyptian guards – or soldiers, Myles couldn't be sure – saluted the three-vehicle convoy as it passed through the exit gates.

Once free from the clutter of the airport, the convoy accelerated onto the main highway to the west. From the passing road-signs, Myles could tell they were avoiding central Cairo. Instead, they headed out to the desert, and fast. Flashing red and blue lights from the front vehicle challenged any car refusing to let the convoy overtake. The SUVs snaked in tight formation along the highway, between overgrown grass verges and kerbstones painted black and white. Myles saw shacks at the side of the road, carwashes which seemed to employ whole families, and a long line of trucks carrying goods from one end of Africa to another. But although some of the scenes were very foreign, many were also very familiar: a stall selling cans of Coke, a teenager in sneakers, and a banged-up Chevrolet. Little bits of America had reached Egypt already.

Inside the air-conditioned SUV, Dick admired the quality and design of the American Embassy vehicle, while Sam thought through their meeting with Juma. 'Professor,' began the Senator, turning to Myles. 'If he comes out with any of his stuff about Rome, are you OK answering it?'

'I'm not a professor, only a lecturer,' admitted Myles. 'But yes, I can deal with the history.'

The Senator nodded. 'OK. And Dick, you don't have a speaking part here. You understand?'

'Understood, Senator.'

Dick called his father Senator? Myles could tell being asked to do nothing was obviously humiliating for Dick Roosevelt. Myles also guessed Dick was used to it. No son could ever shine when their father was as magnificent as Senator Sam, even when he'd just become the hero of New York.

After three hours of travel, as they passed a sign indicating they were close to the Libyan border, the convoy slowed and pulled over.

'Time to cross-deck, Senator. This is as far as the Embassy can take you.'

Five cars were waiting for them, surrounded by more men in shades and combat vests.

Myles saw these men were more heavily armed. And unlike the Embassy guards, they made no effort to hide their weapons. Myles recognised their uniform immediately: Roosevelt Guardians.

In the rising mid-morning heat, Myles, the Senator and the Senator's son climbed out of their official government escort. Small bottles of water were passed around amongst them while eager security men formed a protective box around their VIPs.

The Senator watched the Embassy vehicles depart, raising his water to them as a toast.

Dick spoke through a sarcastic smile. 'Who needs government transport when you've got private security which actually takes you where you want to go?' Then he laughed to himself. 'Hey – who needs government at all?'

His father didn't respond. Instead, he made a move towards the car door, and the new convoy prepared to roll out.

Within minutes they were approaching the Libyan border.

There, they were greeted by a single border guard. The man stood in the middle of the road, and waved at them to pull over. He was carrying a very battered AK-47 assault rifle.

CHAPTER TWELVE
Egypt-Libya Border

The convoy slowed to a stop, dutifully obeying the lone border guard. The guard beckoned the cars to bunch up until they were almost touching. Myles saw one of the Guardians step out of the front vehicle, lift his shades and offer a bunch of passports.

The guard took the papers, nodded, and wandered away to a hut made of concrete just out of Myles' sight.

Several minutes passed.

Then Myles heard the driver's radio crackle with a message for the convoy. It was from the car at the back. 'They've just pulled a mine behind us,' came the voice, unnerved. 'We can't reverse. Out.'

Myles turned to see African men with Kalashnikovs slung over their shoulders, who had appeared from nowhere, holding old Soviet-era anti-tank mines. They dropped them near the lead vehicle's forward tyres. Nonchalant, the men pushed the mines until they were exactly in place. Then they moved away. None of the men bothered with eye contact.

The convoy could no longer drive away.

The Senator registered concern. 'Is this normal?'

None of the Guardians knew who was meant to answer. Eventually the driver spoke. 'No, Senator.'

'Well you make sure you're ready to move those goddamn mines if we need to leave in a hurry.'

'We will, Sir.'

Myles kept watching and wondering. He knew something was wrong, but didn't know what.

Several more minutes passed. Myles could see the Roosevelt Guardian standing outside in the sun was beginning to sweat.

Then, out of nowhere, a much larger group of armed men emerged. In two columns, they filed down both sides of the convoy. There they waited for several more minutes, until more men came, holding more mines. These were placed under the three middle vehicles in the convoy. Whatever armour the vehicles had underneath, Myles knew if the mines exploded, the SUVs would be obliterated.

Suddenly, one of the border guards leant forward and pulled on the door handle next to Dick Roosevelt. It opened.

The man tugged at Dick Roosevelt's arm, and quickly dragged him out of the vehicle. Before he knew what had happened, Dick Roosevelt stood confused and blinking in the sun.

The open car door was swiftly closed again, and a message flickered over the convoy's radios. 'Lockdown – Lockdown!'

The cars locked their doors in unison. The men with guns heard the mechanisms clunk and reacted by pulling on the door handles. None opened.

The man holding Dick Roosevelt pointed his gun under the American's chin. Myles saw a disfiguring scar across the man's abdomen, and witnessed how casually he handled his weapon.

The Roosevelt Guardian who was standing outside waiting for the passports moved over. He raised his shades, hoping for eye contact with the man holding the younger Roosevelt. 'Can you release him, please?' The Roosevelt Guardian made his point as politely as he could.

But the man smiled like he didn't care. Myles could see his teeth were rotten. 'We have to search the vehicles,' he said.

'Yes, but can you release this man first, please?'

'We have to search the vehicles,' repeated the man.

The Guardian pressed the radio mic clipped to his collar. 'They say they need to search the vehicles before they release the Secondary Principal.'

There was a pause, then a reply came over the system. 'OK, release the doors.'

The Senator slammed his fist against one of the seats. 'No. That's bad procedure. We sit tight.'

The driver quickly relayed his instruction back over the radio. 'Negative: we do NOT release the doors,' he shouted into the mic. 'Repeat, do NOT release the doors. Sit tight. Out.'

The Senator checked that his order was being obeyed before he started muttering to Myles. 'What sort of security business has this become? We can't release the doors just because some pirate waves a gun around...'

The African man with the scar soon realised what had happened: the Americans were playing hardball...

He waited for a few moments to check they weren't going to change their minds. Then he poked the gun barrel further into Dick Roosevelt's chin. Dick Roosevelt called out, words which could only just be heard through the vehicles' thick bulletproof glass. 'Dad? They want you to open the doors,' pleaded the younger Roosevelt. 'Father?'

The Senator didn't blink. His face simply said 'America can't give in to terrorists'.

Myles saw Dick Roosevelt trying to catch his father's attention, but Sam Roosevelt refused to even turn his head.

Then the African nodded to one of his men, who took Dick Roosevelt from him and led him away, towards a concrete hut and out of sight of the main convoy. The hero of the Wall Street bomb looked terrified.

The gang leader called over the sole Roosevelt Guardian who was standing outside, unprotected. 'Hey, you. Do you smoke?' He asked his question casually.

'Sometimes, yes,' admitted the American private security man, trying to be helpful. He was a tall man with shades hanging round his neck. 'Do you want a cigarette?' He delved in his back pocket, reaching for a packet of smokes. Several of the Africans cocked their guns towards him, wary that he might be reaching for a weapon. But they relaxed when the man's hand reappeared, armed only with a box of twenty. The Roosevelt Guardian held out the pack, offering them to the border guard.

The African waved them away. 'No thanks. You ought to give that up.'

'No use – I've tried,' said the security man, trying to joke. 'It's not so easy.'

With an arrogant smile, the gang leader with the scar leaned back and laughed. 'Oh, it's very easy. I can stop you ever smoking again.'

The crack of a single gunshot rang out and the Roosevelt Guardian collapsed into the dirt, still holding his packet of cigarettes. Myles saw dark blood ooze out from beneath the Guardian's body, soaking into the dust beside him.

CHAPTER THIRTEEN
Egypt-Libya Border

The Roosevelt Guardians inside the vehicles stared in horror at the murder. One moved to jump out, desperate to offer life support to their fallen friend.

The Senator stopped him. 'Stay inside. He's dead – nothing you can do for him.'

'Yes, Sir.'

Myles watched as the border guards ambled around the body. One of them kicked the Roosevelt Guardian to check he had been killed. Another searched his pockets, pretending it was an official check but really just looking for things to steal. They allowed several more minutes to pass, making sure the impact of the murder sunk in.

Then their leader moved forward, his face right up against the bulletproof glass nearest to Sam Roosevelt. 'Senator,' he hissed. 'Open up your convoy so we can search your vehicles…' He spoke his words coldly, then twisted his face on the glass and grinned. 'Or we kill your son.'

The Senator lifted his palm to his forehead. Myles could tell what he was thinking: *How had it come to this?*

Sam Roosevelt had started his 'Guardians' when he was fresh out of Vietnam. By professionalising his private security company back in the seventies, Sam Roosevelt had made his Guardians the market leader. It took more than a decade for his methods to become the industry standard. By then he had captured most of the contracts. Roosevelt Guardians had become a brand. It gave Sam a claim to leadership even greater than the family name. How had Dick let the standards collapse?

Myles had seen the mistakes, too. Dick Roosevelt's door should have been locked. They shouldn't have let the guard with the passports leave the vehicle. The drivers shouldn't have parked so close – they'd allowed the convoy to be boxed in.

These weren't single accidents. They pointed to systematic failure. Under Dick Roosevelt, the Roosevelt Guardians had lost their discipline.

Myles heard the Senator curse himself. 'Resting on our damn laurels...' the old man muttered. It was a phrase from Ancient Rome. Myles guessed Sam Roosevelt probably knew laurels were awarded for military glory – past glory.

One of the Guardians turned to the Senator for guidance. 'Sir? We need to answer.'

'Well, what do your damn protocols say?'

The security man paused. He had no ready answer.

The Senator thumped the seat with his fist. 'What has this firm become? You should have this worked out in advance. OK, what are your choices?'

'Well, sit tight or let them search the vehicles, sir.'

'OK, so what happens in each case?' quizzed the Senator.

'Well, if we sit tight, they'll probably kill the Secondary Principal – your son, sir.'

'And?'

The security guard was shocked by how easily the Senator could contemplate his son's death. 'Sir, after that, if we still sit tight, they'll use the road mines to blow up our vehicles.'

The Senator nodded, then continued with his questions, which were fast becoming rhetorical. 'And are the vehicles armoured to withstand the blasts?'

'Er, don't know. Probably not, sir.' The Guardian wanted to be rescued from his one-man Senate inquiry. He turned to Myles for help.

Myles recognised the mines pushed under the vehicles. They were anti-tank mines, ex-Soviet stock – maybe TM-46s, but he couldn't be sure. 'If these vehicles have B6 level armour or less,' explained Myles, 'the mines underneath us would destroy them completely.'

The Roosevelt Guardian nodded – their armour was level B6.

The Senator bowed his head: the company he had created as a young man hadn't even provided them with the right equipment. Anti-tank mines were an obvious risk, yet the Guardians had done nothing about it.

Myles could tell: the Senator understood he had to surrender. If they held out, the Senator would lose his son. If he held out some more, the gang would destroy all their vehicles. They'd be even more defenceless.

Myles saw Sam Roosevelt check the faces of the people in the car around him before he issued the instruction. 'OK, release the doors,' the old man grizzled.

As the doors were unlocked, Africans with guns up and down the convoy pulled on the handles. The small army of Roosevelt Guardians were taken out of all five vehicles and forced to line up beside the road. There they were disarmed, then instructed to lie face down with their hands behind their heads.

The sun was now almost directly above them.

The Senator and Myles were treated with more ceremony: given water and allowed to remain standing, while the Africans searched through all the vehicles and made sure they had all the firearms. Radios were collected, along with every other device the group possessed – a camera, some satellite phones, a homing beacon, and several GPS units. Finally, the anti-tank mines were pulled away from underneath the vehicles. Some of the Africans climbed inside and the cars were driven off.

Myles, the Senator, and their small private army were absolutely defenceless on the roadside just inside Libya.

One of the Roosevelt Guardians murmured what everybody already knew. 'These can't be real border guards. I don't think they're even from Libya…'

The African gang leader – the small man with the scar and the swagger – approached, his gun loose about his shoulder. He snorted at the Guardian, as if to say 'who cares?', then moved on towards his real prize: Senator Sam Roosevelt. 'Senator, thank you for coming,' he grinned.

'You must be Juma.'

'Yes, I am. And soon you'll wish you'd never heard of me.'

Juma waved his gun at the Roosevelt Guardians lying face down on the ground. You now have a choice, Senator,' he said, staring Sam in the eye. 'I'm about to give you a gun. Either you kill three of your men,' grinned Juma. 'Or I will kill them all.'

CHAPTER FOURTEEN
Egypt-Libya Border

The Senator looked at Juma in disgust. *Was this man serious?*

Juma cocked his head. He was chewing and smiling, as if he had a narcotic in his mouth.

The Senator's eyes squinted in the sun. He was trying to determine whether this psychopath had any humanity about him at all.

Juma let the Senator ponder his problem while he strolled over towards Myles. 'And you must be the great Myles Munro. The man with the strange brain.'

Myles nodded, unconcerned by the insult.

Juma looked up at the Englishman curiously, one eye closed to keep out the sun. 'Myles: kill three men so that ten others may live? What would you do?'

Myles let the issue tumble around in his mind, acutely aware there was no good outcome. He tried to understand Juma: small, arrogant, ruthless – and probably on qat. Juma had just triumphed over the Senator – killing one of the Americans, and forcing the rest out of their vehicles unarmed. Even though he had scored a victory, Juma wanted more.

No way to win this: Myles had to distract Juma. He glanced over to the Senator, before returning to the pirate warlord. 'Do you still have Dick?' he asked.

Juma nodded. He leaned over to someone behind him and gestured with his hand.

A few moments later Dick Roosevelt was led back up to the main group. His clothes were ruffled, and he looked pale and very shaken. Perhaps a bruise around his mouth. But he was safe.

The Senator opened his arms and called out to him. 'Son.'

Dick looked fearfully at Juma before he moved. With a swagger, Juma gave his permission.

Dick Roosevelt crossed over to his father, who put his arms around him, rubbing him on the back. 'Glad you're safe, son.'

Dick Roosevelt said nothing. It was as if he knew his father had contemplated sacrificing him for the rest of the convoy. Then he began whimpering in his father's arms.

BANG.

The unmistakeable sound of a gunshot cracked through the desert. Myles and the Roosevelts, father and son reunited, looked over in unison to where the sound had come from.

One of the Guardians lying face down on the ground had just been shot through the head.

Juma raised his gun up again. 'Twelve left, gentlemen,' he announced. 'The offer stands: you kill three or I kill them all.'

The Senator shook his head in disbelief. 'Look, punk, we came here to offer you a last chance of survival. If you want to play death games then you're going to die so quickly…'

Juma just kept smiling. He walked over to another one of the private security men. The man was quivering in fear. Juma nuzzled the barrel of his automatic weapon into the fat on the man's neck and grinned as he turned his face up at Myles and the Senator. He tensed his finger on the trigger.

'Wait…'

Myles' call made Juma raise his eyebrows in a look of mock intrigue.

But only for a moment.

BANG.

In an instant, another of the Guardians was dead. Blood from his lifeless body began seeping into the dust.

The remaining Guardians were terrified, trying to remain as still as they could, while knowing that they too could be killed at any moment.

Myles couldn't allow this to keep happening. 'What are you trying to do, Juma?' he called out. 'You're trying to threaten America? You're trying to get us to kill our own security guards? Why?'

Juma strolled back, still smiling. 'I'm teaching you about American values, Mr Munro.'

The Senator pulled a face, as if to say, 'American values? Is this guy serious?'

Juma could see the reaction. 'You would rather let twelve men die than save nine if it meant dirtying your own hands.'

Myles hit back. 'Juma: killing unarmed men on the ground is not "Life, Liberty and the pursuit of Happiness".'

'No, it's not, Mr Munro, "sir",' Juma mocked. 'But Americans will happily let Africans die as long as it means you don't get bloody yourself.'

Finally Myles and the Senator could see the point Juma was making.

Myles tried to console the Somali gang leader some more. He realised he had to offer a compromise before Juma restated his ultimatum. 'OK, how about this: you keep these men hostage, while you take me, the Senator and his son wherever you want to take us,' he offered. 'We have our negotiation, then we all leave. OK?'

Juma turned the offer over in his mind. He clearly hadn't expected it. He glanced over at Sam and Dick Roosevelt. Both had expressions on their faces saying 'do it'.

He looked up at the sky: cloudless. Juma knew about satellites and knew he was probably being watched from several hundred miles above by high-tech hardware. Maybe by a lethal drone not so far away.

He nodded. Waving his hand again, one of his men made a call on their radio. A few minutes later a stream of battered Nissan pick-ups drove up – some had rusted bullet holes and most had machine guns mounted on the back. Armed men moved towards the Roosevelt Guardians on the ground. They bound each Guardian's wrists together with wire, then placed blindfolds over their eyes. One by one – each Roosevelt Guardian held by two of Juma's men – they were guided onto the beaten-up trucks. When all the men were loaded onto the vehicles, Juma gave the order and the Guardians were driven away, bouncing around in the back while dust kicked up from the worn tyres beneath them.

Two pick-ups remained, along with Juma and five of his men. Myles, Sam and Dick looked at each other as if to say 'what next?'

Juma, still smiling, flicked his head to one side to indicate the three men should climb into the back of one of the pick-ups. The Senator led the way, followed by Myles and Dick, who was still shaking with fear.

Once all three were aboard, Juma jumped in to join them. Then he bashed the side of the vehicle to indicate the two pick-ups could move off. 'Now it's time for some serious negotiations, gentlemen,' he bragged.

The last two pick-ups drove away from the border, leaving behind three dead Roosevelt Guardians and some scuffled dirt on the roadside.

As Myles saw the last of Egypt disappear from view behind him, he wondered how they could ever escape from the mad pirate leader who was taking them into the unknown interior of Libya.

CHAPTER FIFTEEN
Great Libyan Desert, Eastern Libya

When Myles taught military history to his students back at Oxford University, he often spoke about Libya. The North Africa desert war, 1941-43, had given Britain its first proper chance to fight back against the Nazis. The Nazis had won initially. The Germans rolled along the coast road to Egypt. They even threatened the Suez Canal. There was a sense of 'every man for himself' as Hitler's war machine swept the British troops away. Some feared the Brits had lost their will to fight. But somehow, the British Army had rediscovered its strength. Some said it was codebreakers, which allowed German supply lines to be intercepted. Some said it was equipment from America. Others argued it was the new troop commander, General Montgomery. But Myles lectured that it was something else, something innate. The Brits stopped losing when they rediscovered their sense of duty.

As the battered pick-ups swayed and rolled along desert tracks, Myles caught the faces of people in some of the villages. They were not Libyans but African migrants. Most had been drafted into the country by the dictator Gaddafi and now abandoned. A few had fled here more recently – Myles guessed from Mali, after Al Qaeda had been kicked out of the country by Western troops. Some seemed hostile, some bemused. One or two failed to realise that the three foreigners in the back of the technical were being driven under duress. But most gave a gesture to indicate they were pleased that Juma and his gang had taken in some rich Westerners. Juma puffed himself up at their reaction. He was the local hero.

The vehicle started to manoeuvre down backstreets. They were in Sirte – the coastal town which remained loyal to Gaddafi until his bloody end, and home to a tribe which still rejected the new government in Tripoli. This was the heart of lawless Libya, the place Juma had made his base, and where the years since the Arab Spring had allowed him to make millions through extortion and racketeering.

The vehicle pulled up in a walled courtyard. They had reached their destination.

The journey had probably taken three hours, and the sixty-nine-year-old Senator was looking dehydrated. The old man eyed both Myles and his son. Without words, he confirmed he was still in charge, and that he would lead the negotiations, which were sure to start soon.

Several more armed men approached. Most wore headscarves, some were dressed in old army uniforms, and a few had cheap Western clothes which fitted poorly. Only their weapons – they all carried AK-47s –identified the group as a single militia.

Juma jumped down and shouted orders in a dialect Myles couldn't understand. The Somalis started to unload their three hostages. The Senator tried to brush them away, annoyed at their rough treatment, but was eventually pulled off. Dick and Myles accepted it was time to be led off the vehicle.

When all three men were standing on the dirt, they were ordered to form a line. Then Juma took a headscarf handed to him by one of his men. It took him more than a minute to put it on.

Why does he take so long with his headscarf? Myles wondered.

With his headgear in place, Juma guided them down an alley, around a corner, and into the side entrance of a large concrete building. Myles saw the old bullet holes in the wall and guessed this was a former oil ministry office block, probably built by the Gaddafi regime many years ago. The offices had long ceased to function.

The men were directed up rough concrete stairs to the second level. There, Juma ordered them to sit cross-legged on the floor. Then the armed Libyans stepped back, keeping their guns poised and ready, to leave just their leader sitting next to the three Westerners.

'Welcome to Libya, gentlemen!' Juma said the words with a flourish, and showed his yellow teeth as he grinned at the three men.

The Senator wasn't fazed. 'OK, Mr Juma,' he replied dismissively. 'Tell us what you want, so I can say "no" and you can shoot us.'

Juma laughed, but it was clear that the Senator was serious. Myles saw Dick Roosevelt gulp, afraid that his father's firm line in negotiations was shortening his life expectancy.

Juma said nothing for several moments. Then he raised his hand. Somewhere behind Myles' back there was movement, and several plates of food were brought out. Dried fish, flat bread and an unfamiliar green vegetable were laid out before them. There followed metal dishes, water and some cups. A bowl was passed around, and the three men were invited to wash their hands in it, before drying them on a dirty rag. Still without speaking, Juma started to eat the food, eventually followed by Dick, Myles and, after much protest, the Senator. Silence lasted throughout most of the meal, broken only by the occasional request to pass something or the chink of metal on the concrete floor.

Finally, Juma spoke, still looking down at his food. 'What I want, gentlemen, is this: I want your assistance.'

Senator Sam Roosevelt spluttered on his food. He had been expecting demands – probably something ideological. Something he would have to refuse. But assistance? This was something new. 'You want assistance? You kill three of my guards and drive us here to ask for *assistance*?' He hissed the word through his teeth, as if the idea was as ridiculous as it was offensive.

'Yes, Senator.'

The Senator shook his head in disbelief, looking back down at the food in front of him. 'Well, what sort of assistance do you want?'

Juma's face acknowledged the question. He had anticipated it. He pulled out some paper from inside his shirt, which he unfolded and placed beside him. Myles saw notes were written on it in Arabic. Something about the loopy handwriting made Myles think it had been written by a woman.

Juma started talking from his notes. 'Gentlemen, you know why my people have come to need assistance from America?'

The Senator humoured him. 'Tell us.'

'First, because we have run out of food. The land here grows no more grain.'

The Senator looked dreary: hard-luck stories from people in his state were the worst part of his job. He'd had voters complain about their cars breaking down, their pets dying and their wives running off. Some old Joe trying to make him responsible for their misfortune. When he met these people, he would try to make plain that acts of God were beyond his remit. Juma was just the same. 'I'm sorry to hear about your grain, but I'm not responsible for...'

'Senator,' interrupted Juma. 'You *are* responsible.'

'How am I responsible for grain in Libya, thousands of miles away from my home?'

'Because, Senator, our best farmland was taken over by big oil companies. And the oil companies are all linked to America.'

The Senator was knocked back again. He hadn't expected that. 'So you're asking for food aid?'

'Yes, Senator,' nodded Juma.

'That's all – just food aid?'

'No.' Juma looked down again at his piece of paper. 'Senator, you know we were all in Gaddafi's militia?'

'Yes, he paid you, right?' teased Sam Roosevelt.

'That's right. But we had no choice,' asserted Juma, justifying his actions without accepting he needed to. 'Me and the people you've seen here and in the villages: we're not Libyans. We're from all over Africa. Poor places, like Somalia and Niger. Most of us were invited here by Gaddafi, then we had to become mercenaries for him.'

'OK,' acknowledged the Senator, saying it as though he wanted Juma to continue but not to suggest he had sympathy.

'Well, Senator, I need your help to stop the reprisals.'

'Reprisals?'

'Yes. The Libyans, when they find out we were mercenaries, try to kill us. We need the rule of law.'

The Senator looked Juma in the eye. Was he serious? 'Mr Juma, the rule of law will certainly reach you very soon…'

Juma held the Senator's gaze for a bit, then adjusted the headscarf around his ears before looking back down at his plate.

The Senator levelled up to him. 'OK, Juma, let's assume you're serious. How do you want the rule of law, exactly?'

Juma tugged at his ear again. He paused before he replied. 'Senator, I want American troops on the streets. I want Libya to become safe for my people again. I want all of Africa to become more like America.'

The Senator smiled, then slowly shook his head. Sending US troops to Libya was doomed. It would be just like Iraq or Somalia. Libya would become another costly quagmire. Another Afghanistan. 'If we sent US soldiers onto the streets of Sirte, they'd just become targets,' he explained. 'All the Libyan people would rally against them – just as the people of America would rise up if we had African troops in Kansas.'

Juma paused again. He moved his head to one side, letting his ear rest unnaturally on his hand. 'So that's a "no", then?'

'Correct, that's a no: we can't send US troops into Libya. When we tried something similar where you pirates come from, we got our asses kicked. But we might be able to help you in other ways…' As the Senator was speaking he became increasingly aware that Juma wasn't really listening. Instead, the warlord was trying to fix something to do with his ear and his scarf.

Then the Senator saw it. And in one swift movement – too fast for Juma to respond – he leant forward and brushed off the Somali's headgear.

Juma's guards, who had been standing passively at the back through most of the exchange, suddenly moved forward. Guns clicked. Dick Roosevelt covered his head, expecting bullets to fly.

But Juma just raised his hand.

His militia men, who had been standing guard, slowed up. Gradually they lowered their weapons. As Juma looked at them, they understood, and walked back to where they had been.

Juma raising his hand was more than a gesture of calm. It was also an admission.

It showed to Myles and Dick that, fitted to the left side of head, previously hidden by his headscarf, was an earpiece.

The Senator slowly plucked out the device and held it in front of all their faces.

Despite the old American holding up evidence that Juma was not the leading man he claimed to be, the pirate leader refused to look ashamed. 'Yes, Senator. I have been receiving advice,' he admitted.

'Advice or instructions, Juma?'

Juma didn't respond, as if he didn't have permission to answer.

The Senator smirked, proud to have got one over on his captor. 'Then, Mr Juma, you had better tell us who's really making decisions here.'

Juma said nothing.

The Senator started to get annoyed. 'Who wrote that note?' he demanded, his voice rising. 'Who's on the other end of this wire?'

Still Juma said nothing. Myles sensed growing tension in the room: this was more than an impasse. If Juma kept refusing to answer, the situation would turn nasty.

Dick Roosevelt was looking scared. 'What my father is trying to say, is…' he offered, trying to mediate.

'Shut up, Dick,' shouted the Senator, his eyes fixed on Juma. 'Come on, Mr Pirate, tell us who's in charge here.'

Myles heard a quiet metallic click from behind him: somewhere a safety catch was being turned off.

Juma looked down at his own AK-47. It was still beside him and within reach.

Dick Roosevelt's eyes darted around, checking out escape routes.

Then a door opened behind Juma. Sunlight burst through, making it hard for the four men sitting on the floor to see more than a silhouette walking through it.

The Senator squinted in disbelief: to him, the person approaching didn't look human. Just a mass of flowing cloth, like a dark ghost emerging from a halo of light.

Then he realised: it was a woman, dressed in full Islamic dress. The woman approached, until she stood above Juma. Then she carefully sat down, and lifted her hijab.

Myles recognised her face immediately.

The Senator nodded, as if the woman's appearance confirmed his expectations. He couldn't resist the chance to humiliate Juma one more time. 'So the old saying is almost true,' he mocked. 'Behind every strong man, there's not a strong woman, but a *wrong* one.'

CHAPTER SIXTEEN
Sirte, Libya

Placidia looked just as Myles imagined she would. Her eyes still beamed a fierce intelligence, her face was still determined. The two decades since they had last met had given her dignity. Unlike other beautiful woman Myles had known at university, Placidia had not grown wide-hipped or flabby. Instead, she looked poised, athletic even. Her skin was taut, perhaps too taut, as if the battles she had continually been fighting with the world were finally starting to wear on her.

Myles remembered how radical she used to be. Placidia had led student marches against the massacres in Bosnia in the early nineties, blaming Britain for not doing enough to stop the killing. She had become a vegetarian at university, and led a campaign to make sure the college canteens always offered a non-meat option. She had been a feminist, an anti-poverty campaigner, even an eco-warrior. But unlike most of the students who took up trendy causes, Placidia had followed her convictions through to the end, even when they led to unpleasant places.

Myles and Placidia had not seen each other since those distant days. Their eyes connected, and he remembered the confusing mixture of emotions she had inspired in him half-a-lifetime ago. Even now he felt his pulse quicken. 'Placidia...'

'Myles, hello.' She said his name without any emotion at all.

Myles wasn't sure how to respond. Talking in the presence of Placidia's husband limited what Myles could say – he knew Juma could carry out whatever he was threatening against the USA at any time. 'This is where you live?' he asked.

'Yes. You've met my husband. He and I are determined to do whatever we can to help these people from all over Africa, trapped here in Libya.' Placidia talked as though she was making a speech. 'We want to bring them all the things they should have – all the things to which an American, like me, is entitled.'

The Senator scoffed. 'Ma'am, you may be American, or half-American, or whatever you are. But nobody's entitled to anything unless they make it themselves. Not even Americans.'

Placidia confronted him directly. 'Senator. Americans are entitled to life, liberty and the pursuit of happiness. Do you know what sort of life most Africans are entitled to?'

'Tell me.'

'Most are lucky if they survive childhood. Adult men get sucked into war, where they die. Adult women die giving birth.'

The Senator raised his eyebrows, unsure what to say.

Placidia didn't relent. 'And do you know what sort of liberty most African migrants enjoy?' She barely waited for the Senator to reply. 'None, Senator. There is no liberty of the mind because there is no proper education here. Not for migrants. There is no liberty of the soul because of the war and poverty. The new democratic regime of Libya talks about liberty, but really they just want us to obey them…'

'OK, OK.' The Senator waved his hand dismissively as he cut her off. 'So Libya's a shit place. We can agree on that. What do you want me to do about it?'

Placidia composed herself, reining back her anger. 'Senator, you know when the US constitution was first written, it counted black men as worth only three-fifths of a white man?'

The Senator nodded. Although it was often brushed over in praiseful accounts of the founding fathers, Placidia was referring to a historical truth: George Washington, Thomas Jefferson and the others had signed up to the 'three-fifths' compromise so that southern states weren't over-represented in Congress. The paragraph was only removed from the constitution after the US Civil War, by the fourteenth amendment. 'Correct, lady. And American women had no vote at all until 1920. So?'

'So, Senator, you'll agree with me, that everybody should count as one, and nobody as more than one?' said Placidia, her face open, as if to pretend there was no trick in her words.

The Senator was sceptical, but didn't want to argue the point. 'Go on.'

'So if an African migrant here in Libya dies, it's just as much of a tragedy as if an American dies. If you can help these landless people, then you have a duty to, sir.'

The Senator looked down, paused for a moment, then shook his head. He sympathised with Placidia's situation. He cared for the African migrants trapped in Libya, as he cared for people all around the world. But he couldn't do much to help them. 'Placidia, we can't send US troops here. It wouldn't work.'

She began quoting him. '"The laws of the land should reach beyond the sea" – your words, Senator.'

'They are my words, yes,' he admitted. 'But that doesn't mean we can help.'

'I thought you'd say that,' replied Placidia. 'Which is why the only way for our people – these hard-working migrants – to get the life, liberty and happiness they deserve is…' She paused before the punchline, making sure she held the Senator's gaze as she delivered it. 'Senator, for you to let them settle in the continental United States.'

The Senator raised his hands, as if to gesture what a ridiculous idea it was.

Myles, Dick and Juma all turned to Placidia, wondering how she would react.

Placidia faked a smile. 'So that's a "no", then, Senator?'

'Goddamn right it's a "no",' confirmed Roosevelt. 'The voters in the US would never allow it. Any elected official who proposed mass immigration into America would be kicked straight out of Congress.' The Senator was half-laughing at the idea as he spoke.

Placidia nodded. She had anticipated this, too. 'Then the US will have to be forced to live up to its duties, and to the Constitution of which it is so proud.'

'Lady, you can't force the United States to do anything.'

'Yes I can. I will bring down the United States as the Roman Empire was brought down. Call it the last prophecy of Rome if you like: that the American Empire will share its fate.'

The Senator sat stunned.

Placidia rammed home her ultimatum. 'Last chance: let our people settle in the continental USA, or your country is doomed.'

CHAPTER SEVENTEEN
Sirte, Libya

The Senator squinted in disbelief. He was becoming increasingly certain he was dealing with a crackpot. The only question was whether he should humour her or tell her straight. Being Sam Roosevelt, he had to tell her straight. 'Lady, you're mad.'

Placidia had obviously prepared for such a response. 'Really, Senator? You accept that America was created with the Roman Republic in mind? That's why the rule of law – a very Roman invention – was placed at the centre of the US Constitution. That's why you sit in the Senate, modelled on the Roman Senate. That's why you have the Capitol building, like the Roman Capitol, and a President who controls the armed forces like the Roman Emperor. That's why you offer US citizenship as a prize, just as the Romans offered citizenship to the bravest foreign slaves and soldiers. That's why you cleared the Native Americans from their land, like the Romans wiped out local tribes…'

'Enough.' The Senator raised his hand. He had met women like Placidia before. He hated their self-righteousness. 'Nobody disputes that America was based on Rome,' he acknowledged. 'What makes you mad, ma'am, is that you think you can bring America down.'

'You don't think we can bring America down, Senator?'

'No, I don't. I reckon you could bring down some of our passenger jets. You might smuggle a few bombs into our country and kill some ordinary folks who are going about their business. That's what terrorists like you do. But it barely scratches us. We lose more people in road accidents every single week than we have in all the terrorist attacks since – and including – 9/11.'

Placidia exhaled dismissively. The Senator clearly hadn't got it. 'I'm not talking about small bombs, or even big ones, Senator.' This wasn't terrorism, she explained. It was about making the United States stay true to its principles. Then she looked him squarely in the eye. 'America is in decline.'

Sam Roosevelt jerked back his face. He raised an eyebrow, accepting that she may be half-right. He allowed her to continue.

'You know America's in decline, Senator. And the American people are starting to realise it too: most of them are working harder than their parents did just to get by. Many know their children will have less than they had. Just like Rome before it fell. So, to help America help itself, I'm threatening to speed up that decline until the United States stays true to its constitution.'

Myles shook his head. This was a different Placidia to the idealist young woman he had known at university. 'You're threatening to kill Americans if you don't get your way?' he said, trying to hide the disbelief from his voice.

'Don't you see, Myles: I'm trying to *save* people. I'm trying to save these poor people from Chad, Somalia, Sudan – all over Africa – so they can live peacefully in the US. And I'm trying to save Americans, too, to stop the country going the way of the Romans.'

'And you're doing that by threatening to kill people?'

Placidia's face showed she was disappointed with Myles. 'Don't you remember what we learned together about the Roman Empire? Have you forgotten everything in *The History of the Decline and Fall of the Roman Empire*? Everything you need to know about Rome is in that book – and if you want to save America, you should look at it again...'

Calmly, the Senator gestured to Myles that he should be quiet. Sam Roosevelt decided that if Placidia wanted to give a history lesson, he should let her. He invited her to speak.

Placidia told the story of Rome. From a humble village in a country on the western edge of the known world, it grew in size and strength until it challenged the great powers of the day. Just as the US had faced down the Soviets, the Romans defeated the once-mighty empire of Carthage. Just as America emerged from the British Empire, adopted much of their culture and then overtook it, the Romans did the same to ancient Greece. Rome, like America, was proud to be a republic, led by free men and slave-owners. It became the world's first superpower.

At its height, the Romans controlled the whole of civilisation, since beyond its huge borders lived only primitive tribes and marauders who couldn't hope to match the quality of life enjoyed within the Empire. A system of roads, laws and taxes brought peace. For many centuries, Roman society was the most prosperous the world had ever known. 'Just like twentieth-century America,' explained Placidia.

'But in the year 376, war in the east drove a group of Goths and Huns from their land, and the refugees sought sanctuary in the Roman Empire. The Romans put them in what today would be called concentration camps, where they froze. They were denied shelter or food,' she recounted. 'Some of the Roman soldiers sold dog meat to the starving refugees in exchange for their girls, who became personal slaves.'

Myles nodded. He knew what happened next, and listened to Placidia complete the story. 'So the Goths and Huns made a mass escape, and started fighting the Romans from inside the Empire's borders. Within fifty years they had raided Rome itself, and within a century the Empire was gone.'

Dick Roosevelt shook his head. 'OK, Placidia. Your people have it tough,' he accepted. 'But nobody's demanding they sell their children to get a Green Card.'

Placidia's voice became firmer as she addressed her captives. 'Senator Roosevelt, Richard Roosevelt and Myles: you all need to understand why the Roman Empire fell, because otherwise the United States will fall in the same way. But the real reason the Roman Empire collapsed has become a secret. Powerful people have hidden it, and given us the official verdict of history, which is untrue.'

The Senator tried to ridicule her. 'Well, missy, can you give us a clue why Rome fell?'

'Yes, here's a clue, Senator: Emperor Valerian,' announced Placidia. 'Valerian went into battle in the Middle East in 260AD but was taken hostage. Rome found a new emperor, and Valerian never returned. He died as a prisoner.'

The Senator guessed what was coming next. 'So you're taking me prisoner?'

'Yes, Senator. You and your son are the closest thing there is to America's imperial blood.'

The Senator wasn't fazed. He just asked: 'And Myles?'

'Just as Valerian's advisors were sent back to the Empire with the terrible news,' said Placidia, 'Myles will be sent back to America to tell them of our ultimatum.'

CHAPTER EIGHTEEN
Sirte, Libya

Juma poked his gun into Myles' ribs, forcing him up.

Myles obeyed. He bent down to shake hands with the Senator and his son, unsure whether either would survive. 'Good luck, Dick,' he said to Richard Roosevelt, who replied with a thin smile but no words. The young hero of New York had much on his mind.

Myles turned to Sam Roosevelt. 'Anything you want me to tell people back in the US?'

'Yeah,' huffed the Senator. 'Some of the suits in Langley will try to keep this quiet. Don't let them: the people of America need to know they're under attack.'

He said the words looking straight at Placidia. Placidia nodded – she had no plans to keep this secret, either.

Myles was escorted from the room by Juma and two of his militiamen. He caught sight of Placidia as he left. She glanced at him with a confident look, as if to say 'we'll meet again soon'. Myles was too stunned and confused to respond.

Outside, the sun was about to set. Myles had to step carefully down the uneven stairs from the building which led to the ground. There Juma punched his thigh, indicating he should get into a bashed-up taxi which was waiting for him.

It was as Myles was climbing in that Juma demanded he take something with him. 'This is for the people back home…' laughed the Somali pirate as he handed it over, then turned his back on Myles and swaggered away.

Myles looked down at what he'd been given: a bottle of All-American Steak Sauce. He checked the bottle was normal – it was – then shook his head in bemusement: Juma was clearly mad.

One of the militiamen sat down beside Myles and the taxi driver was waved off. Myles was being driven away.

The swift dusk soon gave way to the full dark of the night. By then, Myles was well on to the open roads and being driven east, back to the safety of Egypt. It was a long journey, but there was no time for sleep. He had too many questions.

Myles still couldn't understand Placidia. She had always seemed so idealistic, naively so. So how could she threaten to bring down America? It would mean thousands, probably millions of deaths. Where was the idealism in that?

And how had Placidia become married to the psychopath, Juma? Myles tried to separate the question from his own feelings for the woman. It was true: he had liked her very much at university. He had hoped their friendship would become romantic – properly romantic. Physical. He remembered once inviting her for a coffee after their tutorial together. Myles had wanted it to lead somewhere, but she had been too involved in her latest student protest. Despite the obvious, almost electric attraction, they had never been able to engage at an emotional level. Myles wondered if Placidia could relate to anyone in the normal way. She was always too driven, too motivated, too determined to save the world.

Then there was the biggest issue: the threat itself. What would Placidia and Juma do to America? Clearly they thought they didn't need to carry out much of their threat to make America concede. But, on this, Myles thought they had made a serious misjudgement. America was not the sort of country to be bowed by threats. The opposite was true: the more America was bullied to do something, the less likely it was to do it. Surely Placidia could see that? Myles knew Placidia was astonishingly intelligent. How could she have made such a mistake?

Myles tried to remember his history. What *had* brought down the Roman Empire? He stared up at the stars as the taxi drove along the desert highway. Vague memories wafted through his mind. Why *had* Rome collapsed?

He was startled by the door of the taxi slamming shut: the militiaman who had accompanied him had jumped out on a dark corner just before the Egyptian border. This was a different border post to the one Myles had passed through on his way into the country.

The taxi driver already had Myles' passport, and showed it to the official border guard as they left Libya, and again to the police as they crossed into Egypt. Myles watched the signposts on the road: he was being driven to Alexandria.

DAY III

CHAPTER NINETEEN
Egypt

Myles became bleary again, and only woke fully as the sky began to lighten. The bottle of steak sauce given to him by Juma had fallen onto the floor of the vehicle and broken open. The taxi driver saw it too, but didn't seem to mind. He was opening Myles' door. 'Mr Munro, I leave you now,' said the driver, patting him on the back and handing him his passport. 'American Embassy – that way.'

The man pointed at a heavily fortified building set back some way from the road. Myles recognised it: the American consulate in Alexandria. It had been strengthened since Al Qaeda had destroyed the US embassies in Kenya and Sudan in 1998.

Myles stumbled alone on the road as the taxi drove off. One of the Egyptians guarding the consulate saw him and came over, offering a bottle of water. 'Can I help you, sir?' asked the guard.

Myles nodded, acknowledging that he was dehydrated. 'Yes, I need to report a very serious threat to America.'

Myles was soon welcomed into the consulate by the Senior Political Counsellor – a middle-aged man with thinning hair and a relaxed manner. After his passport was checked, Myles was guided along corridors and through several different secure doors into an underground debriefing room. Sparkling table water and perfectly cut sandwiches were set out for him, and he was invited to eat as he talked, even though the crumbs from his food disturbed the antiseptic atmosphere of the room.

As he recounted the events of the day before, the Counsellor used a speakerphone on the table to summon ever greater numbers of people into the room: first a security expert to hear how the Roosevelt Guardians had been hijacked at the Libyan border, then a consular official to make contact with the hostages' families, and an expert on terrorism to take notes on Juma and Placidia. Myles had been interviewed for more than twenty minutes when a voice came back through the phone, asking to clarify a point. Only then did Myles realise even more people had been listening in to the whole of his talk.

The Senior Political Counsellor apologised. 'Sorry, it's Langley,' he said. 'Go ahead, Langley.'

Just as the Senator had predicted, the CIA men from Langley wanted the whole issue kept quiet. 'We can't afford this to get out,' came the voice on the line, squelched by the telecommunications equipment which made the call impossible to intercept as it was beamed across an ocean. 'It'll cause panic.'

Myles shook his head. 'Gentlemen, the Senator was very clear: the people need to know that they're under attack.'

'Sorry, Mr Munro,' said the official. 'Policy.'

Myles screwed up his face in disbelief. What did 'Policy' mean? It sounded just like the sort of word the CIA could use to cut off debate and justify whatever they liked.

There was a pause, and someone summoned Myles' host out of the room.

He returned a few minutes later, frowning in concern. 'Myles, we're going to fly you back to the States for a full debriefing,' explained the Counsellor. 'We need you there as soon as possible. OK?'

Myles realised he had little choice in the matter.

He was soon being driven to a military airfield where a large C130 cargo plane awaited him. He climbed aboard, accompanied by three very tall marine guards. The plane taxied along the runway, and, minutes later, he was flying out west, back across the North African desert and the Atlantic.

Back to the States.

From the conversation in the consulate, Myles was expecting to be flown to a large military base in the US where he could be kept confined, so he would not be able to tell the world about the threat from the African migrants of Libya. So he was surprised when the C130 landed in a commercial airport. Only once the main door opened did he realise which one: it was JFK. He was back in New York.

Myles was even more surprised to see a loving face waiting to meet him. Helen ran up to him as he climbed down the steps. 'Myles, you're safe!' She gave him a hug. Myles held her close. Without words, he smiled, then kissed her.

Only then, as they embraced on the tarmac, did Myles realise Helen was not the only person waiting for him.

'Is the Senator still alive, Mr Munro?'

'Mr Munro, how serious is the threat to America?'

Myles squinted as artificial lights were beamed into his face. Journalists.

Several New York policemen were holding back a crowd of thirty or forty media people, all scrumming for attention. Cameras flashed and microphones were pointed towards him. Myles recognised at least two famous faces amongst them – anchormen from major news channels.

'How did they find out?' Myles asked.

Helen looked at him, bemused. 'The video, of course.'

'What video?'

But before Helen could answer, a car drove up and stopped in front of them. Myles and Helen were invited to sit in the back seats. Through the window, Myles could see the journalists hunch back in disappointment – they had failed to get their interview.

Sitting beside him on the back seat, Helen eyed Myles up and down: her Englishman looked battered and weary. Then she noticed a stain on his ankle. 'What's that?' she asked. 'Looks like you went to a barbecue – is that Steak Sauce?' She started to pick at it, confirming that it was indeed All-American Steak Sauce.

Myles gave her a look which said, 'You wouldn't believe me if I told you...'

Shaking her head, she took out her mobile phone, retrieving a film file from its memory, and setting it to play.

Myles watched as the screen went black, then faded up to show a street scene from Arab North Africa. Two children – both obviously malnourished – were picking something from an open sewer. Then the picture changed to show a wide shot of buildings in downtown Sirte.

The voiceover began. 'This is Sirte today.' It was Placidia's voice. 'Our children die from diseases which could be cured with nickels. Gunmen destroy our homes. Oil companies from America have stolen our best farmland...' Then Placidia herself appeared, pleading to the camera. 'North Africa is like this because the people of America have made it this way.'

Helen looked across at Myles, gauging his reaction. Myles just kept staring at the small video screen.

The image cut to show Senator Roosevelt looking resigned and weary. Standing outside, in front of a concrete wall, the old man started reading from a sheet. His tone was rich with sarcasm, just to make absolutely clear he didn't believe anything he was saying. 'My name is Senator Sam Roosevelt,' he recited. 'And I agree that the United States is doomed like the Roman Empire. That's why we need to change the way we behave and be true to our constitution. And that's why we need to let the Africans trapped in Libya settle in the continental USA...'

The picture changed to show Richard Roosevelt standing loyally by his father, and looking more resolute than when Myles had left him. The younger Roosevelt read his script more seriously. 'My father and I are now prisoners here in Libya. The people holding us have said they will inflict on America the same fate as the Roman Empire unless their people are allowed to settle in our country.' Richard Roosevelt looked up at the camera and smiled nervously before continuing. 'I don't know exactly what they're planning. Sam and I will keep trying to convince them not to do it until they kill us. So, I ask all of you…'

Richard Roosevelt paused, then turned towards someone out of shot and frowned, with a 'Do I really have to read this?' frown. He stalled for a moment while he heard the reply – inaudible on the video – then shook his head in refusal. He screwed up the paper in front of him and threw it at the camera in protest. Almost immediately, a rifle butt was thrust into his face and he fell to the floor. Senator Sam was bending down to help him as the picture faded to black.

A final scene appeared. This time Juma, standing with some of his gang, out in the scrubland far from the city. 'We people of Libya have the right to bear arms, too,' shouted Juma.

The men behind Juma held up their guns and cheered.

'We like America and we want to be good Americans,' chanted the Somali pirate leader.

The men cheered again.

'But if you don't let us in, there won't be much of America left.'

The video panned down to the body of one of the Roosevelt Guardians murdered at the checkpoint, then froze.

Helen looked up at Myles for a reaction, but Myles was too stunned to speak.

CHAPTER TWENTY
Sirte, Libya

When he was fourteen, Richard Roosevelt had been given a copy of Winston Churchill's autobiography, *My Early Life*, by his father. The Senator had intended it to be an inspiration to the teenager. Instead, it just made him feel inadequate. Dick Roosevelt dutifully read about how the young Churchill had been shot at in Cuba, dislocated his arm in India and, most sensationally of all, escaped from captivity in South Africa. Captured during the British Empire's war with the Boers and holed up in a prison camp, Churchill had sneaked over a lavatory roof and dodged sentries to get out. Hundreds of miles behind enemy lines, the young man had first smuggled himself aboard a night train, then hidden for a week in a mining pit, before finally making it home to safety. Churchill's African escape was headline news that established him as a daring patriot. It set up the young man for a parliamentary career.

Now Richard Roosevelt understood: this was his chance to make his own African escape, and become a Churchill himself.

The second full day of their captivity was drawing to a close. Since the video had been taken the day before, Richard Roosevelt and his father had been left with just two armed guards in the same second-floor room of the ministry building in which they had met Placidia. The food was poor: chicken stewed in oil and tomatoes, with rice and flatbread. It had given Senator Sam diarrhoea. Dick knew that he too would be weakened soon. If he was going to escape, he had to escape quickly. But how?

He confided in his father. Instead of being impressed, the Senator just shrugged. 'Might as well,' huffed Sam Roosevelt. 'Your chances are no lower than if you stay here with me, enjoying the Sirte Hilton…'

After more muttering – out of earshot of the guards, at least one of whom understood English – Sam Roosevelt agreed to help.

That evening the Senator confessed to a numbness in his left arm. It was an odd sensation – part pain, part painlessness. It had been building up over several days. Now it demanded attention.

When he told the guards they did nothing. He hadn't expected any more from them.

Then, suddenly, the Senator clutched his chest. He fell back on the floor, screeching in pain.

Dick Roosevelt bent over him and tried to issue first aid, pumping his father's heart.

It took a few moments for Juma's guards to react. They weren't sure what to do at first. One came over, then the other, and Dick was pulled away. Both gunmen looked down at the Senator and tried to work out what to do.

It was while the guards were arguing with each other in a foreign language that Dick Roosevelt took his chance. Calmly, he moved towards one of the glassless windows. He climbed through it and stood on the ledge. Still unnoticed, he glanced back at his father writhing on the ground, then gauged the distance down to the ground, and jumped.

The drop could easily have caused an injury, but Dick Roosevelt was lucky: below him was a taxi. He landed with both feet squarely on the roof of the vehicle, which crumpled safely but loudly as it took his weight.

The noise alerted the gunmen to his escape. They moved over to the window and saw their former captive scrambling away.

One of the men fired off some bullets, but Dick Roosevelt was already round the corner. The other guard tried to jump onto the taxi roof, but landed with a twist. His ankle was gone.

Dick Roosevelt found himself running through an unfamiliar city, trying to find his bearings as the evening light faded. He knew the guards would alert more gang members soon. He didn't have much time.

He sprinted down an alley and onto a wider street.

Gasping, he barely had time to think which way to go, how to escape, what to do…

The few people on the street were all local: he was white and dressed very differently. They were already looking at him. There was no way he could blend in.

He surveyed the street: all the buildings were made of concrete, some decorated with bullet marks. He might be able to hide for a while, but not for long. He would soon need water and food. He'd have to contact local people, and he couldn't trust them: they'd sell him back to Juma's gang. What could he do?

Then he saw a seagull, and realised: he was close to the Mediterranean shoreline. He could even smell it. And where there was sea there would be a boat. Given that he didn't have any other options, it was worth a try.

Above him was an old street sign, punctured with bullet holes, which pointed toward the harbour. He ran, and within half-a-mile, he was there. Thankfully, still out of sight of his pursuers…

Now, drenched in sweat, and with the daylight disappearing by the minute, he looked around for a seaworthy vessel.

And there it was: an open skiff, empty except for a high-powered motor on the back. Dick smiled: it had probably just been used by someone. A prize escape.

Exhausted, he jogged towards it and checked nobody was watching before he slipped in.

The tank was full, the engine was ready, and there was even bread and water on board. All Dick needed to do was pull the cord.

Then he saw one of the Nissan technicals screeching along the harbour road. The headlights were on, and the back loaded with gunmen. They were after him.

Dick ducked, and tugged the cord as hard as he could.

The motor spluttered, then started – first time.

Roosevelt looked upwards and crossed his chest, thanking God.

But the engine noise had alerted the gang members: they knew which boat he was in.

Dick Roosevelt moved his body as low as he could while bullets flew above him. Some hit the skiff, rattling the whole structure. He felt shards of wood fly off just above him. He covered his head in his hands, desperate to remain safe.

It took just one minute for his boat to speed out of range of the guns. Juma's gang would need another skiff to chase him now.

But Dick was lucky. Out on the dark sea, there was no way they could chase him. All he had to do was steer his stolen pirate skiff a few miles out to sea, then turn east and hope he made it to Egypt.

Shaken by the boat bouncing over the waves, he began to feel a little sick. But he ploughed on through the night, and by morning guessed – correctly – that he was now in Egyptian coastal waters.

He actually came ashore on a beach full of tourists. His face pockmarked by the splinters and his shirt ragged, he struggled to climb out of the skiff. Several beachgoers used their phones to capture what would become iconic images: Dick Roosevelt, hero of New York, completing his escape from terrorists in Africa amid sunbathers and beach balls.

He found someone who worked for a hotel, and told them to fetch the police.

Within minutes he was on his way to the American Embassy just outside Cairo. Within an hour he was being debriefed by friendly Embassy staff. And by the end of the day, the story of his astonishing escape was exploding through news broadcasts all over the world – aided by the social media videos of Dick Roosevelt emerging onto the beach. He was lauded as a brave hero for the second time in a week.

And his father was beaten hard by Juma's guards when they discovered he had feigned his heart attack like a professional actor.

CHAPTER TWENTY-ONE
JFK Airport, New York

Helen watched Myles' reaction to Placidia's terror video. She realised that, to him, this was more than just an attack on the United States. 'The woman in the video,' she asked. 'It's her, isn't it?'

Myles nodded, not sure how much he should say.

Helen digested her partner's reaction. 'So, the woman you used to "know" at university is now a terrorist mastermind?' She said the word 'know' as if Myles' knowledge was carnal.

'It's more complicated than that,' admitted Myles.

'What's more complicated: your knowledge of this woman, or her being a terrorist mastermind?'

'Both.'

Their car pulled up near a windowless building within the airport complex. The driver climbed out, ready to open the door for Myles and his partner.

Myles and Helen were led inside, where they were met by three young officials – two men and a woman, all with fixed smiles.

'Good morning, Mr Munro,' said one of the men. They seemed to have been trained in being courteous.

Myles acknowledged the greeting as he looked around at the perfect furnishings. Small table lamps provided neutral lighting. Superficial artworks hung on the off-white walls. It was the sort of place he hated.

'Mr Munro,' continued the man. 'We're here to make sure you can relax, and recover completely from what you've been through.'

'Why? What do you think I've been through?'

The officials giggled as if Myles had told a brilliant joke. 'Very good, Mr Munro. And of course, your partner's welcome to stay here, too.'

Helen was just as uncertain as Myles. 'If I *want* to stay here,' she said. 'What is this place?'

'It's the rest and recovery suite, madam. A special lounge offered for situations, well, just like this.'

Myles was already inspecting the sign on the door. It read 'Deportation and Recovery suite'. 'Two-way traffic, then?' he asked.

The officials nodded nervously as they confirmed the room was also used to expel people from the USA.

Myles' eyes were drawn to the twenty-four-hour rolling news coverage on a TV in the corner. A food factory in Kentucky had just blown up as flour – or some other powder, the authorities didn't yet know – had been fanned around the inside of the building. It made a very explosive mix, apparently. Junk TV.

Myles came to the point. 'Look, I don't need to recover,' he explained. 'I need to pass on what I know so this whole "Roman Empire" business…'

Myles was still searching for words when a woman in a suit entered. It was Susan – the Department of Homeland Security secondee to the Senator's office. She seemed more confident than the first time Myles had met her. 'All in hand, Mr Munro,' she said. 'We've got a team just about to go in and rescue the Senator.'

'Special Forces?'

Susan nodded but her eyes were wide – she was scolding Myles for revealing classified information, and imploring him not to say more.

Myles shook his head. 'Don't send them in. It's a mistake.'

'I think that's for the experts to judge, don't you, Mr Munro?'

Susan moved away before Myles could reply. Helen put her hand on Myles' back to remind him to calm down. Myles tried to put his point more softly. 'Look, a Special Forces raid is just what these people are expecting,' he warned. 'In the backstreets of Sirte…'

'The Senator's not in Sirte, Mr Munro,' said Sarah without looking at him. 'We traced the Senator's mobile phone signal,' she explained, keeping her voice hushed and looking round to check they weren't being overheard, 'to a rural area several miles in from the coast.'

Myles nodded. 'And you think the Senator's still with his phone?'

'We have another source to verify that, yes, Mr Munro. Dick Roosevelt overheard the gang members planning, while he was their prisoner. And you saw the pictures in the video, Mr Munro,' Susan continued. 'We think we've matched the background behind Mr Juma and his gang to a particular point, which is where our Special Forces team are heading.'

Myles was impressed but still unconvinced. 'You don't think this is another trap?'

Susan laughed. 'No. We trust our source and we trust our technology.' She was looking him in the eye again. 'Now we just have to trust our Navy Seals. The Senator planned this raid before he left, in case anything went wrong. He'll take pride in being rescued by his old unit.'

Myles realised why she was more relaxed than before: it was because the Senator was elsewhere. Susan was able to take charge in his absence. Able to be competent.

He accepted a cup of coffee brought over with great care and handed to him by one of the three young officials. 'So if you'll wait here, sir,' said the professional greeter, 'we'll bring you news of the Senator's release as soon as we have it.'

But Myles wasn't listening. He was watching Helen as she began wandering down the corridor. It was the journalist in her: she always wanted to explore. Myles looked again at the room around him and decided he would rather be with Helen than with the officials. He followed her, the young official chasing after him.

'Excuse me – sir?' called the official.

Myles just turned and handed back the coffee. The officials stood bemused, mystified that someone might turn down their perfect hospitality.

Helen had found the deportation section. As Myles joined her, they both overheard an exchange from somewhere above. One man's voice, clearly American, was trying to calm the other, who was terrified and spoke English poorly.

'No, I cannot go back. They kill me,' said the foreign accent.

'Please return to your seat, sir,' came the reply.

'No, they kill me if I go back…'

Helen and Myles moved closer to where the conversation was coming from.

'I not go back. Force me, then I die here,' intoned the accent, sounding afraid. 'Better to die here than the Libyans killing me.'

Myles and Helen started running to where the voice was coming from.

They discovered an African man at the top of the stairwell, three floors above them. He was holding on to the rail with just one hand and threatening to jump.

CHAPTER TWENTY-TWO
JFK Airport, New York

Myles and Helen ran up towards the man who was threatening to jump. As they approached, they saw a group of uniformed men and women edging towards the deportee. None of them seemed to know what to do.

The American border official who seemed to be in charge looked unnerved to see Myles and Helen in the out-of-bounds area. Then he recognised Helen from TV. He felt he had to explain himself. 'He's an illegal,' said the official, apologetically. 'We were going to fly him back home but....'

Helen nodded, acknowledging the point.

Myles decided to approach closer. Holding his hands out, palms down so it was clear he wasn't carrying anything, he shouted over to the distressed man. 'Why don't you want to go back?'

'They will kill me if I go back.'

'Who would kill you?' asked Myles.

'The militia, the gangs, the tribes – any of them. Even the new government,' pleaded the man, sweat forming on his malnourished skin. 'It was safe when we had the dictator. Now law and order has gone. No one is safe...' The man explained how he had fled with his family from the violence in Darfur to the relative peace of Libya. But now it was dangerous even there. All of Africa seemed lethal to him.

Myles locked his eyes on the man, telling him without words that he didn't need to explain any further. But eye contact was all he had to offer. Myles nodded to the man while he tried to think.

Myles looked around: there was no way the border officials would let this man go. Whether the African jumped or was sent back, the man would surely die. Then Myles had an idea…

Keeping his eyes fixed on the African deportee, Myles called over his shoulder. 'Helen, can your phone get footage of this?'

Helen paused before answering, unclear why Myles had asked. 'If you need it,' she replied.

Myles could sense the uncertainty in her voice. But when he turned round he was glad to see her pulling her smartphone from her bag. 'Good,' he said. 'And can you get the pictures of this through to some of your producer friends?'

Helen nodded, pressing a pre-dial button while she kept filming.

Myles returned his focus to the desperate man. 'What's your name?'

'Mohammed,' came the reply. 'My name's Mohammed.'

Myles nodded again, trying to reassure the man. 'And do you have a family, Mohammed?'

Mohammed nodded. 'Yes, three children, and my wife.'

'And what do you do for work, Mohammed?'

'I clean toilets. In the mall, I clean toilets.' The man's eyes were flipping around him, unsure why the strange Englishman was asking him questions. Myles could tell Mohammed was wondering whether he had said the right thing: should he have admitted to being a toilet cleaner?

Myles saw one of the border guards move behind him. Quickly he turned round. 'Stay back,' he insisted.

The border guards froze again, his eyes still fixed on the deportee.

'We're going to do this properly,' Myles explained. He called over to Helen. 'OK, Helen, is this live?'

'Yep, you're on national TV.'

Briefly Myles imagined the millions of viewers in homes across America whose daily programmes he was interrupting. He tried not to let it distract him as he turned to speak into the camera-phone. 'OK, people,' he began. 'Some of you are proud of your country, some of you less proud. This man is so desperate to work here and help his family, he cleans toilets in the mall.'

Myles paused, trying not to freeze on national TV, and wondering whether his British accent would make it hard for him to appeal to the American spirit. He turned to Mohammed, looking for inspiration. Then he turned back to the camera. 'Some of you think there are too many foreigners in America. Some of you might think that America needs people like Mohammed to keep your toilets clean. Some of you might be happy for Mohammed to be sent back to Africa, where he could die.'

Myles looked to Helen, just behind the camera, for permission. Helen nodded. 'So, viewers, this is your chance. In a few moments two telephone numbers will appear on your screen. Call the first number if you think Mohammed should be sent back to Libya. Call the second number if you want his case to be reviewed by an appeals panel.'

Then Myles spelt it out as clearly as he could: 'Call the first number if you want Mohammed to die. Call the second number if you want him to live.'

Helen kept the images flowing, holding the camera as still as she could. On TV screens across the country, the pictures were accompanied by the caption: **Live: Incident at JFK airport, New York. Man fights deportation back to Africa.**

Swiftly a research assistant set up the phone-in lines. Just as Myles requested, two numbers appeared on the screens. By the first number, the words 'send him back'. By the second: 'give him a second chance'.

A TV in one of the offices nearby picked up the broadcast, and someone turned up the volume.

Helen called out from behind the camera-phone. 'Mohammed, you're live on national TV. Do you have anything to say to make your case?' she asked. 'This is your chance to try to persuade people.'

Still terrified, Mohammed took a few seconds to register what Helen was saying. Slowly, he tried to find the right words. 'Yes, my name is Mohammed,' he began, talking slowly. 'I work here so my family has food. I was born in Darfur, Sudan, but when my family's house was destroyed I moved to Libya, where my father and uncle were killed in the war which killed Colonel Gaddafi.' Mohammed looked over to check the border officials were still some distance away before he continued. 'And if I am sent back, I will be killed, too. I clean toilets here in America. Please let me stay to clean toilets. Don't let them send me back. For my family, please let me stay.'

Mohammed's sincerity came through. Myles saw the man was close to tears.

A ring of airport police had formed behind Helen and the deportation officials. Alerted to the events, they wanted to keep onlookers away. They didn't want this situation to be interrupted.

Within the ring of policemen, for several minutes, nobody moved. Helen kept filming while Myles stayed close to the deportee. There was still a chance one of the border guards might make a rush for the man, but none of them tried. The force of phone-in TV was far more powerful than the orders of their supervisor. They understood: this was an extraordinary situation, which meant their supervisor's instructions could wait, at least until the results of the phone-in vote.

Myles also understood: this was evidence that Placidia was right – modern America was more like ancient Rome than most people realised. Whichever way the TV phone-in went, this would be like the Roman games, where emperors decided whether a gladiator who had been defeated in combat lived or died. They indicated with gestures still used today: thumbs-up for 'he lives', or thumbs-down for 'he dies'. Myles didn't know whether modern Americans were cruel enough to deport a man like Mohammed when the fate awaiting him was death, but he was sure, like ancient Romans, they would be compelled by the spectacle.

When Susan discovered what was happening on one of the airport televisions, she marched up and ordered the ring of policemen to let her through, which they obediently did. With her back to the camera to keep her face hidden, she moved to stand between Myles and the deportee, Mohammed. 'Enough,' she called, her hand raised.

Myles, Helen and the border guards looked around, not sure how to react. Mohammed looked back over the rail, knowing this might be the moment when he would have to jump.

Susan turned to the man. 'Mohammed: your case will be reviewed. I don't care about the vote on TV. OK?'

Mohammed nodded, letting out a breath as he became slightly less terrified. Myles repeated the words loudly to make sure they were picked up by the camera-phone. 'So his case is going to be reviewed. Thank you.'

Susan wafted her ID card towards the uniformed men, who accepted her authority and understood their new instructions: to get the man down safely. Mohammed moved away from the railing and volunteered himself into their custody. The drama was over.

Helen turned the camera-phone to herself to wrap up the live broadcast. She owed it to the viewers to summarise what had happened, and to explain how a decision on Mohammed's life had been taken before the votes were counted. She thanked everyone who had phoned in.

As Mohammed was led away and the crowds gradually realised the situation was over, Susan turned to Myles. 'You should come with me,' she instructed.

Myles followed as he was led along corridors within the airport, through several sets of security doors and towards a suite of computer screens where a huddle of security experts was waiting for him.

The TV pictures from the deportation drama was nothing compared to the live video footage he was about to see.

CHAPTER TWENTY-THREE
Undisclosed Location, North-east Libya

The Chinook helicopters were in the air. Warm air blowing up from the desert was mixing with the hot blast from the engines. It was too loud for the men to talk to each other, and the preparation was all done. There was nothing to do but think.

Captain Morton remembered this time from his last mission. That had been a success: a quick flight into Lebanon to rescue a scrawny Canadian journalist, then out again before the Lebanese government could complain about the unlicensed breach of its borders. Morton hadn't lost any of his men, but the hostage-takers had been ready with night-vision goggles.

Night-vision goggles: they used to give US Special Forces the edge. Now they were available over the internet and in half the shops on Main Street…

When the journalist – the very man they had rescued – had written about the Lebanon raid, he had warned that America was relying on its reputation. The things which used to make it the supreme fighting country were slipping away, he said. Its technology had spread to its enemies. Worst of all, it had lost its fighting spirit – a generation brought up on TV and hamburgers was no match for jihadists and radicals.

Captain Morton hadn't liked the skinny Canadian: instead of being grateful for his release, the first thing he had done was complain. In particular, Morton remembered how the journalist had mocked America's capacity to take casualties – 'casualty aversion', the generals called it. In the Second World War, the US had lost 300,000 men without blinking. In Vietnam, it had lost 68,000 and been humbled. In Iraq, according to the Canadian journalist, it had lost just 4,000 and been humiliated.

Casualty aversion was why they were sending only two Chinooks-worth of Navy Seals to rescue Senator Roosevelt. Morton had argued for more – and lost.

For all his lack of gratitude, perhaps the journalist had been right: casualty aversion *was* crippling the American armed forces.

'Two minutes,' called the flight controller.

The words were inaudible over the noise of the helicopter, but it didn't matter. The assault team were watching for his signal, and responded when they saw it.

Backpacks were buckled on, body armour tightened and helmets checked. Captain Morton took a final sip of water from the pipe attached to his shoulder. He remembered his pre-mission briefing session. He was glad to learn that parts of the mission had been planned by Sam Roosevelt himself before he left. Morton had queried why Juma had taken the Senator away from the city. After all, a hostage rescue in a city would be far harder. His commanding officer replied bluntly. 'Because they're dumb, that's why.' As he sucked on the water tube, Morton knew he would soon find out if his commanding officer was right.

'One minute…'

The helicopter manoeuvred down, and angled forward as it began to dive. The men held their seat-straps, ready to unbuckle them the moment the wheels touched the ground.

A blast of air rushed into the body of the Chinook, filling the interior with dust. Captain Morton could just hear the voice of the flight controller shouting, 'Go! Go! Go!'

With the front wheels still off the ground, the men ran down the centre of the machine, out into the downdraught from the rotor blades. Into the midnight desert. There they fanned out, running from the wind behind them, until they lay on the ground. Within seconds, the Chinook had risen off again and was gone. Captain Morton and his men were alone.

Morton's SOPs – his Standard Operating Procedures – dictated a five-minute 'soak' period: time when the men were meant to remain still and tune in to their surroundings. Five minutes was easy to wait during training, but this was the real thing. They were too anxious. This time they were rescuing a Senator, no less. Five minutes was far too long for them to wait. Most were twitching after two or three.

A large insect crawled onto Morton's neck. He couldn't see it but only feel it as it climbed onto his face. Frozen still, he tried to ignore it, but it moved towards his nose. He had no choice: in one quick motion he brushed it off, and kept at it until his face was clear. He had to jump up as he did so. Instantly the men stood up with him. Three-and-a-half minutes, and they were all eager to move. No point waiting any longer. It was time to go.

Morton's team had been dropped off four miles from the Senator's mobile signal. Those four miles were enough to hide the noise of the Chinooks: their arrival would be a surprise to Juma's gang. But it meant Morton and his men had to do a little light exercise before battle.

Four miles: a thirty-minute run. They set out, careful not to run too fast.

Morton wondered what his commanding officers were making of the feed from their helmet cams – the little cameras attached to the head of every one of his team. *Hope you're enjoying the pictures, folks…*

Perhaps one day he'd be able to enjoy war from a sofa, watching helmet cam pictures as he sipped a latte somewhere on the East Coast.

Something flipped Morton's mind back to the present. He was worried about the operation. Something wasn't right.

As he and his men ran along the single track road, he felt eyes watch him from the shacks and scrub which dotted the desert on either side. He swung round in his night-vision goggles: nothing. His team kept on running.

One of the Navy Seals tapped his GPS. The monitor glowed in the dark to show they were halfway along the track. Just two miles to go.

They passed old concrete farm shacks, one on each side of the road.

Morton's senses were screaming at him: something was very wrong.

He looked at the buildings: why make farm shacks out of concrete? And why build farm shacks in a desert? There was no farmland here.

There were two more of the concrete huts ahead, and more in the distance. Morton and his men were surrounded by them. In the dark he could just make out slits beneath the roofs.

He held up his fist, ordering his men to stop. They obeyed instantly, and the slap of boots on the dry mud stopped with them. Silence.

The silence enabled Captain Morton to make out the unmistakeable scratching noise of a gun barrel being repositioned on concrete. Others heard it too. Instinctively, they ducked down onto the ground, readying their weapons as they did so.

But it was far too late: they were already trapped.

With heavily protected firing positions on all sides, Morton's men were caught on flat and very open terrain. Their efforts to shoot back into the concrete huts were useless. Juma's men – Morton knew that was who it must be – were too well guarded. Bullets whizzed over Morton's head. He heard the muffled sound of fast metal penetrating flesh. The soldier beside him took a chest wound. His men were too professional to scream when they were hit, but it didn't stop them dying. The blast of gunfire came from all directions. When one of the men at the back tried to escape he was cut down.

Captain Morton didn't have time to think about how disastrously the mission had turned out, or how Juma had been able to set such a perfect ambush. His fears that the Navy Seals were living on their reputation alone were proved correct.

Then he saw a chance to escape....

CHAPTER TWENTY-FOUR
JFK Airport, New York

The live feed from the helmet cams was streaming back to the US, and to the secure computer suite within JFK airport where Myles and Susan were watching.

It was tragic: within seconds, most of the helmet cams became still, indicating the Seal who was wearing it had ceased to move. Some of them stopped showing pictures at all, because the cameras themselves had been hit.

Susan leant forward, peering at the screens. She couldn't believe it.

Myles watched the few screens still moving. One showed tracer rounds of outgoing fire: the Seal was firing straight into one of the concrete huts. Then he had to turn, probably to cope with fire from behind.

Another showed a Seal trying to crawl through the bodies of his comrades, looking for cover. He managed to escape the main group, into a desert bush. But some of the foliage had been set alight by tracer rounds. The Seal had to move faster to avoid the flames, which probably meant he was seen. Soon a tall Somali pirate with an AK-47 was running towards him. The Seal raised his rifle to shoot the African, but the pictures from his helmet cam tumbled until they too were still. Myles and Susan knew that this man had become another casualty.

Susan scanned the wall of images, looking for hope but shaking her head. She leant forward again. 'Any of them still alive?' she asked, pressing the button on a microphone as she spoke.

It took a few seconds for an electronic voice to come through – military but subordinate. 'Yes ma'am, screen five. Er, it's Captain Morton.'

Myles and Susan zoomed in on screen five. At first the pictures seemed as still as the others. Then they noticed the images were gradually moving – rising and falling with Morton's breathing. Clearly the man was trying to hide amid the bodies of his men. Then, slowly, he managed to slip into a shallow ditch.

Susan pressed the microphone again. 'We've got to help this guy,' she demanded. 'What have we got?'

There was another pause before the disembodied answer came back through the speakers. 'We've got the Predator, ma'am, or we can send in the helicopters again.'

'OK, give me the images from the Predator.'

One of the dead camera-feeds was replaced with an infrared image. The high-altitude Predator unmanned aerial vehicle, or UAV, was clearly circling the scene. The gangmen wouldn't have known it was there – it was circling with a six mile radius, and flying at 14,000 feet.

'OK, I've got the pictures from the Predator,' reported Susan. 'It's got Hellfires, right?

Myles suddenly became animated. 'Hellfire missiles?' He tried to get Susan's attention. 'You're going to use Hellfires?'

Susan nodded. Clearly she didn't share Myles' concern. Ignoring the Englishman, she turned back to the microphone. 'OK, let's give Captain Morton some cover. Send Hellfires into the concrete huts.'

Myles grabbed the microphone from her. 'Cancel that. No Hellfires.'

Susan locked eyes with Myles. She was trying to gauge the strange misfit who seemed to be causing ever increasing amounts of trouble. 'What the hell are you doing? We've got to help the surviving member of our mission.'

Myles was breathless as he answered. 'Then send in the Chinooks. Or an A130 gunship, or anything,' he pleaded. 'But not a Hellfire. If Juma's men were ready for the Seals, they'll be ready for a drone missile.'

Susan accepted Myles was sincere, but didn't share his doubts about the technology. 'I don't want a debate about this. The Chinooks would take ten or fifteen minutes to get there. The Hellfire just needs seconds.' She moved back to the microphone. She was about to give the order again when Myles touched her shoulder, more calmly this time. 'There's a US Senator out there,' he reminded her. 'And he could be being held in one of those huts. If you send in a missile…'

Myles could tell he had made Susan think. She was scratching her head, looking desperately at the screens for several seconds.

The subordinate military voice came back over the system, sounding confused. 'Ma'am, do we have a decision on the Hellfire?'

Uncertain and now quivering slightly, Susan pressed the microphone button again. 'OK, we've got to make a call on this,' she conceded. 'Is Richard Roosevelt listening in to this?'

There was another pause. Then Dick Roosevelt's unmistakeable accent came through the speaker. 'Roosevelt Junior here.'

'Mr Roosevelt, sir, we're ready to send a Hellfire missile into the area. It could enable our last surviving Navy Seal to escape. But, if they're holding your father there, it could also lead to his death. Are you happy for us to go ahead, sir?'

Silence as everybody waited on Richard Roosevelt's thinking time. Then his answer came back. 'What are the other options?'

Unsure she was doing the right thing, Susan graciously handed the microphone to Myles.

Myles thanked her with a look, and then tried to make his case. 'Dick, it's Myles,' he began. 'The Somali gang were ready for the Navy Seals, so they'll probably be ready for a Hellfire missile. The only way we can help this Morton guy is by sending in Chinooks. They can fire on the area and pick up any survivors, including any wounded.'

'Good to hear your voice, Myles. How long would a Chinook take?'

Myles shook his head as he tried to answer. Susan took the microphone back. 'Up to ten minutes for a Chinook,' she said. 'Less than a minute for a Hellfire, Mr Roosevelt.'

This time the pause was short. Richard Roosevelt's voice didn't seem troubled by the decision: he was confident in his choice. 'Then it's the Hellfire. We don't have ten minutes.'

'OK, then launch the Hellfire,' commanded Susan. 'Lock onto the huts.'

Susan's instruction was relayed through the system to the Predator's flight controller, who sat by a computer screen in Louisiana. Moments later the image from the drone's cameras juddered upwards slightly, twice, indicating it had released two of its Hellfire missiles.

Myles and Susan stood transfixed. Even though they both had reservations, they knew this had to work.

On the screen, infrared images were slowly beginning to emerge from the concrete huts. The firefight was over. Juma's guys were about to inspect the bodies.

'Twenty seconds to impact…'

Once the target of a Hellfire has been chosen and the missile fired, the missile was designed to drop from aircraft and glide in mid-air for several seconds – enough time for the helicopter or jet which dropped it to move away. Only then did the main rocket ignite with a powerful flash, and the weapon accelerate towards its target.

Out in the cloud-free desert of rural Libya, Juma was ready. He had sentries watching out for anything else the Americans might send, knowing whatever they tried would probably be airborne. The bright flash of a Hellfire missile igniting was unmissable in the desert sky, and several of his men raised the alarm at the same time.

The warning went out, and Juma's gang immediately started fleeing in all directions.

'Ten seconds to impact…'

Susan couldn't believe what she was seeing. 'They're scattering,' she whispered. 'Why are they scattering? What the hell…'

'Five seconds…'

Susan grabbed the microphone again. 'Disable the missiles,' she called. 'Disable them. Call them off.'

There was silence on the net. Everybody knew it was far too late to deactivate the Hellfires. All they could do was watch as the rockets drove into their targets, sending up a bright plume which blinded the infrared feed from the Predator.

Susan couldn't wait for the image to clear. She had to know what had happened.

There was another pause – almost a minute – while technicians checked the images from Captain Morton's helmet cam.

Then the subordinate military voice relayed the conclusion over the net. 'Er, looks like we've lost Captain Morton, Ma'am.'

Susan lifted her palm to her forehead, then slammed the microphone down. The base shattered with the force. She leant forward again, 'And all Juma's men escaped?'

Images still coming from the Predator showed Juma's men starting to return to the destroyed huts, and regrouping.

'Yes, that's right, Ma'am… And still no sign of the Senator.'

CHAPTER TWENTY-FIVE
JFK Airport, New York

Myles could tell Susan was very shaken. She scratched her head again. 'Was there anything I could have done? Could Morton have been saved?'

'You did your best.'

Susan was grateful for Myles' support. 'OK, so what do we do now? The CIA assessment said you were exceptionally bright: do you have any ideas?'

Myles measured his words as he spoke them. 'We need a different approach,' he replied. 'These guys may be primitive, but we won't beat them with technology. We've got to out-think them.'

'"Out-think" them?' Susan said 'out-think' derisively, as though Myles was proposing some sort of chess competition.

Myles tried to answer. 'I don't mean mind games. I mean we've got to work out what they're planning,' he explained. 'They say they're going to inflict on us the fate of the Roman Empire. That should give us some clues.'

Susan nodded, then went back on the network. 'OK, we're going to form a brains trust to plot our next moves. Mr Roosevelt – we'd be grateful if you could be involved.'

Richard Roosevelt's voice came on, surprisingly unperturbed by the Hellfire strike which could have just killed his father. 'OK, you got me,' he said.

'Good,' said Susan. 'Then I need just one man from each unit. Don't send me the most senior. Send me your brightest – anyone you have who can think outside the box. We'll meet in the academy in…' She glanced at her watch. 'Five hours.'

Only as the message confirmations came through did Myles realise just how many units had been listening on the net. Susan answered further questions, and took suggestions for people to attend the 'brains trust' meeting. It seemed to offer her consolation after the doomed rescue mission into Libya.

Five hours later, Myles found himself in a familiar place: at the front of a lecture hall. But this was in America's most elite military academy. He had been driven to West Point in upstate New York, where the US trained its most promising military men and women.

If he were more sentimental, he would have revelled in the history of the place: this was the cradle of the American military spirit, the training ground for their best – and worst – military leaders over two centuries, including several past presidents. But it passed him by. History mattered much less to him now – now he was caught up in history being made, although it gave him no pride at all.

Before him were more than forty of the military's best intelligence specialists, covert operations experts, and military PhDs. Even some of General Petraeus's human terrain anthropologists were there, including several fresh back from the field. Richard Roosevelt sat in the front row, still glowing with relief after his daring escape. Myles shook his hand warmly.

Myles scanned the crowd – it was a very different audience to the university students he was used to teaching – and stood up to speak. 'Thank you all for coming,' he announced. 'Here is the situation. A gangster initially from Somalia called Juma…'

A long-distance photograph of Juma appeared on the screen behind him.

'…has taken hostage Senator Sam Roosevelt,' explained Myles. 'Juma threatens to destroy America "as the Roman Empire was destroyed". Our job is to stop Juma and his pirates bringing down America, and save the Senator.' He saw a hand go up at the back of the hall and invited the bespectacled naval officer to speak.

'Sir, how was the Roman Empire destroyed?' asked the Navy man.

'Good question,' said Myles, nodding to accept it. 'There are lots of theories – at least two hundred of them. Nobody's really certain. There were probably several things which brought Rome down. But Juma's wife, Placidia…'

A picture of Placidia taken from her recent video displaced the image of Juma.

'…is a top scholar on the subject. Perhaps *the* top scholar. It's her opinion that counts, both because she's probably right, and because she's got a strong influence over Juma and his gang of pirates, mercenaries and migrants. Placidia is half-American, by the way. She knows us a lot better than we know her.'

Another hand went up – a woman in army fatigues. Myles nodded at her. She moved in her seat as she spoke. 'Sir, why Rome?'

'Rome is the country on which the American nation was based,' replied Myles. 'The founding fathers deliberately modelled their experiment in government on Rome, which had, until then, led the most powerful empire the world had ever seen.'

The army woman shook her head. Myles had misunderstood. 'Yes, I get that,' she said. 'But why Rome as a threat? There are lots of ways these people could have threatened us. Why threaten us with a fate nobody really understands?'

Myles acknowledged the point: the woman was right. 'That's something we need to find the answer to.'

In the front row, Richard Roosevelt caught Myles' eye. Myles motioned for him to speak. 'Myles, you've met Juma and Placidia,' said Roosevelt, 'and you know Placidia well.'

'Knew, Richard, knew – I don't know her now.'

'OK, you *knew* Placidia. What do you think they're trying to achieve? I mean, do they really think they can take on America and win?' The question raised a murmur around the room. Dick Roosevelt had his father's gift for making points which won over the crowd.

Myles recognised the sentiment and tried to give as honest an answer as he could. 'Placidia – when I knew her at university – was amazingly bright,' he said. 'Probably more gifted than anyone in this room. And very idealist. So idealist she was almost naive, but determined with it. I don't know what's made her change, but I'm sure her husband, Juma, had something to do with it. Juma has been assessed as a psychopath.'

Dick nodded: he thought Juma was a psychopath, too.

'So, we're dealing with an idealistic mastermind and a madman,' continued Myles. 'It's possible that neither of them have looked at this situation as we would look at it. I'm not sure they're even trying to win. Placidia will probably have a very clever motive. Juma may have no motive at all.'

There was silence. It gave Myles an opportunity to make one last point. 'And there's another thing for us to consider – which is that we *could* concede to their demands. They want many thousands of African migrants trapped in Libya to be allowed to settle in the continental United States. Perhaps we should let them…'

The lecture theatre exploded into furious debate. Myles let it run for a few seconds. Then he shouted instructions over the noise. 'Break into three teams, and come back here in one hour with some answers. We need to know how they're going to attack us, what we should do about it, and anything else which might save America from the fate of Rome.'

Myles allowed the groups to disperse, most of them still arguing furiously. When the last uniform left, Myles was completely alone again.

He absorbed the silence. It helped him think. Why *had* Juma and Placidia threatened the US? He leant back, letting his mind muse on, trying to make progress but failing.

Myles realised: this puzzle was like an optical illusion – the more he thought he understood, the less he really knew. Placidia's 'last prophecy of Rome' – that the United States would be brought down in the same way as the ancient superpower – all depended on Placidia's unique view of history.

Everything he'd learnt about Rome he'd learnt with her, and he hadn't focussed on the history during those lessons because he'd been too focussed on her. And now her puzzle was teasing him for it.

Images of Placidia drifted back into his mind. Emotions were displacing logic: Myles was too close.

His knowledge of Placidia, all those years ago, meant he was the worst person to work out how to stop Juma's plans now.

CHAPTER TWENTY-SIX
West Point Military Academy, New York State

After fifty-five minutes, the first team started coming back. Still discussing their conclusions, there were clearly very different views amongst them. Myles often used break-out groups in his lectures. They forced the students to think. He didn't interrupt: he knew less thinking would be done if he interfered.

The first team was soon joined by another, this time more confident of their material. Gradually the room started to fill up with a diverse collection of uniforms, all busily taking their places and finalising their presentations.

After fifty-nine minutes the room was almost full, and as the minute hand hit the hour the last group rushed in, apologising for being late.

'OK, let's start,' called Myles. 'Who wants to go first?'

A naval lieutenant stood up, holding a large sheet of paper on which his group had scribbled out their thoughts. Myles thanked him for volunteering and invited him to the front.

Slightly awkward, the lieutenant held up the paper and tried to explain what it meant. 'We looked at how the US could be attacked. Our nation's key vulnerabilities.' The navy guy pointed to a long list on the paper:

Internet attack... Dirty bomb... Terrorist attack on the transport system...

The audience nodded – they were familiar with the list. The register of US critical vulnerabilities was published every year.

'Then we went through it and worked out which risks we shared with ancient Rome,' explained the lieutenant.

The speaker uncapped a red marker. Then he struck through the first item on the list, and the second, and the third. The audience watched as most of the list was crossed off. 'So that left these issues for us to focus on.'

Everybody peered at the things which remained. Just three points. The speaker used a blue marker to underline them.

Biological/Viral attack/Plague
Chemical attack/poisoning
Economic attack

Then the lieutenant explained each one. 'For biological, we thought Juma might try to spread diseases which resist antibiotics.' He scribbled "antibiotic resistance" next to "Biological/Viral attack/Plague".

Next the lieutenant reminded the audience that Colonel Gaddafi recently manufactured weapons of mass destruction – mainly mustard gas. Whether or not the stocks had been destroyed, there were still technicians in the region with dangerous skills. He wrote "gas" next to the second item on the list.

Finally, the lieutenant wrote "oil" next to "Economic Attack", as he explained that Juma might engineer a price spike. 'Our economy is still vulnerable to oil shocks. Maybe the US relies on imported oil as the Romans depended on imported food...'

The lieutenant indicated that was as far as his team's thinking had progressed. Myles thanked him and the naval officer returned to his seat.

The next presentation was from a woman in regulation army camouflage. She came to the front with a co-presenter who held up a flip chart. 'OK, so in our group we looked at this problem historically,' she began. 'What destroyed the great Roman Empire?'

'Good,' said Myles. 'If you know the answer to that I'm sure there are a lot of people who'll be impressed.'

The woman smiled, acknowledging Myles' point, then continued. 'We reckon the Roman Empire was knocked down by three things. First, lead poisoning – the aristocracy used the metal in sauces for their food. But these condiments literally drove them mad because lead is toxic, and causes changes in the brain. Roman leaders made some terrible decisions. So Juma might try a similar mass poisoning strategy of some sort, perhaps targeting America's decision-makers.'

There was a murmur of respect around the room. 'Second, fertility levels dropped in ancient Rome just as they are dropping now in the West. Sperm counts in Europe and America are now less than half of what they were forty years ago – we wondered whether the attack might already be happening.'

The audience could tell the woman felt slightly embarrassed talking about the reduction in male fertility. But they respected her point.

'The final issue,' concluded the woman. 'Economic collapse. Rome's currency lost its value. Our dollar is vulnerable in the same way. If the dollar ceases to be the international reserve currency, then our economy will suffer big time.'

Myles thanked the woman as she returned to her seat.

The next speaker was more confident, but also seemed less thoughtful than the other two. 'In our team, we used a classical military approach. We started with Centre of Gravity analysis,' he declared.

Myles had often told his students about Centre of Gravity theory: the centre of gravity was the single thing which, if destroyed, would neutralise an enemy's capacity to fight. It was a sensible concept – an idea developed by Clausewitz, the great military theorist on whom Myles was Oxford University's leading expert. The trouble with Centre of Gravity analysis was that it invited military minds to think of physical things – buildings, people or communication networks. Often, the real Centre of Gravity of an enemy was much harder to pin down – a belief or an attitude which Western forces couldn't reach.

'OK, so we looked at their Centre of Gravity, and we reckon it's their leaders: Juma and Placidia. So we recommend targeting them.'

Myles checked he had understood correctly. 'You mean taking them out?

'That's right, sir. Yes.'

Myles cast around the room for a reaction. It was mixed. Most of the audience accepted that targeted assassination was more complicated than it sometimes appeared. There had to be good intelligence on where the leaders would be, an assessment of collateral damage, a consideration of the wider consequences…

There were also moral issues, and Myles knew men in uniform often relied on euphemisms: using a word like 'targeting' when really they meant kill. He turned to Richard Roosevelt. 'Dick – would you be happy with assassination?'

The Senator's son slowly shook his head. He carefully framed his words in his mind before he replied. 'I'm with the sentiment,' he explained. 'But killing these suckers won't solve our problems. Juma's already set his plans rolling, and those plans will keep on rolling even if he's dead.'

The enthusiastic speaker understood: killing Juma and Placidia was not enough. 'OK,' continued the presenter, 'so then we did

Centre of Gravity analysis for the US. We reckon our Centre of Gravity is our social cohesion – in other words, how we stand together as a nation…'

Myles was impressed: the military planner had defined a Centre of Gravity for the US which wasn't a physical object. Centre of Gravity analysis might actually be of some use after all.

'And if social cohesion is our Centre of Gravity,' continued the man, 'then it can be attacked in three ways: by getting religious groups in America to attack each other, which happened in Ancient Rome. By making people distrust their rulers and leaders, which also happened in Ancient Rome. And by removing people's confidence in their currency, which happened in Ancient Rome, too.'

The speaker turned to Myles, asking permission to continue. Myles used his eyes to indicate the officer should talk on – this was useful. 'So, it's hard to see how Juma can do anything on the first two – religion in the US and distrust of rulers and leaders. Which means we reckon he'll go for the currency. And there's a high-level summit about the international currency system, nine days away. It's the obvious target, because the meeting is in Rome.'

The room spontaneously applauded: the argument was persuasive. Juma must be heading for Rome.

Richard Roosevelt stood up to thank the speaker with a warm handshake, then interjected. 'Thanks for that,' he said. 'As most of you know, as well as being the son of someone famous, I'm CEO of Roosevelt Guardians. What some of you may not know is that my private security firm is actually responsible for the conference. I don't know whether to thank you for the warning or blame you for making my job more difficult.'

The room laughed at Dick Roosevelt's humility.

'But what I think it means, is that I need help,' continued Roosevelt. 'I need someone to check we've made the currency conference safe. Ideally, one of you guys with a brilliant mind who can out-think Juma.'

The lecture theatre was nodding in agreement: if Juma was going to attack the Rome conference then the assembled brains trust should send someone to pre-empt what he might do. But who should go?

Someone tried to encourage the woman who had given the second presentation to go, but she clearly wasn't keen. Someone else was being talked about, but for some reason everybody decided they weren't suitable.

Then there was a suggestion that the brightest person in the room should go. Another voice said it should be the person who got their thinking this far. They needed an expert in military theory, and also someone who had met Juma and Placidia.

It took just a few more moments for the lecture hall to come to a consensus as to who should accompany Dick Roosevelt in reviewing the arrangements. As he felt the eyes turn towards him, Myles accepted that he didn't really have much choice.

Myles was going back to Rome.

CHAPTER TWENTY-SEVEN
Las Vegas, USA

Paul Pasgarius the Third's cabriolet had been washed and polished by illegal migrants while he slept – migrants he felt no obligation to pay – and now glinted in the setting Nevada sun. He swung the vehicle round the junction, and began to cruise along the boulevard.

Paul raised his shades to admire two women walking beside the road. He slowed the car. When the women glanced down at the sidewalk, deliberately ignoring him, he just put more gum in his mouth and accelerated away. Those ladies didn't know what they were missing, he grinned to himself.

It was just a short drive to his office. He left his car with an attendant and sauntered in. His three staff were already working, monitoring screens, but not too busy. He grunted an acknowledgement to them, then strolled into his own private room, and closed the door behind him.

From the notifications on his screen, he already knew there was no unusual activity. Or at least, not an unusual amount of it. As always, a few clever novices were trying to scam the online poker, and some guys were getting lucky on the slots. It always happened at the start of the evening. But Paul Pasgarius the Third's computer algorithm told him what was really unusual. It watched for certain tricks: special betting patterns, and evidence of card counting or accomplices on the staff. None of that was happening. The clever novices would soon find the online settings turning against them. And the lucky guys on the slots, unless they had the rare courage to quit early, would end their night with less money than they started.

It would be a quiet few hours. And that meant, for Paul, lucrative ones. He leant back in his chair, and peeled open a magazine. The headline article was about scams used by gamblers in ancient Rome, and how some of today's most common con tricks harked back to the imperial city.

He was about to start reading when an alert flashed on the corner of the screen. He frowned, disconcerted by the words 'Unknown Caller'. Whoever it was, they were cloaking their location. It wasn't one of the big casinos. Probably no one in Las Vegas at all. He put on his headset and answered.

'Er, Hello.' Paul listened carefully, waiting for words to emerge from the static.

When the voice did come through, it was garbled. Very garbled. 'Paul Pasgarius the Third.'

The voice was so heavily disguised, Paul couldn't tell whether it was a man or a woman. He also wasn't sure whether he was being told his name or asked a question.

'Er yes, this is Paul Pasgarius the Third,' he replied. 'CEO of Nevada Fair Play Computer Monitoring Systems Incorporated.'

More silence. Then a single word: 'Good'.

'How may I help you?'

'I need certain electronic material to be loaded onto a computer.'

Paul paused, trying to understand the command. 'Er, your computer?'

'No,' came the response. 'I think we both know what we're talking about here.'

'Ah,' said Paul. He put more gum in his mouth, giving him time to think. 'Nevada Fair Play Computer Monitoring Systems Incorporated is licensed by the Nevada Gaming Control Board,' he said, rushing the words out in case he was being tested by someone official. 'I comply with all the state regulations and laws.' He almost added the words, 'And I operate according to the highest ethical standards,' but it was too much of a lie, even for him.

'You will not have to breach any laws or regulations – in Nevada,' came the reply.

Paul clutched the headphones to his ears. 'OK,' he mused, slowly.

'Good,' came the reply. 'Because that means no one will ever get to hear about…your activities.' The voice trailed off.

Paul Pasgarius the Third gulped, wondering how the anonymous caller had learned about his misdemeanours.

'You know what I'm talking about?' asked the voice.

Paul thought of trying to bluff it out. Or pretending there was nothing wrong with the special 'parties' he went to – parties he paid to attend and where he was guaranteed a good time, usually with very young girls. But his licence was at stake. It wasn't worth the risk. 'Maybe I do,' he admitted. 'What do you have in mind?'

Then he listened while the voice gave precise details on what they wanted.

'OK,' concluded Pasgarius. 'I can do that for you. Just once, you understand. And, your name – what can I call you?'

He still wondered whether he was talking to a man or a woman, and hoped the caller's answer would settle his curiosity. But the one word response from the voice just left him even more puzzled than before.

'Constantine.'

'Constantine, huh?'

'You got it.'

Paul Pasgarius the Third frowned. He swung his chair round, and gazed across at the fountains of Caesar's Palace opposite. 'Wasn't there an Emperor called that?' he asked.

But the caller had already gone.

DAY IV

CHAPTER TWENTY-EIGHT
JFK Airport, New York

Helen managed to say goodbye to Myles in the airport's secure departures area – there was no time for them to enjoy each other's company properly. 'Myles, it feels funny you going back to Rome without me,' she said.

'I wish you were coming along…'

The final call for Myles' flight came over the tannoy. Myles felt Helen's fingers intertwine with his. He pulled her close, then kissed her. He could tell she was nervous.

Helen gripped his hand tightly, and leant back so she could inspect his face. 'Call me – every day – OK?' she asked.

'I will. And you call me if I forget – right?'

'You got it.' She let him go, and kept waving at him until he had disappeared from view.

Myles wasn't sure what he had become involved in, but he felt duty-bound to see it through. Especially with the Senator still held hostage. But he also knew he had only seen part of the problem so far. In particular, there were three things he still couldn't understand: Why was Placidia trying to destroy America? How had the idealistic young woman he knew at university become a terrorist? And could she really make the US fall like the Roman Empire?

He hoped this trip to Rome would help him unlock the puzzles. But he also knew there was a fourth puzzle, one to which he didn't want the answer: his feelings for Placidia. The thought of her still stopped him from thinking. And he needed to think, he told himself, if he was to stop whatever Placidia and Juma had planned.

Dick Roosevelt helped Myles with his bags at Rome's Ciampino airport. There was also a Roosevelt Guardian car waiting for them, ready to take them to the conference venue in the city centre – a short drive. As they had been trained, the private security men treated Myles as a VIP – opening doors for him, calling him 'sir', and making sure newspapers and other material were ready for him inside. Although Myles found it more amusing than flattering, he could see how seductive it could be. 'This is how you treat all your guests?' he asked.

'All part of the Roosevelt Guardian service, Myles,' replied Roosevelt junior. 'All part of the service.'

Myles and Richard Roosevelt relaxed in the back seats of the firm's armoured limousine as the vehicle swished towards the centre of Rome. Through heavily tinted windows, Myles could see Italian daily life, and wondered how much had changed since imperial times. A mother disciplined her child, old men chatted at an outside table, and a trader stacked boxes of fruits for market. As they drove further, Myles saw foreigners from all over Europe and America who had come to see the city sights for themselves – just as people from all over the Empire travelled to Rome in its heyday. It could all have happened two thousand years ago.

As they neared the city centre, Myles saw more of the historic architecture: paving stones, statues and arches, all worn down by two millennia of weather and events. Famous columns to honour senators and nobles, the central forum, a victory statue… The car passed the famous Victor Emmanuel monument – not two thousand years old but barely one hundred, completed to celebrate the unification of Italy and lauded by the Italian dictator Mussolini in his doomed attempt to create an imperial legacy of his own. It was another reminder that Rome had gone through some tragic episodes since its most glorious days.

Myles saw huge churches – this city was the epicentre of the Catholic faith.

When they turned down a narrow medieval street, Myles saw buildings which had probably been built in the Renaissance. Tourists threw coins into a fountain, smiling as they made a wish.

Rome was a place of beauty and charm, forged by its history. The city's past was dominated by its Empire. And that imperial legacy was always shaded by one fact: that it fell.

He tried to remember his tutorials – his lessons with Placidia… How did *she* think the Roman Empire fell?

He was still wondering as they arrived in the forecourt of the conference centre.

Myles' car door was opened for him. 'Welcome to the Barberini Conference Centre,' said a woman in uniform.

Myles stepped out, and looked up at the building in front of them. It was modern and impressive, but built within a much older stone frame – thoughtful architecture.

The Barberini Hotel in Rome was an obvious choice for a conference. Its central location meant delegates could spend time between sessions visiting the city's famous sites. It already had an extensive CCTV system, making security easier. And, by being in the middle of small and winding streets, terrorists hoping to ram the building with a car or truck bomb would not be able to build up much speed.

The main entrance to the hotel opened out onto a piazza. Currently a car park, the area would be cleared of vehicles before the conference was held.

'We'll have an outside screening point – you know, a walk-through scanner, like in airports,' explained Roosevelt. 'Then another check when people actually get inside.' He detailed how he'd double up the safeguards. Myles was encouraged.

Once inside the building, Roosevelt showed Myles the corridors which led off to the left – to a café and toilets – and right, with stairs ahead of them. There were also lifts to the upper floor. 'Let me show you to the CCTV room. The nerve centre…' offered Roosevelt.

Richard galloped up the stairs then along an upper-level corridor. Myles followed. They approached a normal-looking door, which the young Roosevelt held open for the Englishman. 'Hope you're impressed.'

Myles was. Roosevelt Guardians had managed to fill the room with computer equipment of all sorts. There were TV screens on the walls, phones, whiteboards and communications kit. The two men already there – a Roosevelt Guardian drinking a coffee and a technician making final changes – immediately recognised their CEO and jumped to attention. Roosevelt barely noticed them. Instead, he extended his arm and wafted it across the room, showing it off to Myles.

'And we've connected all the CCTV feeds through to here, too,' said Roosevelt, picking up a computer keyboard. He started flipping through the images from different viewpoints around the building. Myles found himself absorbed in the pictures.

Then something caught his eye. The CCTV image from the main entrance showed two Italian police vans pulling up in the piazza. The doors opened and uniformed men started climbing out. Some were armed.

'Is that normal?' asked Myles.

Richard Roosevelt squinted at the grainy computer image. The Guardians at the entrance were reacting as though the Italian police were unexpected.

Richard Roosevelt asked his employee what was happening.

'Don't know, sir,' came the reply.

Roosevelt changed the feed and switched to a different camera. The central staircase came into view, distorted by the fish-eye camera lens. Within moments the Italian police were there, running up the stairs as Myles and Roosevelt had just minutes earlier. Several of the policemen stood guard. For whatever reason, they seemed determined that no one leave the conference centre.

'What do they want?' asked Roosevelt.

'Don't know, sir.'

Richard Roosevelt turned to Myles. 'Do you know what this is about?'

Myles shook his head. He was as confused as his host.

Moments later a group of Carabinieri burst into the room. They had automatic guns, which they deliberately pointed at the floor. Four of them fanned out, cocking their weapons and making sure no one moved.

The Roosevelt Guardian and the technician froze. Myles stayed still, too. Only Richard Roosevelt reacted. He looked angry and confronted the Italians. 'Who are you?' he demanded. 'What are you doing here?'

'You must be Richard Roosevelt,' replied one of the men, obviously in charge of the special Italian police and smiling from behind a beard.

'Yes I am. And who are you?'

The policeman looked relaxed, and gestured to his men to ease their posture. 'Captain Perrotta. Italian Special Police.'

'Where's your ID?'

Perrotta had the look of a family man: when he made an effort to retrieve a plastic card from his inside pocket, Myles half expected him to pull out a confiscated toy. Roosevelt held out his hand, demanding to inspect Perrotta's credentials.

After a few seconds Roosevelt handed the card back. 'OK, so you are Carabinieri,' accepted Roosevelt. 'I have to check – you know, in post-invasion Iraq there were lots of armed gangs pretending to be policemen…'

But Perrotta had already lost interest in the American. With his plastic ID card safely stowed back in his jacket, he gently brushed Roosevelt aside. He was walking past him.

Richard Roosevelt was incensed. He didn't know how to react.

Then it became clear who the Carabinieri were really after.

'And, sir, are you Mr Myles Munro?' asked Perrotta.

Myles confirmed that he was.

'Then, Mr Munro,' said Perrotta, his head slightly bowed, 'you are to come with me.'

Myles was shocked. He made eye contact with Roosevelt, who looked like he was about to explode.

Roosevelt put himself between Perrotta and Myles. 'Do you have a warrant to arrest this man?'

Perrotta's expression said he didn't care.

Suddenly Myles and Roosevelt felt their wrists being pulled from behind. Roosevelt was just held in place while Myles was handcuffed with a plastic snare.

Roosevelt was only released once Myles had been marched out of the room and along the corridor. Myles heard the American shout as he was led away by the policemen. 'I'll get you a lawyer, Myles. The police will have to release you soon…'

Myles tried to call out a 'thank you' back to him, but he was halfway down the stairs when he said it. Roosevelt probably didn't hear him.

'Can you say why you're taking me?' asked Myles, as they walked outside.

Perrotta just shook his head.

Although Myles was baffled by his arrest, he wasn't worried. He knew he hadn't committed any sort of crime, and he assumed that as soon as the Italian policemen realised that fact, he would be released. Even when he was being led into the Carabinieri police van he assumed he'd be treated properly.

He hadn't expected what was to come.

CHAPTER TWENTY-NINE
Rome

Myles was transported in a police van from the conference venue along the crowded streets of Rome. It was scenic, even pleasant. Perrotta, sitting next to him, pointed out some of the city's landmarks as they passed: the National Gallery of Ancient Art, the San Paolo 'within the walls' church, the Opera House, the National Museum of Rome… If his hands hadn't been bound, Myles could have imagined he was being given a guided tour.

After a few minutes the vehicle pulled into the modern courtyard of an office building. Perrotta made sure Myles could climb out safely, helping him with his balance, and Myles was led inside: a police station. After being signed in by Perrotta, Myles was guided through two sets of secure doors, and finally into an interrogation suite. 'We have some English teabags. Would you like a cup?' offered Perrotta.

'That's kind. Thank you. I'd prefer coffee if you have any.'

Perrotta nodded respectfully and departed. Myles was left alone in the room.

He took in his surroundings. Natural light was coming in from a skylight in the ceiling. There were small posters and notices on the walls. Myles tried to decode the Italian and guessed they were advertising events in the city. He even had a comfortable chair. It was a room for polite questioning – not interrogation.

Myles had experience of interrogation from his short time in the military – from the other side of the table. He guessed Perrotta would ask what he had to ask, find out what he needed, then probably let him go free. Myles had nothing to hide, so he assumed it made sense to talk freely – to clear up the confusion which had led to his arrest, and get back to stopping Juma.

He studied the room some more. The only thing which marked it out as a place of questioning was a camera above the door.

Myles stared at it. Nothing happened. Was someone watching him, or was it just recording?

Myles stood up and moved to the side of the room. When the camera swung sideways with him, he knew he was being watched.

Perrotta returned, opening the door with his back to avoid spilling the two coffees he held in his hands. Myles, his wrists still bound, held the door for the Italian until he could put the drinks down on the table.

'Thank you, Myles,' said Perrotta. 'May I call you Myles?'

'Certainly. Myles is fine.'

Myles was impressed by Perrotta's English, even though the policeman's accent clearly marked him out as an Italian.

'Myles, have you lost your computer recently?' asked the policeman.

Myles thought for a moment. He'd taken his laptop to America, and he had it with him at West Point, but had left it with Helen. He'd not brought it with him to Rome. 'No. No, I left my computer in the United States. Why do you ask?'

Perrotta raised his eyebrows with a shrug. He gave the impression that the question didn't really matter. 'It's OK. And you work in Oxford?'

'Yes.'

'How long have you worked at the university?'

'I've been a lecturer there for about five years.'

'But you also visit warzones?' asked Perrotta, trying to clarify things.

'Sometimes I do. History of war – it's what I teach.'

Perrotta nodded. His style of questioning was very relaxed, more like a conversation than police questioning. Certainly not an interrogation. 'And, in Oxford, you teach about new forms of warfare, too,' continued the Italian. 'Unconventional warfare.'

'That's right. Old-style warfare – big tank battles, infantry marching towards capital cities – doesn't happen much anymore. Wars are different now.'

Perrotta could see Myles becoming animated. Clearly the Oxford lecturer was passionate about his subject, and probably a popular teacher, too.

'Is that asymmetric warfare, Mr Munro?'

Myles paused before he answered. 'Some people call it asymmetric warfare, but that's a bad description,' he explained, trying to be careful with his words. 'All war is about asymmetry. An asymmetry is just a difference. All generals seek an asymmetry – more men, more force, better tactics. The ultimate asymmetry is when one side wins and the other side loses. Wars which aren't asymmetric just become stalemates. Usually very bloody.'

Perrotta nodded respectfully. He pulled his hand over his beard as he framed his next question. 'So you're not an expert in terrorism?'

'I don't teach it, if that's what you mean, no,' answered Myles squarely.

Perrotta nodded again, leaning back. Myles could see him wondering whether to keep up on this topic or switch to another. 'And you did your undergraduate degree at Oxford?' Perrotta was changing topic again.

Myles explained how he'd read history and philosophy. It wasn't a normal course at the university at the time, but they let him study both.

'It must have been interesting for you, Myles.'

'Yes. Both subjects – fascinating.'

Perrotta had got Myles relaxed again. Myles knew from his own experience as an interrogator this was good practice. It meant the questioner could register the reaction when they moved back to more sensitive questions.

'And you knew Juma's wife, Placidia, when you were at Oxford.'

Myles tried not to react, but he found his mood change involuntarily. 'I did know her, yes.'

Perrotta probed further. 'How well did you know her?'

Myles hesitated.

'You would have liked to know her more?' offered Perrotta.

Myles paused again. Silence. It was an answer in itself.

Perrotta moved his head to confirm he wasn't going to press Myles on it. Instead he moved on again. 'So, you weren't in touch with Placidia after she left Oxford, all those years ago?'

'No. Not until I saw her again in Libya last week.'

'And you've not been in touch with her since then?'

Myles found the question disconcerting. 'No, not at all.' Of course he hadn't been in touch with her. Placidia had become a terrorist.

'You're sure, Myles? Not at all?'

'Yes, I'm sure.' Finally Myles was starting to get a little angry as he wondered where Perrotta's questions were leading.

Perrotta remained silent, waiting for Myles to say something else. The silence invited Myles to speak. But Myles knew the tactic. He just stayed silent too.

Perrotta slowly ran a finger on his chin, onto his beard, thinking. 'When you were in Libya,' he posed, 'did you wonder why you were released but Senator Roosevelt and his son were kept hostage?'

Myles just looked blank. No, he didn't wonder. Myles had wondered about all sorts of things, but not that. 'They sent me back so people heard about their ultimatum.' He'd seen several bureaucratic mix-ups over the years, but this was one of the most peculiar.

Perrotta, still relaxed, took a final swig from his coffee and stood up. 'You'll excuse me for a minute, please.'

Myles nodded.

Perrotta left the room, leaving Myles to think back through the questions. Asking about his relationship with Placidia was reasonable, but why the quiz about his computer? And why ask about what he taught? Perrotta had known a lot about him, but had not used notes. Impressive.

It was almost ten minutes before Perrotta returned. When he did, he was as polite as ever. 'Thank you, Myles, for all your answers today,' he said. 'You've been very helpful.'

'Thank you. Can I ask what the questions are about?'

Perrotta shook his head in apology. He seemed genuine. 'I'm sorry, no.'

Then Perrotta tipped his head to one side to explain. He could explain a little. 'Perhaps you've been working with someone in America's Department of Homeland Security recently?'

'Yes, Susan.'

'You don't know her second name – just "Susan"?'

'Yes. Why?'

Myles still spoke like a man who thought he was innocent. Perrotta had seen it before. The Italian weighed his words before he answered. He knew they would strike Myles hard when he said them, so he tried to speak as gently as he could. 'Well, it seems the Department – Susan – has some evidence to suggest you've been helping terrorists conspire against the United States.'

CHAPTER THIRTY
Questura Centrale Police Station, Rome

Myles was stunned. He didn't know what to say. He knew he was innocent, so how could the Department of Homeland Security have made such a mistake?

Myles remembered the people he'd interviewed in Iraq, and how they reacted when he presented them with evidence. Some were guilty, some innocent, some only half-innocent – it was usually easy to tell which were which. But it was the ones who couldn't really engage with the accusation, because it seemed too bizarre, that Myles felt sorry for. Myles felt like that now.

Perrotta escorted Myles to a car, which drove him to a private airport. There, he accompanied Myles to a small jet plane, and Myles was signed over to some British police officers. Although Myles' hands were bound, Perrotta still shook them as he departed. 'Good luck, Myles,' he said. 'I hope you'll be able to return to Italy soon.'

'I hope so, too,' replied Myles. 'Is there anything else you can tell me?'

'No. You're in British hands now. They should give you access to a lawyer.' Perrotta's words were directed to Myles' new escorts as much as Myles himself. But the British policemen seemed uninterested in the suggestion – they kept Myles close but refused eye contact with him. They were acting as if Myles was some kind of terrorist mastermind. Getting legal advice for the accused came a very distant second to public safety. They really seemed to believe Myles was plotting to bring down America like ancient Rome.

Perrotta waved as he left Myles on the aircraft. Myles lifted his bound hands to return the gesture.

After the bumpy two-and-a-half hour flight, Myles was carried off the aircraft under a blanket at another small airfield. He caught a glimpse of the weather as he disembarked. The light rain and cold confirmed he was in Britain.

Then another journey – this time in a secure police vehicle with blacked-out windows. The journey lasted almost an hour.

Myles tried making conversation, but his escorts weren't interested. They seemed to be reasonable people, but their job – their organisation – had made them surly. It reminded him just how much he hated bureaucracies. He was back to where the bureaucrats were in charge.

When the van stopped in an anonymous garage in the dark, Myles' watch was confiscated. Then the binding which tied his hands was cut, and he was led along a corridor from the basement garage into a police cell.

He called out to anyone who was listening, 'Can I have a lawyer?'

No answer.

'Can you tell me what I've been arrested for?'

Again, no answer.

'Well, have I been arrested?'

Still no answer.

Myles kept asking while the prison door was closed in his face, and he was left alone in his cell.

After a few moments of standing and listening – half-hoping the whole thing was a mistake or a warped joke, and he was about to be released – he slumped down.

He ignored his bleak surroundings, and tried to think back. How could anyone even imagine he had helped terrorists? He'd only met Juma once, and only seen Placidia one time since… all those years ago.

He remembered that time. Their last lecture together on Rome – Myles' mind drifted into his memory…

The lecturer turned to the blackboard and wrote up the word:

S-A-N-C-T-U-A-R-Y

He put down the chalk and turned back to his audience. They were all writing the word in their notes. All except one – the young woman in the front row, his star student. She was typing it. The only foreign student in the room, and she was the only one with a laptop. The lecturer was still puzzled why she carried around a heavy computer instead of a simple pen and paper.

He waited until everyone was looking up again before he continued with his talk. 'Sanctuary was not available to the early pretenders,' he explained. 'The many men who aspired to be emperor – in the third century, for example – could expect execution if they failed.' The lecturer drew his finger across his neck to make the point. 'Their heads were sometimes shown in public – to prove they were dead and to deter others. But sanctuary became important later. As the Roman Empire officially became Christian – a process started by Emperor Constantine in the 320s, and which took about eighty years to complete – failed pretenders would seek sanctuary in churches. Some stayed there and prayed. It was thought no truly Christian emperor could kill someone praying in a church…'

The tall boy sitting next to the girl seemed to be writing a note for her.

The lecturer ignored them and continued. He lifted up a much-read copy of *The History of the Decline and Fall of the Roman Empire*. 'This book,' he said, raising his voice, 'has much to say about Christianity and its impact on Rome – it was one of the reasons why, when the first volume came out in 1776, it was so controversial. The author, Gibbon, angered the Church establishment, because he blames part of Rome's decline on the adoption of Christianity...'

The lecturer could see the girl unfold the boy's note. Still talking to his audience, he peered over as the note opened and read it upside down.

Doing the right thing can sometimes be wrong

The lecturer was confused. He tried not to be distracted. 'And so, um, if we look at this year's American Presidential Election,' he continued, 'how does it compare with the battles to become emperor in ancient Rome? It's expensive, like Rome. Between them all, the candidates will probably spend more than a hundred million dollars before the election is over.'

The audience reacted to the figure – the thought of spending so many millions on an election campaign seemed bizarre.

'But in Rome the expense was even greater,' said the lecturer. 'Rivals to become emperor employed huge private armies – often paying mercenaries from outside the Empire. When the challenger loses to the incumbent US President, he can go back to being Governor or Senator. Roman losers faced death – unless they could find sanctuary...'

His star pupil in the front row was shaking her head. She was disagreeing, which irritated the lecturer – to him, the young woman seemed ungrateful.

But the lecturer noticed the clock – it was time to conclude. 'And that brings me to the end of my last lecture for this academic year,' said the lecturer with a flourish. 'Thank you for listening – if you *did* listen.'

There was a small ripple of laughter.

'Good luck with your exams, and enjoy the summer,' he concluded. 'Thank you.'

A few students applauded, but mostly out of politeness. They all moved to leave while the lecturer went through some administrative points.

The lecturer wanted to catch the foreign woman before she left – she was one of the most gifted students he'd ever taught and was sure to have a brilliant future. But she was already at the door, walking with the boy who'd been sitting beside her. The lecturer would have to find her another time.

Outside, the boy tried to guide the young woman towards a café. She didn't seem interested. 'What do you mean "sometimes it's wrong to do what's right"?' she snapped.

'I'm just saying you have to think through what might happen,' said the male student. 'Think of what's at stake. Think of the consequences, that's all.'

The girl shook her head. 'But *they've* been thinking about consequences – the authorities – which is why it's got so bad…' She listed off her complaints. The university authorities had invested in 'evil companies', like tobacco firms. They refused to cater for vegetarians. They squashed new ideas which proved they were wrong.

The boy accepted that one. 'OK, yes,' he said. 'There are professors here who've built up their careers on a single idea, and they don't like it when someone like you comes along and explains why they're wrong.'

'Especially when it's a woman, and she's foreign.'

'I don't think they're doing it because you're a foreign woman,' replied the boy. 'And you're American, which is hardly foreign here.'

'Half-American.'

The boy shrugged. Her nationality wasn't the point. 'Look, Placidia,' he said. 'They've given you this amazing chance…'

'While they take chances away from other people?'

'A chance to change the way people all over the world think about the Roman Empire.'

'And what will that prove?' she asked rhetorically. 'If I do my doctorate here it just means they can control me.'

'All bureaucracies do that,' he said. 'But Placidia, you've got a chance to beat the system. From the inside…' The boy sat down on a limestone wall. He was inviting the girl to sit next to him, but she was too angry.

'Myles, I've actually beaten the system already. I got them to recycle. It was a long campaign, but I managed to beat them.'

'Yes, well done. But the consequences of what you're planning now…'

'Damn the consequences. I've got to.'

'Placidia – they'll expel you.'

She shrugged. 'So?'

The young Myles paused before he answered. He said his words slowly: 'It means we'll be separated.'

Placidia calmly tipped her head to one side. She was squinting at Myles through the summer sunshine. 'You could join me back in America.'

'Do you think that would work?'

'It's better than me sucking up to these idiots,' she said, flicking her head to the lecture halls. 'I can't stay here without trying to change them.' After a few moments, Placidia became slightly calmer. 'Myles, look. We can be together somehow. Oxford University must have an afterlife.'

Myles barely noticed her leave. He sat on that wall for more than an hour, trying to solve the puzzle: a puzzle about people – just one person. A puzzle that he couldn't unlock. When he finally moved away, he walked much more slowly than before.

Placidia's stunt was splashed across all the student papers the following week. It was even picked up by the local TV news. Burning an academic offer letter to protest against the university made good pictures. And Placidia chose to do it at Oxford's Martyrs' Memorial, the site where dissidents had once been burnt at the stake for refusing to accept a much earlier diktat relating to Rome. University bureaucrats faced tough questions, and hostile journalists. Placidia had shamed them perfectly.

But as Myles had warned her, she was expelled the same day – charged with obstructing traffic and causing a dangerous fire. Everybody knew the accusations were false, but it was enough for them to withdraw the offer Placidia had already burned.

The university didn't change because of what she had done. Now, two decades later, Placidia's dramatic gesture was forgotten by everyone – everybody except Myles. To the world, it meant nothing at all.

The only consequence was that they had been separated.

Damn the consequences.

CHAPTER THIRTY-ONE
Sirte Dockside, Libya

Safiq had been born on a farm in northern Chad. When the drought had struck, he had followed his family to Niger. When disease killed off his father's goats, he moved to Algeria where he earned money by filling petrol cans. Then, as a teenager, he was drawn to Gaddafi's Libya, to become one of the two million foreign workers doing menial jobs for menial money – although the wage was the highest Safiq had ever been paid. Over three years he managed to save eighty-two dollars. He hoped it would buy him an education, or maybe even a chance to travel to Europe.

Then the war came. The 'Arab Spring', people had called it. Safiq understood why the people rebelled against Gaddafi – the man had ruled like a cruel and ruthless emperor. But now everybody was missing the law and order Colonel Gaddafi had brought to the country. People had overthrown him for a better life, yet life was worse.

Seeking civilisation, the rebels had threatened civilisation itself.

The war had been very bad for Safiq. When the government bureaucrat who employed him lost his job, Safiq stopped being paid. Soon he was homeless, too. He sheltered with a family from Sudan he knew from the local vegetable store, who lived in a shack next to the old Roman wall. The wall had been built to keep barbarians out of the ancient empire. Safiq spent his eighty-two dollars as slowly as he could, but it soon dwindled.

With nothing for him in Libya, Safiq began to investigate how he could travel to a better life in Europe. He learned from the Sudanese how most of the unofficial passenger ferries were stopped and diverted to the Italian island of Lampedusa, where migrants were sent back to Africa. Many of these ships were overloaded. Some sank, usually drowning everybody aboard. The rumour was that navies from the rich countries didn't even bother to rescue Africans from the sea. He wouldn't go by passenger ferry.

But, by asking questions along the dockside, Safiq did learn of another plan – the 'fast boat', they called it. The boat's captain claimed it had already crossed to Italy several times. Safiq decided it was worth the risk, and paid sixty dollars for a 'ticket' – which was just a scrap of paper.

Departing at night, Safiq found himself with thirty other Africans crammed onto a tiny skiff. His hopes rose as the craft sped out to sea, and the lights from the coast of Libya disappeared beneath the horizon. For at least two hours, the boat sped on, into the darkness. He dreamed he could see Europe ahead, in the distance. He was getting close…

Then the motor stuttered and stalled. The skiff stopped in the water, and Safiq realised the crewman who had steered them out of port was no longer on board. Where had he gone? Safiq couldn't tell. He checked the engine, and realised there was no fuel left. Passengers began to shout and argue. Two young men jumped into the water and tried to swim, but one didn't know how and the other soon tired. They returned to the boat and tried to climb back in. As passengers moved over to help them, the skiff began to tilt. Realising the danger, they tried to move back, but it was too late. The boat quickly tipped and capsized, throwing everybody into the sea.

Safiq and most of the passengers grabbed the upturned skiff, and just held on as long as they could. Safiq saw the woman beside him cry. A father tried to keep afloat with his daughter on his shoulders. The water was cold, and he became numb. Everyone became quiet as they waited in the darkness.

Only when the sky began to lighten were they seen – by an Italian Navy boat. Safiq didn't know how many people were rescued, but he was sure it wasn't all the people who had set off the evening before.

They were taken to Lampedusa, where he stayed for two days, before being transported back to Libya.

Safiq was back in Africa, poorer and much less hopeful than before. He tried to find the family from Sudan he'd known from the vegetable shop, but they'd gone. He tried to find work on the dockside, but only found some plastic sheeting, which he tried to sell.

None of it offered hope.

Then he heard of a new plan – a chance to reach not just Europe, but the United States – and he knew it was a chance he had to take.

DAY V

CHAPTER THIRTY-TWO

Paddington Green Police Station,
Central London

Myles believed it was now a whole day since he had been hand-cuffed in Rome, although he couldn't be sure. Twenty-four hours was just a guess. And nobody had told him anything since he'd left the British police van.

Myles knew from his time questioning suspects in Iraq: when people are left alone, sooner or later they start to think about the worst that could happen to them. Solitary confinement was one of the most powerful forms of pressure there was.

Myles studied the inside of his police cell. He imagined the stories of the people who had been in the cell before him.

His bed was built into the room: a single, body-size concrete step with a dark green plastic mattress on top. The white walls had recently been cleaned – probably disinfected. The strip-light in the ceiling was encased in plastic and protected behind a metal grille. Even if he could reach it, it would not help him at all.

The only way out was through the tall, metallic, painted black door. He gently leant on it and felt his weight rest against the lock. He pressed harder, but the door barely registered his presence. There was no way he was going to barge his way out. He tried to look through the double-glazed peephole, but there was a cover on the other side blocking his view.

Myles realised that he was now completely at the mercy of whoever was holding him. Whoever it was, he had to communicate with them.

He looked around for a camera. Surely they'd be watching him in the cell?

Nothing.

Or, at least, that's what he first thought.

Then he saw, beside the light, a little stud in the ceiling. He stood on the concrete bed to get closer, and realised the stud housed a tiny lens.

He pushed his face towards it, realising that whoever was watching the pictures would probably be seeing a distorted image of his nose.

'Hello?' he called into the lens. 'Can you hear me?'

He watched and waited, but as he expected, there was no response. 'Can you tell my partner, Helen Bridle, that I'm here.' Half-jokingly, he added a 'please' to the end of the request. But there was still no sign of a reaction.

Myles looked around him again. He stepped back down. He didn't want to remain stuck in the cell forever. Surely that couldn't happen.

He remembered Habeas Corpus – one of Britain's oldest laws, the name of which hailed from the language of ancient Rome, Latin. Habeas Corpus was a command to see the body – his right to appear in court.

But if he was being detained under anti-terrorist legislation, would Habeas Corpus still stand? Myles didn't know.

Then he thought of something. Deprive them of information as they deprive me.

Myles looked back down at the mattress and lifted it up. Underneath, the plastic cover was only loosely glued on to the foam. He picked at the seam and managed to peel off an edge of the dark green. It was what he needed.

He bent down, placed his teeth around the plastic, and bit. The small incision was enough for him to tear it. He pulled and the plastic ripped along a straight line. With another bite, Myles was able to remove a small strip of the material. He held it in his fingers, then bit it a final time, tearing it into two halves.

Standing on the mattress, he licked the back of one of the plastic strips and stuck it onto the lens stud in the ceiling. Climbing down, he put the other on the inside of the peephole in the door. If they weren't going to answer, he wasn't going to let them watch.

Myles knew it was a tiny victory, but it satisfied him. It proved he had at least some control over his situation. He lay down on the slightly damaged mattress as he wondered how the authorities would react.

It took just four minutes for the cell door to be unlocked.

Myles was ordered to stand up. His hands were bound again. 'Where are you taking me?' he asked.

One of the prison officials frowned sarcastically, as if to say 'You mean you don't know?' Myles also detected a sense of disgust: clearly the warden looked down on him as some sort of lowlife. 'It's time to see the judge, Mr Munro,' said the guard. 'It's your time in court.'

Myles wondered how they could have arranged a judge so fast. Usually it would take several days, or at least hours. Then he realised: they must have been about to take him to see a judge anyway. His trick with the camera lens had made no difference at all. But he was glad to have confounded whoever was spying on him.

Myles was guided through the cell door. The police wardens were careful to make sure he didn't scrape himself on any part of the lock or door frame. It was as though they were saving Myles for a punishment far greater and far more deserving than a scratch.

In the corridor, Myles got a sense that he was not in a normal police cell. His was the only prison room in sight. His cell was reserved for something special.

Around a corner there were some wide stairs. Still no natural light, though. He was about to climb up when one of his escorts stopped him. 'This way, sir. We're taking the lift.'

As instructed, Myles walked in. Only as he entered and saw they were on floor 'SB' – sub-basement – did he realise he had been kept below ground all this time.

The warden pressed the button for floor three, and the lift started to rise.

Myles tried to make eye contact but the warden looked away.

When the lift stopped and the door opened, Myles was confronted with a sign – stark white letters etched into black plastic: *Paddington Green Magistrates Court.* Below it was an arrow pointing to the left attached to a different sign with a single word: *Defendants.*

So that's where he was. Myles had heard of Paddington Green Police Station before. It was near the centre of London. The place that high-profile suspects were often taken for their first appearance – most terrorism cases were tried here.

Myles was taken in the direction of the arrow, through a door and into an oak-panelled waiting room. There he was encouraged to sit down on a wooden bench while one of the court wardens sat beside him. Once more, his wrists were released.

After just a couple of minutes, a second door opened. A policeman on the other side, his hand still on the door handle, leaned in. His posture indicated Myles should come through, and the wardens nodded to confirm that Myles should go. So Myles stood up and walked towards the door.

He was in the dock of Paddington Green Magistrate's court.

Myles turned to his left, to an audience which had clearly reacted to his appearance. It was the public gallery: journalists were frantically scribbling in notebooks, and a few others were scowling in contempt. One looked like he was from East Africa, a middle-aged gentleman whose expressions made clear he despised Myles.

Then Myles saw Helen. She waved, desperate to make contact with him. Myles raised his hand in return. From her face, Myles could tell she still believed he was innocent. He wished he could hug her, but the policeman standing beside him and a solid partition made it impossible.

Helen silently mouthed the words: 'I love you!'

Myles smiled back, relieved she stood by him.

The judge sitting directly in front of Myles cleared her throat. The dignified wrinkles on her face frowned and her eyes turned down to her desk. It was an indication that Myles' attitude – smiling and nodding to people in the public gallery – was not acceptable. Myles was too relaxed.

He tried to look serious. He straightened his back, and prepared himself for the judge's word. 'Mr Munro, this is a magistrates' court,' explained the judge, labouring her words. 'You have been brought here because a crime has occurred and there is important evidence to indicate you were involved.'

The judge paused to see if Myles would react. Myles remained still. He let the judge continue. 'Therefore, for the purposes of this hearing, I would like you to confirm for me your name: are you Myles Adlai Munro?'

Myles rocked his head forward in confirmation.

'Mr Munro, if you wish to confirm your name, please say "yes" or "yes, I am".'

'Yes, I am Myles Adlai Munro.'

The judge looked down at the papers on her desk before continuing. 'And do you live in Pembroke Street, Oxford?'

'Yes, I do,' replied Myles, trying to comply.

'Accommodation which I believe belongs to the university?' She raised her voice at the end, turning the statement into a question.

'Yes, it does.'

'Thank you, Mr Munro.' The magistrate paused again. The court paused with her. It hung on her words.

After half a minute of silence, the judge leant forward and spoke directly to Myles. 'Mr Munro, you are being held under the 2006 Anti-Terrorism Act. Under the terms of that legislation, you may be held for up to fourteen days without being charged. So far you have been held for only one day. That means you may be held for a further thirteen days before a formal charge is brought…'

Myles could see Helen fuming with fury: the woman magistrate was describing Myles' detention nightmare as if it were a matter of arithmetic.

Myles saw the rest of the public gallery react too. The journalists were wondering what was going to happen next, while the middle-aged African seemed to be bent double in some form of hysteria.

The judge addressed Myles again and he sensed his court appearance was already coming towards its end. 'And so, Mr Munro, I recommend that you be held in further custody while the evidence against you is investigated in greater depth.'

Myles spoke back. 'Can I know what the evidence is?'

The judge checked her answer with an official before she gave it. 'I can assure you, Mr Munro, that the evidence is significant. At the appropriate time, you will be told more about the evidence against you. But under the terms of the legislation, the investigating authority is not required to divulge its evidence before charges have been brought and an arrest made. You, Mr Munro, have not yet been arrested.'

'So, I'm not under arrest?'

'No, Mr Munro. You have been detained.'

Myles was about to query the distinction between arrest and detention, but he was distracted by Helen. She mouthed the word 'lawyer' to him. Myles picked it up. 'And will I be allowed a lawyer?' he asked.

The female magistrate consulted with her official again, this time in more detail.

Myles was turning back towards Helen to thank her for the cue when he saw the middle-aged African man had pulled a long, thin bag from the floor and was lifting it towards him.

Something about the man's face scared Myles. Something was wrong.

It was then Myles realised the man was holding an automatic rifle, and was about to fire.

CHAPTER THIRTY-THREE

Paddington Green Secure
Judicial Hearing Facility, Central London

The officials couldn't believe what was happening. Men in legal gowns stared at the weapon, wondering whether it was real. Journalists in the public gallery froze, completely unsure how to react. Even the men responsible for security in the courtroom were too surprised to respond properly. Was it *really* a gun?

Hardly anyone in the room had seen a real-life weapon fired before, and only one of them had had a gun pointed at him. That man was Myles.

The sight of the rifle triggered a deep instinctive reaction which bypassed the slow but rational thought processes in Myles' mind. Myles' muscles automatically pulled down his head, just as a loud burst of bullets flew towards him. His time in warzones may have cursed him with some peculiar form of post-traumatic stress disorder. But they had also imprinted a reflexive response to danger. That instant reaction had just saved his life.

The first volley of bullets embedded in the defendant's dock above him, showering splinters and other debris. Myles cowered while the tatters of wood burst down.

As soon as the gunfire stopped, the courtroom was filled with screams and panic. Chairs were kicked over in a stampede to escape. People began shouting. Confusion clattered all around. Myles immediately thought of Helen, and hoped she would be able to find a safe way out.

But Myles also understood he was the target. The second volley of fire hit the defendant's stand where Myles was crouching. Its thick wood warped and holes appeared as bullets flew through. The policeman beside Myles was hit – and immediately slumped to the ground.

Myles pushed the policeman's limp body away and rolled through the door behind him, out into the waiting room where he had been just a few minutes before. There he moved past the lift, keeping his head and torso low in case the gunman had a clear line of sight.

Myles had half a second to contemplate what next before another burst of gunfire removed the choice.

Instinctively, he ran down the corridor, following it fast, wherever it led. He turned a corner to find himself moving into another part of the building.

Myles could only wonder what was happening in the courtroom. An alert had been sounded. Myles guessed it was the alarm for an escaped prisoner, since the court couldn't have a pre-assigned signal for a gun in the public gallery.

The security officials in the magistrate's hearing had not been armed. Their large physical presence was meant to be sufficient deterrent against the usual disturbances. But size and weight would mean nothing against this gunman. And if nobody in the building had a gun, how would the man be stopped?

Myles continued sprinting along the corridor. He bumped into a policeman who was emerging, confused, from his office. He ran on, towards two court officials who were blocking his way, too scared to move. 'Let me through…' he shouted as he ran.

The officials flattened themselves against the wall and Myles was clear to run between the two men. It was Myles who the gunman was after. The court officials knew it too.

Screams behind Myles confirmed his fears: the gunman was close. Myles imagined the man jumping from the seats in the public gallery, across the courtroom and into the defendant's dock. The man would have gone through the wooden door and into the corridor just seconds behind him. How could Myles escape?

He realised his chances were slim. As he rounded more corners, he knew the corridors in the building could not go on forever. Soon they would end, and he would be trapped by the man with the gun. A man determined to kill him.

Should he look for the public exit? Myles could hear the crowds moving not far from him and guessed they were being escorted to safety. But crowds meant delay. And trying to hide among them meant putting them in danger. Myles would get caught in the jam. Bullets would kill members of the public, then Myles.

Myles scoured the corridor for something else.

Quickly he pulled one of the doors in the corridor. It was locked. He grabbed the next handle along. This time the door swung open. Myles rushed inside.

He knew he had only seconds. He surveyed the room.

A man with glasses sat behind a desk full of papers. Behind him was a large window with a third-floor view over the city.

The administrator stood up, reacting to Myles' presence – half furious, half shocked.

Myles moved towards him, then edged him aside so he could reach the man's executive chair. He picked it up. 'Sorry...' he said, as he heaved it onto his shoulder. Then he hurled it forward: into the window.

Instantly the glass shattered. Broken fragments followed the chair outside in a long arc to the ground. Myles used his elbow to widen the hole, bashing out the shards.

The administrator started saying something, but became speechless as Myles climbed onto his desk, brushing his papers onto the floor. He was even more shocked when the tall intruder started clambering towards the broken window.

Myles nodded and smiled a 'thank you' to the stunned official as he lifted one foot onto the window shelf. Then he swung his other foot through the hole in the glass and placed it on the outside ledge, kicking glass away until he had a steady footing. He bent down and squeezed his body to move himself outside, holding on tightly with his hands. Finally he brought his second foot through behind him.

Myles was now on the outside ledge of the third floor of Paddington Green Police Station. As he felt the fresh wind brush against him, and looked down to see where the executive chair had landed below, he knew it was too far to jump. He knew the fall would hurt and hurt badly. But as he heard the commotion catching up behind him, he also knew he had no choice.

Myles managed to hurl himself sideways as he jumped off. It meant he didn't go straight down, but instead landed on a small adjoining roof. It was angled – he couldn't land there. But it was enough to break his fall. When he bounced off he wasn't travelling so fast towards the ground.

With his two legs firmly together and his knees bent, Myles hit the concrete hard. He rolled onto the ground, half-winded and with a pain in his feet. It took him a second to gather his bearings, but he wasn't hurt. Not even a sprained ankle. Myles realised how lucky he was, and tried to move off, away from the building.

Policemen and women were busily hurrying around the public entrance to the court. News of the gunman had spread and Myles could hear a wail of emergency sirens approaching. A confused gaggle from the public gallery was being escorted onto the streets close by, while people from the underground station opposite were stopping to watch, although no one seemed to have spotted him yet.

Briefly Myles considered handing himself in to the police. But could they keep him safe? Not with the gunman still close behind him.

Myles knew he had to get as far away as he could. He looked around him and saw a road ahead. He decided he had to get across, and rushed towards it, hoping to dodge the cars driving fast along it.

There was a burst of gunfire behind him. Myles turned to see. He couldn't make out the gunman, but from the faces of the panicked public he could tell that the assassin was already at ground level.

Myles darted between the traffic and sprinted onto the pavement. He began to run as fast as he could.

Then he realised where he was: this was Edgware Road, one of London's major transport arteries. It had been laid down by the Romans – a cultural legacy which had lasted two millennia. Myles knew he was about to become a victim of the Romans again, since they had made all their routes as straight as possible. Running along a straight road with a gunman behind him was madness: there would be no cover, the gunman would get a clean shot.

So Myles darted off down the first side street he saw, desperately trying to keep up his speed while he turned the corner. He knew the gunman could not be far behind.

Too much running: he was beginning to tire and become breathless. Myles contemplated hiding in the buildings he passed: a launderette, a Lebanese restaurant, a small supermarket… The thought of a rest was tempting. But then he heard a scream behind him and realised the gunman was too close for him to stop.

On Myles ran, sprinting for his life. He turned a second corner until he was running parallel to the Edgware Road.

He passed a Roman-looking church – St John's – and panted while he considered hiding in it. Then he dismissed the idea: this assassin had no respect for a courtroom, and would have no qualms about killing him in a church. Religious places could provide no sanctuary for him. There was probably no sanctuary at all.

Myles kept on moving, now desperately short of energy and stamina. He had run too fast for too long. His legs ached, but far worse his heart and lungs were screaming with exhaustion. He knew he had to stop soon. He was running out of everything he had.

He stumbled on to find himself in a place he vaguely recognised: this pleasant square had been on television. The smart Georgian houses seemed familiar. It evoked a sense of power in retreat. Myles remembered cameras here, come to mock a man who once had near-imperial authority.

This was Connaught Square, hidden behind the junction where Edgware road met Marble Arch. This square housed a former Prime Minister. It was also one of the very few places in the capital where the police routinely carry firearms. Only here was the terrorist threat considered high enough to deserve it.

Myles looked over. The guards outside the former premier's London residence were on alert – probably warned about the drama less than a mile away at the magistrate's court. They had their guns ready.

Myles sprinted on. He didn't acknowledge the police. Nor did he want to. He looked towards the far end of the square, hoping he might find some safety ahead.

Then there was a burst of gunfire behind him.

Myles heard the armed police he had just passed shout a single word very clearly: 'STOP'.

But Myles was running too fast to stop. He couldn't stop. He knew that if he stopped he would die. So he just ran on. He was close to cover. Very close. Close enough…

Then there was a very different burst of gunfire behind him. Several bursts from several guns. This time the bullets had hit their mark.

CHAPTER THIRTY-FOUR
Connaught Square, Central London

The Diplomatic Protection Corp assigned to the former Prime Minister had a drill for exactly this sort of event. Three of them remained as they were, their weapons poised. They were watching for the next surprise, ready in case any further threats emerged. Another was on his radio, reporting what had happened to an information hub. Since the former Prime Minister's family wasn't home, they didn't need to escort or protect anyone. That released two men to advance, with their Heckler & Koch G36C semi-automatic carbines held tightly to their shoulders. Carefully, they approached the body.

Fairly soon they decided the man lying face-down on the bloodied concrete surface was not a threat.

The first policeman approached. He kicked the man's foot. 'Armed police,' he announced, following his drill.

No response. With his colleague keeping guard, the policeman bent down to check for signs of life. Putting his fingers on the man's neck, he detected only a faint pulse.

The policeman indicated to his colleague that the body he was examining was only just alive. Death was likely. The colleague understood, and eased his posture slightly. The threat was reduced.

Half-reluctantly, and still wary in case the man suddenly came back to life, the policeman started to pump the man's chest – a half-hearted attempt to keep him alive.

It took just a few more seconds for paramedics to reach the scene. Their ambulance pulled up and first responders jumped out. They rushed to the body and immediately undertook their own tests. They too thought the man would probably die.

The policemen looked at each other. They knew there'd be an inquiry. Questions. An investigation.

But they knew they'd followed policy. The dying man had fired a weapon in the designated area. His gun had landed several feet from his body, and had been guarded – but not touched – since the man fell. They'd issued a warning. They'd not hit anybody innocent.

The policemen relaxed while they waited for a rapid response team. They felt confident.

But Myles didn't feel confident. He'd just seen his would-be assassin gunned down behind him. The anti-terrorism police hadn't shot at Myles, but Myles still didn't trust them.

He knew he had to get further away.

There were probably just two or three minutes before the area was flooded with police. That would mean he would be trapped, caught and returned to custody.

He had to make his decision quickly. Escape or surrender?

He kept running while he tried to decide. Even though his lungs were screaming and his legs worn out, he knew that to stop now was to accept capture.

Myles ran on, out to where Edgware road met Marble Arch. He remembered this site: he was on the last route taken by condemned men. Following Roman tradition, this route used to be lined with voyeurs. Captives were paraded here before they were executed.

Myles lowered his head and immersed himself in the crowds of tourists and shoppers. When the traffic lights changed, he crossed the road with a horde of pedestrians. Walking seemed a better way to pass unnoticed than running.

He couldn't have ran any more, even if he'd wanted to. He bent double, his hands resting on his knees until he caught his breath. He checked behind him: nobody had followed him there, not even any of the Diplomatic Protection Corps, although some of the tourists were still looking at him oddly. He heard the police helicopter – still somewhere above him, but probably assigned to the drama in Connaught Square, where the body of the African gunman was being examined in forensic detail.

Myles was careful not to look up: the police helicopter might have a camera with face-recognition software. Instead he looked around, trying to look like a tourist, still trying to slow his breathing back to a normal rate.

He had reached Hyde Park's Speakers' Corner. Free speech was protected here, although the right to answer back was equally cherished. The verbal jousting was entertaining and attracted many spectators.

While he pondered what to do, Myles wandered through the crowds listening to the speakers. One man was extolling communism. An American in the small audience was answering back, pointing out how the Soviet state locked up dissidents. From what Myles could tell, the American was winning the argument. Myles moved on.

Another speaker was reading from the Bible. Not far away someone else was preaching from the Koran. Myles listened as he passed, wondering why the two men were not addressing each other. The religious freedom they both enjoyed seemed to mean there was no dispute between them.

Would Myles be able to make his voice heard if he gave himself up to the police? He hadn't when they'd detained him in Rome the day before…

Myles thought again of the Senator, and he remembered Juma's threat to America. Could he stop America suffering the fate of Rome if he gave himself in? Could he save America if he escaped?

Then he looked towards the edge of the park, to a bus stop. He often passed this way: it was where the main bus route between Oxford and London offloaded passengers. Myles thought of jumping on one of the buses and taking the ninety-minute journey home: to Helen, to his flat, to his low-stress job at the university – and to where the police would be waiting to catch him.

Myles turned back towards Marble Arch. A small group of policemen were emerging, looking around. They were hunting for Myles.

Myles hid his face. He didn't trust the police. Not at all.

He knew that now he had to decide.

Myles looked again at the bus stop to Oxford, where a bus was about to finish taking on passengers, stowing the last of the baggage into the underside of the vehicle.

He had made his decision.

CHAPTER THIRTY-FIVE
Sirte Dockside, Libya

Huddled under polyester blankets and protected from the wind by sea containers, for many days they waited. Those with passports had already had them stamped – the rumour was that an exit stamp from Libya would make it easier to enter Europe. But most knew that the continent was still very hard to get into. It was almost impossible: all sea-going vessels were being stopped and searched for illegal migrants.

Like Safiq, many had tried to make the journey before. All had failed. They could trade stories on their failures – the lucky ones had been rewarded with a warm meal before they were sent back, the less fortunate ones had faced abuse. Several, like Safiq, had almost drowned. Escaping to a better life in Italy or France was an impossible dream, just as the better life in oil-rich Libya was a mirage.

But now they had hope. So much hope that this time they made sure their families were with them at the dockside. And the hope came from a single rumour – that Juma, the pirate chief from Somalia, had an escape plan.

Safiq saw Juma's convoy of technicals and armoured SUVs sweep into the dockside. He peered to get a look, as the man and the woman beside him were soon surrounded by eager Africans. Juma's militia kept the fans away.

Juma jumped up on a sea crate, trying to make himself look taller. He let his gun hang down from his shoulder as he shouted to the crowds around him. 'My people,' he declared.

The migrants murmured in response. They didn't know what to expect.

'Thank you for being here,' Juma called to the crowd. 'I know that Libya has not been good to you. Africa has not been good to you. And for those of you who have tried to reach it, even Europe has not been good to you…'

Safiq found himself nodding. The audience were listening eagerly. They all agreed, too.

'Well, my friends, I can offer you something better. Much better. I can get you to America!'

Safiq watched while Juma paused. The pirate chief was expecting the masses to cheer. But Safiq and the rest of the people were just confused. The only way to get to America was to fly. How could Juma get planes for so many people? Would the Americans even let them land? He was losing confidence…

Juma pressed on. 'People, all I need to know is which of the young men on this dockside have been trained to fire weapons.'

Safiq recoiled. Whatever this mad Somali was planning, he didn't like it. He didn't want to fight because he didn't want to die. Safiq wanted to live. He saw Juma stare at young men in the crowd. Older family members were holding them back, telling them not to volunteer.

Safiq realised Juma was losing his audience. The Somali reached for his weapon. But then the woman next to him grabbed his hand. Safiq didn't know who she was, but he saw her give Juma a stare and shake her head: no weapons.

Then the woman jumped up on the crate beside him. 'People, my fellow Africans,' she shouted. 'I have made it to America, and you can too.' She had to raise her voice even louder, over the crowd's reaction. 'There will be no fighting. No guns will be fired. You will all be safe, and soon you will all be free.'

Arguments were breaking out amongst the people in front of Safiq. The woman at the front strained to listen to them, cupping her ear to keep out the wind. 'You ask "how?" Let me tell you how: we will travel in a ship that the rich European immigration police will let through,' she shouted. 'It is not a ferry for people. It is not a container ship. People, we will travel in an oil tanker.'

The people around Safiq were listening now.

'And to get through the blockade, we will not travel straight to Italy,' the woman explained, shaking her head. 'Many of you have tried that, and we all know what happens. No – to reach the West, first we will go east. We will reach the shores of the New World through the capital of the Old World: Rome.

A middle-aged man in the crowd raised his voice in reply. 'But how will we sail to America?'

Safiq laughed and nodded. It was a fair question.

The woman tried to laugh too. 'America is too far to sail. Our oil tanker will not sail over the Atlantic. But we have another way to reach America. How we will reach America from Rome must though, for now, remain secret.'

She had them intrigued, hopeful even.

'But I promise you, if you come with me to Rome, I will get you into the United States,' she vowed. Then she closed the deal. 'And even Rome is far, far better than this dockside.'

Safiq was persuaded. Within minutes, he was part of a jostling queue eager to board the Al-Afrique oil tanker. It took more than an hour for the guest workers and their families to embark. Conditions inside the empty supertanker were no better – or worse – than the dockside. Now, though, Safiq and all the other migrants were going somewhere. They had hope, and that hope was leading them to freedom.

The one man who was not free was taken on last. Juma mocked him as he boarded. 'Come on, Senator – I thought you wanted to go home.'

'Be pleased I'm not getting the other things I want,' retorted Sam Roosevelt.

'Like?'

'Like, you dead, Juma.'

Juma tried to laugh. He kicked the Senator to make the point, then ordered that Sam Roosevelt was frogmarched with him onto the bridge.

Juma nodded to his crew, and they radioed to the tugboat in the harbour. The anchor was raised and the moorings released.

Slowly, gracefully, the supertanker full of human cargo, driven by a pirate captain from the slums of Somalia, was hauled out of port into the Mediterranean Sea.

Below deck, Safiq felt the movement of the ship and knew: his journey to America had begun.

CHAPTER THIRTY-SIX
Hyde Park Corner, Central London

The police spread through Speakers' Corner. Some jogged to the edge of the crowd, others tried to seal off the area. The helicopter above radioed down their assessment: the escapee could not have got far.

Then everybody was checked. Policemen systematically filtered through all the tourists, passers-by and families. They even made sure a woman in a hijab wasn't really Myles in disguise. One man complained when his hood was pulled down. A policewoman had to apologise.

Initially they found nothing. So more police cars came, with more officers inside them. Myles, they assumed, had gone to ground, which meant the police had to be efficient. They would check everywhere, looking in every possible hiding place. It was still just a few minutes since their man had been positively identified in Connaught Square – by the anti-terrorism police who had shot the African gunman. So they knew Myles could not be far. Myles would not be able to escape their cordon…

But he already had.

As the police were spreading out through Speakers' Corner, Myles was walking behind the London-to-Oxford coach. As the driver finished stowing the baggage from the pavement side of the vehicle, Myles opened the roadside compartment. He bent down, slipped in, and closed the luggage door behind him. The driver had returned to his seat and started the bus moving while the police were still checking faces in Hyde Park.

Myles escaped just before the cordon was set up.

He wondered whether any of the traffic had seen him sneak aboard. He had stepped in front of a taxi to climb into the underbelly of the coach. But unless the police set up an instant roadblock, it would probably be several hours before the information trickled back. And by that time, Myles would be far away.

Myles felt the vehicle move off, and heard the sounds of London traffic passing by. He used the journey to plan his next moves. He needed to tell Helen he was safe, and for that he would send an email. But he couldn't use his own email account – the police would be watching that. So, when he got to Oxford, he would set up a fresh account at an internet café and contact her through an alias.

He wouldn't be able to go back to his flat – too dangerous. That meant he needed to get clothes, money and food. Since he had an hour and a half in the coach's luggage compartment, he was able to look through some of the bags. In the half-light, Myles was lucky enough to find a fresh shirt and a coat which almost matched his tall frame. Getting dressed in the confines of the moving compartment took longer than he wanted it to – he was jolted and thrown as the bus turned corners – but he managed. He also found a small purple backpack, a cigarette lighter, some sandwiches and some money – euros. He took them all, promising to himself that his actions in the coming days would justify this small act of theft.

Myles realised that leaving the bus might be harder than getting on board. And having rummaged through much of the luggage on board, he had to exit before people collected their bags. So he waited until the bus was starting to drive more slowly, indicating it had reached the busy city streets of Oxford, then opened the compartment. He looked at the streets and saw he had timed it right: he was in his hometown. And when the vehicle was travelling slowly enough, he rolled out onto his feet, stumbled, and fell onto the pavement. He was soon up again and tried walking along the street as if nothing had happened.

No one had seen him disembark, although watching the bus as it drove off, the storage compartment door still open, Myles knew he would be tracked soon. He had to be fast.

First, he went into an internet café frequented by students in the city. There he created a new email account and typed out a quick message:

Helen,
We need a better cursus than this.
Yours.

He left the message unsigned, knowing Helen would look up the word 'cursus' and, when she found out it was the Roman postal system, guess the email came from him. It was cryptic, but Myles hoped she would understand: they needed a code which would allow them to communicate in secret. He knew the police would probably understand the message too, but he had faith that Helen would think of a way to evade their eavesdropping. He pressed 'send'.

Then Myles went to the Bodleian Library, Oxford University's central library. In case the librarian at the door knew he was on the run and might report him, Myles entered through an open fire escape, ducking his head in case the entrance was monitored by CCTV. He made his way to the Politics, Philosophy and Economics Reading Room, where he hunted down the one book he needed most. He scanned along the shelves until he found it – *The History of the Decline and Fall of the Roman Empire* – and carried it to one of the desks.

The first instalment of the book had been published in 1776 – making it exactly the same age as the United States – and had been reprinted several times since. He opened it carefully, then read from the old-fashioned text at the first page he saw.

> The fabric of a mighty state, which has been reared by the labours of successive ages, could not be overturned by the misfortune of a single day...

He soon realised he didn't have enough time to get the information he needed from it now. Even Placidia, perhaps the brightest person he'd ever known, had taken months to get through this book. Myles would need more time with it.

So he nudged each of the six volumes off the desk, and caught them with his purple backpack. Stealing library books was bad. Taking them from the Bodleian would cost him his lectureship. But he knew he had no choice. Casually he slung the backpack over his shoulder and moved back towards the fire exit, unplugging the walk-through scanner which detected stolen books before he passed through.

As he came out onto the street, he saw two of his students. Worried that they might make contact, he walked the other way, where a bus was about to pick up passengers. Instinctively, Myles jumped aboard, even though he didn't know where the bus would take him.

By now he had been in the city for almost an hour, and it was two and a half hours since his unexpected escape from the courtroom. People had already seen him in Oxford – the manhunt would reach him soon. He had to keep moving.

Myles thought through his options: to stay in Oxford would be very dangerous. Even staying in Britain could be risky. But how could he travel abroad? And how could he prove his innocence?

Most important of all, how could he stop the plot to bring down America? The problems ticked through his mind without any sort of solution emerging.

The bus had moved out of the centre of Oxford onto one of the main routes feeding the city. It passed through suburbs and grassy areas. Myles decided to get out at the next stop. He rang the bell, and stepped down as the doors opened.

He was alone again. As the bus drove off, he noticed a small café servicing lorry drivers – their vehicles were parked up next to it, having just come off the motorway nearby.

Recognising it could be his last chance to eat before he was properly on the run, Myles decided to go inside and sit at one of the tables. He was wondering where to go next when he saw a bottle of All-American Steak Sauce. He looked on the label: *Made in the Teutoburg Forest, Germany.*

Teutoburg Forest: where a huge Roman army had been wiped out by barbarians. The imperial army had been tricked then ambushed – the defeat was a complete surprise. It was when Rome was still growing, and ruled by its first emperor, Emperor Augustus. *Teutoburg Forest – the forest that defeated the Empire.*

Myles remembered how Juma had thrown a bottle of the sauce at him in the taxi in Libya. He remembered Juma's cocky expression, like it was a private joke – a 'You'll find out soon enough' kind of joke.

He knew where he was going next.

Like most students, Myles' time as an undergraduate had been about more than just academic study. University had also taught him about the world, and about himself. It was during one of the three–and-a-half-month summer breaks that Myles had decided to explore Europe. Not by train, like most of the other young adults enjoying their time at Oxford – Myles never had the money for one of the 'Eurorail' passes which enabled the bearer to travel on almost any rail service on the continental mainland. Instead, Myles had moved around without paying any money at all. He had procured rides from car drivers all over the continent, right from Bergen in Norway to Spain and Gibraltar.

Hitch-hiking, Myles had discovered, required skills similar to those of an old-school maritime navigator: travelling on winds blowing in all sorts of directions, strong and weak, to reach a particular destination. It meant understanding how traffic flowed over long distances. Better to ask a driver for a major town than somewhere none of the drivers would know. Vehicles using more minor routes tended to be less useful that those travelling on motorways. Motorway service stations were the best place to pick up new rides.

Myles memorised the address label on the steak sauce bottle, then stepped outside and walked along the row of lorries parked there. The number plates gave him the information he needed: there was a German vehicle, but the plate started with the letter M, indicating it was from Munich. Slightly better was a Polish vehicle from Warsaw. That was likely to take a more northerly route through Germany, taking him closer to where he needed to go.

Double-checking he was on the eastbound carriageway – he didn't want to take a lorry the wrong way – Myles bent down to tie his shoelace while he checked no one was watching.

All clear.

Then he quietly hauled his bag on to the Polish lorry and climbed up after it. He took a minute to make room for himself amongst the cargo: boxes of empty beer bottles being taken back for cleaning and refilling. Myles only needed to wait a few minutes more before the driver, who had taken a short toilet break, rejoined his lorry, put it into gear and drove off.

Travelling this way was more uncomfortable than on the bus to Oxford. Myles was also less sure of the route. He thought through what he should do at Dover: should he try to disembark before the truck boarded the ferry? Or should he stay on board and hope no one searched through the cargo? Whatever he did would be risky. Since he wanted to leave the country, he reasoned travelling unnoticed on a Polish cargo lorry was probably one of the best ways to do it. He might as well stay where he was.

Free from the stress of custody and the escape, and despite knowing police and other authorities were searching for him, Myles found himself finally relaxing. Lulled by the movement of the lorry, soon he was asleep. He slept through the last miles of the journey to Dover. He even slept as the vehicle boarded the ferry. He would have been caught if any of the border and immigration officials at the main port scrutinised the vehicles travelling out of Britain as closely as those travelling into it. The modern-day migration crisis was the distraction which let Myles slip away.

DAY VI

CHAPTER THIRTY-SEVEN
Oostende, Belgium

Myles was jolted awake by the ferry bumping against the dockside in Belgium. He had reached Oostende. Here the port officials were more interested in the various cargoes. Myles heard a conversation close to the vehicle and imagined papers were being verified. When the back of the vehicle was opened up, he prepared himself to run. But the check was only cursory. Soon the lorry was back on the road and travelling east.

Inside, there was just enough light for him to read from *The History of the Decline and Fall of the Roman Empire*. Myles knew this book had explained the end of Rome far more comprehensively than any before it. Even though many other histories of the empire had been written in the almost two-hundred-and-fifty years since, all had been based on it or reacted to it. None had bettered it. There must be something in it. Something important...

He scrolled down the list of contents, and skimmed through the sub-headings.

...Thirst of fame and military glory as a vice...

...Patriotism, and its decay and replacement by honour and religion...

...Latent causes of decay and corruption in the long peace of the Empire...

It was clear that Gibbon, perhaps the greatest ever scholar on Rome, traced the roots of the city-empire's collapse right back. He was looking for causes in the Empire's most stable period, the years 96AD to 180AD, three centuries before Rome finally fell.

> ...Imperial government, an absolute monarchy disguised as a commonwealth...
> ...Hereditary monarchy, form of government presenting the greatest scope for ridicule...
> ...Betrayals and dishonesty...

Myles turned again through the pages, and came across one of the book's most famous quotes.

> If all the barbarian conquerors had been annihilated in the same hour, their total destruction would not have restored the empire of the West... The decline of Rome was the natural and inevitable effect of immoderate greatness. Prosperity ripened the principle of decay; the causes of destruction multiplied with the extent of conquest; and as soon as time or accident removed the artificial supports, the stupendous fabric yielded to the pressure of its own weight. The story of its ruin is simple and obvious; and instead of inquiring why the Roman Empire was destroyed, we should rather be surprised that it had subsisted for so long.

Myles pondered the words, wondering what they could mean for the possible decline and fall of the United States, and whatever Juma was planning.

Jostled by the movement of the truck, he couldn't steady his thoughts enough to crack the puzzle. He tried again, but it was no use: smuggled aboard the cramped inside of a beer lorry was no way to read a book like this. He stuffed it back into his bag.

Myles tried to work out when the lorry would next stop: the Polish lorry driver had taken a break in Oxford, about three hours before he reached Dover. He had then been able to take another break while the ferry crossed the English Channel. That meant there would probably be one more major stop before the driver reached Poland, and there was a good chance it would be somewhere in north-western Germany, roughly halfway between the channel port and the final destination.

When the stop came, Myles duly waited a few moments – enough time for the driver to move away from his vehicle – then climbed out of the hole he had made for himself among the boxes. He was in the parking lot of a large German motorway service station. With the sun already past its highest point in the sky, Myles moved over to the main building, trying to walk as inconspicuously as possible.

Myles went to the toilet block and found the showers were freely available. Unsure when the chance would next arise, he took the opportunity to get clean, washing his body with someone else's shampoo, which had been left in the cubicle. He dried himself with paper towels, wondering how other people without a regular address managed to cope. Perhaps they didn't.

Next to the service station restaurant was an internet terminal. He tried to log on, but credit card details were needed to buy time online. So he loitered nearby, looking at the maps and atlases in the shop. From the map, he managed to work out where he was – only about two hundred and fifty miles from the town where American Steak Sauce was produced. Then a mother being distracted by her children left an internet machine with time still running. Myles moved over to the console.

He logged onto his new email account. There was only one message, and it was from someone he'd never heard of – a Dr Neil Bheel.

Myles clicked to open it.

Thanks,

Good to hear from you and glad you're safe. I've got a new phone, so when you've got a chance, give me a call on 001 776 455 410.

Yours, Neil.

He looked at the name again. *Dr Neil Bheel.* It was a surname he'd never heard before, and what sort of cruel parent would choose a first name which rhymes?

Then he understood, and smiled to himself.

He made a mental note of the number – easily done, since 1776 was the year Gibbon had started publishing his masterpiece. 455 and 410 were the years Rome had been sacked by barbarians. Then he wrote back a quick message, saying he would call when he could, and deleted the account.

Hitch-hiking the remaining distance up to the sauce factory was harder than Myles had remembered from his time as a youth. He was older now and looked less innocent to the people who might pick him up. He had to wait almost half an hour at the service station before he was offered his first lift – a youngish-couple in a yellow Skoda – which dropped him about thirty miles from his destination. From there, he was able to take a bus, then another bus. He paid with the euros he had stolen from the luggage compartment travelling to Oxford. The last two miles he had to walk.

Eventually he reached the sauce factory and wondered at the dangers it concealed. An obscure industrial site in northern Germany seemed an unlikely base for a plot against the United States, but Myles reminded himself that he was just a short distance from Hamburg, where an unnoticed terrorist cell had planned the attacks of 9/11.

He approached.

CHAPTER THIRTY-EIGHT
Bielefeld, Germany

Myles wanted to observe the factory first. He needed to understand it, to know just how normal – or abnormal – it was. He knew he would need a good vantage point: somewhere he could wait for a long time without causing suspicion.

He walked around the factory site. There was nowhere obvious to go: no café or bar to sit and drink while he watched the main gate. There was no bus stop where he could wait for a bus which never came. Not even a telephone box.

Myles decided his best option was a newsagent. Wandering in, he picked up a German-language magazine from one of the middle shelves and pretended to make sense of it while he studied the factory gates through the windows. For half an hour he calmly observed the place, trying to work out whatever he could.

It seemed like an old-style operation. As the end of the working day approached, a few people started to trickle away. Many more followed in the minutes immediately after the shift ended. He looked at them. Several were from ethnic minorities – mainly Turkish-looking, and about two-thirds were men. Most were dressed in fairly cheap clothes, some of them had unhealthy-looking skin and many looked unfit. From their faces as they left, he could tell few of them were thinking about the work they had just finished. Instead, they were focussed on getting home or whatever else they had planned for the evening. None of them looked Somali or like they knew Juma, and there was no hint that this was the centre of a plot to destroy a superpower. He was sure almost all of them were innocent.

'Wollen Sie etwas kaufen?' came a voice behind him.

Myles turned to see the stern face of the newsagent. He didn't understand what the man had said, but guessed it was a complaint – Myles had been reading magazines in the shop for too long without actually buying anything.

Myles didn't want to be noticed, so he smiled and put on an apologetic face. Then he drew out a five euro note from the money he had taken from the bus, handed it to the shopkeeper and waited for the change.

The shopkeeper muttered a grumble. Myles pretended not to notice the comment, mainly because he didn't understand what the man had said. If the newsagent realised he had been holding a magazine he couldn't read for twenty minutes it might raise suspicions.

With his change and the magazine, Myles left the shop. Immediately, he faced a row of workers leaving the building he wanted to investigate.

Deciding it was best to be bold, Myles simply walked forward, towards the front gates. Several of the workers watched him but none seemed particularly interested. Myles could easily have had a purpose there. He looked as if he was about to meet someone finishing their shift.

Once through the gates, Myles got a better look at the building itself. The main doors were guarded. Without breaking step, he kept walking. He passed the main door and followed the perimeter wall around on the inside. He kept on walking around the factory buildings. Through one car park, then another…

Myles knew he had to keep walking as if he knew where he was going. To stop would arouse attention. To gauge his bearings would be very suspicious. So he just kept going, careful to duck out of view of the factory's single CCTV camera. After the third of four sides, he wondered whether his luck was starting to fail. If he came back round to the front again, perhaps he would have to leave with the rest of the factory workers.

But then he saw the refuse centre. Four very large bins were waiting for collection, along with other waste in plastic bags. The chance was too tempting. Myles walked straight over towards them. Then he moved behind them.

Gambling that waste-unloading time had finished for the day, Myles spent a few minutes thinking of an excuse in case he was discovered, and wondering whether he could carry it off without speaking German.

But the excuse was unnecessary. Myles waited until the main gates were shut and locked, then kept waiting. He had plenty to think through, and let his thoughts entertain him as he sat amongst the rubbish, caring not at all about the smell of his surroundings.

Two hours later, he slowly emerged from his hiding place, into a half-lit area between the perimeter wall and the building itself. He watched: there seemed to be just one security guard, who loitered near the main door of the building without moving much. Myles couldn't see the man properly, but he noted the guard looked African.

So Myles walked round to the back of the building, testing each window he passed to find one left open. The third one he came to had a small gap. Myles nudged the frame upwards, creating more space. Then, checking around again, he climbed in and closed the window behind him.

Myles was in an office. He hated these places. He tried to concentrate. What should he be looking for?

As he walked from desk to desk, he saw the standard detritus of a sales office – notes and calendars, brochures, a poorly scribbled telephone number, sales cards. All the signs and paperwork were in German. But still nothing seemed out of place, or unusual in any way. He decided to try elsewhere.

After another set of offices – equally uninteresting – he came across the main part of the factory. This was where the All-American Steak Sauce was actually made. Myles looked up in wonderment at the pipes and mixing containers. He could see where forklift trucks drove in supplies from the adjoining warehouse. He saw a giant ventilation fan.

Then he realised where he needed to go.

Following a yellow line on the floor, he walked through some large Perspex doors into the storehouse. This was where the main ingredients were kept. Myles walked along the shelves to see what was there. Glucose syrup, flour, concentrated tomato puree, all labelled in both German and English.

He walked on. A water point, salt, an unnamed type of oil…

Then he saw it and immediately he knew. Carefully, he lifted the tub from the shelf, taking a strange comfort in how heavy it was. The weight proved he was right. He put the container on the floor.

Labelled just 'spice', Myles put his hand in and felt the tiny particles of lead trickle between his fingers. Dark grey, the metal was in powdered form, as fine as dust. It felt like a heavy liquid washing around his hand. He could tell why most of the workers would mistake it for a spice – how were they to know the difference?

So it was that simple: the plot to bring down America like ancient Rome amounted to replacing a popular condiment with a toxic metal powder. Juma's arrogance – throwing a bottle at

Myles – had undermined the pirate's own plan. Undiscovered, the doctored sauce could cause fatal lead poisoning in whoever consumed it, which he guessed was millions of Americans every day.

Amazed at what he had found, Myles checked that he was still alone.

He felt the burning impulse to tell someone, knowing it would be the most dangerous part of his activities for the night, but also the most important.

Myles hurried back to the sales office and picked up the telephone receiver.

He tried a '9' for an outside line. The dialling tone changed. Then he pressed the twelve digit number he had memorised. It was the number given to him earlier in the email from 'Dr Neil Bheel'.

The number rang, then someone picked up. It was a familiar voice, the confident voice of an American journalist. 'Hello,' she said.

'Hello - it's me,' Myles whispered. 'Don't say my name, please. We don't know who might be listening in.'

He heard Helen pause. She was surprised to hear from him. 'Wow – er, hello,' she said. 'Great of you to call. I've just landed in Istanbul – I'll tell you why later. You got my email then?'

'Yes, I did: and "Dr Neil Bheel", quite an inspired anagram.'

'Where are you now…or don't you want to say?'

Myles thought before he answered, not sure how much to say. 'Somewhere in Germany,' he offered. 'In a factory. It's where American Steak Sauce is being made now, and they've started using fine lead particles as an ingredient.'

'Lead?' Helen sounded shocked.

'Yeah – the Romans used to put lead in their sauces,' explained Myles.

'I remember,' said Helen. 'And it made them go mad.'

'Can you wait fifteen minutes until I'm out of here, please, then tell the German police?'

'Certainly. How are you doing? Are you OK? I'm worried about you.'

Myles loved to hear Helen's concern. It was the first consoling voice he'd heard in a long time. As he stood alone in an alien, half-lit office, on the run, he certainly needed consoling. But he also realised this probably wasn't the place. 'Thanks,' he said. 'I'm OK. And you?'

'I think I may have found the next source of trouble,' revealed Helen, proud of her discovery. 'We know Juma's connected with Istanbul. Well there's a plague pit here, where the Romans used to bury the victims of the disease – when an epidemic killed lots of them around the time the Empire was collapsing. I've discovered a new archaeological dig going on near the city walls. I'm about to check it out. It's going under the official name of "Galla".'

'Galla?' queried Myles.

'Yes. I googled the name 'Placidia' online, and it came up with 'Galla Placidia' – the daughter of a Roman Emperor. She married the leader of the barbarian who sacked Rome, then tried to rule what was left of the Empire herself.'

Myles was beginning to remember his history. 'And she almost succeeded.'

'Galla Security, Galla Excavations – I know it, it's them, Myles.'

Myles winced – she had used his name. He was certain the line was bugged by anti-terrorism police, so now they would have a clear fix on him. He began to wonder whether the call to the German police in fifteen minutes would be necessary – they might arrive sooner.

'I think they might be trying to incubate the bubonic plague,' Helen continued. 'They could harvest bacteria from the bodies buried there.'

'Is that possible? When the victims have been dead for a millennium and a half?'

Helen admitted she didn't know. 'But Juma probably doesn't know either, which is why he might try.'

Myles nodded silently. He listened while Helen read out the address: in the Cemetery of the Emperor Justinian. 'Do you think you might be able to meet me here?' she asked.

'OK, I'll go there next,' said Myles, wondering how he was going to evade whatever traps the anti-terrorism police set for him – they'd surely know he was coming. 'Love you.'

'Stay safe, OK?' said Helen.

Myles was about to dismiss the worries when he became very aware of another person in the room. Someone was standing behind him.

Slowly, he put the phone down.

CHAPTER THIRTY-NINE
Bielefeld, Germany

Myles turned: standing behind him was the security guard, a man who looked like the men he had met on his ill-fated journey into Libya with the Senator. A Somali pirate in a security guard's uniform.

Myles quickly tried to work out what the man knew. Was this security guard with Juma? Had the man been putting lead in the sauce? How long had he been listening to his phone call with Helen, and how much had he understood?

The security guard seemed as afraid as Myles. Myles wondered if that was good or bad. He concluded it was probably bad, since it meant the man might do something rash.

Immediately Myles started thinking of escape. He knew Helen would soon be calling the police. He had to be gone before they arrived. He wanted to be gone now.

He smiled at the Somali security guard, and then picked up the phone receiver and pointed at it. 'Hello. I'm here to clean the phones…' he offered.

It was a hopeless effort. Myles made for a very unusual after-hours telephone cleaner. But he could tell the Somali night guard was intimidated.

For a brief moment, Myles wondered about throwing the phone at the man and trying to run. But then he dropped the thought. Somehow the African looked too desperate. He wasn't like the shift-men Myles had seen clocking off earlier. This man would probably chase him and fight him.

Myles tried to make eye contact with him, trying to befriend him. But the security guard just became more intense.

Then the man pulled a pistol from his belt and pointed it at Myles. The balance of power had changed.

Slowly Myles raised his hands. He noticed the Somali's badge: it read 'Galla Security'.

The Somali used his free hand to take out a mobile phone, pressing a preset number, before swiftly returning his gaze to Myles.

Myles remained still. He watched and waited, his hands still above his head, while the security guard had a telephone conversation with someone in a foreign dialect. The man's guttural sounds were the same language Myles had heard spoken amongst the pirates when he was in Libya. The guard *was* linked to Juma.

Soon the phone conversation was over. The security guard pressed the 'off' button on his phone, then put both hands to the handle of his pistol. 'Come,' he said in stunted English.

His instruction, coupled with an unmistakeable pointing gesture from the gun barrel, clearly directed Myles to walk back towards the storeroom.

Now becoming nervous, Myles obeyed. Keeping his hands above his head, he returned down the corridor.

He peeked behind him: the security guard had him fully covered. There was no way Myles could run or duck away, or do anything to avoid a bullet. The Somali could choose to fire at any moment. Myles was within point-blank range of the security guard's pistol.

As Myles arrived in the main factory part of the building, he checked that the Somali still wanted him to continue. The man gestured at Myles to keep walking, and simply grunted 'Storeroom.'

Myles nodded, acknowledging the instruction. Soon he was passing back through the Perspex doors. Then he stood and turned where the main ingredients were kept.

Juma's man gestured for Myles to bend down, which Myles did.

Then the security guard pointed at the lead particles – the 'spice' substitute. The man held out a hand and showed a big scooping motion to Myles. Then he moved his hand to his mouth. The security guard wanted Myles to swallow the lead powder.

Myles pulled a face, querying the request.

The Somali repeated it, and nodded.

Myles shook his head, refusing.

The guard moved closer, poking his gun into Myles' cheek.

Myles froze.

The security guard pushed the pistol harder, cursing him. Then he scooped up a handful of the lead powder himself and rammed it into Myles' mouth.

Myles choked and coughed, trying to get out as much of the lead as he could. The guard pressed it back in, and Myles felt himself involuntarily swallowing some of the tasteless metallic powder. It made him gag.

The Somali kept his pistol rammed against Myles' face. Myles knew he had to swallow again, or he would die instantly: a lead bullet through the cheek if he didn't accept lead powder through the mouth.

Myles reeled back, and used his eyes to talk to the guard. He conceded. He would eat the lead. He just wanted the Somali to give him time. Time to swallow. Time to think...

He gulped, and felt the dry metal powder stick in his throat, knowing some of it had gone down to poison his stomach.

Myles tried to guess how long swallowing lead would take to kill him: several months, at least. He could get medical help. If he could escape.

Swallowing lead wouldn't kill him, but the security guard's sidearm would. Myles had to play along.

The security guard stepped back, keeping his gun firmly aimed at Myles. He allowed the Englishman a few moments for the lead to settle. Then he indicated Myles had to take more.

Myles knew he had to think quickly now. Giving himself as much time as possible, he gradually picked up more of the grey powder.

He checked with the Somali, who still held him at gunpoint. The guard nodded in understanding, almost in sympathy. He was confirming: yes, you should eat it, and yes it will kill you.

Then Myles realised: the guard expected the lead to kill him quickly. It meant the Somali would wait for the poison to work, but then would get angry as Myles continued to survive. Angry enough to kill him.

Myles moved the powder towards his mouth. As he touched it against his tongue, he sized up the security guard. Juma's man was afraid, and clearly wary of Myles trying to launch some sort of strike against him. He was edging back, too. Now five metres away. The man could easily fire off a shot in the time it would take Myles to pounce.

Myles looked around. There was a light bulb hanging from the ceiling, leading to a light switch nearby. Myles could see the turbines of a large ventilation machine – probably used to blow air through the factory in summertime.

He wished he could blow the Somali away, but knew it couldn't happen.

'Eat!' instructed the man, his voice raised.

The security guard was becoming increasingly agitated as Myles pondered the lead dust in front of him.

Slowly, Myles put another handful in his mouth. Again, he almost gagged.

Could he wait until the police came? No. The Somali would probably kill him when he heard the sirens approach. That meant Myles had only a few minutes left.

Myles made a play of gulping hard, as an idea gradually began to form in his mind. He guessed the Somali didn't know the symptoms of lead poisoning.

Roman aristocrats took several years to be made mad by lead… Myles had to convince Juma's man the toxic metal was making him mad in minutes.

Myles started flailing around. In one gesture, he coughed out most of his mouthful, while pretending he had swallowed it. He clutched his stomach, mimicking great pain. He started moaning.

The Somali just kept watching him, with the gun firmly trained at Myles. Briefly the security guard looked around to check they were still alone, which they were.

Myles made a play of standing up but not being able to hold his balance. Without coming close to the Somali guard, he swayed around. Pretending to be grasping for something to hold on to, Myles clutched at the light hanging above him. He squeezed it so tightly that the bulb broke, exposing the filament inside and piercing Myles' palm with shards of glass. Myles winced from his injury, while trying to make out it was less painful than the lead in his stomach. He fell to the floor.

The security guard stepped back again. He seemed surprised how the lead was killing Myles, but happy the deadly metal was so effective.

Gasping on the floor now, Myles tried to stand again. This time he slipped down, moving towards the ventilation machine. Pretending it was an accident, he used his elbow to hit the switch, turning it on. The turbines hummed into action, the fan blades turned, and soon huge volumes of air were bellowing out of the main tubes. The storage room was tight and confined, meaning the air swirled around, cycling and recycling like a small tornado.

Juma's man started to look worried. He kept his pistol pointed at Myles and became even more anxious, and put both hands on his gun. The Somali's eyes were wide with fear. The air blasting from the ventilation machine was scaring him. He motioned again at the lead powder, and this time shouted 'Eat' at Myles over the noise.

Myles nodded, but he still pretended not to be able to control his body. He heaved and rasped on the floor as he struggled towards the bag of lead powder.

Checking his surroundings, Myles looked around for his escape route. There was a window – closed – directly behind him, next to the light switch. Then he checked again on the Somali, who looked about to pull the trigger.

Holding his stomach as if he was very ill, Myles picked up the whole bag of lead dust. He made out he was going to pour it all into his mouth, but he missed.

The powder rained down near the ventilation machine, which whipped it aloft. Within moments the inside of the storage room was thick with the airborne lead.

The Somali protected his eyes. But he could still see Myles through the dust and levelled his pistol at him. Very close range: he couldn't miss. An easy kill. The dust hadn't blinded the man. Instead, he was about to fire.

Myles caught the man's eyes through the swirling cloud and knew this was it.

He dived towards the light switch as the guard squeezed the trigger.

CHAPTER FORTY
Istanbul, Turkey

Helen imagined how Myles would have used the fifteen minutes since they had spoken. It was enough time to clear a scene of fingerprints and make a good escape. She pictured him, tall and strong, calmly walking away from the American sauce factory in Germany.

She took her second phone out again and dialled the code for Germany, +49, followed by 110 – the number for the emergency services in the country.

'Emergency services – police, please,' she said. 'I'd like to report a major crime.'

Helen explained: the crime was being committed in the American Steak Sauce factory, which was somewhere in Germany but she didn't have the address. Then she explained how lead powder was being added to the ingredients, and that stockpiles of the poisonous metal could be found in the food storage room.

'Can I take your name, please?' asked the anonymous voice on the line.

'No, you cannot,' said Helen. She didn't want the tip-off traced to her too quickly. Using a pay-as-you-go phone in Turkey which wasn't registered in her name would make it hard for the police to know it was her. But she knew all emergency calls were recorded. When the recording was played back there was a good chance her voice would be recognised. She was, after all, a frequent contributor to international news broadcasts. Once she was identified, they would ask how she found out about the sauce factory, and that could implicate Myles. In time, it would help the authorities catch him.

As the phone call ended, Helen wondered whether the police would actually investigate. Probably, she thought. And if not, she could find a German newspaper or magazine who would be very interested in the story. Either way, the sauce poisoning operation would soon be closed down.

But Helen wasn't satisfied. Placidia's 'Last Prophecy of Rome' was about more than lead poisoning. After all, nobody thought toxic metal was the main reason why the Roman Empire collapsed. She had to uncover the rest of it. That meant she had to imagine what Placidia had imagined. She had to put herself in the mind of a woman she hated.

Helen also realised she had a deeper, more personal motive for her investigation. She guessed something had happened between Myles and Placidia at university, probably something romantic. She could forgive Myles his past. But something about his involvement with Placidia meant he still had deep respect for the woman – despite what she was doing now. Helen wanted to prove to Myles that the woman was a terrorist, and that she was doing terrible things.

Helen needed Myles to abandon his feelings for the woman completely. That was why she had come here – to Istanbul.

She looked up at the majestic Roman walls which once defended the city. Orange floodlights illuminated the structure while modern roads and buildings overlooked much of the ancient brickwork. Once this had been Constantinople: the second most important place in the Roman world and the eastern capital when the Empire split. This city led a successor empire for a thousand years after Rome fell. Now, Constantinople had become Istanbul, the most advanced city in a country trying to join the European Union. Roman ruins were being overtaken by modern architecture.

If Placidia tried to come here she would surely be arrested. But Placidia could send others, and it was those people Helen had to find.

She walked on, knowing she was now close to the new excavation site. The huge city walls may have kept out the hordes from the east, but they could not keep out the plague. She tried to imagine how the Roman inhabitants had panicked as their population succumbed to the disease. Helen remembered her research – how the Romans had first given dignified burials to the victims, then been forced to place the bodies in mass graves just outside the city walls. Bubonic plague had struck several times. One wave of the illness, in 541 and 542, had wiped out half the population.

Then Helen saw the large canvas tent which was covering the earthwork. The excavation site was exactly where it was meant to be, indicating the paperwork filed in the municipal records office was correct. She watched for several minutes before she approached, pushing her hair behind her ear to listen.

Nothing was happening. It was near midnight and nobody seemed to be working on the site. Perhaps it meant the excavation was genuine, but Helen's journalistic instincts kept her sceptical. She waited for several more minutes, until she found herself distracted by thoughts of Myles. Then she decided to approach.

The entrance to the tent around the excavations was sealed with thin rope. Looking round behind her to check nobody was watching, Helen carefully untied the main knot and unthreaded the cord until the door was open.

She peered inside. It was dark, but she could see a large hole in the middle of the tent, which looked deep. Scaffolding had been placed inside, and an aluminium ladder led down. Also in the tent she saw some benches and clear plastic bags, which seemed to be full of soil, although it was too dark to be certain.

Helen took out her unregistered mobile phone and pressed on the keypad. It glowed and she tried to direct the light towards the interior of the tent. The plastic bags did contain samples of soil.

Then she saw what looked like a large chest, connected to a cable which led back outside the tent. Helen was new to archaeology, but the chest didn't seem like it belonged at the site. It looked too scientific: there were dials and buttons on the front.

Suddenly Helen felt herself grabbed from behind. She tried to wrench herself free, but she was held too tightly. Her mobile phone fell to the floor, and she glimpsed it being kicked into the large hole in the middle of the tent.

Instinctively she slammed a fist backwards, aiming for the genitals of whoever was holding her. She could tell her hit had registered. The grip on her slackened. But it wasn't enough. There were more of them behind her.

She felt something being placed over her head, cutting out what little light there was. She tried to scream, but a hand was placed on her mouth, muffling her cries. She tried to kick, but felt her legs being held then bound with a cord.

She heard voices speaking a foreign language. There was more than one assailant, probably three or four. She kept trying to wriggle, but soon she was tied up – her arms, her legs, and a gag across her mouth.

Then her nostrils caught a terrible smell: something foul had just been exposed to the air. Helen didn't dare imagine what it was. She heard more scurrying and debate between the people who were holding her. It took a minute for their voices to settle. They had decided what they were going to do.

Only then did she feel her right arm being tied at the upper elbow. Moments later she sensed a pain pierce her wrist, as she felt a cold fluid being injected into her vein.

CHAPTER FORTY-ONE
South-eastern Mediterranean

The supertanker had edged along the Libyan coast for almost twenty-four hours. Its human cargo was far lighter than the oil it would usually carry, meaning it floated much higher in the water. This allowed Juma to stick to the shallows, always keeping sight of land as he sailed east.

Juma had hugged the coast for a reason: he didn't want the ship to be challenged. He knew the European Union anti-migration police used satellites to monitor Libya's ports, and that well-armed patrol boats were ready to intercept any vessel which entered international waters – agreed by law to begin twelve nautical miles from land. Juma knew he had to stay less than this distance from the coast. He was ready to fight, but didn't want to fight yet.

He'd been intercepted once before, several years ago. He was a pirate then, directing a container ship from the Red Sea back to Somalia. It was an American Navy boat which had stopped him. But all they had done was confiscate his bounty. Once they had secured the merchant vessel, they had let Juma and his men go. They hadn't even humiliated him. What sort of superpower did they think they were?

He smiled at the memory. *Those pathetic Americans.*

His wife, Placidia, was the only American he knew who wasn't pathetic. But then she was only *half*-American. It was because of her that he had kept men on the bows, scanning the water for deadly, floating bombs, as the supertanker passed along the coast of Libya. The men had long poles to push any mines away, and radios to warn the ship's bridge and engine room if any got near. Placidia had insisted they protect the refugees below decks, and Juma knew he had to obey.

But the ship had not been harmed. The explosives laid by Colonel Gaddafi to guard his main ports had been cleared long ago. And by the time they reached Egyptian waters they knew they were safe.

Now the ship was near Alexandria. Juma sent out a coded radio signal, which his onshore team heard and responded to. Within minutes, a fast-moving skiff was speeding out from the Egyptian coast to meet them. The small boat docked alongside the oil tanker.

Juma and Placidia looked at each other. Without words, they confirmed what they were about to do. Then Juma left the bridge, handing the controls to one of the pirates he had brought with him from Somalia.

Not far away, along a corridor and with a view of the sea, sat Senator Roosevelt. Still in chains, he already accepted he wouldn't be able to escape as his son had done.

He could still fight, but only with words. 'Juma – you haven't drowned yet,' he said. 'Pity.'

'I hope you're enjoying the cruise, Senator.'

'I never knew how sickened I could become on a calm sea…'

Juma ordered the Senator's chains to be removed, and watched as his captive rubbed his skin where the metal had been. 'Time to go ashore, Senator,' he ordered.

'So you're going to kill me now?'

'Not yet,' replied Juma with a grin. 'Probably later.'

The Senator nodded reluctantly. He shuffled along, knowing Juma's gun was behind him, and acknowledging Placidia as she joined them. 'Down there?'

Juma nodded, pointing to the rope ladder with his gun. The Senator peered down to the skiff, then manoeuvred his body over the edge of the tanker. Slowly, he began the long climb down. When he reached the bottom, he was helped aboard the smaller vessel by two young Somalis who made sure the Senator was comfortable but could not escape.

Then it was Juma's turn. When he was halfway down, Placidia repeated her orders to the crew left behind. 'Not a word to the refugees, OK?'

The crew indicated they understood.

She had been absolutely clear: the human cargo mustn't find out Juma, Placidia and their high-value Senator had left the ship. They didn't need to know they were being abandoned by the man and woman who had persuaded them aboard. It would frighten them. The information might even make them do something silly, something which would stop them reaching America. She had promised them America, and she meant it. Keeping her promise to them meant keeping secrets from them, too.

She quickly followed her husband down, and soon joined him and the Senator. Silently, the smaller vessel was untied. Juma allowed it to drift off for several minutes, until it was well clear of the tanker. Then he restarted the engine and headed towards the Egyptian coastline, where a small convoy of SUVs was waiting to take them much further east by land. He didn't want the unmistakeable spluttering of the engine to alert the refugees.

But below deck, Safiq soon knew. He had heard the small engine of a skiff draw close, then stop, then start up again much more quietly a few minutes later. He felt the tanker steer round to the north soon after. And he noticed Juma's crew had become much more relaxed, and suspected – correctly – that it was because the big man had gone.

Even though he knew, there was nothing Safiq or any of the other passengers could do about it. They remained under their polyester blankets, trying to stay warm near the air vents to the outside – the only source of oxygen not infected by the smell of gasoline which stank throughout the ship.

Whether Juma and Placidia were with them or not, Safiq still trusted the couple who had persuaded him aboard.

He still had hope.

And he still believed that staying below the decks of the supertanker was the best way for him to reach a new, much better life in America.

CHAPTER FORTY-TWO
Bielefeld, Germany

As Myles slammed his fist against the light switch, electricity surged into the exposed filament in the broken light bulb. The coil of metal burnt out in an instant, surrounded by the highly combustible swirling cloud of lead powder. The mixture of fine dust and air ignited with a flash, filling the space between Myles and the Somali security guard with a fireball. The explosion roared, creating a shock wave far larger than Myles could ever have imagined.

Myles felt the blast lift and hurl him through the window. Broken glass flew with him, sparkling like glitter. Rolling through the night air, he tried to place his feet on the ground, but ended up skidding on the concrete car park. Large fragments of glass were stuck in his torso and left arm.

Deafened, blinded and stunned, Myles quickly tried to look back to the factory and the Somali security guard. From where he had stopped on the car park, some ten metres away, it was too dark to peer inside. The lead dust had all burnt out instantly, leaving only smoke and a few flames where other things had caught fire.

Myles imagined the blast must have at least knocked his adversary unconscious. He had been near a window which blew out to release the force of the explosion, but the Somali was right in the middle of it, and would have had much worse.

It was no time to wonder. Helen would have contacted the police, and the whole neighbourhood would be calling the emergency services after the explosion: he had to get out quickly.

Myles sprinted towards the locked gates, where he stopped to check no one was watching. Then he climbed up and over, and walked away from the factory as calmly as he could.

Within seconds Myles could hear the scream of approaching police cars. He had to lose himself in suburbia.

He crossed over the road, towards the newsagents, then followed a small unlit path which led directly away from the factory. He wanted to rest, and briefly considered waiting there. But he knew the area would soon be full of policemen, then inquisitive local residents, then journalists. He had to get much further away.

Myles kept walking through the town's streets, staying away from main roads wherever possible. He was careful to keep the factory behind him – he didn't want to walk round in a loop and end up back where he had begun.

After more than a mile he came across a children's playground which had been squeezed into the housing estate, accessible only through footpaths and hidden from the main roads. He looked around to confirm it was deserted. It was. Then he hopped over the small perimeter fence and went to sit on one of the benches. Here he could gather his breath and his thoughts.

Myles ran through what he had just witnessed: a German factory which added lead powder to their recipe for an American sauce. Thousands of people could have been poisoned – mainly Americans. Most of the people at the factory seemed to be innocent – he was sure of that now - although the night guard was clearly involved.

Myles guessed he hadn't consumed enough of the lead to have been poisoned. He'd managed to spit most of it out. But he decided that, to be sure, he would have to make himself sick.

Checking again that he was alone, Myles locked his jaw open and put two fingers onto the back of his tongue. He wretched, vomiting onto the ground between his feet. Spitting until he had cleared out his mouth, Myles breathed deeply to try to settle his stomach.

He waited a few minutes, then put his fingers into his throat again. This time the reflex yielded much less. Myles found himself coughing. Stomach acid seared the route up to his mouth.

He looked around once more. Still alone. Could anybody have known he had visited the factory?

Whoever the Somali security guard had called would have known.

The CIA back in the States may have intercepted Myles' call to Helen. But they wouldn't trace him here. He looked down at the vomit he had left. That was perfectly anonymous: whoever saw it in the morning would imagine a teenager had broken into the playground and been drinking alcohol.

But he had left one big clue behind: his six volumes of Gibbon's *Decline and Fall of the Roman Empire*. It was a clear link with Juma's threat to bring down America. And if they doubted the books were his, they'd soon see the library sheets inside and realise they had been stolen from the Bodleian in Oxford. He might as well have left a signed note with his name on it.

Myles cursed himself – not just for leaving behind something so incriminating, but for having left the book itself. What lessons about Rome had Myles just lost?

A serious setback. More than ever, he needed to understand not just how the Empire collapsed, but how Placidia *thought* it had collapsed. Her words still haunted him: 'Everything you need to know about Rome is in that book – and if you want to save America, you should look at it again…'

He checked his palm for fragments of glass from the light bulb, and eased out two thin slices stuck from the base of his thumb. Pulling them out drew blood. On inspection, he realised the cut was still bleeding. So he raised his hand into the air, where he held it for several minutes, until the bleeding stopped.

The clothes on the side of his torso where he had skidded and landed in the car park were frayed. He lifted them up. The skin underneath was bruised, but otherwise fine. Two shards of window glass had penetrated his flesh, near his ribcage. He drew them out. Fortunately, the incisions weren't deep, and little blood seeped out where they had been. Myles rubbed his shoulder, which was sore, but there was no serious damage. He was probably safe. For now.

Myles desperately needed to reach Helen in Istanbul. If the plot to destroy America was about lead, then Myles had likely stopped it. But if it was about the plague, then Helen would be trying to stop it right now. And if she was only a little less lucky than Myles had been so far, she would definitely need help.

Stealing a car around midnight in the middle of Germany was easy. Myles simply walked along the road, putting his hand to door handles and pulling on them as subtly as he could. The fifth vehicle he tried – a medium-sized Skoda, parked on a driveway set back from the main road – was unlocked.

Quietly Myles climbed in, then spent more than ten minutes fiddling with the circuitry under the dashboard. He was trying to bypass the ignition switch, but it was hard because the manufacturers had clearly done something clever to stop it being 'hotwired'. It wasn't enough to change the way the different leads were connected.

A puzzle: he tried to break it. He could tell there was no computer involved – inserting a key and turning it must be enough to disable whatever anti-hotwiring device had been installed. He saw how the key turned from 'off' through two other positions before it reached the ignition setting. Then he saw each of those positions had a different cable associated with it. Eventually, by working out the order he needed to make the connections, Myles was able to make the car start. He twisted the wires to fix them in place, and moved into the driving seat. The tank was almost completely full, meaning Myles could travel far before he would need to refuel – or steal another car.

There were no roadblocks. If the authorities had decided to set them up, then they were nearer to the factory and Myles was already beyond their reach. He kept driving away from the factory site for more than twenty miles. There, driving onto the German autobahn, he turned south, then south-east.

He was heading for Istanbul.

DAYS VII-VIII

CHAPTER FORTY-THREE
Germany

Istanbul was some two-thousand miles away – impossible to drive in a single stretch, and Myles was already worn and tired. His stomach was painfully empty, and his concentration was fading. He had lost his purple bag in the factory – no more food and water. He decided he would travel only until he was out of Germany before he took a much-needed break.

By first light Myles had reached Pilsen in the Czech Republic, not far from Prague. Here he decided to drive his Skoda into a parking lot, where he climbed out and left it.

He walked for a few streets until he came to more vehicles and did the same as before. He was soon driving away in a Mercedes, which he guessed was at least twenty years old. This he drove some twenty miles, until he abandoned it too, near a farm, where he decided to sleep through the day.

Woken by deep hunger, Myles walked to a nearby village, hiding the side of his body and his torn clothes as much as he could. There he used his last euros to buy smoked meat, cheese and some bread. As he ate his impromptu picnic sitting by the roadside, Myles wondered about Helen, thinking she was probably making good progress with her investigation in Turkey. He understood Helen knew how to take care of herself, but it didn't stop him from worrying that she might be in some kind of danger.

Myles made the rest of the journey to Istanbul through a combination of hitchhiking – with a lorry driver to the border between Romania and Bulgaria – then by stealing a third vehicle, a cheap-looking Ford.

He passed several large camps set up near the Danube for refugees fleeing from the East. The thought of warm soup and other food – perhaps even fresh clothes – tempted him inside. But, like the camps for desperate migrants set up by the Romans, he knew the authorities would try to keep him inside. He'd be kept away from Helen. They might even recognise him and send him back to court. He had to keep moving.

He drove the Ford into Turkey – the only border where they asked for his passport. When Myles pretended he couldn't find it, he was made to wait on one side, then managed to drive through when the guards changed. He soon reached Istanbul itself, parking the car in the outskirts of the city before he enjoyed the last of his bread and meat. The thought of meeting up with Helen again made him smile.

Istanbul – he'd made it.

Stopping at a public payphone, he tried to call Helen's unregistered mobile. No answer. He tried again. Still no response.

Next he dialled her normal mobile. That went straight to answerphone. Myles decided the phone was probably being monitored, so it was best not to leave a message.

He thought again, and remembered the name of the plague cemetery Helen had mentioned: the Cemetery of Emperor Justinian.

He found a shop which was selling guidebooks of the city. One of the books contained a map. Carefully Myles unfolded it and tried to orientate himself. From a small index in the corner of the paper, Myles found the cemetery: the excavation was just outside the city walls, probably about three miles from where he was currently standing.

Back in the car, Myles drove past the Roman heritage which still propped up the city. Temples, old marketplaces and ancient government buildings were everywhere. All empires leave a legacy. The Romans had left much more than most. What would be left of modern civilisation, if Juma managed to destroy it?

He was also puzzled by why Helen hadn't answered either of her phones. There could be a simple explanation for it, but Myles suspected something more sinister. The joy of a reunion with her was becoming clouded by fear.

He drove on to the ancient cemetery, where he saw the canvas tent which covered the excavation site. Deliberately, Myles drove past, then parked up and watched.

Nothing seemed to be happening. So Myles climbed out, closed the car door behind him and walked towards the tent.

The entrance was tied up with thin rope. Myles listened from the outside until he was content no one was inside, then started to loosen the knot. The flap was soon undone and Myles could enter.

Despite the eerie feel, the inside of the tent appeared to be empty. Myles moved further inside. He could see a peculiar scientific-looking chest and some benches.

Then he moved towards the large hole in the centre of the tent. He leant over to look down. Some of the excavated soil surface was reflecting light, indicating it was wet. But there was something else, too. Myles squinted and saw a faint light. Something was glowing down in the ruins.

Myles quickly climbed down the aluminium ladder, to the bottom of the excavation site, several metres below. He moved towards the glow and confirmed it was a mobile phone. He picked it up: one missed call. The call was timed to just over an hour ago, from a number in Istanbul. He flicked through the call log. There had been a call from Germany, and a call to an unusually short number in Germany about sixteen minutes later. The Germany emergency services: it was Helen's unregistered phone.

It meant that either Helen had lost it or, more likely, she was in trouble.

With only the faint light from the phone, he could see old Roman tombs and broken architecture all around him. He realised this was one of the earlier graves for plague victims. Later ones were more hurried and less ornate.

He touched the surface of the stones. Most had decayed beyond recognition. But one seemed to have letters carved into it which he could still make out. There was clearly a 'C' followed by 'M', then a space or a bump – hard to tell – but he thought it was probably an 'X'. Next came another 'X' followed by 'II'. Then a space, and three more letters: 'AUC'. Vaguely, he remembered 'AUC' was short for 'Ab Urba Condita' – Latin for 'from when the city was founded', usually taken to be 753BC. It was how the Romans counted years before they reset their system to the birth year of Jesus Christ. So this tomb was from before the Empire converted to Christianity. He worked through the Roman numerals: CMXXII – nine-hundred and twenty-two. Quick maths: 922 minus 753BC made it 169AD. The numerals spelt out the year of one of Rome's great plagues. He was touching the gravestone of one of its victims.

But something didn't fit. He was in the Cemetery of Emperor Justinian, but this grave was about three and a half centuries older. It was an earlier plague. A half-memory from tutorials with Placidia flickered into his mind. What was he missing? He needed to remember…

Then he noticed movement on the floor of the excavation pit. He turned to look closer: it was a human body, covered in a cloth and bound in ropes, lying alone on the floor of the site.

Carefully, Myles approached. Then he saw a half-exposed face. It was a face he recognised immediately, and a jolt of horror suddenly passed through his entire body.

CHAPTER FORTY-FOUR
Cemetery of Emperor Justinian, Istanbul

Myles rushed over to Helen's body, unsure whether she was unconscious, asleep or dead. He grabbed her and lifted her into his
arms, shouting into her ear, 'Helen, Helen…'

She was still warm, but her body was limp. He registered the
rope tied around her wrists but ignored it. Instead, he pushed
back her hair to shout her name straight into her ear. She still
didn't respond. He kissed her on the lips, pushing his mouth
to hers as hard as he could. Desperate, he slapped her face and
shook her.

Slowly Helen started to stir.

'Helen – wake up!'

She half-opened her eyes and saw Myles. Her face relaxed as
she recognised him. Then she gulped and looked queasy.

She grabbed his shoulder, then strained as she turned away.
She was kneeling on the floor. Myles looked on, feeling helpless.

Then Helen retched. Vomit flew out of her mouth onto the
dusty floor of the excavation. She tried to regain her breath while
remnants from her stomach dribbled down from her mouth.
Then she hurled again, expelling much less this time. She spat
out what remained in her mouth until her mouth was clear. Then
she wiped her face and looked up at Myles. Her expression was
an apology for what she had just done.

'Are you OK?' he asked.

'I don't know,' said Helen. 'They injected me with something.' She gestured to her arm.

'Who?'

'I don't know.' Helen was speaking much more weakly than usual. 'Juma's people, I guess.'

Myles rubbed her head and neck, trying to wake her some more. Then he peeled off the tape which was binding her wrists together. He lifted up her left sleeve to see a needle mark on her arm and ran his fingers over it, feeling a bump where the skin was inflamed. Trying to disguise his reaction, he put the sleeve back in place.

After untying the cord around her ankles, he noticed Helen was shivering. Myles pulled her close and tried to warm her body with his. 'What do you think they injected you with?'

Helen didn't answer. But they both knew what they feared: they were in an excavation for victims of the bubonic plague. Known as the Black Death when it had struck Europe in the 1340s and killed about forty per cent of the population, the bacterial illness had struck the Roman Empire several times, often with an increasingly terrible impact. Plague helped bring down the Roman Empire. Was Juma about to unleash it into the world again, with Helen as his first victim?

Helen changed the subject. 'I know how they did it,' she said. 'How they got you.' She could tell Myles was confused. 'The information about the Navy Seals going into Libya,' she explained. 'The stuff they found on your computer.'

'They found stuff on my computer? That was their "evidence"?'

'Yes, that's why they arrested you,' said Helen, nodding. 'The raid turned out to be an ambush – Juma's men had been warned the Special Forces were coming. So Homeland Security tried to work out how, and they found the secret plan for the raid was on your computer. But it had been planted there remotely.'

Myles paused before responding. Helen was sick and he didn't want to disappoint her. 'That's good news,' he said. 'But we already know any information like that must have been planted somehow.'

Helen rolled her head. Myles didn't get it. Then she coughed. 'Myles, your computer was accessed by someone trying to set you up, and I know where it was accessed from.'

'Where?'

'From Iraq. One of the computer guys in the studio identified internet traffic that went in before the Special Forces raid,' she explained, desperate to get the words out despite her condition. 'And he got an IP address, too.'

Myles understood. 'So you know who did it?'

'Sort of,' said Helen, less confident this time. 'The IP address belongs to a Private Security firm in Iraq, based out in the Western Desert. It's in Anbar Province.'

'Does Roosevelt Security operate there?'

'No. It's a rival. A small start-up called "Galla Security".' Helen smiled weakly as she said 'Galla Security' – she'd been right about Placidia.

Myles pondered. 'Have you found out anything about them?'

'There doesn't seem to be much. Probably a local militia group which got a licence to become legal. They're not big.'

Myles put his hand on Helen's forehead. It was cold. 'How long ago did they inject you?'

'I don't know,' she replied. 'It was soon after you called me from Germany.'

Myles looked down at the patch of vomit, which was already half soaked up by the dust on the ground. If Helen did have the plague then she needed treatment fast. 'We need to leave,' he said. Then, more gently, he asked, 'Do you think you can climb the ladder?'

Helen looked up at the aluminium steps. She nodded. But the way she moved her head made clear to Myles that she wouldn't reach the top without help.

He steadied the metal frame and placed one foot on the bottom rung to keep it firm. Then he put one arm around Helen's back and another under her knees, and pulled her close. She collapsed into him. Clutching her limp body to his chest he turned back to the ladder, and slowly started to haul himself up. He had to poke his elbows into the ladder as he climbed.

Eventually they made it to the top. Trying to climb out onto the ground he slipped, but managed not to fall. Soon he could place both her feet firmly on the earth, where she staggered and sat down.

Myles looked around the inside of the excavation tent for ideas. Antibiotics were what he needed. The plague was a bacterial disease, so it could be treated with antibiotics. But there were no antibiotics in the tent.

He stood up and helped Helen to her feet. 'We've got to get you to a hospital,' he said. 'And fast.'

He put his arm under her shoulder and helped her stand. They started walking.

Then a beam of light shone straight at his face. Myles was temporarily blinded. He tried to shield his eyes but still couldn't see who was holding the torch. He called out. 'Hello?'

After a few seconds a voice replied. 'Stand still, please, Mr Munro.'

The torchlight moved closer. Then he saw the needle of a syringe glint in the beam.

Myles knew what was about to happen. He was about to be injected with the disease too.

He had to think quickly. No way to escape. No good going back down into the excavation pit. No way to fight back...

Then he whispered to Helen. 'Lick my hand.'

'What?'

Without waiting for permission, Myles pushed his fingers into Helen's mouth. Her head reeled back in shock but didn't resist.

The torchlight and syringe approached closer. He heard someone else coming from behind, about to grab his arms.

Myles spun round. Two Somali men were there, exposed by the torch now shining from behind Myles. One looked squat, the other nervous. Both froze as Myles squared up to them.

Then Myles jabbed his wet hand straight towards them.

One... Two...

Quickly, he poked his fingers into each of the men's mouths. The men stood stunned, unsure how to react.

Myles turned back to the man holding the torch. Although the light made it hard to know exactly where the man's mouth was, Myles made a guess. He stabbed his fingers forward.

Three.

Myles could see the men stop. Their attack was over. They knew what he had done.

He saw the syringe fall to the floor as the man holding it tried to wipe out his mouth – desperate not to become infected.

Helen realised too, and tugged at Myles. She could see the men were distracted and wanted to use the opportunity to escape.

Myles shook his head. 'No,' he said. 'If we leave to get the cure, these guys will spread the disease before they die. The plague will get out. There'll be an epidemic.'

He could see the reaction on his assailants' faces: they were shocked there was a cure, but terrified that they would die without it.

Two of the men started arguing in an African dialect. One pulled a knife from his belt, but the other ordered him to put it back. The third man was still wiping his tongue, vainly hoping he could remove any trace of the plague bacteria.

One of the men who had been arguing gave Myles a macho nudge. It was a way of showing he was still in charge. But Myles knew that really it meant the power dynamic had changed. They faced death in two or three days, just like Helen and him. More than that: since he had mentioned there was a cure, he had gained power over them. Time for a bargain.

The Somali nudged Myles again. It was more like a push this time, intended to provoke. 'You give us the cure,' demanded the man.

Myles shook his head. He could see what was going to happen next, but he needed it to play out so the three men understood the situation too. Next would be threats…

'You give us the cure or we kill you,' said the man.

Myles shook his head. 'I've been infected with the plague,' he replied. 'I will die in two or three days anyway.'

The man who had held the syringe grabbed Helen, who was visibly becoming weak again. She did not resist. 'You give us the cure or we kill her…' said the man, smiling as if he thought he had found Myles' weak spot.

But Myles' logic was too robust. 'She also has the plague. She will die soon, too.' Myles shrugged, as if to say 'it doesn't matter what you do'. He had disarmed them.

The three men looked at each other. Finally, they realised: they needed to cut a deal. Eventually one of them spoke to Myles. 'OK, what do you want for the cure?' he asked.

Myles paused before he answered. Then he raised three fingers. 'Three things,' he said.

The leading Somali raised his eyebrows, stunned by Myles' audacity. Then he motioned for Myles to make his demands.

'First,' said Myles, 'I want you to agree that Helen gets the first dose. She's been infected for longer than any of us. She needs the medicine most of all.'

'And your second demand, Mr Munro?'

'Do you agree to the first?'

The Somali gang men looked at each other. One of them started speaking in a foreign dialect, but the other cut him short. Then, based on only eye contact between them – eye contact which made Myles sceptical – the leading African nodded. 'OK, we agree: she gets the first dose.'

'Good,' said Myles. 'Second, I go free.

'Agreed – on the condition that we get to go free too,' said the Somali. 'We're not going to the police.'

Myles accepted the point. 'OK, agreed,' said Myles. 'And third, you tell me who sent you.'

The three men looked at each other again. This was a hard one. Another foreign-language argument ensued. It began to look as though the answer was going to be no – they would refuse to say who they were working for.

Helen broke in. 'Look, guys. We know you were sent by either Juma or Placidia,' she said. 'So who was it: Juma or Placidia? Or do you want to die of this disease?' Helen coughed as she finished her sentence. It was a guttural cough and she bent over double. The men looked frightened just watching her.

Myles was sure he knew what the answer would be: plague was a mass killer. Placidia-the-idealist wouldn't use something so indiscriminate. They would have been sent by Juma-the-psychopath.

Then the answer came: 'Placidia.'

Myles' eyes widened in disbelief. He tried to hide it. 'Placidia? Really?'

The Somalis all nodded in unison. One of them even explained how Placidia had told them exactly which tomb to open, after studying some old books.

Helen glanced an 'I told you so' look at Myles, before coughing again.

Myles was stunned. He checked again, but the men seemed convincing enough. They were sincere. 'Why were you so unwilling to say who sent you a few moments ago?' he asked.

'Because Placidia has our families and she will get them American citizenship if we succeed,' explained one of the men. 'But she said that if her name was mentioned then we would get nothing, and our families may die.'

Myles tried to make sense of it. Was Placidia really so sure of her plan that she thought she could promise US citizenship? And more importantly, was Placidia really planning to infect millions with a deadly illness? What had happened to Placidia to make her change?

One of the Somalis tugged at Myles' arm, distracting him. 'Mr Englishman. So we get the cure, right?'

Helen could see Myles was still stunned by the confirmation that Placidia was willing to commit mass murder. She stepped in. 'Yes, you have a deal,' she said, erupting into more coughs. She collapsed to the floor, still coughing.

The Somalis turned to Myles. They wanted him to lead them to their cure. For Myles, the power he had over the three men standing around him gave him no satisfaction at all.

Myles realised that the woman he loved was very close to death.

And the woman he had loved in the past had become a psychopathic mass-murderer.

CHAPTER FORTY-FIVE
Istanbul, Turkey

Breaking into a pharmacy in Istanbul would be easy. Finding the right antibiotics to steal would be harder. Escaping without being caught would be harder still. Doing it all with three un-trustworthy gangsters before any of them weakened from the plague – or infected anyone else – was a huge challenge. Myles wasn't sure it could be done at all. But as he looked at Helen, whose life depended on him succeeding, he knew he had to try.

He led the men out of the excavation tent, and looked around, trying to guess where in the vast city of Istanbul would be the nearest stock of emergency medicine. The light from a road lined with shops was visible just inside the city walls. He gestured towards it: they would walk through the large Roman gate, then look for an illuminated green cross – the universal sign for a pharmacy, an old symbol dating from Roman times which meant a place of healing.

Juma's men followed Myles eagerly. Too eagerly. They were desperate. Myles wondered how Placidia had sent them here without any protection against the disease they were about to spread.

He was trying to think ahead. They needed antibiotics, but which ones? There were so many types, many of them dedicated to treating specific conditions. A normal pharmacy wouldn't have antibiotics designed to cure bubonic plague, so he'd need to find a general one, a 'broad spectrum' antibiotic. It also needed to be powerful and fast-acting.

He wondered some more. If the Somalis had been sent here without a cure, did they hope to somehow spread the plague without catching it themselves? Or did they know they'd been sent on a suicide mission?

As the team of four approached the floodlit gate in the city walls, now left permanently open for traffic, Myles reflected on just how absurd his situation was. He had infected with a fatal disease the men he was now leading, yet they were following him for a cure. They had been sent here by Placidia, who knew about antibiotics – but had not bothered to supply them with any.

Myles knew he was missing something. Something wasn't right, but he couldn't work out what.

The men entered the city and started walking down the street of shops. No pharmacy was in sight. As they continued – down a hill and round a corner – more shopfronts came into view ahead of them. Still no pharmacy. Myles began to wonder how long it would take.

Then one of the Somalis tugged on Myles' arm. The man said something in his mother tongue.

'A green cross, he says,' came the translation. 'Down that side street.'

The man pointed, and he was correct: on a street which branched off to the right, partly hidden by the curve of the road and a bus stop, was the sign for a pharmacy.

Myles sensed the expectation amongst the three men. They imagined the sign meant they would survive, but Myles knew it was far too early to be sure.

The four of them jogged to the shopfront. A large window display was advertising a slimming drug. None of them could read the promotional material, which was in Turkish, but the message was obvious: these pills will help you lose weight fast. Another display was promoting vitamins at bargain prices, and there was an offer on teeth-whitening products.

Myles looked past them all, towards the back of the shop. There he saw a counter and shelves full of more conventional remedies. Vanity products at the front, medicines at the back.

Myles knew he would need to get properly inside the pharmacy to get the antibiotics they needed. 'We need to break in,' he whispered.

The Somalis indicated agreement. Myles checked no one else was around, then inspected the door lock while the others looked around for something to break the glass. One of them found a metal bin a little way down the street, and wrenched it from the bolts which fixed it in place. He dragged it over and threw it at the glass.

It bounced off. None of them was surprised: the glass was thick and the rubbish bin light.

The metal bumped noisily onto the ground. It rolled near another of the Somalis, who also picked it up and tried to hurl it towards the window.

Even though the throw was much harder this time, the metal bin only managed to scratch the glass a little.

'It's thickened glass. The bin's not heavy enough to break it,' explained Myles. 'We have to use the bin with our weight.'

The Somalis looked unsure. Myles clarified. 'We use it as a battering ram, OK?'

The men nodded. Myles told them to stand a few metres back from the middle of the largest window, then got them to link up with him, in two lines of two. Myles held the bin at the front, pointing the base squarely at the window display. 'Three, two, one…'

The four men rushed forward, straight into the glass. The window flexed then shattered. Myles and the man beside him fell forward, their elbows caught in the dieting promotion. Broken glass was everywhere.

Then a loud alarm screeched out.

Myles tried to clamber into the shopfront window. The Somalis supported his legs, trying to help but actually making it harder. Eventually Myles was in, his ears punished by the sound of the alarm which was even louder inside the shop.

It took several seconds to get around the weight-loss pictures and signs, which had fallen on their sides. He had to wade through broken glass, then out of the window display to reach the main part of the shop. Then he rushed to the back, to the medicine counter.

Quickly he scanned the shelves for antibiotics. The labels weren't helpful – some were in Turkish, others just listed commercial brand names.

He pulled out the drawers. The first was empty. The second one contained a file folder which he lifted out and opened. The file listed conditions and recommended medicines next to them. Myles scanned through it.

Acid reflux
Actinic Keratosis
Acute Anaemia…

There were too many to choose from – but, of course, no listing for 'Bubonic Plague'. He skipped forward.

Feline Carcinoma
Feline Hypothyroidism
Fever Blisters Treatment…

The alarm kept ringing. He needed to do this faster. The police would be here soon. He thought of bringing in the three men, still waiting outside, but realised that would only slow him down. He needed to think. What common condition was the bubonic plague most like?

Myles tried to shut the alarm from his mind. Then he flicked towards 'S', near the end of the file.

Syphilis: prescription – Penicillin

Myles spun round to the drawers of medicine behind him. Within moments he spotted the name of the drug he needed and jumped onto a plastic stool to collect it from the top shelf. There was plenty there. He grabbed as much as he could carry – easily enough to cure Helen, himself and the three Somalis – then headed back through the shop.

The alarm had been going for almost two minutes. Outside, he could see the three Somalis waiting for him, and looking very anxious. 'Did you get it?' asked one.

'Yes, I got it,' said Myles, clambering forward.

They were blocking the hole in the window.

'Show me,' one of them demanded.

Myles held up the packets. There was a picture on them to indicate it was a treatment for venereal diseases. Myles had remembered: syphilis was bacterial and treatment for it was once the most common use of antibiotics.

The noise of the alarm was joined by the faint scream of police sirens – distant, but approaching fast. The four men would need to exit the scene immediately.

Two of the Somalis offered Myles a hand to help him climb through back out through the window. Myles moved towards them as best he could, hindered by a clumsy manner and his tall frame in the confined space.

Then the Somalis pushed into the window display. The display knocked him to the ground. They grabbed the antibiotics from his hand as he fell. The life-saving medicine for Helen: gone. Within moments they had run away.

By the time Myles was back on his feet and clambering out of the window, the Somalis were too far away to catch.

Worse, Myles could hear the police sirens. The authorities were just round the corner.Myles knew he had just moments to decide what to do. Should he take some more medicine from the pharmacy, or hide from the police?

He heard one of the police cars stop nearby. Instinctively, he jumped down, out of the shop window and into the street. Instantly he regretted it. He should have got some more antibiotics for Helen.

But it was too late for that. He had to hide.

Two doors down was a narrow alleyway. Myles ran towards it. There he crouched in the dark passage, hoping no one would notice him. It was a second later that he saw two Turkish policemen walk down the street, looking up at the pharmacy with the smashed window. They were adjusting their hats as if they had just come from a car.

Myles wondered what to do. He desperately needed the medicine for Helen. And every minute mattered.

The alarm stopped. Everything became quiet again.

From the gloom of the passageway, Myles heard the squelch of a radio. The policemen seemed to be reporting on the scene before them.

After a few more seconds, the radio controller came back with instructions. It was in Turkish. Myles wondered what they were being told: guard the premises? Reinforcements on the way? Myles hoped the police would just cordon off the crime scene with tape, then leave to write a report or do whatever else the bureaucrats demanded of them. He waited and hoped, desperately thinking of Helen, and wondering how long she could survive.

He wondered whether there was something else which could save her, and remembered the tomb. Why had the Somalis dug up a grave from 169AD in a cemetery that was famous for a much later plague? He hoped their mistake meant Helen had only a weaker version of the disease.

Briefly he thought of giving himself in. He could tell them about Helen and she'd get proper treatment. But they might not believe him. When he told them she had bubonic plague, they definitely wouldn't believe him. At best there would be a delay, and to Helen the delay would be fatal.

Myles waited another minute. The problem tumbled through his mind, while he wondered how quickly the plague would weaken him. He wasn't feeling weak yet. He still had a chance…

In the half-light of the alleyway, he searched for – and found – a way to climb up the back wall. Silently reaching the top, he peered over: parking spaces, fed by a narrow lane, only just wide enough for most cars. Since the parking spaces and lane must be connected to one of the streets, Myles decided to take the chance. He jumped down, cushioning the noise of his landing as much as possible.

He listened around him: there didn't seem to be a reaction from the policemen. He had managed to exit unnoticed.

Bent over to keep low, Myles followed the lane. It went round two corners, then emerged onto the main street.

Straight ahead of Myles was a police car: the vehicle used by the officers now guarding the pharmacy.

Myles checked again. Still no one around.

Then he approached the car. The front passenger door was open. Myles leant inside, reached for the handbrake, then released it.

He leant back out again, closed the door behind him, and walked to the back of the vehicle. Gently, he gave it a push.

As the police car started moving, Myles darted back to the relative cover of the lane. He waited and watched. The policemen came running from the pharmacy, chasing the police car as it rolled down the hill. This was Myles' chance.

Quickly he ran back along the side street, to the pharmacy. He crawled up through the hole in the front window, and to the back of the store. Up again on the stool, he grabbed some more antibiotics. This time he stuffed a few packets into his pockets in case he was robbed of them again. He also took some injectable vials of an emergency anti-viral drug as a precaution, and grabbed a few strips of the slimming pills advertised in the window. Not to slim, for something else…

Then he jumped down, and went as far back into the store as he could. There he found a green bar across a small door: the fire exit.

Myles pressed onto the green bar and peeked outside before stepping through: he was back in the lane and the parking spaces. Still alone. So Myles closed the fire exit behind him and made his way out, returning to the spot on the main street he'd been only a few moments before.

The Turkish policemen were within sight but distant. They seemed to have managed to climb into their car as it rolled, stopping it. But now they were arguing with each other.

Coolly, Myles ignored them. He walked out of the shadows, up the main street and towards the gate in the Roman walls. Neighbours woken by the commotion of police sirens and shop alarms may have noticed him. They may have remembered him because of his height. But none of them would have connected him with the crime scene. Only the policemen could have done that, and they were too busy quarrelling about their runaway car.

Once through the Roman gate and out of the inhabited area on the edge of the city, Myles checked no one was watching or following him. Then, confident he was alone, Myles ran the remaining distance towards Helen in the excavation tent. He knew he had to get to her as soon as he could.

As he ran, history flickered back into his mind. He tried to remember what was special about the plague of 169AD…

As he approached the tent, Myles saw shadows moving on the canvas. He could tell there was not just Helen inside. There were voices. Anguished voices. The Somalis.

Myles had to confront them. In one swift motion, he lifted up the flaps on the entrance to the tent and leapt inside.

CHAPTER FORTY-SIX
Cemetery of Emperor Justinian, Istanbul

As Myles entered the tent, he immediately saw the three men who had taken the antibiotics from him. They were clutching their stomachs and arguing. They seemed to be in pain.

Beside them, lying on the ground, was Helen, who looked pale. Myles rushed over and lifted her head. He tried putting two of the antibiotic pills in her mouth and crunching them between her teeth. Then he took out some of the injectable anti-viral drugs. They were hard to use. Eventually he managed to plunge three doses into her thigh.

There was no immediate reaction. He shook her. Still no response. He couldn't tell whether or not the medicine was reaching her bloodstream. He rubbed her leg, hoping to spur the antibiotics into her system.

'Helen, I know you're going to survive,' he called into her ear. Then he lowered his voice so the Somalis couldn't hear him. 'You've got septicaemia, but not the plague…'

Then an angry voice called to him from behind. 'You have poisoned us,' it jeered.

Myles shook his head, still tending to Helen as he spoke. 'You poisoned yourselves,' he said. 'You overdosed.'

The Somali grabbed his shoulder, pulling him away from Helen. 'But we're sick now. You made us sick.'

Myles could barely bring himself to answer the Somalis. They had stolen the antibiotics from him in the shop window, and left none for Helen, whom they had promised would get the first dose. 'You've just taken too much medicine,' he said. 'It means you won't die of the plague.'

Myles could see his response hadn't satisfied them. The three were stirring towards him. They were about to attack.

Myles dug his hand into his pocket. There he found the slimming pills which he had taken from the shop. He held up the thin strip of tablets. 'Look,' he said. 'I've got medicine here which will cure your overdose.'

The Somalis peered sceptically at the packet. The writing on it was too small for them to read from where they were standing.

The three men edged closer. 'I'll cut you a deal,' he offered, holding the strip of tablets higher. 'You get these tablets if you allow Helen and I to leave.'

The men looked unsure. Myles could see them wondering: would this Englishman really trust us again? Was he a fool?

One of the men started to grin. 'OK,' he said. 'You give us the tablets and we'll leave you alone.'

Another one joined in. 'Yes. You give us the tablets first.' The man was holding out his hand, looking up at Myles. Smug and insincere: there was no way Myles would trust them.

With a single backhanded motion, Myles flicked the packet of pills through the air as if he was throwing a frisbee. The pills flew high, hitting the roof of the tent, then dropped down towards the large excavation hole. Both Myles and the Somalis saw the last glint of light reflect from the packet as it smacked into the side of the hole, spun around, then fell down to the bottom.

Myles waved his hand towards the hole. 'You've got a deal,' he said. 'The pills are down there…'

Myles turned back to Helen, half-expecting the Somalis to pounce on his back. But they had taken the bait. They were ambling over to the excavation hole and arguing over who should climb down first.

Taking the opportunity to go while he could, Myles put one arm under Helen's knees and one beneath her shoulders. Then he lifted her limp body and carried her through the flaps of the tent.

Out in the night air, which was colder than the inside of the excavation site, Helen seemed to revive a little.

Myles ran holding her, stumbling over the ground where it was uneven.

'I've not got the plague?' she asked, blearily.

'I'll explain soon,' said Myles, still running.

He headed back towards the old Ford parked just a few hundred metres away. When he reached it, he leant down to open the front passenger door, then manoeuvred Helen into the seat. She could barely sit upright, so he put a safety belt on her to make sure she stayed in position. A few seconds later he was driving off, back towards the Roman gate and the site of the pharmacy break-in.

The policemen were still there. He drove up to them and lowered his window. 'Vandals,' he told them, pointing behind him. 'Back in the excavation tent, just through the gate over there. Vandals, destroying the Roman ruins. You should investigate.'

One of the policemen nodded as he thanked Myles in rusty English. The other was about to ask follow-up questions, but Myles was already driving away.

He watched them in his rear-view mirror as he accelerated away. They seemed to have taken his crime report seriously and would probably send someone over to the excavation tent. The trio of Somalis would soon be arrested.

Myles smiled to himself: how appropriate that they should be arrested for being 'vandals' – the tribe that raided the Roman Empire in its dying days.

He kept driving, looking for road signs which might point to a hospital. He glanced across at Helen, and spoke as he drove. 'Helen. Are you awake?'

There was no answer.

'Helen. I'm going to drive you to a hospital,' he said. 'You need proper treatment, but you don't have bubonic plague. None of us do – not even the Somalis. OK?'

Helen still seemed asleep.

'I worked it out from the tombstone,' continued Myles. 'They dug up the wrong plague victims. Placidia sent them to the wrong grave by mistake. The epidemic of 169AD wasn't bubonic plague, it was smallpox. And there's no way they'll be able to recreate smallpox from the tombs – the DNA of the disease is too fragile to survive through the centuries. Other archaeological digs which have looked for smallpox have found only the faintest trace of it inside teeth. Your illness is septicaemia, from having soil injected into your bloodstream.'

He looked back over at Helen. She probably hadn't heard anything he had said.

'Septicaemia isn't infectious, so the rest of us are healthy. But Helen, you still need treatment. Antibiotics for your blood infection, and a medical check for the smallpox,' he explained. Then he paused: the next words were hard. 'But I've still got to track down these terrorists. And if I'm with you, then I can't do it.'

Finally he saw a road sign labelled with a large 'H' and the word 'Hastane', which he guessed was Turkish for hospital. Myles followed the arrows and soon saw a well-lit building. He moved down through the gears as he approached the accident and emergency section, where he live-parked.

Myles froze still for a moment, trying to force himself to move. His body resisted. He wanted to stay with her. But he knew he had no choice.

'Helen, I'm going to have to leave you here,' he whispered, hating himself for it.

Gently, he moved round to help her out of her seat. Then he wiped dirt from her forehead, and kissed it.

Lifting her up, he hugged her close, then carried her towards the reception desk. Seeing that the woman was obviously very sick, two medical professionals in uniforms moved over to take her.

'Thank you, Myles.'

Myles just caught her words as he left the building.

DAYS IX-X

CHAPTER FORTY-SEVEN
Off the Coast of Ostia, Central Italy

Safiq knew the supertanker was approaching land. Italy, some-one had said. Safiq's chance to settle in civilisation was ap-proaching...

One of Juma's crew came down into the oil storage area, where the smell of faeces had displaced the whiff of gasoline. The pirate explained what was going to happen.

Two groups, he had commanded: young men with weapons to lead, and everybody else to follow.

Safiq was one of the first young men to be offered a gun – an AK-47. He remembered his father had once been given a Kalashnikov too, and had cherished the Russian-made weapon, even though he never had any bullets for it. Safiq accepted both, half nervous, half excited by what was to come.

As he followed the others onto the deck of the tanker, he saw how police boats were trying to block the port entrance. Loud speakers were blaring across the water in a language Safiq didn't recognise. Port workers were running away. The tanker was approaching them fast.

Too fast?

Then Safiq realised – it was meant to go fast. The supertanker would ram into the dockside so that none of the Italian police could stop it.

The pirates were pushing the young men with guns to the front. But Safiq reckoned anyone near the bow would be hurt when the ship crashed into the port. He moved through the crowd to avoid an argument with the pirate crew, who were becoming angry. As the dockside of Europe came closer and closer, he barely had a chance to look forward. He was still trying to get to the middle of the ship.

Safiq tumbled over when the tanker hit, his ears deafened by the crunch of metal against concrete. He heard the people around him roar – first in fear and confusion, then in celebration. They had landed in Europe – now they would reach America.

The crowds streamed off, jumping down from the buckled deck onto the harbourside below. They cheered as they ran. The men with guns fired into the air. The families followed, carrying whatever they could and taking much longer to climb down from the ship than the young men at the front.

Safiq realised the great mass of people was moving forward. They knew where they were going. Safiq followed.

Jostled by the crowd, Safiq's AK-47 was knocked and the magazine fell to the ground. He picked it up but it was dented. Still running, Safiq tried to clip it back into place again but it wouldn't stay. He tried holding it there, until he decided he didn't really need it – the gun already had a bullet in the chamber, and that was enough. He allowed the magazine to drop again, and left it this time.

He saw some of the men with weapons taking aim. A rocket was fired at a tower – but missed. A burst of gunfire hit the outside of a house. They were scaring the local people away so they could reach their destination. Threatening civilisation so they could join it.

Safiq pointed his AK-47 at an empty car, holding it from the hip, and pulled the trigger. The single bullet pumped out.

Metalwork near the wheel hub buckled. But the gun was much louder than Safiq had expected and the recoil frightened him. He didn't want the weapon. He let it fall on the roadside and ran along with the others.

He could see people watching the crowd from windows. They were afraid – good. But not that good – Safiq wanted to be like them. To enjoy a home like theirs, food like theirs, a life like theirs…

He kept running with the crowd, all of them desperately hoping they could reach the centre of the city before they were blocked or captured… Then Safiq truly understood: he and the African migrants around him weren't running for their lives. They were running for a *good* life.

And they knew where they were running: to America.

Via the American Embassy in Rome.

CHAPTER FORTY-EIGHT
Istanbul, Turkey

Myles slumped. Deep tiredness infected his muscles. His whole body was exhausted. Three days ago he had sprinted for more than a mile to escape the gunman in London. He couldn't do that now.

Once he had driven clear of the hospital, Myles parked up and tried to think through his next steps. He knew he had some nasty choices to make.

Should he stay near Istanbul? That way he could check on Helen – perhaps visit her in hospital in a day or two, when no one was expecting it. Desperately, he hoped she was OK. Septicaemia, he tried to convince himself, was quite common. The medics would diagnose it quickly. She'd get the right treatment, whether Myles visited her or not. There was probably nothing more he could do to make her safe.

Should he hand himself in? After all, he'd stopped an attempted poisoning in Germany and now a plot to spread the plague – even though the bungling grave robbers had only dug up smallpox. Police would have seen his work in both places and known that Myles had foiled two terrorist plots within a week. They might even let him stay with Helen.

But it wasn't enough. Myles was convinced that Placidia was planning more. The Roman Empire had been weakened by lead poisoning and the plague, but it had not been destroyed by them.

It was barbarians running through the streets of the capital - desperate and hungry, but also jealous and resentful, which had defined the ancient civilisation's final days. The barbarians had ransacked a culture they envied but couldn't understand.

How could Placidia make that happen to modern-day America? There was more going on here. Far more.

He felt sure that if he gave himself up to the authorities they'd quarantine him, or find some other excuse to keep him away from what was happening. Myles would have to keep running. And the best thing he could do for Helen would be follow the lead she'd given him – to Iraq.

He lay back on the car seat. As the back of his scalp hit the headrest he recognised just how tired he was. He was hungry and thirsty, too. His whole body was a wreck. He needed downtime, and he needed to spend it away from danger.

He also realised that he needed to change his car. The Ford had been seen by the policemen near the pharmacy break-in, and also at the hospital. Turkish police were probably looking through CCTV footage to find him while he rested.

Summoning his energy, as if a long-planned lie-in had been cut short, Myles climbed out of his vehicle and walked along the street until he found another row of cars. As before, he checked the doors of several of them until he came to one which was open – a white Fiat. He climbed in, tore open the cardboard hiding the electronics, and again hotwired the ignition. He was able to do it more quickly this time, now he understood how the circuitry in modern cars was arranged. But he still found it exhausting.

He drove on about three miles, until he found a parking lot near a supermarket. Here he parked, and lay in the back of the car under a blanket laden with pet hair he found on the back seat.

He was woken by the morning light, feeling groggy and thirstier than ever.

He opened the glove compartment in the car: insurance documents, a torch, an adjustable spanner, receipts, and an out-of-date coupon for something. No money.

Myles looked up at the sign for the supermarket: they would have food.

He checked himself again: was it really OK for him to steal, just so he could remain on the run? He already felt bad for taking the cars, rifling through the luggage on the bus going to Oxford and breaking into the pharmacy. Each time he had broken the law he could justify it: he was protecting the public…

But stealing food from a supermarket seemed harder to justify somehow. The thought of it made Myles despise himself. Crime rose when Rome declined… If everybody stole – even to save America – the America they saved would be very different. Did he really have to steal?

He thought again and realised, yes, he did. If he was going to have a chance of confronting Juma and Placidia and stopping the plot to bring down America like ancient Rome, he needed to get some food and drink.

Reluctantly, Myles slumped out of the white Fiat and ambled towards the store. It was still fairly early in the morning and there didn't seem to be many customers inside. But he was conscious of his clothes – the tears and faint scorch marks drew attention to him. Myles was used to being a misfit, but standing out had just become dangerous…

He wandered towards the double doors, which opened automatically as he approached. A security guard was waiting as he went in. Myles tried his best to ignore the man. The guard appeared to be only half-interested.

Never having shoplifted before, Myles decided it was best to look as though he was browsing normally. He picked up a basket and surveyed the vegetables near the entrance, plucking a cabbage from the rack to check it for quality. Occasionally he picked more things up to inspect them, trying to sense whether anyone was watching him. There were no cameras in the ceiling. He felt confident he wasn't being observed.

On the corner of an aisle, he found some cartons of milk. In a single swift motion, he bent down and moved one into the inside pocket of his jacket.

Next he came to some cans: tinned meat and, a little further along, baked beans. Again, he made a point of putting them in his coat as nonchalantly as he could.

Finally, he found some cheese. This was easier to take, since the slices of brie were thin. Myles leant over and stuffed several inside his sleeves.

He had what he needed. It was time for him to go.

As he walked back towards the double doors, he wondered how ironic it would be if he were arrested for shoplifting – a small but real crime – after he had just uncovered plots to spread poison and plague in the world.

He continued towards the exit, trying to avoid catching the attention of the security guard. He knew leaving the store with an empty basket was bound to raise concerns. He just had to keep walking.

'Affedersiniz, Efendim...' called a voice. It was the security guard. Myles turned to him, unsure what the man had just said. The guard realised Myles was foreign and offered him the same phrase in English. 'Excuse me, sir...'

Myles nodded. He moved over to the man, trying to smile, and wondering if he was about to be arrested. He started thinking through what he could do. Run – but where to? He couldn't make a fast getaway in the car. Pretend to know nothing about the stolen goods? Not credible. Hand himself in… Maybe.

Myles approached the security guard. 'Yes?'

The man pointed down, his eyes lowering towards Myles' coat pockets.

Myles frowned, pretending to understand what the security man was saying.

'Your laces, sir.'

Myles looked at his feet: his laces were untied. He relaxed his face in understanding.

Bending down subtly, Myles tried hard to keep the cheese slices hidden in his sleeves. Kneeling on one knee at a time, he refastened each lace in turn. One, then the other, making sure to pull them tight. 'Thank you,' he said, weakly.

Myles smiled at the man, who tipped his cap in response. Myles replaced the empty basket by the door and walked out of the store as confidently as he could.

He retreated to his car. Checking again that he hadn't been seen, he collected his takings beside him on the passenger seat. He waited a few more minutes to check before he ate the cheese slices, washed down with the chilled milk. Then he took the adjustable spanner from the glove compartment and used it to squeeze the tin of meat. As he tightened, the metal buckled then split. Myles scooped out what he could, catching his finger at one point, causing a small cut. The cold baked beans opened more easily, but some oozed out of the can before he could eat them. His clothes had become messier than ever.

The food satisfied only his stomach. The fact that it was stolen made him feel sick.

Doing the right thing had been important to Myles ever since his mother had died. As a fourteen-year-old, he'd decided that his extraordinary brainpower would be wasted on maths problems or the puzzles of physics. Perfect solutions lost their appeal. It was the human world which mattered: accepting it could never be perfect, the right thing to do was to make it better. Was Myles doing the right thing now?

He wondered. Justifying theft in an effort to stop a terrorist plot was a bit like taking up Juma's deadly offer from when they had first met at the Libyan border: kill one man himself to stop Juma killing more. It might be the best thing to do, but did that make it right? Myles couldn't work it out.

The puzzle was as nasty as Myles' current situation, although now even more was at stake. Much more. He cursed himself, and tried to rest.

After several hours in the car, interrupted only by a toilet break, Myles was confident he had no contagious diseases. Placidia's mistake in picking a grave from the Antonine Plague of 169AD – rather than the much more lethal Justinian Plague of 541-542AD – was lucky for him.

He remembered Placidia at university. She would have never slipped up like that. It was a relief to know Placidia was making mistakes now.

He wondered where to go next. His only lead was from Helen. She had identified the IP address of a computer which had placed files on his laptop, files which detailed the Navy Seal rescue operation in Libya, files which had led to his arrest in Rome. He had to track down the address. That would clear his name, and might help uncover more of the plot to destroy America.

He remembered Helen's drowsy words: the IP address belonged to Galla Security, based near An Nukhayb in Anbar Province, Western Iraq.

So Myles connected the ignition on his Fiat, moved into gear, and prepared himself for a day and a half's drive to Turkey's south-eastern border with Iraq.

The first half of the drive was uneventful. Myles had enough fuel to drive past the modern capital, Ankara, and along the highway into the mountainous central region of Cappadocia. There he decided to abandon the Fiat, parking it on the roadside, and begin hitch-hiking. He didn't have to wait long in the sun: he was offered a lift by an elderly couple from Denmark who were touring the area. They took him to Diyarbakir, where he managed to get picked up by a long-distance haulage lorry about to go over the border into northern Iraq.

At the Iraqi border post, Myles noticed the signs of recent renovation. A new shiny metal roof now shaded part of the road. The gates and bollards were clean and had just been installed. The entry system was computerised. There was even high-powered air-conditioning for the offices. Myles knew where the money for the upgrade had come from: it was American money.

There was also a deeply sinister presence overshadowing the border post: the threat of Islamic State extremists. It meant Turkish military hardware was on hand, and stationed in depth, in case the jihadis tried to stream across. The barbed wire had been strengthened recently, and there were new CCTV cameras covering all the crossings. Several men loitered around, probably Turkish intelligence staff, gathering whatever they could find. Myles tried to avoid them all.

Getting to Galla Security near An Nukhayb involved crossing from the benign Kurdish-dominated northern part of Iraq to the much more volatile western area, where Islamic State held sway. Anbar Province was dominated by Sunni Arabs, who had a reputation for taking up arms against the Americans and, more recently, official government forces. The west of Iraq was wild.

Myles was taken by the lorry driver into Iraq and as far as Zakho, the border town in the north. There he found a pool of long-distance drivers all working for firms which had won large contracts from USAID, the American international development agency. One of these was driving to Al Kut, and offered to pass him to someone else driving towards Jordan. Myles accepted, and the driver duly did as he promised. In return for what the driver called, in broken English, Myles' 'honourable nature', he gave Myles some water and much appreciated food – chunks of chicken meat in pitta bread sandwiches.

The last lorry driver was a former dentist from Mosul called Mustafa, who had four children. He took Myles to the outskirts of An Nukhayb where he wished Myles farewell with three cups of tea, consumed by the busy roadside. Myles tried to be as generous as he could in return, although he had nothing to repay him with other than good company.

After shaking hands with Mustafa, and watching as his lorry drove away on the dusty tarmac highway, Myles walked along the road, conscious that his height, skin and features marked him out as a Westerner. Anyone wanting to act out their grudge with America might see him as a legitimate target.

But again, Myles was lucky, or at least it seemed that way. He was able to walk for more than a mile without any attacks or other violence from vehicles passing by. He also found the place he was looking for. Corralled by an unfinished breeze-block wall which defined the very large perimeter for the site, Myles could see the buildings and the offices of Galla Security in front of him. He wondered whether the premises had ever been inspected by a government official and guessed they probably hadn't.

It was from here that someone at Galla Security had sabotaged his computer.

Myles sensed much worse things had been done here, too.

CHAPTER FORTY-NINE
An Nukhayb, Iraq

Myles paused to survey the outside of Galla Security. Built on the edge of the town, the site seemed to consist of a few low buildings by the road, then a long and fairly thin sliver of land leading off into the desert. The breeze-blocks which defined the perimeter were unpainted and uneven. Myles guessed the whole structure was less than three months old.

He pondered climbing into the site, but it was daytime, and he suspected there would be security cameras. Even if he waited until dusk, it looked as though there was no cover inside the breeze-block walls except the buildings themselves. Breaking into the premises without being caught would be far harder than the factory in Germany – and he had been caught there.

Myles brushed the dust from his clothes which had been gathering since he entered Iraq. He pulled his collar taut and tucked in his shirt, trying to hide the tatters on one side. Unusually for Myles, he wanted to look smart, even though there was little he could do about it.

He walked on towards the metal front door of the walled compound. There he found a small plastic button connected to a painted wire leading inside. He pressed it firmly.

After a few seconds he heard a sharp voice with a thick Arabic accent. 'What is it?'

Myles cleared his throat. 'Er, hello? I'd like to have a look at your premises.'

'American?' queried the voice.

'English.'

There was a pause. Myles eventually heard the squeak and clank of a gate opening in one of the buildings. Footsteps, then the metal of a bolt was slid back, and the door in the perimeter wall was opened enough for a face to push through. The man looked aggressive, and had an AK-47 on his shoulder. Myles could tell the man wasn't local. He looked East African. Myles guessed he was from Somalia, like Juma.

'Hello,' said Myles, trying to be respectful. 'I'd like to look around your site.'

The Somali guard clearly understood but didn't know what to make of the request. 'You want to hire our security men?'

'I may need you for some work,' lied Myles. He tried to look as agreeable as he could.

The guard still looked sceptical. 'You are alone?'

'Yes, I am alone.'

The guard peered behind Myles to confirm he was telling the truth. There was no car waiting for Myles, and no burly mercenaries with their weapons poised. Although this made things safer for the guard, it also made him more suspicious. The Somali gunman frowned and squinted at Myles, noting his tattered clothes. The man was wondering whether Myles was mad or just naive to travel in this part of Iraq without protection.

The Somali decided to frisk Myles for weapons. Myles held his hands up, so the guard could pat him down and, once he was satisfied Myles was unarmed, allow him through the metal gate. Myles had to duck his head to get inside.

Ahead of him was a newly built office building. The security guard led Myles to a walk-through metal scanner, which wasn't working. Hardly the grand entrance of a major security company…

Then Myles was invited to sit in a reception area. There he was brought tea, heavily laden with sugar, by another Somali-looking man, who soon disappeared again. The security guard seemed to lose interest in Myles, too, focussing once more on the perimeter gate.

Myles waited. Several minutes passed. As he drank his tea, Myles wondered if he was being ignored or forgotten. But the tea was very refreshing. Myles realised there was no reason to hurry his hosts for their attention.

On the table in front of him was a brochure. Myles picked it up and started browsing.

It was the company report for Galla Security. He flicked through the pages. The document had been produced cheaply, and probably printed locally. Myles saw the posed photographs of security guards aiming their guns into the distance, as if they were defending against an unseen foe. In poorly translated English, it listed 'Services Offered By Us':

Protecting People
Protecting Sites
Other Services

For this third category, clients were invited to telephone a number or send an email with their request, explaining what their 'other service' was. All prices were negotiable.

Myles flicked to the back, where there was some detail on 'company information'. It said that Galla Security was certified by a trade association. There was a poor quality close-up of a signature, with the name of an official underneath. The document seemed to imply that this was a sufficient guarantee of quality.

Then there was a reference to the 'Alliance of Iraqi Private Security Firms'. Apparently Galla Security was owned by this conglomerate.

Myles logged the information in his mind. The amateurish nature of Galla Security was oddly comforting. It made the firm seem genuine. And that made his question more puzzling: Why would someone from this firm upload files onto his computer? And how would people here get the information in the first place – information about a Special Forces raid into Libya?

Myles turned back again to look at the security guard. Myles could easily imagine the man was connected with Juma.

Then he turned back to the pages of the brochure. The security men in the first picture looked like oversized cops from the southern states of America, probably retired. Other photos showed more beefy Westerners. He saw a few home-grown Iraqis with guns on other pages. None appeared like the men in the building with him now. Even the picture of the offices looked like it was staffed by Iraqis and white men, portrayed as working harmoniously together. He peered closer. Half-hidden by an outstretched sleeve in the office picture was a logo. Myles could make out some words: 'Alliance', 'Iraqi' and 'Security'.

The Alliance of Iraqi Private Security Firms.

The brochure had been compiled by the conglomerate which owned Galla Security. They'd even used their own picture library to put it together.

Myles wondered why Helen hadn't discovered the link to the holding company, the Alliance, when she'd first investigated the firm. Helen would have been thorough, so Galla probably kept their link with the Alliance of Iraqi Security Firms off their website. Was that deliberate?

It was still possible it was a genuine private security firm, perhaps set up by amateurs and bought out by the larger 'Alliance', whatever that was. But it could also be a money-laundering front, pretending to receive revenue from clients when really their cash came from more sinister sources.

It could even be worse.

Myles was caught up in his thoughts. He went to take another sip of tea, but realised he had already drunk it all. He wondered what to do next.

The man who had brought him the drink appeared again, poking his head around a pillar. Myles tried to catch the man's attention, but he was gone before Myles could speak to him. Something about the man's movements made Myles think he was checking up on him. Myles looked down again at his empty cup. Clearly the man hadn't come to offer him more tea.

Then Myles saw a door open at the back of the office. A woman appeared, completely shrouded in a translucent birka, her head bowed as she approached.

Myles recognised the figure immediately. His eyes widened in alarm, and he sensed his pulse pump fast in his neck. Despite the air-con, he felt sweat break out all over his body.

Reflexively, Myles stood up to hug her.

But the woman lifted up her veil to confront him. 'You made a mistake coming here,' she said.

Placidia's eyes were as fierce as ever.

CHAPTER FIFTY
Galla Security Offices, Iraq

Myles tried to hide his reaction. He forced himself to remember what he had learned from the factory in Germany and the excavation site in Istanbul: Placidia had sent several men on missions which were sure to kill them. She had tried to poison the world with lead, and infect it with a deadly plague. He was standing in front of a ruthless woman – a woman who had committed herself to destroying America and crippling civilisation.

But the sight of her face also reminded him how he used to feel. He remembered their long conversations, and sharing coffee with her. He remembered trying to make her laugh, and trying to distract her from her high-minded causes.

Placidia kept staring at him. Myles returned her gaze. They stood opposite each other for several seconds, neither of them speaking.

Then she touched him on the shoulder. With a tilt of her head, she indicated they should walk towards a more private inner office. Myles was unsure whether he should accept her invitation, but found he was already following her.

The inside of the office was plain with the rough walls painted white. Myles realised it had no outside windows – only a skylight. There was one desk in the room, which had three computers on it, all plugged in with several cables.

Placidia closed the door behind them as they entered. Two sofas faced each other, divided by a low coffee table. She directed Myles to sit in one seat while she sat opposite.

They were alone.

Myles realised this was the first time they'd been alone together for almost twenty years. His head started calculating exactly how long it was – how many years, months, days, retreating for protection into a world of numbers.

If Placidia had found more time to be alone with him all those years ago things could have turned out so differently...

Placidia sat looking at him, still silent. She was sitting with one leg crossed over the other, her head on one hand, while she rested her elbow on the back of the sofa. It was how a Western woman would sit.

'So, Helen Bridle is your partner, now?' she asked with a faint smile.

Myles nodded.

'She seems nice,' said Placidia. 'I knew you'd do well for yourself, Myles.'

The conversation was making Myles uneasy. He wanted to fire back, but knew he shouldn't. He spoke as casually as he could. 'And you're married?'

Placidia nodded.

'How long have you known Juma?'

'A few years, now,' she replied, briefly looking down at her wedding ring.

Myles knew he ought to compliment her husband somehow – to be polite, and to show he respected her choice. But he couldn't – there was nothing pleasant to say about him.

Placidia filled the silence. 'I know what you're thinking Myles: he's not the sort of husband you expected me to pick at university.'

'That's true.'

'You're surprised?'

'I'm sure he's…' Myles struggled for a nice word. 'I'm sure he's…capable.'

Placidia leant back and laughed. It was a strained laugh. It soon stopped. 'Yes, he's very *capable*. Capable of killing, piracy, terrorism. Torture every now and then.' She spoke with a resigned smile, still staring straight at Myles. 'And before you ask, yes, he's very good at what he does.'

The next question was obvious. For Myles, the ultimate puzzle. His pulse still racing, he couldn't resist asking. 'So, Placidia: why did you marry him?'

Placidia remained silent.

'Love?' suggested Myles, offering her a get-out.

She shook her head. Her smile faded and her gaze turned down. This time she resisted eye contact with Myles as she spoke. 'I've always tried to do what's best. Marriage offered me a chance to do just that.'

Myles listened as Placidia slowly raised her eyes to meet his.

'Myles, you know at university I was committed to changing the world for the better, right?'

Myles found himself nodding involuntarily.

'Well,' she explained, 'what better way to make a positive difference than to find a powerful man and persuade him to do good?'

Even though her thought process was bizarre, Myles sensed Placidia was being sincere. 'So you married Juma hoping to change him?'

'To change him and a part of Africa where hundreds of people die each day – yes.' She shrugged.

Marrying a psychopathic pirate chief to make the world a better place would be absurd from anybody else, but from Placidia it was logical. Myles knew she had a habit of taking morals to their extreme and beyond. Perhaps she was naive. Myles accepted Placidia really did think she was doing the right thing.

'And have you saved lives, by marrying Juma?'

'Yes, I think I have,' replied Placidia, nodding. 'He's killed fewer people because of me. I've made him help poor migrants from all over Africa. I've done far more good than if I'd stayed on the East Coast of the States working for some charity, or complaining about things.'

She could see that Myles was unconvinced.

'Think of it this way, Myles – other people work for NGOs like Doctors Against Disease, or Mothers against Drunk Drivers,' she explained. 'Well, I've created Pirates against Poverty, and it's saved many, many more lives.'

The conversation fell silent while they both thought.

Placidia moved in her seat, putting her hand through her hair. 'So Myles. This is a historical question, and you're a historian, right?'

'Right.'

'Do you think we might have become a proper couple at university?'

Myles squinted, trying to understand where Placidia was coming from. 'Historically, Placidia, I wanted that,' he said, trying to be honest while he hid his emotions at the same time. 'As I remember, it was you who didn't. You never had time for me. Your campaigns to change the world were always too important.'

'Sorry.'

Myles shrugged, pretending it no longer mattered to him. But he still needed to say more. 'You know, when I read about you leaving Oxford I wrote you letters, but you never replied.'

Placidia shook her head blankly. 'I never received them.'

Myles raised his eyebrows, surprised. Part of him wanted to tell her what he'd written. To replay his emotions, now he was finally with her. But he couldn't. 'If you had received them,' he asked, 'would you have behaved any differently?'

She paused before pulling a face which said she probably would have ignored the letters anyway. 'I was an arrogant young girl in those days, Myles. We only recognise our flaws after they've done their damage.'

'Sometimes our flaws keep doing damage.'

'Sometimes,' she accepted, pausing again. 'Did you *really* send me letters?'

Myles didn't need to answer her question – his face had answered already. *Yes, of course he'd sent them.*

Placidia looked mournful. For the first time in their meeting, Myles felt truly sorry for her. Had her entire life turned on a failure to receive his messages? Perhaps – many other people's lives turn on less. But someone as gifted as Placidia? Someone with all the wonderful opportunities she had? Could she really have been that vulnerable?

Placidia moved her legs in a gesture which was half flirtatious, half hopeless.

Myles wanted to hold her. But he still couldn't forgive her for what she was doing now. 'Placidia: was it you who planted files on the Special Forces raid onto my laptop?'

Myles looked straight at Placidia, who stared back in return. They gazed at each other for a long time, both refusing to surrender.

Then she broke off the competition and turned to her desk. Pulling open a drawer, she removed an old scrap of paper, which she carefully unfolded and passed to Myles. Myles read the handwritten words. It was his handwriting.

He remembered that piece of paper. He couldn't really argue with it. She read it out, just to make her point understood. '"Doing the right thing can sometimes be wrong".'

'Yes, Myles, those files passed through this computer,' she admitted. 'We had help from a computer guy in Las Vegas. It was wrong, but it was done for very good reasons.' She could see Myles was sceptical. 'You don't believe me?'

'No, Placidia, I do not,' answered Myles, his heart still pumping too fast for him to behave normally. 'Those files caused me to be arrested, questioned, shot at in court…'

'I didn't send the hitman.'

Myles stopped. He checked her face. She seemed to believe what she was saying.

'So who did send him?'

'My husband, Juma. I didn't want you to…'

'To die? To be killed?' Myles offered.

'No. I tried everything,' she pleaded. 'I tried as hard as I could to persuade Juma not to send that man. But Juma sent him anyway.'

Myles understood. 'So marrying a powerful psychopath doesn't always allow you to do good, then?'

'No, it doesn't,' she accepted. 'Not always, no.' She changed her tone, from defensive to apologetic. 'I'm glad you managed to escape, Myles.'

'I've been on the run ever since. Almost a week now.'

'Myles, you do understand: if I hadn't uploaded those files onto your computer, you'd be in even greater danger. Probably dead.'

Myles looked at her squarely. 'Explain.'

Placidia shook her head. 'If I did that, it would cost more lives.'

Myles squinted sceptically at her. 'So you're saying, you can't tell me who wants to kill me because it'll cost lives.'

'Yes.'

'My life or the lives of others?' asked Myles.

'Both.'

'How many others?'

Placidia shrugged. 'I can't say.'

'Can't say or won't say?' asked Myles, frustrated.

'Both… Look Myles,' she said, trying to level with him, 'there are just some things it's best not to know. This is one of them.'

Myles shook his head – he wasn't letting it go. 'Tell me: who wants me dead?'

'OK. My husband wants you dead,' Placidia admitted.

'Why?'

'Because it'll make him look strong to his men. Because we knew each other at university… Because he's mad, I suppose,' she shrugged again. 'There might be other reasons, too.'

'Thank you. Why couldn't you tell me that before?'

'Myles, there are more important things than this.' She was pleading now, desperate to be believed.

'More important than someone trying to kill me?'

'Yes,' she said. She was nodding, and her face seemed very sincere. 'Don't you see? The whole of civilisation really is at stake here.'

'From Juma?'

Placidia refused to answer directly. 'All I can say, Myles, is that this is the most idealist cause I've ever worked for.'

CHAPTER FIFTY-ONE
Galla Security Offices, Iraq

Myles realised Placidia was serious. 'OK, Placidia,' he said. 'So what's the most important thing, then?'

Placidia invited Myles to come towards the desk, while she turned on one of the computers. Slowly the machine made noises to indicate it was booting up.

'This is just a normal PC,' she said. 'We got the software from the man in Las Vegas. It's all quite easy, really.' She clicked the mouse over to an unnamed folder, which opened. Inside she clicked on a file marked 'Senate Dump'. 'This programme...' Her words trailed off as she concentrated on the keyboard. A box appeared on the screen with the options 'Start' or 'Cancel'. Placidia moved the mouse over to 'Start' and clicked.

She paused to check the programme was working, then seemed satisfied that it was. 'Done,' she announced. 'I've just started a programme which puts images of naked children onto the personal computers of fifty-five US Senators.'

Myles was aghast.

Placidia offered to explain. 'It's not all the Senators. Just those who voted against the recent immigration bill – the ones who made it harder for Africans to settle in the United States. In a few days I'll let the media know and they'll investigate.'

'But nobody's going to believe half the US Senate is into...' Myles could barely bring himself to say it, '...into *that*.'

'You think? They believed the files about the Navy Seal operation on your computer.'

'But that was just me,' said Myles. 'Not a bunch of highly respected Senators.'

Placidia shook her head. 'Myles, Congress is decadent. Everyone knows it.'

She could see Myles was still in shock.

'You don't understand how bad it's got, do you?' said Placidia. 'Like ancient Rome, America started as a republic and a democracy. But they've been bought. Senators spend their time sucking up to people with money who can fund their campaigns. Like Rome, the system has become corrupted.'

'But Placidia…'

'Power without responsibility,' insisted Placidia, refusing to allow Myles to interrupt. 'Just like Roman senators before their empire collapsed – decadence comes before decline.'

'They'll trace how the files were uploaded – just as Helen found the files on my computer were from here,' said Myles.

'I've found ways to do it differently now. There are better ways to hide the IP addresses. It'll look as though the Senators browsed the web and downloaded the files themselves.'

Myles still couldn't believe what he was hearing. 'Look, Placidia… I know you have a…a very unique sense of right and wrong. But what can be right about putting sexual images of children onto the computers of Senators? Some of them are good men and women. If they're found with child porn they'll be locked up.'

'You were locked up because of what I put on your computer and, believe me, it saved your life,' she said, smiling. 'It's true, Myles. Putting child porn on Senators' PCs will save lives too.'

'Someone's trying to kill the Senators?'

'No. Other people's lives. The lives of African people, who die every day. The reputations of a few Senators for thousands of lives. African lives – I know they count for a lot less than American lives…'

'But, Placidia, that's…just wrong.' Myles was struggling. He tried to define exactly what was bad about Placidia's 'Senate Dump' programme: 'OK. Let's just suppose that this plan works,' he said. 'The fifty or so Senators who voted to keep immigrants out of their country get discovered with child porn on their computers. They have to resign and new ones come in. It doesn't mean new laws will get passed.'

'No, but it makes it more likely.'

'What would you say to a Senator who worked really hard for the people in his state? He's done nothing wrong, no scandal, nothing. Then he has to resign over child pornography.'

Placidia raised her chin, looking unashamed. 'I'd say, he shouldn't vote to condemn many thousands, perhaps millions of people, to their deaths, by denying them the right to settle in America. Sometimes you have to break a rule to save the system of rules – to save the principles which made Western civilisation.'

Myles shook his head. He just couldn't accept her logic. He wiped the sweat from his forehead and tried to exhale deeply. Fury and long-buried emotions made it hard for him to focus.

Placidia looked at him, concerned. Her voice became quiet again. 'Myles, there's more at stake here than even the lives of thousands of people who want to become US citizens. Do you know what happened to the Empire's population when Rome collapsed?'

Myles looked blank – he didn't know.

'The population collapsed, too,' explained Placidia. 'To just one-twentieth of what it had been. Nineteen out of every twenty people just couldn't survive any more. And the end of the Roman Empire brought about the Dark Ages. Knowledge was thrown away,' she said, using her hands to emphasise the point. 'Cities disintegrated. Life everywhere became more basic, more brutal...'

'And you think that's about to happen again now?'

'It's happening already. Myles, I did a lot of research to find out what brought down the Roman Empire.'

Myles nodded. 'I know,' he said. 'I tried to get hold of your thesis, but couldn't.'

'There'll be a reason for that.' She smiled. 'Look at this,' she said, turning to the computer and double-clicking on another icon. This time a home-made video appeared. It started with Placidia walking around some Roman ruins, then faded to black as nine words appeared on the screen:

The Decline of America and the Fall of Rome.

Myles peered intently at the screen. It was another of Placidia's public broadcasts – half history lesson, half taunting terrorist propaganda. 'Is this going to be released soon?' he asked.

'In a few days,' said Placidia, her eyes fixed on the screen.

The words faded and the picture returned. Placidia was stepping between fallen stone columns in an abandoned Roman town. Apart from some weeds which had taken over the collapsed architecture, she was the only living thing in the picture. She began speaking to the camera. 'When we look back at history, we try to explain what happened,' she said. 'Rarely do we ask how things could have been different. The people who went through the amazing events of the past were often surprised by them. Most people thought things would continue as they always had done. Then, as now, most big changes were only visible with hindsight – after they happened.'

Placidia turned to Myles for approval. Myles was too engrossed to return her glance. He kept watching the video.

The Placidia on the screen was opening her arms, pointing at the collapsed architecture around her. 'This used to be a vibrant Roman city,' she explained. 'It had commerce and government. It could afford great monuments. The people had baths and public games. It could even afford to send its sons off as soldiers to fight in the Middle East. Rome – like modern America – had the greatest army on earth.'

The video cut to some graffiti on one of the Roman stones. Placidia's voice continued as voiceover: 'None of these Romans expected their civilisation to collapse. But collapse it did, suddenly and completely.'

Then Placidia spoke squarely to the camera. 'I'm warning you that America could very soon face the same fate.'

The picture cut to a graph labelled 'US Share of World Trade'. The line peaked in the late 1960s at just over half, then tumbled down in the subsequent years. 'Just like the Romans, you are losing your dominance of world trade…' came the voiceover.

A second graph labelled 'US Social Mobility' appeared. Again, it showed a clear downward trend. 'The Roman Emperor Diocletian passed laws which made men take on the same occupations as their fathers,' the voiceover continued. 'In modern America, it is college fees and the who-you-know economy which mean the best jobs stay in the same families more than ever.'

Next came a graphic labelled 'US – real median income'. It was a bumpy flat line, declining slightly since the late 1970s. 'Rome, just like modern America, used to say it was getting richer every year. But towards the end, only the rich got richer in Rome, just like in modern America. To buy a home and a car and their groceries, most Americans now need to work harder than they used to thirty or forty years ago. And it's going to get worse, not better…'

The video cut back to Placidia, walking pensively through the Roman ruins. 'Some people think that Rome was brought down by lead poisoning or the plague, or by barbarians rampaging through the streets of the capital. Some say it was a costly war with the Persians in Mesopotamia – modern-day Iraq and Syria. Some blame the decision to make Christianity its official state religion, because until just a few years before it fell, the Romans had been careful to separate Church and State…'

Then Placidia spoke straight to the camera. 'But what *really* changed was its people. Roman people became different. Rome was built by citizens who were prepared to sacrifice everything for their empire. By the time it collapsed, crowds were pleading for permission to eat human flesh. The Romans had become cruel and selfish. Some said they deserved to die out…'

Pictures of great Roman buildings appeared like a series of holiday photographs. 'It is my belief that most Romans would have become better people if they knew what was coming to them,' she speculated. 'And the same is true of America today. Most Americans are addicted to things they don't need – huge houses, holidays, take-away food. And they're determined to keep out non-Americans who are prepared to work really hard for just a small part of what Americans can enjoy. You're not even helping us enjoy an American way of life in Africa. Just condemning us to death. And what you don't realise is that really you're condemning *yourselves* to death.'

Placidia reappeared on the screen to conclude her remarks. 'There are lots more similarities between the end of Rome and the forthcoming end of the United States. You'll find out the biggest one in just a few days. My point is,' said Placidia, her tone making clear she was about to conclude, 'it's *not* inevitable. You can change it. Tell your Senators to reach out to people like us. Please, help us survive. Because, if you do not, then your country will die next.'

Placidia's haunting image slowly disappeared from view as the picture faded away.

Myles silently watched the video close, stunned by what he had seen.

Eventually he turned to Placidia. 'So that's why you think the Roman Empire collapsed? The people just became too cruel and selfish?'

Placidia tilted her head and raised her eyebrows. She was pondering. 'It's a big reason,' she accepted. 'Look at adverts on American TV today – and in Europe, too. Most of them ridicule someone and say 'buy this product to feel superior'. No advertiser could sell something because it was good for civilisation. Even patriotism has gone out of fashion. And when they sell something that's good for charity or the environment, they just offer to make people feel smug. "Ask what you can do for your country" became "ask what your country can do for you",' quoted Placidia, well aware she was reversing one of President Kennedy's most famous phrases.

'And it was like that in ancient Rome?' asked Myles.

'Yes. In the early days, people were proud to fight for Rome. People made sacrifices for their civilisation. By the end they were cutting off their thumbs to avoid the draft. Everybody felt they deserved wealth and security, but no one would work for it.'

Myles was still sceptical. There was something she wasn't saying. 'So you think that by doing all this – sending a car-bomb to Wall Street, poisoning people, digging up the plague – you can make Americans come together again?'

'It wasn't the plague,' interrupted Placidia. 'I made sure those men dug up something else – an illness they had been vaccinated against. And it was a disease which wouldn't have survived underground anyway.'

'It was deliberate?' queried Myles, confused.

Placidia nodded as she confronted him. 'You still don't get it, do you?' Her eyes were wide, like a teenager desperately trying to be believed. 'Look, America is in serious danger. Really, it is. Believe me, I can't tell you exactly why, but if you don't help me…' She leant forwards, about to make a gesture to Myles. She put her hand on his cheek. Myles wondered whether she was about to kiss him.

Then they were disturbed…

CHAPTER FIFTY-TWO
Galla Security HQ, Iraq

Myles and Placidia turned to see Juma swagger in with a grin on his face and an AK-47 in his hands. Juma made a point of leaving armed guards at the door, which he closed behind him. 'Hello, ladies,' he mocked.

Both Myles and Placidia nodded respectfully, acknowledging his presence.

He turned to his wife, looking cocky. 'So, has your history-professor man agreed?'

Placidia's eyes turned down as she shook her head. 'I've not asked him yet,' she said.

Myles checked both of their faces. 'Asked me what?'

Placidia paused before she explained herself. 'Myles, you know that Rome was besieged before it was first ransacked in 410. The Goths who stormed the city that year just wanted a homeland, like us. They surrounded Rome for almost two years, stopping food going in and people going out. As the city began to starve, the Senate of Rome agreed to pay off the Goths in return for them lifting the siege. But the Senate couldn't raise the funds because the rich people in the city just hid their gold and silver, so there was no wealth to collect. Most of them buried it.'

Myles found himself nodding. 'That's why archaeologists still find treasure buried in central Rome.' He saw Placidia nodding, and began to imagine what she had in mind. 'But Placidia, people have paper money now, and stocks and shares. You can't bury that in the ground.'

Placidia was about to reply when Juma interrupted her. 'It's like this,' he declared. 'I've got hundreds of people who need to be paid off. This private security company, for a start.'

'Your mercenaries, you mean?' asked Myles.

Juma smiled and started speaking more slowly. 'Placidia's already given me my own personal history lesson. She told me that the great Roman military which won an empire was gradually replaced by mercenaries, but they eventually lost it.'

'Paying for mercenaries pretty much bankrupted ancient Rome,' confirmed Placidia, underwriting Juma's words and nodding as she spoke.

Juma began to grin. 'See – it was private security companies like mine which came to rule the Roman Empire.' He poked a finger towards Myles' face, then slowly dragged it across his chin. Myles' chin was covered in hair and stubble. He hadn't shaved for several days. 'So Myles, I need you to become our fundraiser.'

Myles didn't answer with words, although his body language was responding with a very clear 'no'.

Juma turned to Placidia, mocking surprise. 'The professor doesn't like the idea?' he said. Then he caressed Myles' jaw again, slowly rolling his fingers around Myles' face. Suddenly, he grabbed it firmly, and thrust his face towards Myles. 'Would you prefer a bullet in that beautiful head of yours?'

Myles took Juma's hand away, then tried to defuse the situation with his humour. 'I'd be a hopeless fundraiser – I can't even get myself a pay rise.'

Juma grinned, exposing his rotten teeth.

Placidia stepped in, more serious than ever. 'Myles, the stakes are high here.'

Myles remembered what she had just told him: *Juma wants you dead.* The stakes were very high.

Juma started lecturing him. 'Myles, as the Roman Empire weakened, the imperial mint started putting less and less gold in their "gold" coins. A few emperors tried to stop it, like bringing in fixed prices for basic foodstuffs or decreeing how much gold there had to be in the coins. But it didn't work. The Romans had to establish what's called a "fiat" currency – a currency which only had value because the government said it did…'

Myles could tell Juma was just reciting what Placidia had taught him, but he didn't want to interrupt.

'Well, America is like that now,' said Juma. 'Forty years ago the dollar stopped being exchangeable for gold. Now they just keep printing dollar bills. Congress can't raise taxes, and they can't afford to spend less on the military or other federal programmes, so the deficit just keeps growing.'

Placidia was nodding along. 'It's even worse than in ancient Rome,' she explained. 'In Rome, only the Emperor could mint coins. But in modern America, the banks create money and they've bought off the government. The system's already out of control.'

Juma grinned again. 'And we just need them to print a little more for us. Easy.'

Myles shrugged in resignation. 'You know, ever since the Boston tea party, the Americans have taken badly to Englishmen asking them for money.' He squared up to Juma. 'I can't do it,' he said.

Placidia interrupted before Juma could answer. 'Myles, you don't have to do much. There's the big currency conference coming up. You just need to explain the history of Rome. Tell the rich bankers and the governments to offer up some cash. Make them do what the Roman Senate and the Emperor failed to do and put the future of civilisation before themselves. Please, Myles.'

'You want me to help blackmail the world economy?' said Myles. He shook his head. Whatever was at stake, he just couldn't do it.

Juma smiled – the Englishman was as straight-talking as he was. Then the Somali pirate grabbed a tuft of Myles' hair and pulled it sharply to one side. 'That's OK, Myles,' he said. 'That's what we thought you'd say. I can deal with the currency conference without you. I'll go there alone. It's not a problem.'

Placidia glared at Myles, desperately urging him to reconsider. 'Myles, think about what you're saying. Could we reach a compromise on this?'

But Juma had already swung his gun into Myles' ribs.

Myles bent over and stumbled, almost falling to the floor.

Juma cocked his weapon. 'It's OK, Placidia. Time for me to give this man a history lesson of my own.'

Juma quickly lifted his gun onto his shoulder, then grabbed Myles' shirt. Myles felt himself flung against the wall.

Placidia tugged on Juma's arm. 'Let him go,' she pleaded.

Juma shook his head.

Placidia tried again. 'If you kill him, they'll try to kill us.'

'They'll try to kill us anyway,' replied Juma. He whipped his hand over Myles' face. Then, with Placidia watching in shock, he kicked Myles – a high kick, in the stomach.

Myles bent double, then felt himself flung out of the room. He caught a last glimpse of Placidia – she was almost tearful – only the second time ever that Myles had seen her show real emotions. Myles could tell: Placidia really believed his life was in danger.

Juma slammed the door behind him, then stood over Myles. Three of Juma's men came in, clearly knowing what was going to happen. Myles heard them boasting to each other in their African dialect, taking pride in what they were about to do. Juma took command. 'Stand up, Englishman,' he bellowed.

Half frog-marched, half jostled, Myles was taken through the remaining offices of Galla Security towards an exit at the back. The door opened out onto a bright car park. Juma directed him towards a white Toyota Corolla. 'Sit,' he commanded, as if Myles were a dog.

He was manoeuvred into the back section of the vehicle, where grinning Somali gunmen sat either side of him, with a third opposite. Juma took the driver's seat and turned on the engine.

Myles sized up the men around him. One of them offered qat leaves around. Myles declined, but the other men gladly grabbed some. Tiny pieces of half-reduced leaves stuck to their teeth. They showed decaying gums when they grinned. Qat, Myles knew, took two hours to have maximum effect. In two hours, these men would want to demonstrate their machismo. He had just two hours to escape.

The Toyota Corolla drove through a back entrance in the breeze-block perimeter wall, leaving Galla Security behind. The vehicle bumped the passengers as it started to accelerate, making its way onto the highway.

Myles was surprised when, after less than half a mile, the vehicle turned off the main route. The gap in the kerbstones led to a vague side road. Soon they were completely off-road. No more buildings from here. Juma was taking Myles into the desert.

Myles could not react and began to wonder if he was there at all. It was a sensation he had read about: an out-of-body experience. As danger increases, people begin to imagine themselves from a distance. The mind detaches from a frightening situation, trying to take the body with it. Myles was mentally removing himself from the car now.

Snap out of it, he thought. But he couldn't snap out of it. He sensed the bravado of the men beside and opposite him. He looked at one of them, who grinned back.

The men leant and lurched as the Corolla started to reel over the uneven ground. When the front wheels impacted against a bar of half-dirt, half-sand, Juma's men whooped in delight. For them it was like a fairground ride, or a hunting expedition. A hunting expedition with a guaranteed kill.

Myles tried to focus on what could well be his demise. How could he save himself? He knew that, because he was cooperating, they weren't guarding him as tightly as they might. He kept trying to think through his situation. If he tried to escape and failed, he wouldn't get a second chance.

He would have to play along until a good chance came. To stay obedient until he knew he could escape.

Was there any chance to fight back? No. Was Juma going to try to kill him? Probably, but it wasn't certain. What could Myles say which would make Juma think twice?

After a couple of minutes where the track had become rougher, the Toyota halted. Myles heard the engine stop and the vibrations cease. Juma was instantly out of the door, standing close to where Myles was sitting. He dropped the back flap of the vehicle.

'Down,' instructed Juma.

The Somali gang men obeyed instantly, and jumped down. Myles had no choice but to follow.

He was poked in the back by the barrel of a gun, and found himself led towards a slight slope in the desert. He tried briefly to look around: nothing but dirt and sand in all directions.

'On your knees,' barked Juma.

Myles turned to Juma and tried to talk. 'I can help you achieve what you're trying to achieve,' he offered.

Juma rocked his head back, laughing. 'I know, Mr Munro. You're about to. Down.'

'Juma…'

'Down.' Juma's instruction was absolutely clear. Myles started opening his mouth to offer more but was immediately deafened by a burst of automatic gunfire. Bullets drilled into the ground in front of him, spitting dirt onto Myles' shins.

Juma leant close to Myles, and looked at him wide-eyed. Then he slowly mouthed the word again. 'D-O-W-N.'

Reluctantly, Myles started to put his knees on the slope. He tried to kneel facing Juma and his three accomplices, but Juma made clear he wanted Myles to be facing away. Myles swung himself around until he was looking at the sand.

There were a few moments of silence. Then Myles felt the nuzzle of a gun barrel pressing on the back of his neck. It was pushing his head down. He duly lowered his face, until his nose and chin were firmly against the slope in the desert.

Then Myles felt the pressure of the nuzzle pull away. He understood he was expected to stay in position. He'd been lucky so far – could he be lucky again?

Some distance behind him, he heard quiet words being exchanged between the four Somalis.

The discussion stopped, followed by almost ten seconds of silence.

Very slowly, Myles tried to lift his face from the slope. Deep down he hoped the men might have departed. Perhaps he had been left alone in the desert.

He turned to look. He wasn't alone.

Juma's gun was raised to his shoulder, and Myles was looking down the barrel.

He saw a flash leave the end of the metal tube, and sensed a huge noise as a bullet shot towards him.

The last thing he felt was the pressure from the pulse of air which accompanied the bullet as it left Juma's gun. He never felt the bullet hit. Instead, he slumped lifelessly into the dirt slope.

CHAPTER FIFTY-THREE
Capitol Hill, Washington DC

As a journalist, Helen used to keep away from press conferences whenever she could. It was a statement of independence: she didn't like being summoned by a public figure, and she hated to help them promote themselves. Press conferences were old-fashioned and pompous. They were for losers.

But now her lover's reputation was at stake. He had saved her life in Istanbul. She had to do all she could for him.

Myles needed her. Even though press conferences were for losers, it was better to be a loser than to lose *him*, she thought.

And so, through a contact, she booked a meeting room in the Senate. She called her colleagues in the press corps, and prepared all the information a journalist would want to cover the story.

When her friends arrived, they were given a pack of evidence: the material found on Myles' computer, an affidavit from a respected Silicon Valley tech firm saying how the files had been planted, and details on exactly where in Iraq the files had been sent from.

She knew it was a good story – if she were a journalist, she would have covered it. Except, she was a journalist, and she couldn't cover it because she was part of it. That was why it felt so odd to walk into a room full of her colleagues and sit in front of them. It made her less of a journalist than she used to be.

'Thank you all for coming,' she began. 'You know, I used to avoid press conferences like the plague. But since I almost caught the plague recently, I thought I'd give press conferences a go, too…'

There was a little laughter around the room. 'You better not be contagious anymore!' heckled one of her friends.

'Thanks,' acknowledged Helen, accepting the joke. 'Actually, it turned out to be a blood infection, and I'd like to express my respect and gratitude to the highly professional doctors and nurses in Turkey, who gave me such excellent medical treatment.'

She began going through the evidence in the information packs, holding up each piece of paper in turn. 'Myles Munro has been trying to *save* America, not destroy it,' she explained. 'He's done all he can and he's not even from this country…'

Hands went up. She picked someone from the front row. 'Helen, who do you blame for all this?' came the question.

'Well, it looks like someone in the Department for Homeland Security made the wrong conclusion about the information on Myles' computer,' said Helen, trying to be fair.

'So you blame Homeland Security?'

'This isn't about blame. It's about tackling threats to America. For that, Myles Munro needs to be able to work with the authorities. He shouldn't have to run from them.'

Several journalists shouted at once. Helen chose a woman reporter from a rival network. 'Do you think Homeland is doing enough to stop Juma's plot?' asked the woman.

Helen nodded. 'I think the plot is real. Juma is ruthless – we know that. And his wife is absolutely crazy. She may be clever, but it's an evil sort of cleverness. She's an expert on ancient Rome. Perhaps she's the greatest threat here.'

'But do you think Homeland is doing enough?' repeated the questioner.

Helen shrugged. 'I don't know what Homeland's doing,' she admitted. 'Apart from keeping Myles Munro on the run.'

The rival reporter looked down to write notes. Her face was dismissive.

'Where is Myles Munro now?' asked a print journalist.

'I don't know that. I'm sorry,' said Helen.

'But you were with him in Istanbul…'

'Yes, he saved my life there,' acknowledged Helen. 'He may have been heading to Iraq. But I don't know whether he reached the country.'

'So he could be working with Islamic extremists in Iraq?'

Helen shook her head. 'No,' she insisted. 'And the headline which called him a "Runaway Terrorist" is about as wrong as it could be.'

She was beginning to feel outnumbered. Even though she knew many of the journalists, it didn't stop them asking nasty questions.

Then a tall frame entered at the back of the room. Helen saw him first and smiled as if she had just been saved. The press pack saw she was distracted and turned to see who it was.

The man strode towards the front of the room, bypassing cameras, careful not to knock any of the broadcast equipment. He wore cowboy boots and an open-neck shirt.

If this press conference wasn't news already, it was now.

Helen welcomed him to the front. 'Ladies and Gentlemen,' she announced, the relief obvious in her voice. 'The Chief Executive of the Roosevelt Guardians and son of the Senator in whose name this room is booked. Dick Roosevelt.'

Roosevelt junior knew how to make the best of theatre. He held his hands up in a 'you got me' gesture as the media shouted out to him.

'Any news on your father, Richard?'

'Do you agree with Ms Bridle about Myles Munro, sir?'

'Your Roosevelt Guardians are managing security at the currency conference in Rome – will it be attacked?'

'How safe is America, Dick?'

Instead of answering the questions, Dick Roosevelt just let them come. He had a natural ability to relax in the spotlight – just like his father. It's the picture that matters.

He made a point of allowing each person in the room to speak, pointing at them in turn. Only once the press conference had exhausted itself of questions did he volunteer some words of his own. 'More questions than I ever got in school,' he quipped. 'I'll try to give you more right answers than I gave my teachers.'

Some of the journalists chuckled.

Then Roosevelt became more serious. 'Look, I'm helping out this fine woman here because our country is in trouble,' he said firmly. 'There is a plot to destroy America as Rome was destroyed, a plot led by some very mad and bad people – hell, I should know, I've met them. And we're not doing enough to keep America safe.'

He paused to find one of the broadcast cameras. He levelled at it. 'Now there are two brave men out there. They're in harm's way. They're missing in action. They're probably suffering big time. Myles Munro is a hero, and so is my father. America needs to find them, and we need to help them.'

A journalist interrupted him with a question. 'What do you think about the African refugees in Italy, Mr Roosevelt? Should we let them into America?'

Roosevelt tried not to be fazed by the question. He paused and looked thoughtful. Then he began to recite something:

'Give me your tired, your poor,
Your huddled masses yearning to breathe free,
The wretched refuse of your teeming shore.
Send these, the homeless, tempest-tost to me,
I lift my lamp beside the golden door!

'That's the poem on the Statue of Liberty,' he explained. 'The words which greeted our great-grandparents arriving in America, right?'

There was much nodding in the room – they recognised the quote.

Roosevelt carried on: 'Well, sometimes America is a victim of American values,' he said. 'Our hospitality can be abused. Our doors have opened so wide we've let in people who aren't really poor. We've even let in terrorists. And – hell – we're already full up.'

'But is that a *Christian* attitude, sir – "No room at the inn", sir?'

Roosevelt smiled again. He made clear he didn't have much respect for the questioner. 'Look, I'm a Christian,' he said, nodding. 'And I want this to be a Christian country. I believe Christian values ought to be taught in schools – that was the one mistake our founding fathers made, and we're suffering for it now. But being a Christian does not mean letting an alien religion invade our country…'

Suddenly Roosevelt lost his audience. He wondered whether it was something he said, but realised he was being upstaged.

Helen noticed it too: it was something else. All the mobiles in the room – switched to silent for the press conference – seemed to be vibrating.

The reporters at the back immediately started talking on their phones, breaking the atmosphere of the event. A few dashed out of the room while others started to pack up. In just a few seconds Helen, Myles and the Roosevelts had gone from being the lead story to old news.

Dick Roosevelt put up his hands again – his 'you got me' gesture seemed particularly appropriate. Roosevelt caught Helen's eye – no point continuing until they had the journalists' attention again.

Helen agreed, suspecting she had been right about press conferences – they *were* for losers after all. She asked one of her journalist friends what the breaking story was, and was shown the message which had just come through:

> *'Department of Homeland Security announces it is impounding the personal computers of all members of congress and their staff. Indecent images have been found on at least fourteen machines...'*

Dick Roosevelt saw it too, then quickly whipped out his phone and dialled one of his contacts. 'Get Susan, the Homeland Security woman who used to work for my father,' he commanded. 'Tell her to find out what the hell is going on.'

CHAPTER FIFTY-FOUR
Western Desert, Iraq

Myles had always been curious about religion but never attracted to any particular one. He loved the thought of an afterlife. He longed for a place beyond the world as explained by science. He always wished for a fundamental reason to do things, and hoped religion might be able to deliver.

There is no afterlife.

But he had always been disappointed. Religions might offer comfort, but that was all. To Myles, it was all just empty calories. Why believe in a religion for a spiritual world when you could just believe in a spiritual world anyway?

There can be no afterlife.

And did God, or a spiritual world, or an afterlife, make sense? Could they ever? Since death was by definition the end of life, 'life after death' was a contradiction. If there was such a thing, it couldn't be his life which was continuing.

There is no such thing as an afterlife.

And yet Myles sensed something. Not with his eyes: they were blurry. Not with his ears: they were recoiling. He had even lost his sense of gravity: he no longer knew which way was up. But somehow he was still aware.

Myles foundered. Where was he? Not heaven. Not hell...

Vaguely he became aware of voices. Laughing voices. Male voices.

No holy book described where he was now.

He found his lungs straining, and reflexively pulled back his head. He gasped for air, then tried to spit dirt from his mouth. *He was alive.*

Myles' eyes began showing him the bank of dirt. He was where he had been before he had been shot.

Someone grabbed at one of his legs. He felt his arms being pulled taut. He was being tied up.

He understood the laughing voices now: Juma and his acolytes were prostrate in hysterics. A mock execution. The bullet had missed. Deliberately.

Myles bent over to see his wrists being bound with cheap wire. The Somali man who was doing it looked up at Myles, still intrigued by the Englishman's reaction. The man opened his mouth, revealing gums covered in half-chewed qat.

Only as his ankles were tied did Myles feel he was back in the real world again – half happy to have survived, half terrified by the knowledge that the mock execution might be repeated at any time, perhaps next time for real. He was completely at Juma's mercy.

Juma slung his weapon on his shoulder, moving his gun as if it completed his display of marksmanship. 'It's all right – you're still alive,' hissed Juma. 'For now.'

Juma's men laughed again. Myles refused to react.

Myles' height meant it took all three of the Somalis to carry him out from the dirt and back into the Toyota Corolla. They didn't offer him a seat this time. Instead, they just lifted his body onto the metal floor of the pick-up and pushed him forward until they could shut the flap at the back. Juma's men climbed in, glaring down at their prey.

One of them kicked him and sniggered, as if he were a plaything. Again Myles refused to react. Then the vibrations of the vehicle's engine started again, and the pick-up started rolling.

Unable to see in any direction other than straight up, Myles didn't know where they were going. From the position of the sun in the sky, he guessed they were travelling north or north-west. But it didn't really matter. It was all desert round here. He was just being driven even further away from any sort of habitation. Even less chance of escape than before…

As the vehicle bumped and rocked on the uneven desert terrain, Myles was jostled around on the floor of the pick-up. He tried to test his bindings, disguising each movement as an unavoidable jolt from the journey. Both his wrists and ankles were very tightly secured. No way to loosen them.

The butt of an AK-47 was just inches from his head. He considered trying to grab it and use it somehow, but it was hopeless. Myles couldn't even get to his feet. It was no way to escape.

The journey lasted about half an hour, although the timing was hard to tell. The Somali gang men passed drinking water amongst themselves several times – water Myles desperately wanted for himself – before the vehicle stopped and the ignition ceased.

Someone bent down to cut the binding on Myles' ankles. His legs were released. Myles didn't know whether to thank the man or kick him, but he quickly realised the three Somalis guarding him weren't interested in him anymore. They seemed to be looking around. It was as if they had found some scenery in the desert. Myles could only imagine.

They followed the same routine as for the mock execution: Juma out, the back flap down, and everybody else out too, with Myles being dragged off last of all.

But this time they were definitely *somewhere*. This wasn't just a random spot of desert. This was an abandoned town. An old Roman town.

Myles had read about these: there were several of them through-out modern-day Syria and Iraq, most of them well preserved by the dry desert climate. Settlements like the one he was in now had been created by the ancient empire and thrived for several hundred years. Then they had been left – either when the ground was lost to the Persians in the eastern wars between 200AD and 350AD, or when the Roman Empire itself collapsed in the century which followed. They had been abandoned ever since.

Myles squinted as he looked around: fallen columns and carved stones lay everywhere. The Toyota Corolla had parked on the remnants of an old Roman road. He was not far from a circle of stone benches, a mini-amphitheatre where 'games' had kept people entertained almost two thousand years ago.

Suddenly Myles recognised where he was: it was where Placidia had filmed her second video – the video she had shown him earlier, which explained how the Roman Empire had died.

As he blinked in amazement at his surroundings – a response which made Juma lean back with a grin – he turned to see the one modern structure in the whole area. It was a tent, just like the one over the excavation site in Istanbul.

Juma saw Myles had noticed it. The pirate leader made a gesture to someone. Myles didn't know who.

Then the tent flap opened from the inside, and an old man was forced to march outside, into the light and heat of the desert afternoon.

Myles and the old man stood staring at each other. Like Myles, the man's wrists were bound. The man had not shaved, and his sunken cheeks suggested he had not been given the food and water a 69-year-old needed to remain healthy in the desert heat.

As the man walked up to Myles, lifting his face in defiance of Juma and ignoring the Somalis who stood around with their guns, Myles greeted him with respect. 'It's good to see you, Senator,' he said.

The Senator nodded and clenched his jaw against the desert heat. Although the man had been weakened by his captivity, Myles could tell Sam Roosevelt had lost none of his will.

Myles and the Senator tried to shake hands, but the wire around their wrists made it difficult. They managed as best they could. Myles noticed the Senator's forearms: they had become thin, almost skeletal.

The Senator squinted up at Myles. 'I thought they'd let you go,' he said. 'Did they double-cross you, too?' Roosevelt emphasised the words 'double-cross', accusing Juma and his team as they listened in.

Myles thought of explaining everything he'd been through – in New York, his arrest in Rome, his escape in London, the factory in Germany and the excavation site in Istanbul. Then he decided there would be better times for all that. 'They did let me go,' he acknowledged. 'Then they tried to kill me a few times, then they captured me again.'

The Senator smiled. 'So we're captives again.'

Myles nodded. 'The only difference is that this time we're in Iraq,' he said.

Without dropping his outward show of confidence, the Senator was clearly struck by something Myles said. He turned his face and lowered an eyebrow. He leant in to Myles and spoke more quietly. 'Iraq? You sure?'

Myles nodded again. Briefly he explained how he knew they were in Iraq's Western Desert. They couldn't have travelled long enough from An Nukhayb to have crossed a national border.

'How come there's no military presence?' asked the Senator. 'We trained Iraqi troops. They should be here. I've seen Senate papers on this.' The Senator slumped. His life's work in the Senate had just been devalued. There was more evidence from the Romans two thousand years ago than of Americans who had just left. 'So this is what we leave behind when the United States retreats?' he lamented.

'Where did you think we were, Senator?'

'They took me on a boat to Egypt, then east through the Sinai. I assumed we were in Jordan or Syria. These guys must have gotten into Iraq without even climbing over a fence.'

Juma came over and imposed himself on the two Westerners. 'Gentlemen. I'm sure you've got lots to talk about.'

'We have, Mr Juma,' retorted the Senator, 'but not with you.'

'That's OK,' gloated Juma. 'I've brought you both here to give you even more to discuss.'

'We're not running out of material.'

Roosevelt's caustic defiance was missed by Juma, who had already turned to some of his men. They started opening the doors of an SUV with blacked-out windows, which had been parked for some time behind the tent. A Somali man was dragged from inside. Like Myles and the Senator, his wrists were bound.

Myles recognised him at once: the security guard from the factory in Germany. Somehow, despite the explosion, he must have survived. But Myles couldn't tell whether the man had escaped to Juma, or been captured by him.

Juma turned back to Myles. 'Englishman – you've met this man before,' he said.

Myles confirmed that he recognised the man.

'Then you know how useless he is,' huffed Juma. 'You know what the Romans used to do with people like him?'

Myles didn't respond. The Senator answered for him, kicking back his head as he spoke. 'I know what the Romans would do with people like you, Juma.'

Juma laughed. 'Except that the Romans respected power, Senator. And that's what I have and you do not, gentlemen.'

'For now.'

Juma shrugged. 'Yes, but when else matters?'

The Somali pirate wandered towards the hapless guard, who was now shaking. 'Senator, the Romans would have used this man for entertainment,' he explained. 'They put slaves, Christians and criminals in a ring and made them fight to the death. It was a spectator sport. If death fights were shown on American TV today they would draw in huge audiences.'

Juma turned to Myles. 'This man almost killed you. Do you want your revenge?'

'No, I don't.'

'That's very Christian of you,' mocked Juma. 'Maybe I should put you both in the ring and just let him have the weapon. Give him a second chance. What do you think?'

Myles remained silent.

'Senator, you're in favour of capital punishment,' said Juma. 'This is your chance to be an executioner.'

'It's too early for capital punishment,' replied the Senator. 'He's not been on death row for fifteen years.'

'Former Navy Seal and super macho Senator Sam Roosevelt – afraid to kill?' Juma said his words with a taunting tone, teasing the Senator for a reaction.

'Juma, there are lots of people here I'm not afraid to kill at all. It's just that he isn't one of them.'

Juma ambled away, smiling thinly to cover his lack of a reply. 'OK, so neither of you will help me entertain my men by killing this man?'

Myles and the Senator refused to respond.

Juma ignored them. 'Then I'll have to make him die myself.'

The Somali gang leader lifted his Kalashnikov and aimed it at the man, who collapsed to his knees. The prisoner was whimpering, begging Juma not to fire.

Myles called out as Juma cocked his weapon. 'Don't, Juma.'

Juma looked at Myles with a sarcastic expression on his face. 'Of course I wouldn't kill him with a gun. Where's the entertainment in that?' Juma shook his head. 'My men have seen thousands of fatal bullet wounds. No. I want to offer them entertainment. Just like the Romans: *entertainment*.' He emphasised the word 'entertainment' as if he was reciting it from a textbook, as if he had done the research himself. Myles had seen many academic pretenders at Oxford. Juma's words confirmed how little the pirate leader really understood – except about killing.

Juma's men brought out a cloth bag. This was placed over the man's sobbing face, down as far as his nose. They pulled it tight and tied it at the back, leaving his mouth exposed. Then he was fed what looked like a string of four yellow sausages. An instruction – a single word – was yelled at him, and he began to eat them. Although he tried to chew and swallow, the soft sausage-like tubes were hard to consume. When he gagged, he was kicked until he continued. Terrified, the Somali security guard kept going for several minutes. Finally he finished the 'meal'.

'Good. Now, take off his hood,' ordered Juma.

The hood was untied and lifted off.

Then Juma called out some words. The men who had fed the guard the sausages understood immediately and ran away as fast as they could. The guard himself looked wide-eyed in a mix of disbelief and terror. Then he tried standing up, desperately looking where to go.

Juma laughed. 'Gentlemen, I've explained to this man that he's just eaten a remote-control bomb…'

The terrified man started running around, at first not sure what to do. Then he decided it was best to go near to some of the other pirates. He hoped that Juma wouldn't trigger the device if it meant killing some of his other men at the same time.

Myles protested. 'Let him go, Juma.'

'I have, Mr Englishman. Look – he's running free!'

The man tried to clutch one of Juma's men, but the Somali drew his AK-47 and fired it into the desert ground to keep the man away.

The man tried to approach Juma, but Juma just laughed and spat at him.

Finally, in absolute desperation, the man decided to run away as far as he could, hoping either that Juma was bluffing or that he could get out of range of whatever device the pirate warlord was planning to use.

While Juma's men laughed at the man's efforts to escape, Juma was handed a small radio-like transmitter. He offered the button to Myles and the Senator. Both refused to press it.

Finally Juma laid his thumb on the button and looked up as he pushed. Instantly the running Somali exploded into a red cloud. The spectators, both voluntary and captive, crouched in reaction to the blast.

When they looked to see where the man had been, there was hardly anything to see. Just one limb and half a torso seemed to remain visible. Every other part of him had disintegrated in a mist of tatters and debris which would soon be covered by the desert sands.

CHAPTER FIFTY-FIVE
Las Vegas, USA

Even though Paul Pasgarius the Third had heard nothing more from 'Constantine' for well over a week, he guessed the caller would contact him again.

This time he was ready with special software, so he might have a chance to locate the anonymous voice. After all, if the voice tried to blackmail him again, he guessed his best hope would be to try to blackmail Constantine in return.

So when his computer flashed that there was another incoming call, again from an 'Unknown Caller', he switched on his tracking programme before he answered.

'Paul Pasgarius the Third speaking,' he said with false confidence, one eye on the location programme as he spoke.

'Good evening, Paul,' came the voice.

'Constantine – hello,' replied Paul. 'I hope you've called to report one hundred per cent customer satisfaction.'

The heavily disguised voice seemed to chuckle a bit. 'Yes, it worked,' said Constantine.

'Good,' said Paul, guessing the voice was more male than female. And whoever it was, they sounded more commanding than they had last time. It was a voice of authority.

'Now there's one more thing for you to do,' continued Constantine.

'You can't blackmail me now,' said Paul, chewing his gum near the microphone on his headset. 'Haven't you seen the news? Half of congress has been doing what I've been doing.'

'You're right, Paul,' replied Constantine. 'Which is why this time I'm going to pay you. Cash.'

Paul hadn't expected that. He chewed his gum more slowly. Perhaps he was lucky to hear from Constantine again after all.

'What I want you to do, Paul, is help me clean up a few computer trails. There are some tracks which need to be covered.'

'And the cash?'

'I'll be giving that to you in person.'

'How much?'

The garbled voice laughed again. 'You don't get to ask how much. More than enough is the answer.'

Paul stared hopelessly at his software programme. It had stopped searching, and simply come up with the answer 'Source location unknown'. He shook his head, annoyed. 'Where will I meet you?' he asked.

'In Rome,' came Constantine's answer. Then he commanded, 'Buy your own air ticket.'

CHAPTER FIFTY-SIX
Western Desert, Iraq

Myles had been briefed about 'consumable' bombs when he was with military intelligence: as deadly as a suicide vest but much harder to detect. Al Qaeda had sent a man with a bomb inside him to assassinate an important Saudi royal in 2009, and he had managed to detonate himself in front of his target. It was just a technical flaw with the bomb which had allowed Prince Mohammed bin Nayef to survive. Now it seemed that Juma had adopted the technology. Worse, the Somali gang leader had made it work effectively.

Juma was still grinning. 'It's good, huh?'

Myles and the Senator glanced at one another, each inviting the other to speak. The Senator offered the first retort. 'So good, Juma, I think you ought to try it yourself.'

'Thank you Senator. I'm glad you found it entertaining.' Juma gave a false laugh as he swaggered around. 'You know what this place is?'

'Tell me, Mr Juma,' asked the Senator, his tone making plain that he didn't care for Juma's games. 'What is this place?'

Juma didn't answer immediately. Instead he redirected his question towards Myles, feigning an overeducated accent. 'Mr Oxford Academic, sir. Do you know what this place is?'

'Looks like an abandoned Roman town,' offered Myles.

'Correct. Well done – you've done your reading.' Juma's voice was overloaded with sarcasm. 'Yes,' he said, talking as much to his men as to Myles. 'This rubble used to be one of the last outposts of the Roman Empire. The Persians did to this town what I'll do to America. The Romans had to abandon it. And do you know what they did here?'

Myles didn't respond.

'You don't know, Englishman?' taunted Juma.

'No, I don't.'

'The Oxford brainbox doesn't know? I'll tell you what the Romans did here,' said Juma, ambling closer. 'They kept eunuchs here.' Juma put his hand on his crotch and jumped around howling. His men all laughed at him, reacting from fear as much as humour.

Then Juma swung round and grabbed Myles' crotch. 'And are you a eunuch? Mr Myles, sir, Mr Munro? Mr Oxford University?' Juma's voice had become serious and threatening. He pushed his sweating face into Myles' and breathed his words at him. 'Is that why you didn't "do" my wife? Huh?' Juma tightened his grip. 'You couldn't do it for her?'

Juma pressed hard. Myles suddenly bent double – he was no eunuch.

The Somali warlord lifted his knee into Myles' face, knocking him to the ground. Myles rolled on the desert scrub. His wrists still tied, it was hard for him to recover his balance.

Then Juma stepped towards the Senator. 'You won't go down as easily as him, will you, Senator?'

Roosevelt was opening his mouth to answer when Juma swung his forearm back, and punched squarely into the Senator's stomach. The Senator, like Myles before him, bent over. Then Juma pushed him onto the ground too. Roosevelt landed awkwardly on his side.

Juma stood over them both, watching them writhe and gloating at them. 'Gentlemen, it seems you both like the floor,' he teased. 'The Romans used to teach their gladiators how to die. When a gladiator had suffered a fatal wound, he was expected to drop to his knees then fall to his right. It let spectators know when to look away. Isn't that thoughtful?'

Myles and the Senator were recovering, but there were still guns pointed at them. There was no chance of them being able to take Juma by surprise.

'Drag them into the ring,' Juma ordered to his men. 'Time for some fun.'

Myles and the Senator were both grabbed by their bound wrists and pulled across the rough ground. A ridge of stone bumped out of the desert floor. The two men were dragged across it. They were dropped in the middle of a broken circle of old Roman limestone.

They were in the arena.

Juma was still feigning a half-laugh. He nodded to one of his men who flicked open a cheap handheld video-recorder. A small red light appeared on the front of the device, which was pointed at Myles and the Senator. Myles noticed Juma's men had pulled back.

Slowly Myles started to stand up again. Once on his feet he offered his bound hands to the Senator, helping the frail man to stand beside him.

The pirate leader giggled in expectation, but it was clear that little was happening. Juma's men were hoping to watch something violent, but there was no sign of it yet. He called out to the two Westerners, trying to mock them with his sarcasm. 'Time to fight each other – if you please, gentlemen.'

But Myles and the Senator refused to perform.

Juma raised his gun and fired a burst of bullets into the air. 'Fight!' He shouted his demand towards both men, but neither had any inclination to obey.

The Somali warlord was beginning to look powerless in front of his men. He lowered his gun barrel and pulled the trigger again. This time a splattering of metal skimmed off the ground near the Senator's feet.

Myles and the Senator recoiled from the noise, but still refused to move.

The pirate marched over to them. He grabbed each man by the neck and pushed their heads towards his. Then, speaking through his teeth, he said in a quiet but chilling tone: 'If you're lucky, I'll let one of you out of here alive,' he said. 'But unless you start fighting each other, I'm going to have to kill you both to keep my men happy. And if you just pretend to fight, or try to fix it so you both survive, then I'll make sure you both die. Do you understand?'

Myles and the Senator shared a glance. Just by their exchange of eye contact, it was clear that neither of them had any intention of following through with Juma's request. No way would they fight each other.

But Myles also knew how dangerous it would be to disappoint the Somali psychopath.

CHAPTER FIFTY-SEVEN
Western Desert, Iraq

With a sense of ceremony, Juma knocked the two men's heads together. He was looking as confident as ever: finally, the two men would obey. Then he raised his voice to the sky and shouted as loudly as he could. 'Fight!'

As his men started to cheer, Juma eyed Myles and the Senator in turn. His gaze underlined his threat: 'And if you both survive, then both of you will die.' He turned his back on the two Westerners and started to walk to the edge of the arena. Myles and the Senator were left isolated in the middle.

The Senator murmured to Myles. 'Got any ideas?'

'Only that we've got to get out of here.'

'Agreed,' said the Senator. 'Then we pretend to fight until we can think of something.'

Myles nodded.

As Juma reached the edge of the stone circle, he turned and stared at the two men.

No one was moving. Then Juma fired another burst of gunfire into the air. 'Only one of you can leave that ring alive…'

Finally, Myles and the Senator rammed into each other. Because their hands were tied, as their shoulders collided they both lost their balance. The two men spun down to the ground.

Juma's men cheered.

Myles and the Senator scrabbled around in the dirt. Slowly they began to get back on their feet.

Myles looked around as he stood up again, keeping his voice down. 'Could we run into the desert?'

'Not fast enough,' whispered the Senator. 'Could we steal some of Juma's weapons?'

The men slowly wheeled around, pretending to spar. Really they were scanning all around them, looking for something – anything – which might help them. Myles eyed Juma's Toyota. 'His vehicles?' he suggested. 'We'd need to distract his men, though.'

The look on the Senator's face said he agreed. The old man was recalling his combat experience. Myles could tell he was trying to imagine solutions. There was nothing obvious.

The two men charged into each other again. They had less energy than before. Again they tumbled to the floor. The audience enjoyed it less the second time. They were running out of time.

The Senator whispered to Myles while they were in the dust. 'Juma doesn't care which one of us comes out of here alive,' he said. 'The survivor won't be ransomed or released. He'll be killed. Juma wants us both dead.

Myles nodded: he agreed with the Senator's analysis.

As the two men were returning to their feet they were both distracted by a cry from the audience. 'Fight like you mean it!' came the call, followed by a laugh. It was Juma's voice.

Then the pirate lobbed a bayonet into the ring. Myles had to side-step fast to avoid the falling blade. It landed near the Senator's feet.

Myles and the Senator both looked down at the weapon: Juma wanted to speed things up. Whoever picked up the knife would be able to stab the other.

The Senator bent down and grabbed the handle of the bayonet with his tied hands. But he refused to attack Myles. 'Our wrists,' he said.

As he slowly moved opposite Myles, the Senator spun the blade in his hands until it was pointing towards him. He sawed away at the bindings on his wrists for several seconds. Eventually the wire was severed and fell onto the arena floor.

The spectators started to whoop as the Senator brought his hands apart. They could see him about to attack Myles, whose wrists were still bound.

The Senator threw the blade from one hand to the other, catching it easily each time. 'Run at me,' he said.

Suspicion flickered through Myles' mind. *Run at a man holding a knife?*

He hesitated. The Senator repeated himself. 'Come on, man. Run at me. I'll drop the knife and you pick it up. Run at me.' The Senator was holding the knife down, ready to impale Myles as he approached.

Who was the Senator trying to fool – Juma or Myles?

Would Sam Roosevelt kill Myles to survive, or drop the knife as he promised?

The Senator could see Myles was unsure what to do. 'Myles, you gotta trust me,' he said. Then he turned on his convincing voice – the perfect all-American accent that had won over millions of voters and almost won the US Presidency. 'We're all going bust if we ain't got trust.'

Roosevelt was speaking like an old-school politician. A statesman who really cared for more than himself. Something about his manner was convincing.

Gradually Myles nodded. The Senator braced himself. Then Myles rushed.

The two men collided. The Senator fell backwards. Pretending to be caught off guard, he let the bayonet fall from his hands.

Myles quickly rolled on the ground and returned to his feet. He rushed for the bayonet and grabbed it. The Senator barely moved – there was no contest for the weapon. Roosevelt had been true to his word.

As the old man stood back up, Myles quickly rubbed the blade against the wire on his wrists. He was too clumsy to break through easily. He tried to push harder, but it only meant the knife slipped out of his hands. It fell to the dust. The Senator gave Myles space, allowing him to pick it up and try again. Eventually Myles cut through and, as with the Senator before him, the binding dropped away.

As the audience saw Myles' hands were also free they cheered again. The contest had become even more exciting.

Myles held the weapon while he stood opposite the Senator, both men still circling slowly, pretending to look for a weakness in the other.

The Senator wiped sweat from his face. He was trying to hide his moving lips. 'OK. I've got a plan.'

'Tell me, Senator.'

'There are rocket-propelled grenades in the back of that vehicle, right?'

Myles checked behind him to confirm which vehicle the Senator was talking about. 'Yes. Go on.'

'OK, then you chase me over there. I'll grab an RPG while you escape. I'll be able to hold them off long enough.'

Myles didn't quite understand what the Senator was proposing. 'But they'll kill you. While I'm driving away, they'll kill you.'

The Senator gritted his teeth and spoke with his best sarcasm. 'Son, in case you hadn't noticed, they're going to kill us anyway.'

Then Myles realised: *the Senator was offering his life for Myles'*.

Myles gulped, slowly accepting it was the best course of action. He mouthed the words 'thank you' to the Senator, who accepted them graciously.

'Just swear to me you'll bring this guy down.'

'I will, Senator,' Myles promised.

Carefully, Myles advanced, pointing the knife towards the Senator, who stepped back. The audience were enthralled.

Myles walked forward again. Again the Senator withdrew, his face bearing the expression of someone who was prepared to die. The Senator turned to check his bearings. To Juma and the men watching it looked like the glance of a desperate man trying to see how much further he could retreat. But Myles and the Senator both knew he was working out how far he had to run to get to the Toyota Corolla.

The Senator turned back to face Myles. He knew where he needed to go. Through his eye contact he indicated he was prepared. The Senator controlled his breathing, as if he was gearing up for his last fight. He was ready.

Myles' face thanked the Senator again. It was time.

Then Myles raised the bayonet and started to lurch toward the Senator. Roosevelt turned his back and ran away as fast as he could. Straight towards the vehicle.

At first the audience cheered. Myles had run the Senator out of the arena. They watched as the Senator jumped over the stone boundary which marked the edge of the decaying Roman circle. Roosevelt seemed to be fleeing for his life. Close behind was Myles, holding the bayonet firmly in his hand and thrusting it towards the Senator. The old American had been beaten by the young Brit.

They hollered and whooped.

Then they started to realise: the two men were not just running out of the arena. They were running towards the vehicles. Their vehicles.

Myles maintained the pretence of chasing the Senator for as long as he could. The Somalis were checking themselves. Had the Westerners tricked them?

The Senator just reached the Toyota. Myles was yards behind.

Then gunfire scattered towards the two men, just missing them and kicking up dust from the desert.

Myles turned to see Juma's men running towards him. Most were lowering their AK-47s, ready to fire.

Juma himself was the only one not moving. He seemed to have been most shocked by Myles' and the Senator's trick. 'Kill them both,' he called to his men.

Myles ducked into the cabin of the vehicle as fast as he could. Keys were dangling from the ignition. Myles fumbled with them before he managed to turn them. The Toyota's engine whirred into action.

He was about to crank the gearbox when the windscreen was shot through and shattered in front of him. Myles had to shield his eyes as glass exploded all around him.

Then a single word cut through the noise. 'Juma.' It was the Senator's voice.

Myles turned to see the old man standing behind the rear wheels of the Corolla. Roosevelt was holding a rocket-propelled grenade to his shoulder.

Juma's men paused. The pirate who had been firing at the windscreen relaxed his trigger hand and looked uncertain. Most of the others just stood still. They were waiting to see what the Senator did with his weapon, or whether Juma would renew the order to attack.

The Senator called over the chaos. 'Let's talk this through, Juma,' he said.

Myles could see that Roosevelt was sweating. He had repositioned the sight of the RPG launcher to his eye, trying to ensure he had a clear shot. He flexed his fingers on the trigger mechanism.

Juma's voice shouted out from the back, hidden by a wall of his men. 'We can talk if you want to.' His voice sounded as though he was still gloating. 'Do you have any final words, Senator?'

The Senator's breathing was strained. He kept the rocket trained on the bulk of Juma's men as he prepared his reply. 'Juma, I'll let your men live if you let me and the Englishman go,' he bargained.

There was a silent pause. Then Juma replied with a phoney laugh. 'So you want to negotiate with us "terrorists", Senator?'

The Senator called back, shouting over the back of the Toyota. 'Juma, this is your last chance. Let us go or I'll fire.'

Juma paused slightly before he replied. Eventually he came back with, 'Will you let us settle in the United States?'

The Senator paused also. 'We can talk about that,' was the reply.

'We're talking about that now, Mr Senator Roosevelt. Yes or no – will you let us settle, Senator? If you won't give a clear answer now, when we have you at gunpoint...'

Juma's words trailed off, overtaken by a bizarre whooshing noise.

It was the sound of a rocket-propelled grenade shooting through the air. The Senator had fired.

The RPG blasted into the ground in front of Juma's men. Myles and the Senator were knocked back by the fireball. Fragments from the casing of the rocket flew towards them. Instinctively they ducked, allowing the vehicle to take the shrapnel.

Smoke and flames caused chaos. Myles glanced towards the crater where the grenade had exploded. Dead bodies and limbs were mangled with screaming flesh: but some of Juma's men were still alive. Myles could also hear the clatter of automatic weapons being cocked.

Myles turned back to the car, but the engine had stopped. He turned the ignition again – nothing.

He tumbled out to see the Senator had almost fitted another rocket onto the launcher.

Then, behind the Senator came a voice they all knew. 'Stop now.' It was Juma.

Although Myles could not see Juma himself – the car was in the way – he could see the Senator, and could tell the Senator was facing him. Juma's voice was even and unstrained: he had not been hurt by the explosion, and Myles guessed the pirate leader's Kalashnikov was pointing straight at Sam Roosevelt's head. Juma was probably twenty or thirty metres away, but it was close enough to be sure of a kill.

Senator Sam Roosevelt looked down at the rocket-propelled grenade launcher he held in his hand. He hadn't had time to fit the new missile head on properly. The grenade was only loosely attached.

Slowly, the Senator rotated the launch tube until it was upside down. He was pointing the missile towards the ground.

The Senator turned to look at Myles. He had a resigned look on his face, but also a sense of urgency, as if he was warning Myles. There was something he wanted Myles to do.

Myles tried to understand, but the Senator couldn't use words to say what he meant – he would have been heard by Juma. The Senator was trying to point somewhere with his eyes. What did he mean?

The Senator made the expression again. Myles tried desperately to make sense of it.

Then the Senator squared back to Juma. 'You asked me whether I had any last words,' he said. 'Well I don't. Last words are for fools who haven't said enough during their lifetime.'

Something about the Senator's tone and manner had changed. The power balance between him and Juma had tipped again. Myles knew what the Senator was about to do.

In those last moments, Myles crouched. He tried to protect himself. He was tense with anticipation, unsure whether he would survive what now seemed inevitable. Was there anywhere he could hide?

He looked around. Finally, he saw where the Senator's eyes were pointing…

Moments later came the explosion – far larger than the first. The Toyota was tossed sideways. The survivors of the first grenade, and the bodies of those whom it had killed, were blown into the air. Even Juma was knocked off his feet, and the gun flew from his hands.

But the sixty-nine-year-old Senator, war-hero and twice Presidential hopeful, who was far closer than anyone else to the centre of the blast, knew none of this. He had finally escaped his captives. Indeed, he had killed many of them off.

His last act had confirmed his refusal to give in to terrorists.

The Senator had proven his determination with his life.

CHAPTER FIFTY-EIGHT
Western Desert, Iraq

Juma was dazed: he had been thrown down against the desert floor by the blast. His body was still in shock from the pressure of the explosion. Air had been forced from his lungs and it took him time to recover his breath.

But he had been lucky: he had just been far enough away when the grenade detonated. Although fragments from the outer casing had shredded some of the warlord's clothes, his wounds were only superficial. One side of his body was grazed and bleeding, but that was all. Once he had gathered his senses, Juma was largely unharmed.

The Somali pirate chief got back on his feet and surveyed the aftermath of the rocket-propelled grenade. As with all explosions, the impact of the Senator's second munition seemed to have been random. Devastation was interspersed with areas which remained untouched. Some of the desert floor was torched and charred. Other parts looked exactly as they had before. Dead bodies from the first explosion had shaded some areas from the second.

Juma looked down at his men. Several bodies were in pieces. Charred limbs and torsos were mixed with broken weaponry and tatters of clothes. It was hard to know exactly how many people had been killed.

Juma noticed one Somali pirate near the middle of the crater who was missing a leg and arm. The man started to howl for help as he recovered consciousness and recognised his leader. Juma stomped towards him, lifted his head and shook it, then put it down again, swiftly concluding that the man had no hope of surviving. When the man called out again, Juma returned to him, then kicked him hard in the face. The man lost consciousness once more, never to regain it.

Two other men appeared to be alive but severely wounded. They were careful to remain quiet. Two more, who had not been with the main group, were on their feet by this time. Like Juma, they were largely unhurt, and explored the wreckage with him.

To check both his captives were dead, Juma was keen to examine the Toyota: it had been blown upside down and landed on its roof, which was crushed. The African gang leader bent down to check no one was alive inside. There was certainly no movement. No one could have survived, he concluded. Although he couldn't see properly, Juma was content to leave the vehicle containing Myles' corpse where it was.

Juma missed the satisfaction of killing him, but knowing the Englishman was dead was almost as good. He shrugged, then turned away.

Then he saw the Senator's body, which had massive wounds to the chest and neck. Sam Roosevelt was definitely dead. Juma called over to his two surviving accomplices. When he had their attention, he put his boot on the old man's face and stamped it into the dust. The pirates laughed as Sam Roosevelt's head was pressed down, deformed and bloodied. Juma stepped away satisfied.

Content that he had surveyed the danger, Juma replaced the magazine in his AK-47 and made the gun ready to fire. Then he levelled the barrel at the bodies of the men near the crater. He aimed at the two who were alive but severely wounded. Although they tried to ask for a chance, Juma shot them through with bullets. They died instantly.

Juma stepped back, and fired a short burst into the Senator's body near his feet. Then he clambered back over to the wreck of the Toyota.

Once more he examined the twisted remnants of the vehicle. Juma couldn't see the Englishman's body. He was beginning to doubt his earlier conclusion. Could Myles have survived?

To make sure, he readied his weapon for a final time, and sprayed the whole front section of the Toyota Corolla with bullets. He exhausted the whole of his magazine, and his gun clicked to let him know he was done. Then he crouched down to examine the bullet holes. A good spread: there was not a single space within the mass of the vehicle which hadn't been hit. A cat couldn't have avoided the bullets, let alone someone as tall as Myles.

No movement from inside.

Juma waited. Still no movement.

Finally, he was convinced: wherever Myles Munro's body was, there was no way he could still be alive. His limbs must be amongst the twisted and charred cadavers near the crater of the explosion. Juma was content. He stood up and chuckled at his work: he had killed both of his Western hostages.

He beckoned over to his two fellow survivors, who came in beside him. The three men walked away from the wreckage, careful to step between the corpses rather than on them.

With their guns slung back on their shoulders, Juma ordered his men into a second car, parked further away from the main scene. They climbed inside, Juma enjoying a last glance at the scene of the Senator's demise so far from the American soil that he loved.

Soon Juma and his men were away, and the pile of wreckage and dead bodies was left behind in the cooling desert afternoon sun. Within hours the scavenger animals of the desert would pick at what was left. Within days it would be half-covered by desert dust. Perhaps some of the scene – the twisted metal of the overturned vehicle and the Somali guns – would be preserved for as long as the Roman ruins of the abandoned town. But to Juma, it didn't matter. He was heading off to rejoin his people. Placidia's people. The last obstacle had been overcome, and he was about to achieve his grand ambition.

CHAPTER FIFTY-NINE
Via Veneto, Rome

Safiq had arrived, but what sort of civilisation had he reached?

He was in a fine street, with rich architecture and lovely trees, somewhere in the centre of Rome. It seemed like a wonderful city. He and a mass of hundreds of other Africans, a few of them still armed, crowded outside the American Embassy.

But the embassy was protected by a strong fence. They knew the fence was strong because they had attempted several times to knock it down and failed. Someone had been badly crushed when they tried. Safiq understood: there was no way in.

In every direction, including the route the throng had taken from the ship, roads had been blocked. The Italian police were containing the crowds. Safiq was wondering whether the Italians would advance – for now, they were just waiting. Waiting, he guessed, for the Africans to tire and give up.

Like the Africans, a few of the Italian police had guns; Safiq had worked out the armed ones wore special 'Caribinieri' uniforms. He made sure he kept his distance from them.

Safiq had no food and, like the others, he was hungry. The only nearby café had closed and been locked up. They'd all managed to drink from a water hose when they first reached the embassy, but now even that had been turned off.

So here he was, in the middle of civilisation but still desperate. He was standing right next to the US Embassy, which someone had told him was officially American territory, but his American dream was further away than ever.

Life was still harsh, like it had been on the windy dockside in Africa.

And he knew that soon it would get even worse.

CHAPTER SIXTY
Western Desert, Iraq

Myles waited for more than an hour before he moved again. When Juma had fired bullets into the overturned Toyota, he had cowered. He had strained to hear the distant sound of the Somali's vehicle driving away. But he needed to be sure it wasn't another of Juma's games. He had to know Juma wasn't waiting for him.

Blood had trickled into his hair. Myles silently walked his fingers up his scalp to trace the source. There was a sensitive spot near the top of his head. Probably just a small cut, he told himself. Head wounds give out a lot of blood.

Although it was dark, Myles felt sure he wasn't concussed. He was too alert to be dazed. He would deal with his head wound later.

Myles listened again. Still no noise from above. Had all of Juma's men gone?

Or had the pirate left a watchman to make sure there were no survivors?

Slowly Myles edged along the mosaic floor, sticking tightly to the walls. He looked at the overturned Toyota suspended over him, blocking the way he had come in – half dived, half fallen, at the moment the Senator had pulled the trigger. Unless Juma and his men deliberately moved the vehicle, they would not find Myles' new hiding place.

He felt safe from them.

The Toyota pick-up had given Myles the cover he needed to slip down a hole into this buried Roman room. The underground room which the Senator had seen – the last act of the great Sam Roosevelt had been to save his life.

But the day was ending, and the dim light in the space where Myles was hiding was becoming dimmer. Myles knew he could not stay underground forever. He needed to escape. He also needed food and, more urgently, water.

Drops of clear liquid were falling from the front of the vehicle onto the mosaic floor. Myles looked down at the dusty puddle. He held out his palm and caught some drops, then put them to his tongue. Immediately he spat it out: it was soapy windscreen fluid. Nothing he could drink.

He moved back into the Roman room. Was there anything here he could use?

The paved floor of the chamber depicted a well-dressed Roman man – perhaps an emperor – holding a sword at the neck of another man, who had a dark face and was kneeling in submission. The body of a beheaded man lay on the ground beside them both. The emperor seemed to have taken the throne. Given there was blood on his sword, he may have killed for it. Myles marvelled at the image – the beheaded man reminded him of the Senator.

Myles stamped on the floor: it was solid. The room was professionally built – probably by artisans who expected their civilisation to survive for many more centuries.

He walked around the walls of the room, thumping them with the side of his fist, looking for a way out. Nothing presented itself.

The only item in the room was at the end furthest from the entrance, and so furthest from the fading light. Myles' eyes had to adjust to see what it was. There seemed to be a stone bench with a head-shaped indentation, and space for chains in case someone needed to be tied in position. Above the indentation was an iron spike mounted in a large stone, itself attached to a rod. The rod reached down into an axle through the bench. Myles touched the stone, then pushed it gently. As the stone tipped forward, it began to accelerate with its own weight, forcing the metal spike to crash down onto the head-shape indentation on the bench.

Clang.

Myles looked behind him, worried that the noise could have alerted Juma's men. He waited, listening in the dark. Several minutes passed, but there was nothing.

Myles was definitely alone.

He returned to the device. The head-shape indentation, around where the spike now rested, was slightly darker than the rest of the bench. Very old bloodstains.

Now Myles recognised what the machine was. He remembered reading about them when he had studied with Placidia. Wounded or defeated gladiators would have been brought down from the arena and their head laid on the bench. Then the spike would have been allowed to fall, piercing their skulls. For mercy killings…

This was how the Romans dealt with their entertainment after it no longer entertained. Far easier to use than a sword, this was a Roman killing machine, the pre-industrial equivalent of a guillotine.

Myles withdrew his hand, leaving the spike where it was, and trying to respect the many people whose lives had ended here. Ancient Rome had become truly brutal before its collapse.

Myles looked around the remainder of the chamber, checking it again for nooks and weak points. He pressed and checked every surface he could reach, especially where the stone crumbled. But there was no way out. The only exit was the entrance, and that was covered by the Toyota.

He stood again below the overturned vehicle, and tried to work out how he could climb up into it. The crushed roof was almost within reach. He jumped and grabbed the engine cover, but it came off in his hands, and Myles fell back down onto the floor.

He looked up again: the engine block was above him now. No way through it. And round the sides the Toyota had wedged itself in solidly.

Again, Myles jumped up and tried to grab hold. He swung his legs up and tried to kick through.

No use. He wasn't even close: the Toyota was very firmly in place and there was absolutely nothing he could do to move it or get through it.

He felt a chill. The temperature was dropping, and he wandered whether he would catch hypothermia. Dehydrated, he knew he'd succumb more quickly.

He jumped up and grabbed a seat belt, then pulled himself towards the dashboard.

He checked the radio – dead.

He checked the fire extinguisher – empty.

He checked the battery – useless.

Nothing. With each passing thought he also felt himself weaken. His arms were losing strength and he had to allow himself to drop back to the floor.

Daylight was almost gone. He felt the wound on his head again: it was still bleeding. His thirst was beginning to subside as his dehydrated body started to shut down. He felt faint.

He tried to tighten his muscles, forcing his body to keep up his blood pressure. He was trying to think of ways to escape, almost as a distraction, knowing that he needed to keep his mind busy, knowing that to fall asleep might be deadly.

He tried to imagine Helen, the best reason of all to escape. She should be cured of septicaemia by now, he thought. She should be safe – probably back in America. He wanted to be with her. Would he ever see her again?

He still hoped that, together with Helen, he could stop Juma. If only he knew *how* they were planning to bring Rome's fate onto America. If only he could get out of here.

As the last glow of sun disappeared from the chamber, Myles found himself immobile on the ancient mosaic floor. Involuntary shivers twitched through his body.

His last image was of the killing machine used by Romans for fighters who, like him, had been defeated. And like all those exhausted gladiators so many centuries ago, his resistance had left him.

DAY XI

CHAPTER SIXTY-ONE
Rome

Paul Pasgarius the Third's trip to Italy was the first time he'd ever left the United States. It had been a struggle to get from the airport to the place he had been told to meet Constantine. Just as he had been warned, security cordons were everywhere.

He glanced anxiously at his watch. Constantine was late. Had he been scared off – or stopped at one of the checkpoints? Paul wondered how Constantine would carry the large bag of cash he had promised.

Then he felt a hand on his shoulder. He turned around, and saw an unexpected face.

'Constantine?' he asked.

The man nodded. 'Thanks for coming, Paul.'

Paul recognised Constantine immediately, from all the news about the terror threat to America. He tried to pretend he hadn't, swallowing hard to hide his nerves. 'Can we make it quick, please?' He looked Constantine up and down, disconcerted that the man didn't seem to be carrying a bag of currency. 'Do you have the money?' he asked.

Constantine nodded. 'I do,' he said, reaching into his pocket. But instead of cash, he pulled out a packet of gum and presented it to Paul as if they were two friends passing the time.

Paul instinctively took the stick he was offered, unwrapped it and folded it into his mouth. 'Thank you,' he said.

He was surprised to see Constantine put the packet back in his jacket pocket, and equally surprised by the gum's strange taste. 'Er, you're not having gum yourself?' queried Paul.

The man shook his head. Within moments Paul understood why, as he felt his throat tighten.

'No gum for me,' said Constantine matter-of-factly. 'Some people would say gum-chewing is disrespectful, and disrespect for authority can bring down empires,' he mused. 'But for me, I just try to avoid gum which has been dipped in strychnine.' He sauntered away.

Paul Pasgarius the Third's dead body slumped behind him.

CHAPTER SIXTY-TWO
Western Desert, Iraq

Darkness closed in. Myles felt his body drift, as if it had lost its weight. He imagined himself rise out of the chamber which had threatened to become his tomb. He was floating.

Visions invaded his mind. Dreams from ancient Rome: he pictured the Hun, the barbarian warriors from the east who had outmatched the Romans in battle. He remembered the descriptions of them – narrow-eyed, with squat heads and flat faces. The Romans had always described the Asiatic horsemen as ugly, using words of intolerance. He remembered how the leader of the barbarians, Attila-the-Hun, had held civilisation to ransom. When Rome couldn't pay, the 'eternal city' was ransacked and it never recovered from the rampage of 455 AD. It meant that Rome's last military expedition – to Libya, in 468 AD – was a fiasco, and soon the Roman Empire was formally declared dead. An imperial order was the death certificate, signed in 476 AD.

Myles imagined the Hun presenting the official paper to him now. He was being asked to sign the end of the Roman Empire. To sign away civilisation, to sign away his life… Myles refused to take the pen, but someone grasped his wrist. He was being forced to sign.

Myles mustered his strength. He tried to move his arm, to keep it away from the paper, but he was too weak. Finally, he just managed to throw his arm sideways. Whoever was grasping it was knocked to the ground. The paper was taken away. Myles knew the Empire's death certificate would be brought back to him soon.

He became aware of the person who had grabbed his wrists. The person, who Myles had thrown to the floor, was in pain. Myles looked over and recognised the narrow Asiatic eyes described in the ancient texts.

Myles had been captured by the Hun.

He became aware of his surroundings: the flat walls of a nomadic tent, the sort used by the barbarian horseback riders, who had been ancient Rome's final adversary. The tent had been painted green, like the steppes of Asia from where the horsemen had come. Then he saw another Hun approach him with a spear. Myles could not resist. He felt pain as the weapon was plunged into his arm. Then he felt weak. His entire being was slipping away. Like the Roman Empire, he was passing into history.

The thoughts dribbled away until he could think no more.

It took many more hours for the drowsiness to pass, although Myles had lost his ability to feel time passing. Only gradually did Myles realise he had conjured pictures of ancient Rome and imagined himself there. History had mingled with the present.

Slowly, Myles recognised he was in a sick bay. The tent was not the home of barbarian horsemen, but a green surgical curtain. It surrounded the stretcher-bed, to which he had been strapped.

'Hello?' he asked, although he wasn't sure who he was asking.

An Asiatic health orderly came to Myles' bedside. She was soon joined by a more senior-looking doctor with a peculiar logo on his breast pocket. The doctor's face also marked him as from the Far East. Myles saw a few Chinese characters on some well-kept medical equipment.

'So you're awake, then?' said the doctor in an oriental accent.

'Yes, thank you,' Myles replied – awake but groggy. He wasn't sure what to ask first: where was he? How had he got there? Who was looking after him?

The doctor saw his confusion and smiled. 'It's all right,' he said. 'You've been with us for a while now, and there's no sign of any problems at all with your head.'

The doctor reached over for an MRI scan and passed it to Myles. Myles tried to understand the image, which was on a large sheet of photographic film. It just looked like a picture of a brain in shades of grey. He looked back up at the doctor. 'Er, thank you,' he said, turning it sideways to see if it made more sense. It didn't.

'We did other tests on you as well,' explained the doctor. 'You've got elevated levels of calcium in your blood, and it looks like you've been exposed to some sort of disease recently, but it's nothing too serious,' he said, smiling. 'Basically you're fine.'

Myles barely absorbed the doctor's words. He was still staring at his brain scan, and pointed at the edge of the scan, where his skull looked like it was nicked.

'Yes, it's a small fracture,' said the doctor, nodding. 'Probably caused by the explosion – or the fall. But you were lucky. You were the only survivor we found.'

Myles was obviously still very confused. He was sure Juma was still alive. 'You only found one vehicle?' he asked.

'There may have been others, but they would have driven off before we arrived.' The doctor explained how workers had seen two fireballs in the desert, just over the horizon. They'd gone to investigate – taking heavy security with them, of course. There they had found the dead bodies and the single overturned vehicle, which they pulled away to discover Myles. He had been lifted out on a stretcher, semi-conscious the whole time. 'It's not our business to ask whether it was an accident or what you Americans call a "shoot-out",' said the doctor.

'I'm not American,' said Myles. He wondered about his words as he said them. He wasn't American, it was true. But in his culture, his attitudes and his outlook on life, he realised he had much in common with many from the United States. He was even in love with a woman from New York. He was certainly more American than the medical team who had just saved his life.

'You said "workers",' he added. 'How many workers do you have here?'

'We have about fifty managers from China, then about two-hundred-and-fifty locals working on the rigs,' said the doctor.

Suddenly the commercial logo on the doctor's clothes made sense: oil. 'So you're the guys that bought up Iraq's oil after the American troops left?' asked Myles.

'That's right,' nodded the doctor. 'You guys did the fighting, we're making the profit.' The doctor smiled apologetically. Myles thought about arguing the point, but realised there was no need. The doctor already understood many Americans resented China buying up Iraq's mineral resources.

'Doctor, you know the Romans towards the end of their Empire relied on grain being shipped in from abroad, from North Africa,' Myles explained. 'When those lands fell to the barbarians they lost their last chance.'

'You need rest.'

Myles accepted the doctor was right. Only now did he realise how tired he was. Not since he had been in custody in London had he had a proper night's sleep. The medical team had wired him up to a drip, providing him with fluids which his body craved. His muscles were sore. Myles knew he was a wreck.

'You said I had high levels of calcium in my blood,' he asked.

'Yes,' said the doctor. 'Looks like you've been eating chalk!'

Myles paused to absorb the information. 'Not lead?'

The doctor smiled. 'No, lead and other heavy metals were fine. The elevated calcium won't do much – it might even strengthen your bones. It is abnormal, but not dangerous. It needs to come down, and it will in a few days.'

'Calcium, not lead?'

The doctor looked slightly offended. He was wondering why the tall Westerner was querying his medical advice. 'Yes, calcium,' he confirmed again. 'Your lead levels were absolutely normal. Should they not be?'

Myles' mind was still ticking over. 'And you tested my blood for infections, too?'

'Yes. You'd recently been exposed to smallpox, we think, but because you were vaccinated against it, the disease didn't take hold.' The doctor leant back and became authoritative. 'You definitely need rest,' he said. 'Now, is there anything I can bring you? A book? TV?'

Myles was still digesting the information: it meant that in Germany he hadn't been exposed to lead after all, just harmless calcium. He turned back to the doctor. 'Do you follow the news? Has there been anything about Helen Bridle?' he asked.

The doctor shook his head in ignorance. 'I don't know,' he admitted.

Myles wondered what else to try. He pondered for a moment, then queried, 'Can you download books here?'

He saw the doctor nod.

'Then, doctor, can you get me a book, please. It was first published in 1776, and written by a man named Edward Gibbon.'

'I'm not sure books that old are available online,' said the doctor. 'I'll try. What's the title?'

Myles' face opened into a smile. 'You should be able to get this one. It's called *The History of the Decline and Fall of the Roman Empire.*'

Ten minutes later the female orderly returned and presented Myles with an electronic book reader. Myles took the device eagerly and thanked her. Immediately Myles started to scroll down.

History of the Decline and Fall of the Roman Empire
By Edward Gibbon, 1776

The Asiatic woman plumped up Myles' pillow, so he could sit up and read. Seeing Myles already thoroughly absorbed in the book, she leant over to a television suspended from the ceiling. Quietly she swung it into place and put the remote control near her patient. But Myles was too busy with the electronic reading device to notice.

Myles kept pushing his thumb down until he reached the text itself.

> *...peaceful inhabitants enjoyed and abused the advantages of wealth and luxury. The image of a free constitution was preserved with decent reverence: the Roman senate appeared to possess the sovereign authority, and devolved on the emperors all the executive powers of government.*

The words were formed in the same language as the American Declaration of Independence. Perhaps not surprising: the book hailed from the same year. Substitute the word 'president' for 'emperor', and the book could apply to the States. Gibbon had even spoken of a 'revolution' when he explained the purpose of his masterpiece:

...to deduce the most important circumstances of Rome's decline and fall; a revolution which will ever be remembered, and is still felt by the nations of the earth...

Gibbon seemed to fear democracy. He had opposed the 'colonies', as they then were, breaking away from the British Empire.

Under a democratical government the citizens exercise the powers of sovereignty; and those powers will be first abused, and afterwards lost...

But it was not democracy which caused the decline; Gibbon seemed to blame corruption.

Corruption, the most infallible symptom of constitutional liberty, was successfully practised: honours, gifts, and immunities were offered and accepted...

Myles jumped down to the events which actually brought down the Empire, when the city itself was sacked.

The fabric of a mighty state, which has been reared by the labours of successive ages, could not be overturned by the misfortune of a single day... The union of the Roman empire was dissolved; its genius was humbled in the dust; and armies of unknown barbarians, issuing from the frozen regions...had established their victorious reign over the fairest provinces of Europe and Africa... Its fall was announced by a clearer omen than the flight of vultures: the Roman government appeared every day less formidable to its enemies, more odious and oppressive to its subjects.

Then he found a vital sentence.

If all the barbarian conquerors had been annihilated in the same hour, their total destruction would not have restored the empire of the West: and if Rome still survived, she survived the loss of freedom, of virtue, and of honour.

He paused, then lowered the book. The words rang through his brain. Why had Placidia told him to look at it again?

Myles wondered: Was ancient history like this really so important to the present day?

He remembered the lectures he'd given at university. History needed to be humble. 'Some people say they study the past so they can learn from it,' he often told his first year students. 'They're wrong. We study history to learn whose mistakes we're copying.' It made his undergraduates laugh.

History mattered, but Myles knew it was the present which mattered most. Juma was heading for Rome. He might already be there. And he was going to destroy the currency conference, now just days away.

Myles picked up the remote control and pointed it at the TV as he pressed. The screen came on. The picture showed a man and woman sitting behind a desk with a map of the world's new superpower behind them – the news in Chinese.

He scrolled through the channels until he found an English language TV station. Instantly he recognised the voice of the presenter. It was Helen. She was back at work.

Myles stared at the image of her. He longed to be with her. As he studied her face, he saw there were no scars from the smallpox, and she didn't even seem pale: the doctors in Turkey had cured her of septicaemia completely. Knowing she was safe made Myles' whole body relax in relief.

He tuned his ears to hear her report, which he guessed had been recorded in the last few hours. From the way she moved as she read the news, Myles could tell she was even well-rested.

'Confirmation that his father was killed in Iraq came with only a modest consolation for his son, Richard, who has been named as his successor by the State Governor,' reported Helen. 'The new Senator, still shocked by his father's death, has pledged a return to Christian values, and to continue his father's work protecting America from terrorists…'

There was footage of Dick Roosevelt being jostled by cameras and reporters.

'…and since the recent Congressional scandal, in which indecent images were found on roughly half of the computers in the Senate, Dick Roosevelt – whose IT equipment was given the "all-clear" – is even being talked of as a future contender for President,' continued Helen's voiceover. 'Although the US Constitution requires candidates to be thirty-five years old before they can run for that office…'

Myles was interrupted by the doctor rushing in, worried. 'We logged your name earlier as Myles Munro – is that right?' he asked. The man raised his voice at the end of his question, as if there was genuine doubt in his voice.

But Myles knew – there was no use pretending anymore. He had been on the run long enough. 'Yes, I am.' Myles guessed the doctor had just made the connection, and was about to have Myles arrested. But instead, the Chinese man just said, 'Mr Munro, we have a call for you.' He pressed a button on the TV remote, and glanced up at the screen, which went black for a few moments, while the doctor departed.

Then a new picture appeared. Sitting in a video-conferencing studio very far away was a familiar face.

CHAPTER SIXTY-THREE
Western Desert, Iraq

Myles adjusted the volume and sat up in bed. The picture on the video conference was slightly hazy, and the image seemed to follow half a second behind the sound. But Myles didn't mind. To see Helen again made him feel alive. From being in the middle of a strange hospital room, it seemed as though Myles had suddenly returned home. 'Helen,' he smiled to the image on the screen.

'Myles – you're alive!'

'And so are you! Sorry about leaving you at the hospital.'

'It's OK,' she accepted. 'You did the right thing. You saved my life.'

The words made Myles feel much better. 'Thank you – I hope we're together again soon.'

'Your head?' she asked, squinting at the camera.

Myles was aware that Helen was looking above his face. He put his hand on his head and felt bandages. 'It's from yesterday,' he explained. 'The doctor here reckons no lasting damage.'

'You sure, Myles?'

'I think so. Look – they gave me the scan to prove it.' Myles held up the picture from his brain scan.

Helen twisted her head to see it more clearly, but, like Myles, she soon concluded it only showed a brain. Without expert knowledge it could mean anything. Myles waved it away, agreeing the scan picture didn't help.

He became aware someone was sitting next to Helen. Dick Roosevelt leant into view, and towards the video-conferencing camera. It made him slightly out of focus.

'Dick Roosevelt here,' he said. 'You OK?'

'Sure, Dick. And you?'

'Thank you, yes, I'm OK,' he said. 'Bearing up.' Dick was still shocked from the death of his father.

'I'm sorry about your father, Dick. If it's any consolation, he died as bravely as he lived,' reported Myles, remembering Sam's last moments. 'He gave his life to save others.'

Dick Roosevelt nodded thoughtfully. 'Juma killed him?'

Myles felt uneasy about giving too many details to a son still so obviously in shock. 'I'll give you the full story later,' he said. 'But yes, Juma was to blame.'

Helen started speaking again. 'Myles, in case you're still wondering, you've been cleared. Homeland Security have accepted those terrorist plans were planted on your computer. They know you're innocent.'

'How did they know?'

'Internet tracks. Computer forensics told them you were set up. They knew the classified information was planted via the IP address in Iraq, although they still haven't traced how the people in Iraq got the files.'

To Myles, it all seemed so long ago. It took him a while to understand the implications of it all. 'So I'm welcome back in civilisation again?'

'Yes, Myles. And we need to take a really big holiday together.'

No longer being on the run was a huge relief, but Myles knew it was too early for a break. 'We can't take a holiday yet, even though I'd love to. Juma's still dangerous and he's still out there.'

Dick shook his head slowly. 'Don't worry about him, Myles. We're wise to the threat he poses, and we reckon we're safe.'

'He's a psychopath,' warned Myles. 'Don't underestimate him. He's committed to bringing America down like Rome, and he's the sort of person that does what he says he's going to do – no matter how crazy.'

Helen sensed Myles and Dick Roosevelt were sparring a little. She tried to calm them down. 'Myles, don't forget Juma bluffs, too. It wasn't bubonic plague in Constantinople, only smallpox. And in Germany, it wasn't lead.'

'I know – calcium, right?'

Helen and Dick both nodded.

'But that doesn't mean the threat's over,' said Myles. 'The plague and the lead – that was Placidia, not Juma.'

Helen noticeably tensed up. She still reacted negatively to any mention of Placidia.

Dick tried to unpick Myles' thinking. 'You're saying Placidia and Juma, even though they're husband and wife, are working to different agendas? Why?'

Myles wasn't quite sure. 'Placidia's very, very intelligent,' he explained. 'She's the expert on ancient Rome, and she's the one who always wants to minimise death.'

Helen reacted with sarcasm. 'By threatening to kill people, right?'

'Threatening to kill, but not actually killing them,' said Myles. 'Hence the calcium and smallpox, rather than lead and plague.'

Dick was nodding now. 'And Juma?'

'Juma actually enjoys causing suffering,' explained Myles. 'And I'm sure he's going to blow up the currency conference in Rome.'

'Why do you think that?'

Myles shrugged. 'Because he told me he would.'

Dick still looked sceptical. 'You know, it would be very difficult for Mr Juma to bring any harm at all to the conference in Rome,' he said. 'You've seen some of the security plan for the event. It's even stronger now.'

The new Senator waited for Myles to reply, but the Englishman remained silent.

Helen moved towards the microphone. 'Myles, I want to be with you. I want to be with you right now.'

'I want to be with you, too, Helen.'

Dick Roosevelt looked slightly embarrassed at the couple's show of affection. 'You two, if you want to meet up, I can arrange for you to get together in Rome. Myles, if you're still worried about security at the conference, you're welcome see more of it. I'll show you around myself, and I won't let the Italian police interrupt you this time.'

Both Helen and Myles soon found themselves nodding.

'OK, then. That's agreed,' concluded Dick. 'I'll get you flown out of there and we can all meet in Rome in a day or two.'

Helen blew Myles a kiss. 'I love you, Myles,' she said.

'Love you too.'

Then Dick leant forward to press a button on the screen. For a moment his jacket shrouded the camera, dark and out of focus, before the picture went black.

Myles felt alive again: he'd been cleared by the authorities and he had spoken with Helen. Soon he'd have his vitality and he would be returning to civilisation… If he could stop Juma destroying it.

DAY XII

CHAPTER SIXTY-FOUR
Western Desert, Iraq

Myles tried to get out of bed. His muscles were sore and he fell back. But he knew he had to get to Rome quickly. 'Hello?' he called out. The female nurse ran into his room. 'I need my clothes,' he told her. 'I need to leave.'

'Are you sure?' asked the nurse, concerned.

He made clear that he was. The nurse ran out to fetch the doctor, who returned to find Myles standing beside his bed.

'Thank you. Doctor, I need my clothes, please…'

The doctor looked rather apologetic. He explained that Myles' clothes had been cut off his body when he was unconscious. 'You can have your clothes, Mr Munro, sir, but if you tried to wear them in Europe you may be arrested for being underdressed.'

The nurse blushed and tried to hide a smile. She delved inside a plastic waste sack and pulled out Myles' old clothes. With wide eyes, she held them up: they were tatters and rags.

Myles acknowledged the point. 'OK, well do you have any other clothes I can wear?'

The doctor nodded and led Myles to one of the storerooms. He tried to gauge Myles' height – tall for a Westerner but abnormally tall for someone from the Far East. He picked out the tallest boiler suit he had and gave it to Myles. Myles climbed into the garment. The height was right, but it was far larger – fatter – than Myles' body and hung loosely around his waist. Myles flapped his arms.

The doctor laughed. 'I'm sorry, sir. It's the best we can do.'

The doctor looked up at Myles' head, which was still bandaged. He bent down to the bottom of the cupboard to pick out a grey cloth cap, which he then placed on the Westerner: Chairman Mao headgear.

Myles thanked the doctor. Although the boiler suit looked odd, they were the first fresh clothes he had worn for many days. The food and medical care at the Chinese oil rig may have saved his life. Being rescued from the desert certainly did. 'Please pass on my thanks to everybody here,' he said.

'Thank you, sir.'

Within minutes the deep flutter of a helicopter came into earshot. Moments later, Myles found himself blasted by the downdraught. He shielded his eyes from the sand lifted up by the rotor blades as the vehicle came to land at the helipad next to the rig's offices.

But this was not a military helicopter – the US military and their allies no longer operated in this part of Iraq. This was a smaller, privately owned helicopter, and on the side of it were emblazoned two words in English alongside their Arabic counterparts: Roosevelt Security.

Dick had come good on his promise.

Myles pressed on, and ran towards the aircraft, whose rotors slowed but never stopped. He was soon buckled in and rising above the oil plant. The doctor and nurse waved up at him as he ascended.

Inside, the co-pilot proffered Myles some headphones. He gladly put them on. Only as he did so did he realise how loud it was inside the craft.

'Welcome aboard, Mr Munro,' said the co-pilot. 'Senator Roosevelt sends his compliments. We understand you don't have a passport with you, sir?'

Myles nodded.

'No problem – we'll be flying to a private airport just over the border in Turkey,' explained the co-pilot, unfazed. 'From there we should be able to get you a jet to Rome.'

'Thanks – that's great.'

'So lay back, relax, and enjoy the flight, sir.'

Myles nodded his gratitude. The vibrations of the aircraft were making him dozy already. He felt like an exhausted child starting to fall asleep in a car seat. But he knew he still had to think. Why had Placidia bluffed about lead and plague when she was planning to bring America down like the Roman Empire? And what was Juma planning?

He looked down at the desert below him: they were flying over an area which was once known as Mesopotamia, the cradle of civilisation. Yet it was featureless. There was no sign of development at all. The civilisation which had once flourished here was completely gone.

They made a desert and called it peace.

Words from a famous Roman historian, Tacitus, explaining how the Romans subdued nations by killing anybody who resisted their rule.

Myles studied the inside of the aircraft. He saw the company's circular logo and all the documents needed to satisfy the new Iraqi aviation authority. He kept turning the issue in his mind. How was Juma going to destroy the currency conference?

What seemed like minutes later, he was woken with a judder as the helicopter landed. He looked outside: he was at a local airfield in the mountains of south-east Turkey. A man from Roosevelt Security was soon opening the door and helping him out.

With a hand on his ducked head, Myles tried to keep his new headgear in place as he thanked the helicopter pilot over the noise. He was quickly escorted onto a small private passenger aircraft.

Propeller-driven rather than a jet, it seemed more rugged than most executive jets. The pilot shouted in a thick but accomplished South African accent that the flight to Italy would take just four hours.

Myles spent the time musing over the situation.

Placidia had always been an idealist – why had she become a terrorist?

Rome had declined over generations, perhaps even centuries – how could America be brought down within a lifetime? Juma was determined to bring down the United States – but what was driving him?

The plane's flight path circled around Syria and Lebanon. It was routed over Cyprus, then the Greek Islands, crossed into Italian airspace near Brindisi, then north-west towards Rome. Myles was finally away from warzones. The luxury was confirmed when the single member of the cabin crew brought out a fine silver plate of seafood and a glass of champagne.

Myles gladly enjoyed the hospitality. But the thoughts which warmed him most were of Helen. It was Helen who had helped clear his name, Helen who had given him the lead to Galla Security in Iraq, and Helen who had trusted him when the authorities did not. She had stuck with him when he needed her most.

And so, as the small propeller-driven plane touched down in Rome's Ciampino airport, Myles could barely wait to remove the seat belt.

As he'd hoped, Helen was standing there, waiting beside the new Senator.

The aircraft taxied to a stop. Myles clambered down the stairs, almost tripping over himself – and his ill-fitting Chinese clothes – as he rushed to meet Helen. She ran towards him too, and they embraced, together at last on the tarmac of the airfield.

Together again in Rome.

CHAPTER SIXTY-FIVE
Rome

Myles and Helen kissed. It was a long and meaningful kiss. When they were last together, each had feared the other would not survive. Now they both felt more alive than ever.

After almost a minute, Helen pulled back, smiling at Myles. She frowned theatrically as she looked up at Myles' headgear. 'What's this – Chinese Communism back in style?' She lifted off his cap as she said it, and was about to toss it away when she remembered the bandages on his scalp. Carefully, she put it back into place. 'We'll get you some fresh clothes when we get a chance,' she said, tactfully.

The young Senator approached, his arm extended for a handshake. 'Welcome back to Rome, Myles. Glad you made it out OK.'

'Thank you, Dick'. Myles paused. 'I'm sorry again about your father.'

Dick looked down and shook his head in respect. 'Was it painless for him?'

'It was quick,' replied Myles. 'And he took as many of them with him as he could.'

'That's my father, the great Sam Roosevelt,' said Dick, making clear he wanted to change the subject. 'Come this way. We can talk in the car.'

Dick Roosevelt had arranged for a people carrier to take them into the centre of Rome. Myles waved a thank you to his South African pilot before he climbed aboard with Dick. Helen followed.

Inside, Dick ordered the driver to go, then turned to Myles for advice. 'You've been through a lot, so I'll understand if you just want to rest. But if you do have any suggestions.' He pointed out of the window. 'As you can see, we've set up a normal security cordon. But this isn't a normal security situation.'

Myles paused before he answered, trying to gather his thoughts. 'The TV news reported that a shipload of refugees from Libya had reached Rome. What's the latest?'

'Reckoned to be about fifteen hundred of them,' replied Helen, nodding. 'Still claiming asylum, still wanting to become American citizens. They're camped outside the US Embassy at the moment, on Via Veneto.'

Myles remembered Via Veneto – it was where he had made a fool of himself, thinking an Italian had hidden a bomb in a washing machine crate. He didn't let the memory faze him.

'And Juma?' he asked.

'No sign.' Helen looked at Dick Roosevelt as she said it. Roosevelt confirmed her assessment: there was no evidence that Juma was anywhere near Italy. They had no information on the Somali pirate at all.

Myles absorbed the information. 'OK, so we have Juma determined to destroy America while one-and-a-half thousand of his people want to enter the country.' He looked up at the other two, inviting them to draw conclusions.

Helen turned to Roosevelt, then back to Myles. 'You mean, something doesn't make sense?'

'Right,' he agreed. 'None of this makes sense.'

Dick frowned. 'So?'

Myles didn't answer. 'Who's coming to the currency conference?' he asked.

The young Senator looked blank, as if to say 'I don't know – or at least no one important'. Slowly, Roosevelt tried to remember the list of attendees he had seen. 'Bankers, including a few central bankers, some managers of sovereign wealth funds...' he said, reciting from memory.

'Any politicians?'

'No, I don't think so.' Roosevelt's eyes roved upwards as he tried to recall the lists. 'Although, I suppose I'm a politician now.'

Myles accepted the answer. 'How many guests in total?'

'I think about one hundred and eighty – just under two hundred.'

'Anyone who Juma might want to assassinate?'

'A few former central bankers maybe. But I can't see how their death would bring about the end of America.' Roosevelt paused again. Then a thought suddenly struck him: could *he* be the target? His eyes asked Myles the question.

Myles raised his eyebrows, then weighed it up. 'It's possible. Juma's already killed one Senator Roosevelt. He might want to kill another.'

Dick Roosevelt inhaled slowly. He was trying to remain calm when clearly he was frightened. 'I don't see why he would want to kill me. I hardly know the guy.' Then he tried to shrug off the danger. He chuckled a shallow laugh.

But the faces of Myles and Helen were serious. Helen leant forward and held his wrist firmly. 'You need to stay in a safe place, Dick,' she suggested.

'I can stay in the CCTV centre at the conference – it's about the safest place there is.'

Myles agreed. But he kept pressing Roosevelt. 'Could Juma hate the Roosevelt Guardians? Or something else you stand for?'

'I've made clear that I'm a Christian,' admitted Roosevelt. 'As a Senator, I'm committed to bringing Christian values to America. There were battles between Christians and pagans in ancient Rome, right?'

'Right,' agreed Myles. 'But if Juma wanted to strike a blow against the Church there would be lots of easier ways to do it.'

Roosevelt paused again. He was thinking it all through. 'Well I doubt it's anything to do with the Roosevelt Guardians,' he said. 'I know Juma has his own militia, but private security firms hardly compete with each other. We tend to work together as much as we can.'

Myles gazed out of the window as the people carrier passed through the city. The streets seemed much more tense than on his last visit. 'Have we heard anything from Placidia?' he asked.

'Somehow she turned up in the middle of the refugees,' answered Helen, tetchily. 'She's become an interview junkie – talking to all the broadcasters she can find about how bad the West has been to "her people".'

'So she's not convincing, then?' asked Myles, smiling slightly.

'No. Ask any woman you know: that lady's a fraud. I asked the Italian police whether they'd arrest her for terrorism. They said they were just waiting for the warrant.'

'I'm sure she's broken the law,' agreed Myles, 'but Placidia doesn't seem to be trying to harm people. She sent us to a plague site without the plague, and tricked Juma's men to put harmless calcium into the sauce rather than lead.'

'Empty threats don't make her harmless,' huffed the Senator. 'And if she uploaded that stuff onto the Senate computers, then she's heartless.'

'Maybe,' said Myles. 'But she's not trying to cause harm. She said she was trying to save America and I believe her.'

'Save America from whom?' asked the Senator.

'She refused to say,' said Myles. He shook his head, still baffled, as he tried to sum up. 'OK, so the plot to bring down America, Placidia's "Last Prophecy of Rome", is this: between one and two thousand malnourished Africans camped in Rome seeking asylum. Meanwhile, we expect an attack against the currency conference – a conference attended by financiers nobody's heard of, and which is already very well protected by Roosevelt Guardians,' he said, his tone indicating they were clearly missing something.

'Not just my men,' added Dick. 'When the threat level rose, I brought in Homeland Security. Remember Susan, who used to work for my father – well she's here. And she brought half the US military along with her.' Dick could see the others were surprised. 'In fact, now they're doing most of it – Marines and Special Forces. Roosevelt Guardians are just doing the minor stuff – like the CCTV. This has become too serious for a private security firm.'

Myles and Helen were relieved. They respected the Roosevelt Guardians, but they trusted the elite US troops more. Myles was impressed that Dick Roosevelt had been sensible enough to call in support, probably missing out on profits. 'That's very public-spirited of you, Dick,' he said.

'Not really – it's more like good business sense,' admitted Dick. 'If I kept this contract just for Roosevelt Guardians, and someone like Juma breaks through, the damage to our reputation would destroy the firm.'

Helen was still concentrating on the Roman angle. 'But how can they do it? Myles: was there a single day or event which brought down the Roman Empire?'

'Not really,' said Myles, shaking his head. 'The city was ransacked by barbarians a few times, but over the course of generations. Romans lost a few battles, but they often won again soon after. Rome fell slowly.'

'So, historically, none of this makes any sense?'

Myles pulled a face. *Some* of it made sense, parts he couldn't say in front of Dick and Helen…

The people carrier was slowing towards the conference centre. They passed an old Roman statue – a much-loved senator killed off by a jealous emperor – now grey with smoke accumulated over the centuries. Myles studied it as they passed it, trying to learn whatever it was willing to teach him.

'Sometimes history makes no sense until it's over,' he said, thinking to himself. 'And then it makes all the sense in the world.'

The people carrier halted in a small queue of vehicles. Several cars ahead, a roadblock was manned by Italian policemen. Roosevelt leant over to explain. 'We're still more than a mile from the conference centre,' he said, apologising. 'This is security in depth. There's another check further up, then the US military scanning people on foot nearer the entrance.'

Myles was struck – security was much tighter than on his last visit.

'Good, huh?' said Helen. 'I did a story on conference security yesterday. I really can't see how anyone could break in.'

The people carrier crawled towards the checkpoint. As they approached, the driver folded down the sun visor. A special pass had been fastened to the underside, and when the police saw it they waved the vehicle through. Roosevelt turned to Myles for a reaction. Myles was absorbed in his thoughts. He noticed the heavy concrete blocks on the main routes as they came nearer the building. It would be very hard to drive a vehicle-borne bomb into the conference centre.

'Have you planned for rocket-propelled grenades, too?' asked Myles.

'Why – does Juma have them?'

'He does, yes. Or at least, he did have in Iraq.'

Roosevelt weighed the idea in his head. 'Good question. It would be hard for someone to get close enough, I think. But it might be possible – just. They wouldn't be able to do much damage, though, and they'd be caught almost as soon as they fired it.'

Myles nodded. As they came closer to the building itself, he saw increasing numbers of police, US Marines and Roosevelt Guardians patrolling key points. Men in plain clothes hung around, watching all that happened. Myles noticed they all had the same lapel badge.

The people carrier was directed towards a parking space. The driver pulled up and Roosevelt led the way out of the vehicle, closely followed by Helen and Myles.

As they walked towards the conference centre they were funnelled into lines. Myles looked ahead: everything was being scanned. The US Marines questioned everybody who went through. One man was sweating and was asked to strip down to his underwear, until the Marine was satisfied he wasn't concealing a suicide-vest of some sort.

Helen was shocked. 'If they ask me to do that, I'm just gonna turn around,' she insisted.

Thankfully they didn't ask her. But they did ask Myles why his clothes were too large for him. 'I borrowed them,' he replied.

'Who from, sir?' asked the Marine.

'It's a long story.'

'Try me, sir…'

Myles was willing to cooperate and was about to explain when Dick Roosevelt whipped out his ID card. The Marine bent down to inspect it, then stood back to salute. There were no more questions for them, and the trio were invited to walk into the conference building itself.

Sniffer dogs at the entrance barked as Myles approached. Myles put his hands up – he had, after all, been near explosives in Iraq. But when the dog handlers saw he was with the new

Senator Roosevelt, Chief Executive of Roosevelt Guardians, he was allowed to pass.

Dick escorted them up some stairs and along a corridor. They passed a guarded door, and were soon in the control room – the room where he had been arrested on his last visit.

Helen and Myles absorbed the TV monitors, computer banks and pieces of paper dotted around the room – there were so many more than before. The people working there seemed busy and efficient. There was even a flip-chart testing out possible flaws in the security for the event.

'This is the Situation Centre – the CCTV room,' said Dick. He moved towards one of the monitors and invited the administrator to flick between views from different cameras. 'We've got more than fifty cameras on this place,' he explained. 'Any terrorists who try to come would be seen long in advance.'

Roosevelt could see even Myles was impressed. But Myles couldn't help thinking they were still missing something. How come Juma had been so sure he could get through? He tried to frame his question. 'Do you think Juma knows about all this? Do you think he'll still try to get close?'

He was answered by a voice behind him. A female voice. 'He'd be mad to come. But then he probably is mad…' It was Susan from Homeland Security. She lowered her head apologetically. 'I'm sorry, Myles. When we detained you, we made a mistake.'

'It was you?'

'Yes. I had you arrested, and I was wrong.'

Myles nodded – apology accepted. 'It's OK.'

'Thank you for being so understanding,' said Susan. 'And we don't want any more mistakes, Myles. Which is why we've filled this place with US Marines, special forces and undercover guys…'

Helen's mobile rang. She apologised as she answered. The call was from her producer. Myles overheard half the conversation:

they wanted Helen to be down with the crowds of refugees. 'Yes, yes, I'll be safe,' she answered dismissively. 'The place is surrounded by police, and the US Embassy is next door – it's can't be too dangerous.' Then she jolted in shock. 'Really? You want me to interview that bitch?'

Myles and Dick looked at each other. Both were listening in now.

'Can I refer to her as a terrorist?' asked Helen, then followed up with: 'OK, but I can *ask* her if she's a terrorist, yeah?'

She nodded as she concluded the call, then apologised to Myles and Dick. 'Sorry, guys – I'm going to confront Placidia, outside the embassy.'

'Should I come?' asked Myles. 'I need to speak to her. There must be a way to defuse this thing.'

'No.' Helen was shaking her head. 'This is strictly journalism. She's got a lot to answer for.'

'OK,' said Myles, hesitantly. 'Stay safe down there,' he insisted.

'Will do. Any special questions you want me to ask her?'

Myles thought for a moment. 'Yes. Ask her about Rome: what was the real reason it fell?'

'That's all? Not, "why did you try to give me the plague?" or "Any more bombs planned?" huh?'

Myles shrugged. 'Perhaps – it would be interesting to hear her answers.'

She kissed him on the cheek, then waved with her fingers to Dick, and was gone.

'Be careful,' Myles shouted after her.

Dick turned to Myles. 'So what do we do now?'

'Just wait, I guess,' suggested Myles. 'Can you get CCTV pictures of the entrance – where people are being scanned?'

Roosevelt duly set the monitor to show the main entrance, then moved to get some coffee at a machine in the corner of the room.

Myles stared at the grainy computer image. He watched as the guests were scrutinised by the walk-through machine. One by one, they went through. About half set off the machine first time and were sent back to remove belts, shoes, mobiles and other items until they managed to walk through without the scanner beeping. Myles could sense the frustration of the people queuing behind: the process was slow. Perhaps they didn't realise just how serious the threat was. Even if Juma made it through, there was no way he could get a weapon in here – surely?

Then he noticed a man in a summer suit. His face was dark and his body small and muscular. Myles stared closer.

The man walked through the machine, then stopped in reaction to something. He had set off the alarm.

Calmly he stepped backwards again. The Marines pointed towards his jacket, which the man slipped off.

'Dick, Dick – come over,' insisted Myles, his eyes still fixed on the moving image. The man set the machine off a second time, but this time removed a pass from his pocket. The Marines inspected it, then waved him through.

Myles pointed at the screen. 'It's him. It's Juma.'

'You sure?'

Juma was wearing glasses and his hair was different, but Myles was sure it was him. 'Yeah. I recognise him.'

Dick Roosevelt rushed over, alert.

'Hey – why didn't the Marine stop him?' asked Myles. 'You sent out the description of Juma, right?'

'It should have gone out, yes,' insisted Roosevelt, resenting the accusation that he'd made a mistake. 'Is he still there? Which camera is he on?' he asked.

Myles tried to point the man out again, but Juma had already disappeared.

CHAPTER SIXTY-SIX
Barberini Conference Centre, Rome

Myles ran towards the doors but Dick called him back.

'Which one is he?' asked Roosevelt, scrolling back through the pictures, reversing the CCTV footage on the screen.

'That one – he's that one,' said Myles, pointing at the computer image, frozen as Juma lifted off his jacket with a Marine on each side of him.

'Got it,' said Roosevelt framing the image. 'I'll put out an alert.' He turned to talk to Myles, but the Englishman had already gone.

Myles sprinted along the corridor, bumping past delegates and almost knocking over someone taking bottled water into the main conference room.

A Marine called after him as he rushed by. 'Slow down, bud.'

'Sorry.' Myles' apology was lost in the rush. He leapt down the stairs, three at a time. Stopping at the entrance, he looked around. He could see the scanner where Juma had been less than half a minute before. He scoured the crowd:

No sign of him heading into the building…

No sign of him standing around outside…

No sign of him in any of the corridors…

It didn't make sense: how could Juma have disappeared so quickly?

Myles approached the Marine with the sniffer dogs. 'Excuse me. Have you seen a, a, man…' He struggled to find a description, and was out of breath from the run.

The dog handlers were smiling. 'We've seen lots of men here, sir, and a few women too.'

'I'm looking for a black man,' said Myles, rushing out the words as fast as he could. 'Er, Somali, small to medium height, glasses, brown jacket. Muscular, very muscular. Scar on his abdomen...'

The dog handlers looked at each other, unsure. 'Perhaps, about five or ten minutes past. The dogs reacted a bit but he was clean.'

Myles shook his head. 'This would have been one minute ago or less.'

'No, then no,' came the dog handler's reply.

Myles put his hand on his head as he tried to think. He became aware the Marines were looking at him strangely. Then he realised the bandages were showing from underneath his Chinese cap.

'You OK, sir?'

Myles nodded, still trying to think. 'Which way did the man go? The man who made the dogs react. Which way?'

One of the dog handlers leant over and pointed down a corridor.

Myles ran down where the man had pointed. More crowds. Myles tried to examine all of the faces as he passed.

No sign.

People just looked at Myles as if he was odd.

Where had Juma gone?

As he reached the end of the corridor, Myles found the conference café. He tried to check the faces of everyone there too. They all looked relaxed and engrossed in their conversations. The group in the corner laughed at a shared joke. Myles tried to see around them.

Still no sign. Juma seemed to have evaporated.

For a moment Myles wondered if he had imagined it. Could it have been someone else? After all, the man didn't look exactly like

Juma. The person he'd seen was wearing glasses and had different hair. But if it wasn't Juma, where had the innocent lookalike gone?

He looked around the café again. He was looking for someone who was agitated, but realised the most agitated person there was himself.

He searched over the heads of the delegates, peering all the way back to the corridor. He could just see towards the dog handlers at the entrance. If it was an innocent man, Myles would have found him by now. Juma must be hiding.

Myles was about to walk back up the corridor when he noticed something out of place – something nobody owned. Hanging over the back of one of the chairs was a jacket. He looked more closely: it was the jacket he had seen Juma wearing on the CCTV.

He moved towards it and picked it up.

He held it up in the air, unconcerned about making a spectacle of himself. 'Is this anybody's jacket?' he called out.

Heads turned, and for a moment the earnest conversations paused. Some men queuing for coffee wearing just shirts seemed particularly interested, but soon they dismissed it and returned to what they were doing.

Myles held it high for everyone else to see. Still no one claimed it.

One delegate looked at the jacket then at Myles' clothes and sniffed – as if Myles was asking to take something that wasn't his. Myles ignored the man. He felt the pockets. There were things inside. Myles delved and pulled out some car keys. They seemed normal, and were attached to a remote control locking device. Then he noticed they were for a Toyota. A Toyota Corolla. Significant, or was he imagining it?

He moved the car keys into his own pocket and kept searching through the jacket. There was a pen, which he placed down on the table. Then he found a packet of pills. He examined the box:

laxatives. He looked inside – several had already been popped through the foil. The pack was half-empty.

He began to question himself again: Juma didn't seem like the sort of man who would take pills for minor ailments like constipation.

Myles spun the jacket around to check the other side. There was a large piece of paper, which he lifted out and unfolded. This was more interesting: a map of the conference venue.

Myles studied the map closely. Had He wasn't sure whether it was standard issue for all the conference delegates been given one? Or had maps been kept from the public as a security precaution, in which case this was more significant?

Myles was just about to reach for the final thing in the jacket, which felt like a credit-card size rectangle of plastic, when he realised eyes were focussing on him.

Myles lifted his head to see US Marines closing in on him from three directions.

Without looking down again, Myles slipped the plastic rectangle into his palm.

'Hands up, please, sir,' came the instruction.

Myles did as he was ordered. As he lifted up his arms, the plastic card fell into his sleeve, passing his wrist towards his elbow. The US Marine patted him down, but knew it was a formality: everyone in the venue site had already been checked for weapons. The Marine queried the Toyota car keys Myles had just found, only giving them back when he was sure they were normal. Myles' new map of the conference venue was confiscated.

'Can you come with me, please sir?' demanded the Marine.

Myles nodded. 'Certainly, but something important is going on, and we need to stop it fast.'

'There's already a security alert out, sir, and you match the description.'

Myles shook his head. Typical. 'Well, where are you taking me?'
'Follow me, sir.'

Myles found himself marched through the corridors where he'd just been running. Back to the dog-handlers, back up the stairs. Something about the calm attitude of the Marines made him relax. It was obvious the Marines didn't really think Myles was a security risk.

Then he realised where they were taking him.

Myles continued with his escort along the upper corridor. When they reached the door to the CCTV room, the leading Marine stopped and held the way open for Myles, who walked in.

There was Dick, crouched over a different image: this time it was a live television feed.

'Sorry for calling you back like that, Myles,' said Dick, only half apologising.

'I was on his case – Juma…'

Dick ignored Myles' protests. He kept watching the TV. 'Myles, You gotta watch this…' he said.

CHAPTER SIXTY-SEVEN
Barberini Conference Centre, Rome

Dick was transfixed by the live feed from CNN. Myles and the Marines escorting him were immediately hypnotised by the images, too.

They showed hundreds of African refugees gathered in Rome, not far from the conference centre. They all looked tired, many desperate. One was shouting in anger about something, his face covered in sweat. The refugees were trying to get into the US Embassy, which was now protected by a single ring of Roosevelt Guardian security men. The private security guards, massively outnumbered, had their guns ready. Their message was clear: if the refugees tried to push their way into the embassy – which international law regarded as American soil – the security men would shoot.

Dick shook his head in disbelief. 'This is wrong,' he muttered to himself. 'This is so wrong.

Myles tried to console him. 'Surely the Roosevelt Guardians have been trained well enough. They're not going to fire, are they? They'll just keep it under control – surely…?'

'I don't know, Myles, I don't know…' He turned to Myles. 'I'm in charge, I'm responsible. I've got to get down there.'

Myles could see the fear on Roosevelt's face. 'Can't you just radio through? It'd be quicker – just tell them to back off?'

'It wouldn't work, Myles. I've got to be there.'

'Then stay safe,' conceded Myles.

Roosevelt registered the comment but his mind was already thinking ahead. The young Senator ran towards the door, clearly determined to resolve the chaos on the streets of Rome. That left only Myles to track down Juma.

Myles still couldn't work out how Juma had managed to escape so quickly. Within a minute of seeing him at the scanner, Myles had run down to confront Juma at the entrance. But in that minute Juma had somehow made it into the conference centre, past the sniffer dogs, along the corridor and into the café, where he'd left his jacket, then disappeared. Myles had to find him. And fast.

He turned back to the computer screen showing the CCTV feed. 'Anyone know how you play back images on this?' he called out to the room.

Susan came over. 'Yes, press control-delete on the computer to get the controls up, then use the cursors.'

Myles nodded his thanks then followed her instructions, concentrating on the screen. Instantly a time-stamp appeared at the bottom of the image.

Susan squinted at it, then looked up at a clock on the wall. The times didn't match. She seemed puzzled. 'Our clock's fast,' she said, frowning.

Myles wondered too, then he understood. He shook his head. 'No,' he replied. 'The images are slow. Five minutes slow.'

They hadn't been watching a live feed, but a delayed image with a five-minute lag. Myles had reached the entrance within a minute of seeing Juma at the scanner, but that was really almost six minutes after Juma was there – plenty of time to escape. 'Can you get me a feed from other cameras?' he asked.

Susan pressed something which brought a rectangle up on the screen. It contained three columns with four images in each.

She pointed at them to show how Myles could click on each one to enlarge it, then use the cursor keys to fast forward or rewind.

Myles selected the image for the main entrance. He fast-forwarded until Juma appeared in his summer suit, then played it. It was definitely him. The dogs reacted to him, and one of the Marines made him take off his jacket. The low-quality images showed the Somali being padded down by the soldiers.

The soldiers seemed to find nothing. Then Juma asked them a question, got directions, and went out of shot towards the café – now carrying his jacket...

Myles clicked on the image of the café. The chair where Juma had left his jacket was clearly visible in the left-hand side of the screen. He rewinded the image, then played it when he saw himself. He was going through the pockets of the jacket, then the Marines approached him.

Myles went back further. It showed him arriving, looking around, then seeing the jacket.

He scrolled back two more minutes. The jacket wasn't there. He fast-forwarded until he saw Juma enter, then pressed 'play'. The Somali leader still looked calm. He scanned around, peering at the coffee queue. Then he put his jacket on the chair. He took out the pills – laxatives – and popped several of them into his palm, knocking them back into his mouth. Juma put the half-empty packet of pills back, and looked around some more.

Suddenly Juma reacted to something. It was his phone. He pulled it from his pocket and answered it. *Someone had warned him.* Quickly, Juma jumped to look down the corridor. Then he ran away from view, towards the toilets.

Seconds later Myles appeared in the image, searching for him.

Myles thanked Susan. 'You need to get a message out: they need to seal off that café area,' he said. 'Tell them to look out for this man.'

Susan understood and moved towards the radios.

Myles turned to one of his Marine escorts – a tall man who looked more intelligent than the others. 'And you need to come with me,' said Myles.

The Marine nodded, and Myles and the Marine darted out of the room. For the second time, Myles ran along the corridor, trying to bump into as few people as he could, but this time with a US Marine closely behind him. Down the stairs, past the entrance and the dog handlers, along the second corridor, to the café.

The Marine stayed close. Already the message had got out, and other Marines were alert and on duty, actively guarding the café.

Myles and the Marine stopped opposite the door to the toilets. Checking they were both ready, Myles silently pressed on the door. It swung open. Myles held it for the Marine, who used hand signals to instruct his colleagues: they were to guard the entrance.

Then the Marine followed Myles in.

Inside, an elderly delegate was washing his hands. The man realised Myles and the Marine were looking for something. Myles put his finger to his lips, indicating the man should be quiet. The man understood, exiting with his hands still wet.

Myles and the Marine inspected the cubicles. Only one was in use. Locked.

The Marine bent down to see a pair of shoes on the floor. He nodded to Myles. Myles peered down and saw the same thing.

Silently, the Marine pointed at his boot then at the door. Myles indicated that he agreed.

Taking only a moment to prepare himself, the Marine suddenly gave the door a huge kick.

The door flipped back on its hinges, the broken lock flying against the wall.

Before the Marine could see what was inside, he was knocked straight down, onto the toilet floor.

He had been shot.

A man with a bare torso barged out, jumping over the body of the Marine.

It was Juma.

CHAPTER SIXTY-EIGHT
Barberini Conference Centre, Rome

Myles bent down to check on the Marine. Juma's bullet had hit the body armour on his chest, knocking him to the floor and winding him.

The Marine was moving his head around as if he was dazed. Myles hauled him up until he was sitting on the floor.

Then Myles felt a terrifying presence standing above him. Juma hadn't left the toilets. Instead, he was holding his pistol just a few inches from Myles' nose. 'My Mr Englishman,' sneered the Somali pirate. 'Looks like you just can't get enough of my bullets, can you.'

Myles didn't reply immediately. Instead he made eye contact with the Marine. He could tell the soldier, still sitting on the ground, was thinking of making a move. Grabbing Juma's legs, perhaps.

Quietly Myles shook his head. He knew Juma: the man would kill them both on a whim. The Marine understood and stayed where he was.

Slowly Myles lifted his eyes. Juma's face was sweating and his smile was not as confident as it once had been. As well as his jacket, Juma had taken off his shirt, revealing the scar on his abdomen where his kidney had been stolen as a teenager. His muscles were glistening as though he was feverish. 'Juma. So you made it here,' said Myles.

Juma was breathless. 'I did, Mr Munro. And now I'm going to do what I said I'd do.'

'Bring down America like the Roman Empire? You know this is Rome, not America, don't you?'

Juma pretended to laugh, but he was clearly in some pain. He put his free arm on his stomach. 'Englishman, stand up,' he ordered.

Myles obeyed. Juma indicated to the Marine. 'You, too.'

The Marine came to his feet as Juma walked back, creating extra distance between him and the two men. Myles kept questioning him. 'So come on, Juma, what's your plan?' he asked. 'How are you going to destroy America?'

Juma took the question straight on. 'I'm going to destroy this conference, which will help destroy the dollar,' he said.

Myles shook his head. 'Rome didn't collapse because they devalued their coins – it was the other way around. They devalued their coins because the Empire was falling apart.'

Juma pretended to chuckle again. 'Thanks for the history lesson, Mr Professor. You'll be history yourself soon.' He motioned his gun in a circle. He wanted the two men to face away from him. 'Hands on your heads, please. Both of you walk towards the door.'

Myles raised his hands, but refused to be humbled. 'Which of the conference delegates do you want to kill, Juma?'

'That's easy, Englishman: all of them.'

'But they're all fat, middle-aged bankers. There aren't even a lot of them – America loses more men in road accidents every day than there are here,' said Myles.

'They hold the key to America's economy.'

'Who told you that, Juma?' taunted Myles. 'It's nonsense. They all have deputies ready to replace them, anyway.'

Juma gestured with his gun as Myles and the Marine walked forward, reaching the toilet door. 'And through you go,' he ordered. 'Hands still on your heads.'

As the door opened, Myles saw a crowd of Marines eagerly watching him. Their barrels were all pointed at him – Myles felt the laser beams and gun-sights zero in. All were poised to shoot.

Myles and the Marine beside him couldn't talk. They made faces to indicate they were under duress. The firing squad clearly understood.

Then Myles felt Juma's sweat-soaked hand grab his collar from behind. The Somali gang leader twisted it and pulled. He called out to the crowd, his mouth just inches from Myles' ear. 'Guns down please, gentlemen. All guns down.' It was the voice of a man well used to command.

Juma waited, still only half through the toilet door. Myles could see the security men in front of him were unsure what to do. Several kept their eyes on Juma. Myles could tell some of them were contemplating taking a shot.

Juma shouted again, agitated this time. 'Guns down. Now.'

Silence. Nobody moved. The only noise came from large TV monitors above the café. It was CNN coverage: a live feed from the refugees near the US Embassy, not far away.

Finally an authoritative American voice called out from somewhere – one of the Marine commanders. 'Lower weapons. Everyone lower their weapons…'

The Marines obeyed almost immediately, gradually and more reluctantly followed by the Roosevelt Guardians. As their guns started to drop down, Myles saw the crowd ease up slightly. They would not be firing in the next few moments. The stand-off might be resolved.

Juma called out again. 'Thank you, gentlemen. Now, I want the men standing by the corridor to move to the sides,' he insisted. 'Move.'

This time the men with guns obeyed more quickly. A few weapons clattered as they shuffled their positions. The firing squad in front of Myles had become an armed human corridor.

Juma twisted Myles' collar more tightly, grabbing it firmly in his hand. Myles felt his shirt squeeze around his neck.

For several seconds, silence began to settle throughout the conference building. Then suddenly the noise of gunfire – a burst from somewhere high. Everyone looked up to trace it. It was the CNN feed on the conference TV. Myles heard Helen's voice, broadcasting live. 'Some shots have been fired at the refugees in the square here. Panic is starting to break out. We don't know exactly what's happening…'

The pictures jogged around – the cameraman filming them was taking cover – until they fixed on a wounded African woman lying on a grass verge. The men trying to treat her were ducking their heads.

Juma whispered in Myles' ear. 'We're about to start running together, Englishman.' Aggression hissed through his voice. 'Before you try something, just remember how much I enjoy killing.'

Myles nodded.

Juma called to the Marine. 'You. I want you to run ahead. Go towards the entrance and tell them to drop all their weapons. Go.'

The Marine understood. With all eyes looking at him, he started to jog. Clearly relieved to be away from Juma, he waved his palms down to the floor, making eye contact with people all along the corridor. Everywhere, weapons were lowered and placed on the floor. A few unarmed conference delegates, accidently caught up in the situation, began to press themselves against the wall, terrified.

Soon the Marine had cleared the route ahead. He slowed, then turned back to face Juma, his job done.

Myles could sense Juma was about to move. He braced himself, desperately trying to think of a way of saving the situation.

But he knew Juma was even more desperate than him, and that made the pirate warlord more dangerous than ever. Would a sharpshooter try to kill Juma?

Myles felt Juma push on his collar. He started moving.

Juma began pushing him faster. Myles tried to jog, but found it impossible with his collar held.

Then Juma started to turn Myles around. He was trying to spin, to make it hard for any of the Marines or security men to take a shot without hitting Myles – the hostage.

'Run,' shouted Juma. Myles felt himself pushed and pulled along as they rushed down the corridor. He caught the eyes of the people watching him. They kept their guns lowered, all too afraid to shoot.

'Keep going,' ordered Juma.

Myles and Juma had spun halfway along the corridor. The café was behind them and the entrance to the centre just up ahead.

Myles saw Juma's pistol: a standard-issue security weapon. The sort of gun used by security guards. It pressed into his ribs. He thought about trying to knock it to the ground, but Juma was grabbing him too tightly.

Juma was growing confident again. None of the men around him dared to fire. He started joking into Myles' ear. 'You like waltzing, Mr Englishman?'

Before Myles could answer, Juma had yanked him around as they approached the entrance. Suddenly they stopped spinning and Myles became a human shield in front of the pirate.

The Somali warlord pointed his gun in front of him and shouted at the people ahead. 'Down.'

The dog handlers and conference delegates froze. Many had been about to leave the centre. Now they realised they'd been caught.

'Down!' called Juma again. He glared at them with wide eyes and the face of a maniac. As they caught his stare, the bankers, security men and assistants realised they had no choice but to obey. They started lying down. Juma stared at the Marine who had ran ahead, ordering him to do the same.

Juma turned to the last few who resisted his order, and jerked his gun towards them. Quickly, they copied the others. Soon everyone was on the floor.

Juma checked again behind him, then pushed Myles forward and advanced.

Myles kept thinking: has he only got a gun? He knew that if Juma fired he would instantly be torn down by all the security men. But that would leave Myles dead too. Sacrificing himself like Sam Roosevelt wasn't enough. He already knew the plot to bring down America was about more than just the Somali pirate warlord. Far more. Myles needed to survive.

He called over his shoulder to Juma. 'You can't kill the all the bankers with just one gun.'

Juma laughed. 'Up the stairs,' he ordered.

Myles felt his neck being pointed at the steps, and walked around a terrified conference delegate who looked up at him from the ground. Juma followed on behind.

Juma checked behind him again. Everyone remained on the floor. The Somali pirate started calling out again. 'Where's my Marine? Marine!'

The Marine who had run ahead to clear the way lifted his head from the floor.

'Get up,' shouted Juma. The Marine jumped to his feet. 'Go up those stairs,' continued the Somali, 'and tell the people up there to lie on the floor.'

The Marine nodded then ran up in front of Myles and Juma. On the upper level, he did as Juma had instructed. The delegates started to lie down.

Myles and Juma climbed the steps.

'You've been abandoned, Juma,' said Myles, trying to distract him.

Juma didn't reply. He was watching the upper-level corridors as he led his hostage to the top of the stairs.

A few delegates were lying on the floor in one direction. The way towards the CCTV room was clear. There was no one with a gun who could do anything to help Myles.

Juma grinned. 'I'd say *you've* been abandoned, Englishman – all the security men are downstairs.'

But Myles could sense Juma was disappointed. Whatever Juma's plan was, it seemed to have gone wrong.

They were both distracted by the largest TV monitor in the centre. Helen was questioning Dick Roosevelt on camera.

'Why have your men started firing at these civilians?' shouted Helen over the chaos.

'They opened fire in self-defence, Helen,' countered Dick.

'But these aren't terrorists, Senator. They're unarmed civilians.'

'These people are complicit in terrorism. We've just heard of a terrorist attack at the currency conference…'

The Senator's revelation had clearly caught Helen by surprise. She didn't have the next question ready, and seemed unsure whether to ask about the incident or press Dick Roosevelt more on his claim about the African migrants.

Myles and Juma kept watching as the footage switched away from the interview to the refugees. The bottom of the screen showed the words 'Breaking News – Terrorist incident at Rome Currency Conference'.

Then Placidia appeared. She was standing in front of her people, her arms out, trying to stop any more of the refugees being shot. The audio didn't pick up her voice, but it was clear she was pleading with the Roosevelt Guardians holding rifles.

Myles could see Juma's face – whether it was Placidia or the shooting, he was enthralled. Myles used the distraction to reach inside his pocket. Subtly, he moved his fingers towards the car keys he had taken from Juma's jacket. He clutched them in his hand.

On the screen, Placidia refused to cower. With her arms outstretched, she stood like a crucifix. People behind her flinched as another shot was fired, but she remained in place – defiant.

'You can't protect her, Juma,' said Myles. He sensed Juma's mind switch back to his present situation.

'She can protect herself,' huffed Juma proudly.

Myles knew Juma was wondering what to do next – where to go, where to escape.

If Myles was going to distract Juma, the time to do it was now. 'Juma, you know what Placidia told me?' he said.

'What, Englishman?'

'She told me I was better.'

Almost instantly Myles felt the hand on his collar thrust him forward. Myles was being thrown down the stairs. Juma's voice called out behind him as he tumbled – a single word. 'Die…'

Myles saw the warlord's forearm stretch out. He pointed his weapon down at Myles.

Myles closed his eyes and pressed the button.

CHAPTER SIXTY-NINE
Barberini Conference Centre, Rome

There was just a flicker of recognition on Juma's face before the bomb detonated inside him. His body erupted, and an enormous force burst out from his abdomen. The Somali pirate chief's body was torn apart in an instant. His legs were shot in opposite directions, while one arm and most of his torso spun in the air. Juma's head was blasted away to a distant part of the conference centre, while his gun ricocheted off the steps.

For half a second, a red mist hung in the air, then seemed to disappear. Juma, and all that he threatened, was blown away.

Myles barely noticed blood from the pirate's body spray towards him. The explosion had blasted him towards the bottom of the stairs, and left him convulsed by the shock wave.

Myles still clutched the remote control in his hand, half disbelieving that something so small could have an impact so huge. Then he looked up at the remnants of the man who had terrorised America. *Juma was dead.*

It was hard to believe the pirate leader, the man who had caused such misery, was finally gone. Myles exhaled, still amazed he had survived.

The Marine at the bottom of the stairs was the first to his feet. He rushed over to Myles, very confused about what had happened. 'What the hell was that?' he asked.

Myles was still catching his breath. 'Juma had swallowed a bomb,' he explained. 'He was going to plant it somewhere, then leave before it went off.'

'But he didn't get the chance?'

Myles nodded in confirmation, still staring at Juma's remains.

Other delegates around the entrance to the conference centre began to stand up. The Marines and Roosevelt Guardians who had been near the café were running over, guns in hand.

Myles looked again at the live feed from CNN. The 'Breaking News' message on the screen now declared: *US Marines fail to contain terrorism at conference.*

Myles shook his head in disbelief at the headline. This wasn't about the Marines…

Then he understood. He turned to the Marine beside him. 'This isn't over,' he said, thinking aloud. 'America could still share the "fate of Rome" – I've got to run.'

The Marine frowned, as if to ask what it was all about. But Myles was already gone, leaving the confused security men to clean up the mess and work out what had happened.

The noise of the blast had been heard outside and several Marines and Italian policemen were running to assist. Myles sprinted out of the building against the flow of people. He tried to weave through them, apologising for bumping into them as he went. He had to get to the US Embassy.

Some of the people he passed saw him running and thought there was still danger in the conference centre. Others stared at him and his odd clothes, and wondered whether he was guilty. But Myles just tried to move through them as fast as he could.

Sweating in the sunshine, he approached the security perimeter of the conference. Here he had to slow. A Marine manning one of the scanners held out his hand to indicate 'stop'.

Myles pointed backwards with his thumb. 'There's a bomb just gone off in there,' he called to the Marine. The Marine saw Myles' sweat and assumed – wrongly – that Myles was worried about another bomb in the conference centre. He let Myles pass.

Myles sprinted off again. He hurdled over a concrete road barrier designed to protect against vehicle-borne bombs, ran through the twisty narrow streets, passed tourists and cars and jogged up the steps. Myles knew the route – he had gone this way when he was on holiday with Helen. Now he had to reach her.

As he reached Via Veneto, near the US Embassy, he confronted the next security line. This one was made of Roosevelt Guardians. An outer cordon: to protect the backs of the Guardians who were watching the African refugees.

Myles stopped again. He tried to size up the private security men controlling the way ahead. They looked stern. A pretty Italian journalist was arguing with one of them – she'd just been expelled from the scene and the Roosevelt Guardians weren't going to let her back in.

Myles tried to peer through. He could just see some of the refugees through the lines of men. They were still holding out, still just outside the US Embassy. He had to reach them.

He tried to calm his breathing and wiped the sweat from his face as he walked up to the Roosevelt Guardian who seemed to be in charge. 'I need to go in, please,' he asked, trying to sound polite and respectful, even though he was obviously in a hurry.

'No, sir. No one goes in.'

'Please, it's important,' Myles insisted. 'Lives are at stake.'

'Sorry, sir. Orders,' came the reply, cold and certain. 'No one else in.'

Myles clenched his fist in frustration, but knew a punch would only get him detained.

He looked at the Roosevelt Guardian's face again, trying to judge him. Myles realised telling him about the plot to bring down America wouldn't convince him – the man was just following orders.

Myles tried to speak to him in a chatty tone. 'So you're clearing out the journalists from around the embassy?'

The man didn't answer, but his non-reaction confirmed Myles was right.

Myles nodded knowingly. 'I'm a friend of Dick Roosevelt. The Senator said I should get through.'

'Sorry, sir. No one goes in.'

'Check with Dick Roosevelt,' urged Myles, pressing his point. 'You don't want to countermand his order. Check with him.'

The Roosevelt Guardian looked unsure. He clearly didn't want to annoy a friend of the Chief Executive. But then could Myles really be a friend of someone as senior as the new Senator Roosevelt? The Guardian eyed Myles' ill-fitting Chinese suit with suspicion.

Myles pushed his point home. 'Get on your radio and check with him. Now – it's urgent. Tell him Myles Munro is here and is ready to go through.'

Reluctantly the private security man used his radio. 'Outer cordon control point for Chief Exec's office,' he said. 'Message. Over.'

There was a pause, then a crackle of static and 'Send.'

'We have a Mr Munro here, claims to have permission to enter from the Chief Exec. Can you confirm?'

Another pause, before a radio squelch followed by the words, 'The Chief Exec is unavailable at the moment. Please hold.'

Myles knew if they made him wait too long his chance would be lost. He *had* to get through. 'Dick Roosevelt is unavailable because he's in great danger,' lied Myles. 'Either that, or everything he's worked on is about to be destroyed.'

The Roosevelt Guardian just looked bemused. What was this Englishman talking about?

Myles could see the Guardian was about to react again, when he decided to take the chance: quickly, he vaulted over the barrier. 'You'll thank me later,' he called, hoping his words would confuse the private security guards, as he sprinted on again, this time towards the inner cordon.

The Roosevelt Guardians didn't know how to react. Myles left them standing. The Italian journalist saw what had happened and tried to push through after him. The Roosevelt Guardians stopped her, but it meant they couldn't chase after Myles. They had to let him go.

The men in the cordon in front of him didn't expect him. They didn't even see him – Myles came from behind. He ducked under their line and ran forward.

Before the Roosevelt Guardians could act, Myles was with the refugees.

He quickly took his bearings. He could see Helen and her crew. He could see Roosevelt Guardians manhandling other journalists. And he could see the line of Guardians themselves, now behind him: the inner cordon. They had their weapons ready, and they were about to fire.

Myles was in the thick of the crowd. The Africans had been cornered, and they knew it. Some were trying to move, at least half aware there was nowhere to go. Others were panicking, some terrified. Most looked hungry and desperate.

The Roosevelt Guardians were about to shoot into the crowd…

Myles tried to make his way through. A mother was sitting on the ground, breastfeeding her infant. Myles carefully tried to step over her. He passed an angry teenager shouting back at the Roosevelt Guardians. Some older refugees were sitting down, unsure what to do. But there was no sign of Placidia.

Myles kept trying to pass through. He had to make it over to Helen, who was about to broadcast again. She had her finger on her earpiece and was holding a microphone. Turning to check the image behind her, she paused for a gesture from the cameraman, then started reporting on the scene.

Another journalist was trying to film not far from her. The Roosevelt Guardians were jostling with the cameraman. A scuffle, which Myles made his way around.

Eventually Helen saw him approaching. She indicated to someone that they needed to stop filming, then moved through the crowd towards him. Myles tried to wade towards her.

Finally, their hands touched over the people. They pulled each other in and embraced. 'Myles, you're safe,' she enthused.

'Where's Placidia?'

It wasn't the question Helen had been hoping for. She made plain she didn't know.

But Myles was insistent. 'Quick, where is she?' He looked round again, desperately searching through the crowds. Still no sign.

Helen finally picked up on Myles' urgency. 'Myles, what's happened?' she asked.

'The plot to bring down America like ancient Rome – it's gone wrong,' he explained.

Helen looked confused. 'But…but that's good, isn't it?'

Myles shook his head sceptically. 'There was never a proper plot,' he said. 'I'll explain later. But where's Placidia? We need to find her. Now.'

Helen tried to look around with Myles. Both were taller than most of the crowd around them, but it was still hard to see everybody. 'I don't know,' said Helen. 'She was close by a few minutes ago.'

Helen and Myles were knocked by some of the panicked refugees, who were desperately looking for shelter. Many were shouting or screaming, fearing more bullets would be aimed at them. Helen was almost brought to the ground.

Myles grabbed her, turned her towards him and spoke directly to her face. 'Helen. We need to get into the Embassy,' he insisted.

'The US Embassy?'

'Yes, inside.'

Helen was now doubly confused. 'Placidia won't be in there.'

Myles nodded. 'This isn't for Placidia.'

Helen turned to the building just behind them, still baffled. Myles seemed convinced. She knew she would have to trust him.

Helen beckoned over to her camera crew, who acknowledged Helen's lead and started to follow. She indicated to Myles that they were ready to move.

Myles and Helen started to push through the crowd of Africans. Most of the refugees were already bunched up – they had tried to move as far away from the Roosevelt Guardians as they could.

Helen waved her way through. As the crowd started to realise she and Myles were not a threat, their route to the embassy became easier.

Soon they were approaching the Roosevelt Guardians keeping the African refugees out of the embassy grounds – the line which marked the start of US territory.

Helen tried to shout to Myles over the noise. 'Why the embassy?'

'To protect America,' was Myles' response.

Helen made clear she didn't understand. But she kept moving forward until finally they had passed through all the refugees. She waited for Myles and her two-person production team to join her. Then she faced up to the wall of Roosevelt Guardians.

The Roosevelt Guardians were still blocking the entrance into the embassy. They acknowledged Helen's presence, but refused to move.

Helen turned to Myles. 'What now?'

'We need to get in.'

'But these guys won't let us in,' said Helen, frustrated.

'They have to. You're American,' insisted Myles. 'Show them your passport.'

The Roosevelt Guardians overheard Myles' explanation to Helen. They waited while Helen searched for her passport. Eventually she found it.

She pulled it out and waved it at the Roosevelt Guardians. Her production crew did the same.

The private security men looked unsure. They hadn't been given orders about Americans.

Helen pressed her point. 'C'mon, guys. It's Americans like me you're here to protect…'

Still unsure, one of the Guardians turned to someone for advice. It was enough for Helen to push her way through. Myles and her production team followed. The private security men realised the decision had been made for them and allowed the four to go inside. They quickly closed the line up again. Some refugees tried to push on them, but the line of security men wasn't going to move any more. The Africans were still trapped.

Just as they were leaving the crowd behind them a voice called out. 'Mrs Helen. Mrs Helen.' Myles and Helen turned to see a young African woman, who neither of them knew, holding something out for them. Helen went back to see what it was. The Roosevelt Guardians were reluctant to let the young woman reach over to her, fearing she was going to break through into the embassy. But it was clear the woman had something she wanted to give Helen. She was holding it up, trying to pass it to Helen over the security guards.

Helen tried to reach for it. Her hand was knocked. The young African woman was being moved away by the crowd.

'Throw it to me!' called Helen.

The African woman tossed it as she was pushed away. Helen managed to catch it in the air, and grabbed it firmly. It was an old-style mobile phone.

The young woman called out to her. 'It's from Placidia,' she said. 'Placidia said you'd need it.'

Helen nodded to indicate she had heard, although she didn't understand the message.

She looked at the phone, bemused. Briefly she wondered whether it was dangerous: would it blow up? Helen turned quizzically to Myles.

He took the phone and quickly pressed the 'last dialled' button. Nothing. Then he looked at the messages – the inbox. Again, nothing.

Myles knew he'd missed something. What was Placidia doing?

He frowned in frustration. Another of Placidia's puzzles, or had he forgotten something?

He didn't have time to work it out now. He looked back at the refugees, now in full panic as they realised the Roosevelt Guardians were preparing to fire at them.

Some of the Africans were crying, others shouting. Some jeered at the Roosevelt Guardians, even as the security men raised their rifles. The migrants felt betrayed. They were trapped in a square with no escape. People who were about to be slaughtered like animals…

One of the young men given a gun on the ship raised his weapon to fire in the air. A Roosevelt Guardian sniper hit him almost immediately, also shooting the two women standing beside him. All three collapsed in an instant.

Myles moved over to Helen. 'Come on,' he shouted to her over the noise. 'We've got to get inside the building.'

Helen and Myles moved in through the entrance door of the building. Myles desperately looked around inside. He knew there would be one here…

His eyes scanned the walls as Helen spoke to the worried man on reception. Then Myles saw what he was looking for. He moved over towards it, apologising to the receptionist as he did so. 'Sorry…'

The man wondered what he was about to do. But Myles had already raised his arm.

Myles took aim, then slammed his elbow into the fire alarm.

CHAPTER SEVENTY
US Embassy, Rome

The square of glass in the fire alarm shattered. Instantly a deafening siren rang throughout the building. The doors automatically flung themselves open.

Helen frowned at Myles. 'What have you done?' she tried to shout over the noise of the alarm.

Myles tried to shout back, but realised the fire signal was too loud. He could only give her a one word explanation. 'Sanctuary,' he mouthed.

Helen still didn't understand.

Within a few seconds US Embassy workers started to appear from corridors and stairways. Some in suits, others in chinos or jeans. They began to gather near the doors, wondering whether it was a drill or a real fire.

Myles shouted as loudly as he could. 'Everybody outside.'

He hoped none of them remembered the last time he gave instructions to the embassy staff, but his English accent still caused confusion: why were American diplomats being herded by a Brit?

Helen saw what was happening and backed him up, putting on a southern drawl to make sure everyone got the message. 'Come on – everybody outta here…'

An older staff member recognised her from television and looked uncertain. Helen kept up the pretence. 'Yes, it's a fire alarm,' she confirmed. 'Everybody out. Quick.'

Gradually the embassy staff started to obey. Diplomats and officials, office staff and cleaners all started to leave the building. Once it became clear a few were going the rest followed in a rush.

Myles and Helen found themselves in a swarm of half-panicked Americans, all desperately trying to leave the building.

The receptionist, who had seen Myles slam his elbow into the alarm, tried to approach. He couldn't make it through the crowds, but he caught Myles' eye.

Myles knew the look. He didn't want to be detained again. He grabbed Helen's arm. 'Come on,' he shouted in her ear. 'We've got to get out of here, too.'

Myles led Helen out again, allowing them to leave with the US Embassy workers.

Outside the embassy was chaos. US Embassy workers were flooding out, mixing with frightened refugees. Roosevelt Guardians and the few remaining journalists were caught up in the swirling crowds, just like Myles and Helen. No one could see what was happening.

Then the African refugees seemed to realise the embassy doors were open.

If they pushed through the Roosevelt Guardians they would be safe inside the embassy.

The Roosevelt Guardians were desperately trying to hold the line, but with the embassy staff breaking their line one way, it became impossible for them to hold back the refugees pushing the other. And as soon as a few African refugees were through, the push of the crowd became unstoppable. The line broke, and the refugees streamed towards the embassy doors and inside the building. Finally they had reached American soil.

The refugees were safe at last.

Journalists started to break through the outer cordon. Myles saw the Italian who had been arguing with the Roosevelt Guardian when he had vaulted his way in: she was now taking pictures of the private security men looking dejected. Helen's own broadcast crew started to get footage of the first Africans inside the embassy, as they tried to claim asylum. Paramedics rushed to treat refugees with bullet wounds. The breach in the line meant the Roosevelt Guardians couldn't pretend anymore: they had to let all the Africans through.

Helen frowned in confusion. 'I still don't get it.'

'We've bought some time,' explained Myles. 'But that's all. We still need to find Placidia.'

'Bought who time, Myles?

Myles was still too distracted to answer properly. He searched around for any indication of where she could be. Nothing. He wondered whether she could have been hiding in the crowd, but it was unlikely: if she was still with the refugees someone would have seen her by now.

'She must have gone somewhere,' said Myles.

'Did she escape?' suggested Helen, trying to be helpful. 'Or did someone call her away?'

'Perhaps…' said Myles, pausing. 'Or she called someone else away…' He remembered the mobile, and pointed to Helen's bag.

Helen pulled it out for him. 'I've already checked: there's nothing on it,' she shouted over the noise.

'Not in the inbox…' Myles went into the messages, then clicked on 'messages sent'. There it was. The message read: 'We need to talk. Meet me in the Pantheon. Now.'

Myles scrolled down to 'message details', then looked at his watch. 'Sent fifteen minutes ago,' he said. 'There's still time.'

He passed the device back to Helen, who still looked confused. 'Why did she give the phone to me?'

'Because she knew you were here,' explained Myles. 'Maybe she knew you'd give the phone to me.'

'Well, who's she meeting?'

'Dick. It's Dick Roosevelt,' muttered Myles.

'Dick?'

Myles nodded as he looked ahead, trying to map out the fastest route to the Pantheon. 'Helen, this chaos here – it's not the most important thing. It's not the news story,' he tried to explain.

Helen looked around her: wounded refugees, confused embassy officials, angry security guards... 'Looks like a story to me.'

'No. Listen.' Myles held her shoulders. 'I've got to go. But get your production team ready for another one of those videos from Placidia.'

'No, Myles – she's a terrorist.' Helen was feeling adamant now. 'And she's a bitch.'

'OK. Then just believe me; these refugees are innocent.'

Helen glanced at them. She could accept that. 'But Myles...' She wanted to say something more to him, but Myles was already running. Within seconds he had gone. Helen couldn't see him for all the journalists, refugees and Embassy staff. Then she caught a final image of his tall frame dodging through the crowds. He disappeared behind an Italian fire engine which had arrived on the scene, blocked in by the jam of people.

Helen moved back towards the embassy, towards her production team who were eagerly taking as much footage as they could. The camerawoman clearly wanted her to do a live broadcast, but Helen wasn't going for it. 'Have we had any more terrorist videos from Placidia?' she asked.

The camerawoman shook her head and pulled a face which said she didn't want to be disturbed. She kept filming what seemed like ideal news footage.

'Please check,' insisted Helen.

The camerawoman reluctantly conceded. She pulled out her internet-enabled mobile to go online. It took a few seconds to boot up and get a webpage. Then she scrolled to the site which had shown earlier broadcasts from 'the plot to bring down America like ancient Rome'. She studied it until she was sure, then showed it to Helen. 'Nothing new,' she said.

'Really?'

The camerawoman nodded as she took back the device and prepared to film Helen commentating on the crazy scenes in the embassy.

She was just about to put the internet browser away when she saw something. 'Wait…There is something. Coming through now. It's live.'

Helen and her camerawoman began watching the moving images. Helen recognised the ancient interior immediately. The footage was being broadcast from inside the Pantheon.

CHAPTER SEVENTY-ONE
Pantheon, Rome

It took Myles eight minutes to sprint to the Pantheon.

As he ran across the piazza outside the building he heard a loud bang. The acoustics of the Pantheon distorted the noise, but Myles recognised the sound immediately.

A gunshot.

All the tourists flinched and looked confused. But not Myles – he kept running, past Roosevelt security men standing guard outside, through the large wooden doors, and into the eerie interior of the building itself.

He began to walk forward, into the darkness, towards the centre of the 'Church for All Gods'.

'Anyone here?' he called out, catching his breath.

His words echoed around the building. No response. Then he heard a weak voice call out. 'Myles – is that you?' It was Dick Roosevelt, lying wounded on the church floor.

Myles rushed over. Dick clearly had a bleeding wound near his left shoulder. He was grasping his upper arm with his right hand.

'Dick – what happened?'

Myles bent down to help, unsure what he could do. He lifted Dick's torso into a sitting position, and examined his wound. The bullet had passed through his muscle: serious but not life-threatening.

Roosevelt spoke slowly. 'She shot me,' he said.

'Placidia?'

Dick nodded. His face turned towards the side of the church.

Myles followed his gaze, his eyes still adjusting. Gradually he made out a figure slumped in one of the alcoves of the church. He left Dick and moved towards it, slowly at first, then as fast as he could.

Placidia's body was still warm. Myles lifted it – limp and heavy. He looked at her mouth, her forehead, and her cheeks…and her lifeless eyes. He tried to shake her, but there was nothing. He shouted at her face, 'Placidia?'

No response.

He looked into her eyes again and turned her head towards the dim light inside the building: the pupils didn't contract. He felt her neck: no pulse. Then he held her towards him, hugging her body for the last time. *It had all gone so wrong.*

Myles held her close, helplessly rocking her dead body in his arms.

Dick called out from behind, his voice still strained. 'Is she dead?'

Myles didn't need to answer Dick's question: it was obvious she was. He cut the young Senator out of his mind and ignored his whole surroundings. Instead, he remembered the life-force which Placidia had once been: the tireless campaigner at Oxford, the beauty of their shared tutorials on the Roman Empire, the enigmatic terror behind Juma and the plot to bring down America…

Myles could admit it now: he had loved her. Somehow her spirit would never go.

He looked again at her face. It seemed stuck in an odd expression: it was as if she died in the midst of victory and defeat at the same time.

Myles surveyed the rest of her body. Her breasts were bloody and damaged: a bullet wound to the chest.

Dick's voice called over to him again. 'You think I might get some treatment here?' he asked, sarcastic and pained.

Myles gently kissed Placidia's body as he lay it back on the floor of the church. 'Sure, Dick. I'm coming,' he called as he moved back to the young Senator.

Dick had managed to remove his jacket and bunch it up. He was holding it as a pad against the wound. It was already starting to soak through with blood. 'I guess I finally got her,' he said.

'Self-defence?'

Dick nodded, wincing with pain. 'Yeah,' he said. 'If she had been a better shot...'

Myles examined the wound as he listened. 'Did she say anything before she died?'

'Not much,' replied Roosevelt, looking around as he tried to recall. 'I think she said, "At least I'll kill one American".'

'That's what she said, "At least I'll kill one American"?'

'Something like that.'

'Then she tried to shoot you?'

'Yeah, but I, kinda, moved to the side,' said Dick trying to smile. 'And shot her back.'

Myles pressed firmly into Dick's shoulder wound, freeing up the Senator's other hand. 'She didn't make you drop your weapon first?' asked Myles.

'No. I guess she was an amateur terrorist.' There was a mocking tone in Dick's voice.

'So she held you at gunpoint but let you keep hold of your weapon?' said Myles.

Dick Roosevelt nodded. Then he grabbed Myles' wrist with his free hand. He forced Myles to look him in the eye. 'Hey, Myles. Isn't it great? It's finally over,' said Dick, excitedly. 'The plot to bring down the United States. Placidia's "Last Prophecy of Ancient Rome". It's over. You and I: we saved America. We're real heroes now.'

'You mean, Juma dead, Placidia dead…' said Myles, more soberly. 'And your father: dead, too.'

The mention of Sam Roosevelt's death knocked Dick's mood. He started to become sullen and self-absorbed. 'It was such a pity my father had to die,' said Dick, almost like a confession. It seemed as though he might say more, but the American kept his words back. Roosevelt junior seemed to be thinking something through, perhaps even making a calculation.

After a silent pause Roosevelt changed the subject. 'Well, at least my men are outside,' he said.

'Well, why don't they come in?' suggested Myles, surprised. 'We need to get your wound treated, Senator.'

Dick didn't really respond to the question. He winced again, then turned back to Myles. 'So what do you think Juma had been planning?'

'I guess he was trying to smuggle a bomb into the conference and set it off.'

'Not a suicide bomber, then?'

'No,' answered Myles, shaking his head. 'He only swallowed the bomb to get through security. He was trying to get the bomb out in the toilet when we interrupted him.'

Dick looked pensive. 'And Placidia?'

'I think all she wanted was asylum for her people,' said Myles, looking over at her crumpled body. 'It was her last campaign.'

'Really?' huffed Roosevelt. 'She just tried to kill me.'

Myles didn't react.

Dick could tell he wasn't convinced. 'Come on, Myles. She *was* a terrorist, right? She had to die.'

Myles still didn't answer. 'She had to die' – one of the doctors had said that about his mother's cancer. Then he remembered how Placidia used to be. 'She wasn't a terrorist when I knew her. At university she was idealistic. She believed in good things.'

'Sure,' accepted Roosevelt. 'But she changed. People change. Perhaps by marrying Juma, she became a psycho. Right, Myles?'

Myles shook his head, still concentrating on Dick's wound. 'I don't think so,' he said. 'I reckon she just got caught up in something too big for her to handle.'

'An accidental terrorist, huh, Myles?' joked Roosevelt.

'She wasn't a terrorist.'

'No? So who was?'

Myles wondered carefully about how to respond. But no response was necessary. He felt Dick's expression change, and realised the Senator had picked up the gun with his free hand.

Dick Roosevelt lifted the weapon towards Myles, then pressed it into his abdomen.

CHAPTER SEVENTY-TWO
Pantheon, Rome

Myles froze.

Then, very slowly, he looked down to check he really was being held at gunpoint. He returned his eyes to Dick Roosevelt's wound, then carefully lifted his hands away. The wound didn't seem to matter any more.

His non-reaction was not what Dick had been expecting.

Dick's eyes narrowed. 'You're not surprised, Myles?'

Myles shook his head. 'I suspected before. It was how Juma got into the conference centre that convinced me. He had a Roosevelt Guardian ID card.'

'Did he?' asked Roosevelt, already knowing the answer.

'Yes – I've got it,' said Myles, immediately knowing he'd made a mistake by releasing the information.

Roosevelt grinned, his weapon still trained on Myles. 'Then hand it to me, please, Myles.'

Myles removed from his sleeve the small plastic card he had taken from Juma's jacket in the conference centre. He allowed it to drop on the floor.

Dick didn't react. Instead he poked the gun into Myles' shirt and lifted up the fabric. 'You wired?' he asked.

Myles frowned, confused. He made Dick spell it out.

Dick became agitated. 'You know - a recording device,' he explained. 'You trying to get me to incriminate myself on tape?'

'Surely that would be against the Fifth Amendment, Senator,' replied Myles flatly.

Senator Roosevelt wasn't convinced. 'Take off your clothes,' he ordered.

Myles screwed up his face in disbelief.

Dick confirmed his instruction. 'Take off your clothes and pass them to me, one by one,' he demanded. 'So I can check you don't have a device on you.'

'I'm not that smart, Senator.'

'No, you're not,' conceded Roosevelt. 'But Placidia was. She had something. A mobile phone thing. It was broadcasting onto the web. She was trying to make a secret video of me. Something she could have uploaded like all her other videos.'

'But you got it?' asked Myles.

The Senator nodded, then glanced over at a smashed electronic device not far away. It had been stamped on, and was very definitely broken. 'She had managed to broadcast a few minutes' worth, but nothing incriminating,' he gloated.

Myles realised his last hope was gone: Placidia had failed to record a confession from Dick Roosevelt. He had no more defences left.

Myles began to remove his Chinese cap. But he knew as soon as the Senator confirmed Myles had no audio device on him, Dick Roosevelt would pull the trigger.

Myles had to play for time.

He paused as he undressed. 'Placidia invited you here by text message,' he said.

Roosevelt looked uneasy. 'How did you know that?' he asked.

'I've seen the text,' explained Myles. 'It means people will know you've been in contact with her.'

Roosevelt pondered for a short moment, then shrugged. 'I'll just say I was invited for peace talks. My father got away with talking to terrorists all the time.'

'Maybe,' admitted Myles. 'But they might be able to find all your other contacts with her and Juma. If Placidia was smart enough to try to record her conversation here, you can be sure she kept evidence of your role in everything else.'

The Senator smirked. 'I've been in contact with them for ages. Investigators still haven't made the connection. They probably never will. The guy from Las Vegas I hired to do computer stuff wiped everything clean.' Then he began to laugh. 'And even he didn't know it was me until a few minutes before he died. He just called me "Constantine", like the Emperor. Isn't that sweet?'

'The information planted on my laptop?"

The Senator nodded.

Myles was beginning to understand it all now. 'You must have been in contact with them since before they took your father hostage.'

'From before the first bomb in New York,' boasted the Senator.

'I always thought your escape from Libya was…unlikely.'

'"Heroic" is the official description, Englishman,' said Roosevelt, mocking an English accent. 'It was "heroic".'

Myles had removed his shirt to reveal his bare chest. He wasn't 'wired'. Both he and the Senator were aware that Myles, standing, could easily try to tackle the wounded Senator somehow. The Senator recognised the threat and indicated Myles should move away.

'My trousers too?'

Roosevelt nodded. 'In America we call them "pants". Yes please. And shoes.'

'And socks?' said Myles, starting to unbutton his fly.

The Senator nodded again, enjoying the control. 'I know you're wondering how I'm going to explain this to the forensics? It's easy,' he gloated. 'Placidia, self-defence,' he said, gesturing with his gun towards her. 'You being naked: well, she always loved you. Perhaps she wanted to see you naked before you died.'

'Before *she* killed me?' asked Myles.

'Yes. Before *she* killed you.'

Myles knew Dick Roosevelt meant what he said. The man would kill him as soon as he needed to. How could he get out of here alive? Options tumbled through his mind. Did Roosevelt have another weak spot, apart from his shoulder? He remembered Roosevelt saying his men were outside – could he get them in sooner?

Myles motioned his head towards the pistol. 'How will you explain the shots?' he asked.

'The gunshots?'

'Yes. Witnesses outside will have heard three shots, each several minutes apart. Hard to explain away as "self-defence".'

Dick paused, then accepted the point. 'Thank you,' he said. 'That means I'll have to muffle this next bullet.' He moved his weight as he sat on the floor. He removed the balled-up jacket which he had been pressing into his shoulder wound and tried to hold it over the barrel of the gun. It was awkward, and the blood made it slip in his hands, but he seemed determined.

Myles only had seconds. He raised his voice. 'Your father... your father spoke about you before he died.'

'Yeah?' Dick was pretending to only half-listen. He was still concentrating on using his blood-soaked jacket to muffle the imminent gunshot. 'So, what did my father say?'

Myles looked down at the ground as he put the question back to him. 'What do you think he said?'

Dick was about to give an instant answer. Then he paused, and became more thoughtful. 'Did he say sorry? Sorry for passing on a third-rate private security firm? Or for failing to become President - twice?'

Myles shook his head. He looked around for any hope – anything – which might save him from the bullet. But there was nothing.

'He didn't say sorry,' recounted Myles. 'He said "this is how it ends".'

'"This is how it ends?" – my father's last words?'

'Yeah. He was talking about the Roman Empire,' said Myles, trying to bluff. 'He said "Civilisation collapsed because people became self-centred, and there were too many pretenders to imperial power." Your father mentioned the emperor Constantine, the emperor who made the Roman Empire Christian. When Constantine's own son tried to become emperor, Constantine had him murdered.'

Dick looked pensive. 'So my father knew it was me?'

Myles nodded, bluffing again. 'And, right before he died, he said some people had to make sacrifices for others.'

Dick looked down at his gun, smiling again. He had heard enough. 'Well that's true, isn't it…'

Myles sensed he had overplayed his hand. Dick was going to shoot.

He had no other options left. He had to go for the gun.

Damn the consequences.

But he was too late.

As he lurched forward, Myles felt himself blasted backwards. He collapsed onto the marble floor of the ancient church. His body spasmed as the noise reverberated through the cavern of the church. Roosevelt's jacket had not muffled the noise at all.

Then, in the instant between being hit by the bullet and the searing pain which followed, Myles realised it wasn't the noise of the gunshot echoing around.

CHAPTER SEVENTY-THREE
Pantheon, Rome

Light had broken into the church. The doors had been slammed open and silhouettes with guns were rushing in. Myles' eyes couldn't adjust to see who they were. His body was still in shock from the gunshot wound.

Dick turned to see them too.

Everything had changed. Dick needed to change his story. 'Hey – thank you,' the young Senator called out, trying to sound upbeat. 'This man knows about the terrorist plot to bring down America like ancient Rome,' he shouted.

There was no answer. The armed men were running to surround Myles and Dick, both now with gaping injuries to their shoulders.

Finally it became clear who the men were: Myles recognised their dark blue uniforms, their leather shoes and their accents. He even recognised the beard of the man who was approaching him and the Senator.

They were Italian Special Police. Inspector Perrotta had come to stand over Dick Roosevelt. As Myles and the Senator floundered on the floor, both losing blood from their bullet wounds, Perrotta repeated the Senator's words back to him. 'He knows about the terrorist plot?' he said in his thick Italian accent. Perrotta sounded as though he believed the Senator, who nodded and looked hopeful. Roosevelt loosened his grip on his weapon – the Italians had Myles at gunpoint now.

Perrotta bent down and lifted the pistol from the Senator's hand. 'He knows about the terrorist plot, you say?' Perrotta's tone was more sarcastic this time. He made eye contact with one of his men, who in turn indicated that it was safe for paramedics to come forward.

The Senator clutched his shoulder again, playing up the pain. 'Yes, inspector,' winced Roosevelt, pretending to ignore the sarcasm. 'And he shot me, and that woman.'

Perrotta nodded, unconvinced.

Myles rolled his eyes, from disbelief as much as pain. He was still on the floor and could only hear the words. He groaned at the prospect of being arrested by Perrotta – again – because the authorities were too slow and too dumb. They would follow their rules, their procedures. The police would obey their bureaucrats…

One of the Italian policemen lifted Myles' shoulders and held his head. Something was pressed into the wound to stem the bleeding. Seconds later paramedics arrived and took over. Myles was told the bullet wound was serious, but that he'd live. 'Please try to stay awake, Mr Munro…' said the medic.

Myles lost consciousness a few moments later.

Both he and the Senator were stabilised – emergency measures to reduce blood loss from their wounds.

Myles sensed just a blur of medical equipment and the rush of professionals. He writhed, his naked skin soaking in blood. Only half awake, he dreamed he was paralysed. He imagined being back in the London courtroom with Dick Roosevelt accusing him while he, Myles-the-misfit, wasn't allowed to answer.

Then he started to rise up. He realised he had been strapped to a stretcher. Brought out into the light, his awareness returned. Only then did he know the paramedic was right: he would survive.

The Piazza Rotunda outside the Pantheon was now filled with journalists, onlookers and assorted other people who had realised something interesting was happening inside and wanted to know more. A pathway to waiting ambulances had been roped off. Myles was carried through it at waist height.

Where was Helen?

He hoped – expected – her to run under the rope and greet him. To take his hand and squeeze it. But there was no sign of her.

As Senator Dick Roosevelt was brought out behind him, Myles heard the swoop of journalists shouting questions out to him. He listened out for Helen's voice amongst them, but it wasn't there. Was she reporting on the story from somewhere else?

'When will you resign, Senator?'

'Do you have a political future, Mr Roosevelt?'

'Why did you kill Placidia when she was praying, Dick?'

Myles was confused. Why did the journalists think Placidia was praying when she was killed? And why were they interrogating Dick?

Then he realised – somehow they *knew*. They had worked out that Dick Roosevelt was behind it all.

But how?

The Senator, of course, didn't answer the questions. He was wounded – the perfect excuse to avoid allegations. But the questions sounded tough.

Finally he felt his stretcher lifted into the back of an Italian ambulance. And there, waiting for him, was Helen. 'You're safe now,' she smiled. She kissed him.

Myles was still confused. 'You're not reporting this?'

'I already have,' announced Helen, proud that she was ahead of him on at least one thing.

Myles discovered he'd been given medical treatment in the Pantheon until his condition stabilised, while Helen had broadcast rolling coverage. She hadn't been allowed in to see Myles while he was being treated for his gunshot injury, but hadn't needed to: she had seen the whole thing anyway. Live.

Helen smiled. 'The Senator was behind the whole thing,' she confirmed, looking at Myles' face and his wound.

Myles was still mystified. 'Yes, but what convinced you?'

'Dick arranged it all with Juma in advance. The bomb in New York so he became a hero, his escape from Libya. Kidnapping and killing his father, so he could become Senator. Even the stand-off between the refugees and Roosevelt's Guardians, so he could pretend he was protecting America. And it was Roosevelt who got the files about the Special Forces raid – both to warn Juma and for Placidia to plant on your laptop,' said Helen, now clearly teasing Myles with all she knew.

'Yes, it must have been. But how did you find out?'

Helen smiled again, deflecting Myles' question. 'So the Roosevelt Guardian corporation was linked to Juma's own private security firm, in Iraq?'

'Something like that,' agreed Myles. 'I don't know exactly, but I think the Guardians bought out Galla Security or something. That was how they were connected.'

Helen nodded again. 'Don't worry. The world knows it now. All from Placidia.'

Myles winced in confusion. 'Placidia?'

Helen explained how Placidia had offered Dick Roosevelt a deal: she wouldn't expose him if his Roosevelt Guardians let the refugees into the embassy. 'The tragedy, Myles, is that her people were already safe. You'd already got them into the embassy by setting off the fire alarm. She didn't need to meet him,' she said. 'Placidia could have lived.'

Myles rolled his head on the stretcher. He remembered Placidia's body on the stretcher. Perhaps if he'd been quicker, she would still be alive.

The ambulance was moving now, driving over bumpy cobbles and ancient stone roads through the streets of Rome. Helen tried to hold him steady. 'So Myles, she was trying to do deals with that bastard right until she died.'

'Yes, but she didn't believe in them,' said Myles. 'She always said, "Do whatever saves the most lives". She would have made the deal to protect her refugees. Once she knew they were safe, she would have exposed Dick.'

'And break the deal?'

'Yes,' confirmed Myles. 'But for the best reasons. Placidia's morality was twisted, but it was twisted in a good way.'

Helen combed her hand through Myles' hair, careful to avoid the scar on his scalp. Paramedics had given Myles some fresh bandages.

For Myles, there was still one final puzzle. 'So how did you know, Helen?' he asked. 'And why did a journalist shout out that Placidia had died praying – she didn't even believe in God.'

Helen smiled. She pulled out her mobile, and opened a browser. It showed the inside of the Pantheon. 'Placidia. She set up a monitoring device.'

'A camera? I know,' said Myles. 'But Dick Roosevelt found it.'

Helen shook her head. 'Placidia was ahead of him. She knew Dick would be looking for it, so she had two. She was broadcasting live images onto the net the whole time she was there,' said Helen, sounding respectful of Placidia for probably the first time ever. 'That's how everybody knew. And that's how they saw live images of her praying – praying in church – when she was shot by the Senator who pretended to believe in Christian values.'

'She gave her life to protect America from Dick Roosevelt,' said Myles, completing the epitaph. 'She didn't just die for her refugees, but to save her country, too.'

CHAPTER SEVENTY-FOUR
US Embassy, Rome

Safiq knew nothing of the drama at the Pantheon – at least, not for several hours. When he did, he felt so very sorry for the woman who had died praying. He recognised her image immediately: it was the woman who had persuaded him to board the tanker in Libya. He had assumed she was Muslim, but discovering she prayed as a Christian made no difference to his admiration for her. The half-American lady had been true to her promise: she really had done her best for him and the other refugees. Only now she was dead did Safiq discover her name, and he vowed that, were he ever to have a daughter of his own, he would name her Placidia.

The hours before Safiq saw Placidia on the satellite TV in the US Embassy had been tense and chaotic. It had taken several minutes for him and the other refugees to accept they were safe. US Marines took control – both of the building and the Roosevelt Guardians, who were disarmed and arrested. The refugees were corralled again, but this time within the embassy, which meant they were on US territory. There they were given hospitality, food, and water. For Safiq, it was an unexpected welcome. American generosity was even warmer than he had hoped.

Safiq was one of the first to claim asylum. He had expected his bid to be rejected, and that he would be shipped back to Africa again. After being fired on by the Roosevelt Guardians, part of him feared a terrible fate – like the 'barbarian tribes' which had sought sanctuary a century before Rome collapsed, and which that empire had treated so badly.

But several countries offered to take a share of the migrants. Refugees were resettled throughout France, Spain and Italy, in the area once ruled by the ancient civilisation. And Safiq was one of the migrants to be accepted by their first choice – by the country which had become heir to the Roman Empire.

So, within a week, Safiq was making his new life in a country he loved. Safiq was in the United States. Placidia had taken him to America after all.

DAY XIII

CHAPTER SEVENTY-FIVE
Agostino Gemelli Hospital, Rome

X-rays on Myles' shoulder confirmed his wound was not life-threatening. The bullet had broken through his shoulder blade near the joint. Fragments of bone would have to be aligned so they could heal and Myles' underarm muscles, ripped apart by the exit wound, would take several months to regain their strength. But Myles had been lucky: the shot struck him just a few inches above his heart. Lunging at Dick Roosevelt may have saved his life after all.

The first two weeks of his recovery, confined to a hospital bed, frustrated Myles. He wanted to get out. To see Rome and Italy, and to explore. But daily visits from Helen, which often ran on well beyond the hours dictated by the hospital bureaucrats, made things much easier. It was not the sort of relaxing time in Rome the couple had initially planned, but it was what they both needed.

Myles was also consoled by the rolling news coverage of the story. Although not many new facts emerged, there were several follow-up stories which all got good coverage. It took six days before news channels found a lead item more interesting than the story of the disgraced Senator and the conclusion of Placidia's 'Last Prophecy of Rome'.

Dick Roosevelt recovered from his self-inflicted shoulder wound quickly. It meant, after ten days, he was fit enough to appear in handcuffs, unshaven and in an orange jumpsuit.

Cameras flashed and the videos rolled: he had an image of defeat on his face. Even his confidence was finally exhausted. The evidence against him was overwhelming – he had been filmed shooting someone who posed no threat, passed classified documents to Juma, and conspired in an act of terror against the United States. The final irony was that a federal law brought in by his father – the Roosevelt-Wilson Act – would be used in his trial. His father's legislation meant crimes committed abroad, like Dick's, were tried as if they had been committed in the continental USA.

The political demise of the young Senator Roosevelt had become inevitable ever since the world logged on to the video-stream being broadcast from the Pantheon. Since people now realised how dangerous Dick's firm, the Roosevelt Guardians, had become – a danger to American democracy itself – they had to be disbanded. Other private security firms would soon face strict controls. Myles smiled as he saw Susan, who had been seconded to Sam Roosevelt's office, now back with the Department for Homeland Security, interviewed on the rolling news. She made the point very well: 'Private' had to be taken from 'security', since security was always a public matter…

New private security legislation was championed with the slogan 'Driving standards up to drive the bad boys out'. There was even a cross-party consensus in the US Senate on the issue. It would have made Sam Roosevelt proud.

The Senators were also pleased to be able – finally – to dispel the continuing rumours about pornography on their computers. Once seen as the most innocent amongst them, Senator Dick Roosevelt was now the most guilty. In time, his name would become a byword for sharp practices and behaviour which threatened the constitution of the United States.

After two weeks in Rome, Myles was fit enough to take a flight. He and Helen flew back to the United States together, where he could convalesce in her New England home. Even though they tried to keep the details secret, it didn't stop him being treated as a hero by reporters and well-wishers as he passed – again – through JFK airport.

Myles didn't answer any of their questions. He had already promised his one-and-only interview about the whole affair to a single journalist: Helen.

She interviewed him seated in an armchair, in her own house. He still wore a sling, but didn't need the head bandages anymore, and looked relaxed.

'So, Myles,' she asked, framing the question with poise. 'Many people have said you saved America. Are they right?'

He couldn't help smiling at the question. It was probably the softest interview Helen had ever done. 'No,' he answered. 'The country would have survived anyway.'

'But is the US doomed to decline and fall like ancient Rome?'

'No. Because the US is very different from Rome – different enough. America is set apart by its values. Rome was built on a culture of violence – of empire and aristocracy. Of people killing each other to get to the top, or for entertainment. America is not like that. Perhaps, if America and the West become as cruel as Rome we deserve the same downfall. But it's up to everyone to make sure we stay better than that…'

Myles had answered the riddle of Rome. Not the puzzles set by Placidia in her terrorist broadcasts, but the real riddle: how was the world's greatest empire, a civilisation which had lasted a thousand years, brought down by nomads and barbarians? Myles explained there was no single answer. But the best answers were not about Rome's enemies, but about Rome itself.

The interview continued for twenty minutes. Myles felt able to talk about it now, and he gave one of his best lectures ever. He showed how modern America was partly like ancient Rome, but also very different. He enthralled viewers across the nation as he explained how the Romans lived and died, and how the United States could avoid the same fate.

And as he talked his individuality came through. People could see what Helen had seen before – that Myles was unique. The things that made him unusual were also the things that made him brilliant.

'Thank you, Myles.' Live on TV, she kissed him again. Myles blushed, then took her hand as the interview closed.

Finally, it was over.

EPILOGUE

Over the coming months, Myles would watch the video of Placidia talking to Dick Roosevelt in the Pantheon several times. He always wondered: did she know her people were already safe? If she did, then why did she meet with Roosevelt? And if not, was her death a tragedy that he – Myles – could alone have stopped, if he'd just run a few seconds faster to reach her?

The question was only answered when Myles was fully recovered and preparing to return to Oxford, to restart his academic work.

Exactly six months after her death, he received an email. The address seemed odd, but he clicked on the link it offered nonetheless.

A video file opened on the computer. The format was the same as the YouTube broadcasts Placidia had sent out while she was alive – the broadcasts which had warned of a plot to bring down America like ancient Rome.

Myles pressed 'play', and a picture of Placidia appeared. She was in the Pantheon, and he realised it must have been filmed a minute or two before the main recording, when the meeting with Dick Roosevelt was broadcast live to the web.

Placidia moved back from the camera. She looked nervous, and checked behind her. The sound quality was poor. 'This is a message for Myles Munro,' she said. 'Myles, I don't expect to survive my next meeting with Dick. I think he's going to kill me, which is why I'm making this video. Myles, I think the whole US is in danger. Every aspect of American power: its military, its reputation, its finances – unless something is done to stop Roosevelt, America will share the fate of Rome. Even the once-great democratic tradition is threatened – the more people like Dick Roosevelt rise up, the more the country will go down, and states could start to peel away by 2020. Someone had to take a stand. That's why, when Dick asked Juma and I to pretend to be terrorists, to help Dick become President, I said yes. Not to help him, but to sabotage his plan.'

Myles rubbed his eyes as he watched Placidia. In the video she checked behind her again to make sure Dick hadn't arrived yet.

'But, Myles,' Placidia continued. 'Please believe me. I never meant harm. I always believed in trying to save as many lives as possible. That's why I insisted the lead factory in Germany only used calcium from chalk, and why the men in Istanbul never got near the real plague.'

She glanced away from the camera again. 'You see, Myles. The plot was like this. Dick Roosevelt just wanted there to be Islamic terrorists. But I said we needed smart terrorism. It was me who suggested the threat to "bring America down like ancient Rome". It was the thing I knew most about, so it gave me control. And it meant I could make sure you were brought in. Myles, I thought you'd decode all the references to Rome and understand. And I hoped it might finally bring us together. I never really gave you a chance. I regret that.'

Placidia looked strained for the first time in the video. Myles guessed it was because of what she was saying, not because she expected Dick to be with her soon. 'Rome fell because it had too many civil wars,' she said. 'These didn't just kill off its soldiers. They meant it came to be ruled by selfish, dangerous, nasty people – like Roosevelt. And once the Empire had started to decline, its civilisation could never be restored. Like love, once lost, it was lost forever.'

Placidia reacted to a noise behind her. Myles saw the light change in the background: the doors to the Pantheon were opening. Quickly she leant forward and pressed a button. The footage continued, but now it was the public video – the material which the world had seen. The video of Placidia and Dick Roosevelt talking. The image stream of Roosevelt incriminating himself, then shooting Placidia while she prayed.

For several minutes, he wondered about everything Placidia had said. Could their relationship ever have come to something – at university, or in the years before he met Helen?

And was she right, that America could be doomed by a single bad President? The country seemed too strong for that. The United States had become as permanent as his relationship to Helen.

His thoughts drifted back to the present – the video should be evidence in Dick Roosevelt's trial.

He tried to replay it, but somehow he couldn't. The file was missing.

Myles scoured his computer and his email, but it no longer seemed to be there. It took him an hour to realise, and finally accept: the message had deleted itself.

Like ancient Rome, Placidia's last words to him were gone forever.

LETTER FROM IAIN

Thank you for reading *Last Prophecy of Rome*. I really hope you enjoyed the book.

If you did like it, then please write a review and post it online – reader reviews help other people find good books, particularly when you give a story like *Last Prophecy of Rome* five stars (if you help bring the average above four stars, this book will be recommended to new readers).

Reviews also show your support for books like this one, and some of the ideas within. If you have an opinion on one of the themes in *Last Prophecy of Rome*, then please put it in your review. I do hope some of the characters in the book – especially Safiq, and Dick and Sam Roosevelt – help people reflect upon current events.

And reviews are fascinating: it has been wonderful to read all your thoughts and reactions to Myles Munro's other adventure so far, *Secrets of the Last Nazi*, and I'm eager to see whether you liked this one, too – even if you only write a few words. I've found connecting with my readers is both enjoyable and important. It makes the many lonely hours it took to write this story worthwhile, especially when you give the book a generous number of stars.

As for Myles Munro, he has more adventures ahead. As well as *Secrets of the Last Nazi*, there will be another book starring

Myles Munro – as soon as I finish writing it. If you'd like to keep up-to-date with all my latest releases, just sign up here:

www.bookouture.com/iain-king

So thank you again for your support. Until next time,

Iain

🐦 @iainbking

www.iainbking.com

ABOUT THE AUTHOR

Iain King CBE FRSA has worked in ten conflicts and warzones, including Iraq, South Sudan, and Afghanistan – where he served alongside both of the battalion commanders who became Britain's most senior casualties of the war, and in more frontline bases than any other civilian. Parts of this book were written in Benghazi, Libya, where he coordinated international civilian support during part of the 2011 war. In 2013, he became one of the youngest people to be made a Commander of the British Empire.

Iain King is already the author of two successful non-fiction books: an acclaimed chronicle of Kosovo after the 1999 war, and a jargon-free introduction to moral philosophy which set out a new explanation of ethics. The Myles Munro books – *Secrets of the Last Nazi* and *Last Prophecy of Rome* – are his first works of fiction.

ACKNOWLEDGEMENTS

Thank you: to Andy Bearpark, Lou Perrotta, Mark Russell, and Rob Shenton for keeping the secret; to Jolyon Shotton, Mareike Schomerus, Whit Mason and the Bookouture team for superb support and advice; and particular thanks to Claire Bord, Clare Hulton, and to my family, for all their wonderful wisdom.

EXCERPT FROM
SECRETS OF THE LAST NAZI

Imperial War Museum, London, United Kingdom

Myles didn't turn his head to see the mock-up of the trenches – complete with duck-boards, theatrical mud and artificial smells. The vintage machine guns, both German and British, which had caused so much slaughter in the Great War, didn't register with him at all. He even ignored the Spitfire hanging above him, the old German Jagdpanther tank, and the V1 and V2 'Wonderweapons' used by Hitler in his desperate last months.

That was all history. An outdated vision of war. Misleading, even. War wasn't like that, not any more, as he told his students in some of Oxford University's best attended lectures.

Myles knew. He'd been there.

Even the Cold War had been distorted. The superpower confrontation between the United States and the Soviet Union wasn't what most people said it was. Myles walked right past the big photo-posters showing scenes from 1989, when the Berlin Wall disintegrated in the bright glare of TV lights. Frozen in time, some faces were celebrating, while East German police stood around, not believing the impossible had come true.

The only scene he couldn't ignore was the most sinister: a faded photograph, blown-up into a large display, which showed a bureaucrat in front of a queue of Jewish refugees. The man was sitting at a table, registering details from the families as they offloaded from the cattle trucks. The bureaucrat and his paperwork were in control. The refugees clutched their suitcases and precious possessions, leaning forward to speak to the man at the desk, trying to help him with information. The poor men and women were oblivious that they had only minutes left to live.

Myles shook his head in disgust, cursing the bureaucrats…

He walked on. He had not come here to browse, but to help Frank, his old university friend of almost twenty years.

Myles held the glass door open with his foot as he heaved the last cardboard box inside. 'When do the public arrive?'

'Ten,' replied Frank. 'We've still got time.'

Myles nodded, as he continued through the main entrance area. 'Downstairs with the rest?'

'Yes – thanks. I'll come with you.'

With Frank limping behind him, Myles led the way down the metallic stairs, careful to duck his head under the beam.

The museum's walkways had been designed for children, not tall university lecturers. Frank pointed to a pile of other possessions, and Myles placed the box beside them.

'Cheers, Myles,' said Frank, tapping the box with his walking stick. 'That's the last one.'

Together they stared at the cardboard dump. Half a lifetime: just three boxes.

'Really, that's all you've got?'

'It's all I could salvage before it sank - but on the bright side, if I'd been asleep when my houseboat started leaking, I might have drowned!' Frank tried to laugh, but the chuckles came out flat.

'You sure the museum won't mind you using their space, Frank?' Myles asked.

Frank held his stick while he pushed his glasses back into place. 'I hope not – I am the curator. And if they do sack me, I'll have to ask you for advice…' Then the curator's face reacted, as he had another thought. 'In fact, I think…' He started to limp along the underground corridor, looking up at the small cards which explained what each storage unit contained. He stopped opposite a tall cabinet labelled *Terrorism – UK*, then climbed on a small stool to retrieve a box file. He called back to Myles. 'We've still got it somewhere …'

Myles' fingers rubbed his forehead. He didn't want it. 'It's OK, Frank. I've seen it before.'

But Frank had already pulled out the file. He hobbled back down the ladder, and unfolded the tabloid as he returned to Myles. The headline still screamed at him, all those years later.

Myles Munro: Misfit Oxford Military Lecturer is Runaway Terrorist

Frank was grinning. 'You see – we still have all sorts of war records!' He paused with a half-smile, realising he'd just told an unfunny joke. Then he folded the newspaper back up and patted Myles on the back, realising he needed to change the subject. 'You did well to recover. Very impressive.'

Myles didn't respond. 'Impressive' didn't matter to him.

Frank nudged him. 'Come on – how's it all going?'

Myles tipped his head to one side. 'Predictable, sometimes.'

'Predictable bad or predictable good?

Myles paused to frame his thoughts, tried to explain. 'Most people have very set ideas. Military history just means Hitler to most of them. Even the open-minded ones aren't open to anything too challenging.'

'So you're looking for something else, Myles?'

'Maybe,' accepted Myles. 'Not looking very hard though...'

Myles was distracted by the large vaults looming above them both. 'So what's the Imperial War Museum planning next?' He could see his old friend become enthused.

'My new exhibition: *War and the Natural World*.'

Myles raised his eyebrows. 'Interesting...'

'It's joint with the Science Museum – you know, for kids,' explained Frank. 'We're trying to show how natural events have a big impact on war.' Frank hobbled around, guiding Myles towards a half-finished display called *World War Two and the Moon*. Then he gave Myles a handout to read.

Myles was impressed. 'Looks like fun.'

'Yes – and the displays go right back to Alexander the Great. The eclipse just before his greatest battle was an omen that the Empire of Persia would be defeated – and it was!'

Myles smiled, only half buying it. He let Frank continue. 'And it wasn't just ancient times,' lectured Frank. 'The Crusades, the Korean War – even World War One began with an eclipse, too. Did you know that?'

'No, I didn't.'

'That's right – in August 1914, on the day that German and British troops first clashed. And the centre of the eclipse was exactly over where the first big battle took place. It was probably the most important battle of the whole war.' Frank lifted his stick towards a map of Europe.

'Battle of Tannenberg?'

'Correct – and World War Three started with an eclipse, as well.'

Now Myles knew he was being ribbed. 'We haven't had World War Three.'

Frank chuckled. 'No – but we almost did. Remember 1999, when the NATO commander ordered his troops to take Kosovo's main airport - the one held by the Russians? The attack was only stopped when a subordinate refused to obey. He "Didn't want to start World War Three", he said. Well, I discovered the centre of the big eclipse in the summer of 1999 was just a few miles from... wait for it... Kosovo!'

Myles looked sideways at his friend, wondering whether Frank was taking the eclipses too seriously. Frank hadn't noticed – he was too absorbed.

'And there was also a very local solar eclipse, exactly over Iceland in October 1986, when Reagan and Gorbachev held their big summit there. Some people say it was the summit which ended the Cold War. Did you know that?'

Myles didn't answer, as he realised his old friend had become even more eccentric with the passing years. Trying to find sense in the movement of planetary bodies was not a good sign.

Ting...

The faint metallic noise came from far off, further down the corridor. They looked at each other, surprised.

Both men remained silent for a moment.

Frank shrugged, but Myles couldn't dismiss it. He started walking, then jogging towards the noise – along the underground corridor, to where the lighting wasn't so good.

He stopped to listen again.

Nothing.

His instincts were confusing him. He halted, tried to sense what could have caused the sound, then wondered if he had imagined it. He was about to turn back when he noticed an empty box file on the vault floor.

He picked it up and called over to Frank. 'Was this you?'

Frank indicated it wasn't.

Myles looked at the label on the empty file.

De-Nazification interviews, 1945 – box 4

It must have fallen down somehow – although that didn't explain why it was empty.

He peered into the darkness, looking for a shelf with a space on it.

Something didn't seem right. The shelves were messy, as if someone had been rummaging through the archives. But there was something else, too.

Myles froze, and heard movement close by.

Someone was there.

He peered into the gloom, searching for whatever he could find, whatever didn't belong.

Then he saw them: a pair of eyes.

Scared eyes.

They were looking straight back at him.

Suddenly a man rushed out, ramming into Myles who tumbled to the floor, box files raining down on his head.

He could see the intruder running away. The man had something clutched in his hands. He was heading back towards the stairway.

Myles called out, 'Frank – stop him!'

But Frank was too shocked to react. The thief fled past him. Myles jumped back to his feet and started chasing him down the corridor, pounding up the museum's metallic stairs three steps at a time. His clumsiness made him trip, but he recovered.

Myles raced back past the trench exhibition, ducking under the beam as he ran up the main staircase and towards the ground floor.

He heard Frank's call out behind him. 'I'll get the police…'

But there was no time to get the police.

Myles stumbled again as he reached the top of the stairs, falling onto the polished surface of the main hallway. Quickly he pushed himself back up.

He scanned the exhibits: rockets, the American army jeep, tanks, information displays, a submarine... The museum was full of hiding places.

Then he heard a clank: *the outside doors.*

Myles swivelled to see the exit doors were still moving – the thief must have just barged through them and escaped.

Myles dodged a donations bin near the entrance and grappled with the heavy glass door which swung back in his face, slowing him down. Finally he reached the park outside. At last he could see the thief again. The man was racing away from him – past the souvenir section of the Berlin wall, over the well-kept grass, towards the main road...

Myles tried calling. 'Hey you...'

The thief turned around to see Myles' tall frame at the entrance of the museum, and the man's eyes filled with terror.

Quickly he turned and kept running.

Myles sprinted on as fast as he could. Gradually he was catching up. He could see the thief's rucksack. The man's canvas jacket. His trainers...

The thief was approaching the end of the path, forced to slow down as he approached the busy road. The rush-hour traffic was too fast to cross. Myles had him trapped.

Myles saw the man turn and face him again, his eyes flickering around in panic. Myles was getting closer, still running straight at the man. His arms reached out to grab him, but the thief swiftly stepped aside and Myles stumbled, off balance again.

Myles saw the man dash into the traffic. A small car braked as the thief ran in front of it. Back on his feet, Myles manoeuvred around the stopped car. An angry commuter honked at him, but Myles kept on, still chasing the thief.

Their eyes connected again.

That was when Myles felt the huge force of a van smash into his side. He felt his leg bend, and his body twist away. For a moment, he was weightless as he was flung high into the air. Then agony surged through his leg.

Cars stopped around him, and backed up all along the road. People climbed out and moved towards him.

But Myles soon realised the people were not interested in him. He tried to see through the crowd, through the cars and through the pain and saw people helping the thief, desperately trying emergency medical procedures on his blood-covered face. None of them were any use.

The man Myles had been chasing was dead.

Lightning Source UK Ltd.
Milton Keynes UK
UKOW06f2011160816

280845UK00025B/600/P